ANGELA CHANNING—The dowager queen, whose brutal acts against her own blood are calculated to control the empire that holds first place in her heart.

CHASE GIOBERTI—Heir to half of Falcon Crest, he never wanted to challenge Angela. Now he will be forced to match her tactics if he has any hope of keeping what is his.

LANCE CUMSON—As sexy as he is cynical, he will someday own it all if he plays by Angela's rules. His perilous choice is not to give a damn.

MELISSA CUMSON—Her stock went up when she inherited her father's huge vineyard. But it was not land she lusted after. It was the men she couldn't have.

RICHARD CHANNING—Brilliant bastard outcast, he will use a ruthless international cartel in his obsession to reclaim his heritage.

FOR EACH OF THEM THE
ULTIMATE LURE IS . . .

FALCON CREST

FALCON CREST

A Novel by

Patrick Mann

*based on
the series created by*

Earl Hamner

and on episodes written by

Robert L. McCullough	Irv Pearlberg
Garner Simmons	Kathleen Hite
E. F. Wallengren	Leah Markus
Scott Hamner	Dick Nelson
Stephen Black	Henry Stern
Suzanne Herrera	Kathleen A. Shelley

and Barry Steinberg

A DELL BOOK

Published by
Dell Publishing Co., Inc.
1 Dag Hammarskjold Plaza
New York, New York 10017

Dell ® TM 681510, Dell Publishing Co., Inc.

ISBN: 0-440-12437-9

Printed in the United States of America

First printing—December 1984

FALCON CREST

Part One

Chapter One

Women with as much power and money as Angela Channing rarely get out of bed this early. Yet as the dawn sun flared brilliantly in the east, sending horizontal streaks of orange across the vast vineyards of Falcon Crest, Angie was awake, sipping her morning cup of strong black coffee and gazing out the window at the largest wine empire in California's Tuscany Valley.

It was all hers, Angie thought, or should be. Or soon *would* be.

The pleased look of total power that had brightened her face went suddenly dead as she remembered that Falcon Crest, hers by right, was only half hers. She knew full well what had been in her father's mind before he'd died. Old Jasper Gioberti had but one true heir, his beloved daughter, Angela. As surely as she stood here in her tall-heeled feather mules and the lavishly decorated cheongsam she wore as a dressing gown, Angie knew her father had meant her to own every square inch of this vast holding that bore the falcon's crest.

Me, she told herself, not my weakling brother, Jason. And certainly not his do-good son Chase, her

nephew, who on Jason's death now held half ownership of Falcon Crest.

Angie frowned, then ran a smoothing finger over
the wrinkles in her forehead. She might be a grandmother but she was an attractive woman still, she
knew, and in the battle that lay ahead for her, every
trick, every wile was necessary for victory.

"More coffee, Mrs. Channing?"

Chao-Li stood in the doorway of Angie's immense
corner bedroom, a tray on his arm. His small face
regarded her with simple curiosity. As majordomo
of Falcon Crest's palatial mansion, Chao-Li had witnessed too much of Gioberti and Channing history
to remain in awe of his employers. But Angela Channing knew he stood, if not in awe of her, then in a
state of respect that bordered on fear.

He'd seen her grow from the brilliantly beautiful
woman who married Douglas Channing to the em-
bittered dowager queen of Falcon Crest. Angie felt
that he knew her mind better than anyone else,
sensed its subtleties, its spiderlike patience, its banked
fires of rage. Chao-Li remained respectful, but wary.
In the end, Angie knew, he was sure she would win.

"Half a cup, Chao-Li. Are you certain Mr. Phillip
said seven A.M.?"

He carefully poured the coffee. "Mr. Phillip phoned
at one A.M. to say that he was booking a private jet in
New York. It would bring him to our Valley airport
at"—the Chinese glanced at his watch—"just about
now, Mrs. Channing, six-thirty."

"And you've sent Desi to pick him up at the
airport?"

"I have."

"Mr. Phillip didn't explain the need for all this
rush?"

"To Chao-Li?" His almond eyes crinkled in a smile.

"Whatever news he brings is for your ears alone, Mrs. Channing."

"Quite right. That's all, Chao-Li."

Angie watched the dismissed servant close the doors behind him. Phillip Erikson was an old friend and enemy of hers. He'd become quite a high-powered attorney, thanks to her patronage. It amused her to have Phillip run her confidential errands and remain on hand when she needed an escort. Anything more between them—and there had been a lot more over the years—was a kind of carrot she dangled before Phillip. Be a nice errand boy, she seemed to tell him, and you may once again enjoy my favors in bed.

But what could have happened in New York to send Phillip jetting out here? Couldn't it have been told over the telephone? Or was he saying, not in so many words, that Falcon Crest's own telephones were no longer secure from eavesdropping?

Angie wondered if she had time to dress, then decided there remained only time to make up. She sat down at her wide dressing table and surveyed her face, broad through the jaw, small-nosed, with eyes so big they almost didn't need the liner and mascara she was applying.

What was Phillip's news? Surely in New York he would not have picked up California gossip. The standoff between Angie and her nephew, Chase, was always a shifting thing. At any moment, through sheer lamebrained good-heartedness, Chase was perfectly capable of making a decision that could injure Falcon Crest.

Angie's lips tightened as she brushed on lipstick. That had always been Chase's trouble, and his father's before him. Jason had been too softhearted to be entrusted with an enterprise as vast and profitable as Falcon Crest. Their father had known this. Surely,

Angie reminded herself, he had realized that his own steely power and business sense had been inherited only by his daughter, Angela.

No, the news Phillip was bringing could not be of some new, dim-witted idea of Chase's. It had to relate to something in New York, where the winery's distribution and promotion center lay. 'From here the shipment of millions of bottles of Falcon Crest wine and brandy was worked out, not only for America but for the world, where the label had begun to earn tremendous favor.

In the distance, Angie could hear the low, menacing hum her Mercedes 600 limousine made, like an oncoming act of nature edging closer. She finished her makeup and returned to the window. Miles away, beyond the eastern quadrant vineyards, beyond the pressing sheds, beyond the winery itself with its thousands of casks and fermenting vats, a small plume of dust seemed to race toward the house like a desert whirlwind.

It rounded the corner of the bottling plant. In this vast panorama of nature, grapes ripening in the sun, buildings not yet open for the day's work, nothing stirred but the Mercedes. It seemed a malevolent force to Angie, the sure bearer of bad tidings.

She watched her chauffeur brake the huge limousine to a halt in the courtyard almost below her window. Phillip Erikson was Angie's age, mid-fifties, but he sprang out of the car as spryly as a boy, holding his small attaché case in one hand and glancing up at her window as he approached the house.

Angie nodded to him. Phillip waved and disappeared below. In a few seconds she could hear him ascending the long, curving marble staircase from the main hall to her bedroom. Faintly, with Phillip's footsteps, she could also hear the quiet shush-shush of the slippers Chao-Li wore this early in the day. He was more than a majordomo: he was a bodyguard as well. As faithful an assistant as Phillip Erikson might be, Chao-Li would never dream of giving him unobstructed access to his employer's bedroom.

The Chinese knocked at her door, then opened it. "Mr. Phillip is here."

"Send him in."

"Angie, darling!" Phillip's tall frame hurtled through the door, every lock of his silver-gray hair perfectly in place. Arms outstretched, he made for her.

"Chao-Li," Angie said matter-of-factly, "coffee and toast for Mr. Phillip."

As the servant left, Phillip encircled Angie in his arms and aimed a kiss at her mouth. She maneuvered it to a position somewhere beneath her left ear.

"So it's good news you're bringing," she said then, pushing him away from her and sitting on an embroidered chaise longue in the broad bay window.

"Did I say that?"

"Your behavior is positively boisterous." Angie indicated a straight-backed chair opposite her. "In other words, it's bad news and you're trying to distract me with all this youthful display of affection."

Phillip's face grew grave. He stared at her for a long moment. Then: "Richard Channing is back," he announced.

Something fierce snapped behind Angie's eyes. Her own face went grim.

"In New York?"

"He's taking the morning flight to San Francisco. That's why I had to beat him here. Angie, he's assuming control of the *Globe*!"

"What!"

"He somehow found the money to exercise his father's purchase options. What I mean is, he now owns damned near half the newspaper."

The two sat in silence for a long moment. Angie hadn't seen Richard Channing in decades. He'd been a meddlesome little pest when Angie's late husband, Douglas, had suddenly sprung him on the family as his own bastard. It was a situation that hardly appealed to what maternal instinct there was in Angie.

She'd borne Douglas two daughters, Julia and Emma. To be told that some unknown prostitute or paramour had whelped a third brat—and a son at that—hardly kindled much sympathy in Angie for this too-curious little boy. She'd treated him abominably, as she felt she had every right to do, and forced Douglas to send him abroad for his education. She hadn't even let Richard know when his father had finally passed on.

No, there had been no love lost between Angie and this boy. Nor, she was sure, did the boy—now a man in his early thirties—have any reason to feel anything but hatred toward her.

And now he was back in California, was he? And, what was worse, assuming control of the Channing family newspaper?

"There can only be one reason for this," Angie said at last.

Phillip nodded, assuming an air of superior knowledge. "To make trouble."

"Oh, more than that, Phillip. Trouble?" Angie asked scornfully. "You don't know Richard Channing. Trouble is only the beginning. This will end, you may be sure, in chaos, destruction and death!"

The silence that followed Angela's dire prediction seemed to swirl about the large room, engulfing them.

A look of horror seemed frozen on Phillip's face, his eyes locked helplessly with Angie's. She gave him a small, tight smile, with no hint of mirth in it, and crossed her legs on the longue. The full side slit of

the cheongsam fell open. Phillip's glance traveled
downward to take in the long, smooth sweep of
Angela Channing's still-shapely leg.

There was a discreet knock and Chao-Li entered.
"Coffee, Mr. Phillip?"

Chapter Two_____

There are VIP lounges in most major airports around the world. Diana Hunter had been in more than a few. There are seven VIP lounges at New York's Kennedy Airport and Diana was finding this one perhaps the most depressing she had ever experienced.

Not that she was doing any more than waiting for the morning flight to San Francisco. Mr. Denault had made sure of that. He'd more or less banished her to the window area, where great triple-paned sheets of plate glass gave out onto an utterly eerie scene in which giant jets roared and smoked their way skyward in utter silence, seemingly without making the slightest sound.

"You wait over there," Henri Denault had ordered her. "I have a few parting words for Richard. He wouldn't enjoy me saying them in front of a witness."

So, across the almost empty lounge, fully fifty feet away from her, the two men stood by the coffee bar, locked in what appeared to be the most deadly of discussions. Like the great jets outside the window, their conversation was totally silent. They were even too far away for Diana to read their lips.

It was just as well, she reminded herself. The Cartel was organized on a need-to-know basis. Mr.

Denault told you only what he thought you needed
to do your job. And not a bit more. At least, that was
the way he treated Diana. It was obvious that he had
much more to say to Richard.

Diana soon tired of the sterile view through the
lounge windows. Moving along a wall of smoked
mirrors, she headed for the ladies' room to freshen
her makeup. As she walked, she could see herself
reflected darkly in each mirror, moving like a ghost
in a haunted house, her slim young body gliding, the
shadowless sunlight giving her blond hair a kind of
foggy look piled atop her head. She sat down at the
built-in makeup table in the ladies' room and stared
at herself.

Clever face. The trick was never to let anyone
know *how* clever.

Perhaps only Mr. Denault would ever know. Before one joined the Cartel there were endless examinations, intelligence tests, psychological evaluations.
One couldn't even apply for a job without showing
proof of a brilliant college career. And, even then,
Denault demanded much more information before
he hired someone new.

As she redid her hair, piling it more tightly, Diana
reflected that joining the Cartel must be something
like joining a very strict holy order. Not that there
was anything mystical about what the Cartel did:
investments, pure and simple, in almost anything
that made money, from oil and gold mining to cur-
rency exchange and electronics. No, it wasn't the
work that made the Cartel such a fortresslike, reclu-
sive place. It was the discipline.

Like a holy order, it had its hierarchy. Henri
Denault was the supreme ruler here in New York.
But there was someone above him, in Europe, a
Pope never referred to by name. "Number One" was
this world ruler's only designation. And the others,

like Denault, who ruled the Cartel's work in places like New York or London or Frankfurt or Hong Kong, were subservient to no one *but* Number One.

As Diana left the ladies' room, she realized she had taken a different return path. She was, in fact, coming up almost directly behind the two men whose conversation she was not supposed to overhear. It was all quite by accident, of course. She stopped short, watching them in one of the eerie smoked-glass wall mirrors. They couldn't see her as long as she remained motionless. If she moved, it might attract their attention. She froze.

"—nothing of the kind," Richard Channing was saying, not in an argumentative voice but more of a pleading tone. "There is no way this project of mine could be considered independent of the Cartel."

"Not only independent," Denault contradicted him, "but a damned wasteful ego trip on your part, Richard. You don't belong in California and you know it. You belong here with me."

"But the stakes. Think of the stakes!" Richard's eyes almost glowed in the darkly reflecting mirror walls. Diana watched his handsome face seem to light up with enthusiasm.

God, he *was* handsome, she told herself. There wasn't a weak line in his face. It was all angles, all powerful, deep-cut grooves of power. And yet, far from seeming bleak or forbidding, he was criminally good-looking, the kind of man who turns heads in a crowd. And not just women's heads, she remembered.

As for Denault, who had the power to cancel Richard's new project, he seemed curiously unwilling to do anything more than caution against it. The whole thing was so unlike the hard, grim investment banker. He was used to barking orders, not reminders. Yet here he was, not telling . . . asking.

"I'm well aware of the stakes, Richard," he was

saying. "Or, at least, I'm aware of your promises about them. What was it you said?" He smiled almost sneeringly. "Nothing less than the whole wine industry of California?"

"Precisely," Richard responded. "With control of the newspaper I have the leverage to begin breaking apart the whole Falcon Crest empire. Let me put down roots in Tuscany Valley, and within a year I can hand you the whole operation on a silver platter."

"Tempting, I admit."

Denault was silent for a long moment. Diana couldn't see his face, except in profile, but she could see that searching, laserlike glance of his as it seemed to bore into Richard Channing's eyes.

"Just tempting enough," the older man went on. "I can't escape the thought that you've deliberately made it tempting so that the Cartel would finance your takeover of the newspaper."

"A straight business deal, Henri."

"Quite. You had your father's stock options. We had the money. By rights, those options belong to the Cartel."

"You needn't remind me." Richard's voice got a strangely hoarse quality to it, as if he were straining to utter his thoughts. "I don't need to be reminded that everything I am today is due to you."

"Hardly."

"As my adoptive father, you—"

"That has nothing to do with it," Denault cut in brusquely. "If you know me at all, Richard, you know there is no room in my life for sentiment."

"Yet, when I needed a father's guidance, you were there."

"Perhaps. And perhaps I would have been equally helpful to a total stranger, providing he had your abilities."

"Abilities you nurtured."

Henri Denault stood silently. Then: "It does no harm," he said in a dry tone, "to flatter one's superior officer, Richard. I am, as you know, immune to flattery, but still it does no harm." He produced a noise meant to be a chuckle; the result, however, was devoid of any warmth. "Just as long as you remember what you told me a moment ago—that you owe everything to the Cartel."

"That's not what I said."

"Never mind. It's what you should have said." The older man's finger gently prodded Richard's chest. "And here is something you should have added to that statement."

"Yes?"

"That what the Cartel gives," Denault said ominously, "the Cartel can take back."

"Those," Richard said in that strained voice, "are the rules of the game."

Denault's nod was curt, forceful. "I know some of the traps waiting for you in California," he said then in a softer tone. "There's the whole nostalgic thing of coming back to the place you were born. Of revisiting scenes you remember only from when you were a boy in your real father's arms. And, even stronger, there's the mystery of your true parentage, isn't there?"

"Yes." Richard's voice was very grave now, strained. "There's that."

"The whole question of who your real mother was. And the violent animosity of the woman who could have been your stepmother, if she hadn't chosen instead to cast you out of your father's life."

Neither of them spoke for a long moment. Richard's handsome face tensed, the smooth muscles clenching, as if swallowing something nasty.

"That bitch."

He paused and cleared his throat. "But, Henri,"

he said in a lighter voice, "it's the very existence of Angela Channing that guarantees my success and yours. I never wanted to humble anyone as I do her. I never wanted to wipe anyone off the face of the earth as I do her. And she ... *is* Falcon Crest. Destroy her and all of it falls to us."

"Flight 412, nonstop for San Francisco, now boarding at Gate Seventeen."

The announcement over the loudspeaker startled Diana. The two men turned away from the mirror wall and she quickly retreated along a different route until she emerged from the direction of the ladies' room.

"Diana," Denault called across the lounge. "I'll say good-bye here."

She joined the men. There was a moment of slight uneasiness. "You two needn't look so grim," she kidded them. Richard took Diana's arm as they picked up their small carry-on bags. "Henri?" The two men shook hands.

"I'm sending my best man with you," the investment banker said. "That she happens to be an attractive woman"—his austere face seemed to crack in a wintry smile—"is what we must call a fringe benefit, eh?"

He took Diana's hand and shook it firmly. "Take care of him, will you?" he ordered. "He thinks this will be child's play. I know different."

"The pair of you," she said, trying to lighten the situation. "So serious. After all, this isn't a funeral."

"Diana," Henri Denault said softly, "that ... is where you're wrong."

Chapter Three _____

Maggie Gioberti occasionally wondered what her life would have been like if she hadn't married into this turbulent family with its gigantic stake in the rich, productive Valley and its commanding position in the world of wine-making. But on a morning like this—clear, cool and brilliantly sunny—she forgot her doubts.

For a woman with two grown children, she looked amazingly young. Dressed in jeans, sneakers and a pale mauve tee shirt, Maggie knelt in her garden and carefully trowled the earth around her azaleas, breaking up clods into light, airy soil. It was scarcely breakfast time but she and her husband, Chase, had been up and working about the place for some time now.

The rural life, she thought, brushing back her thick mane of blond hair as it swung forward over her cheeks. It really is early to bed and early to rise.

It didn't apply to either of her children though. Both Cole and Vickie were still in bed and would probably remain there until late morning. As for Chase, he always piled enough work into his daily routine to occupy three men. As county supervisor, his responsibilities were regular and steady. But as half owner of Falcon Crest, his day was filled with emergencies, sudden problems that required instant solutions, and, overall, the steady, deadly implacable enmity of his Aunt Angela.

Maggie looked up through the line of slender lemon trees she had planted herself. Beyond, glittering in the morning sun, the Gothic pile of the family mansion rose out of its wraparound veranda to sharp, pointed spires and cupolas quite like some enchanted castle in a Disneyland devised by mentally disturbed architects.

She smiled. Not a bad image, she thought. She wasn't the kind of writer who hoarded up phrases for later use. The stories and screen plays Maggie wrote had to do more with the interplay of characters. The film script she was working on now, for example, concerned just such a locale as Tuscany Valley, with its tensions between rival families of vintners. Maggie called it "Tangled Vines."

She smiled a bit lopsidedly at the irony of the title, got to her feet and slowly walked back toward the gardening shed to replace her tools. On such a day it felt good to be alive. She had her work, a good man for a husband and two attractive children who might, one day, if they ever got out of bed, amount to something.

From the shed she could see her own home, a much more modest affair than the witch's castle in which Angie Channing lived. Yet it was big enough for the four of them and quite attractive in its lively way. Maggie drew in a long, full breath of clear morning air and exhaled slowly with some satisfaction.

Beyond her garden, in a small grove of orange trees planted on Falcon Crest property, something moved. Something white, or pale, wraithlike, seemed to flit between the trees under the thick cover of small dark green leaves and sweet-smelling blossoms.

Maggie watched. Then she saw her wraith again. Even at this distance she could tell it was Melissa, the tall, dark girl whose pregnancy had not yet begun to show through the . . . ? What on earth *was* she wearing—a nightgown?

"Melissa, is that you?"

The apparition seemed to melt into darkness behind the trunk of an orange tree.

"Melissa? Are you all right?"

Slowly, almost fearfully, Melissa's dark, pretty face appeared. "Maggie?" Reluctantly she emerged from the darkness, as if summoned by a séance. Maggie walked toward her.

"Are you all right?"

"Mm. Yes. Fine." The words came haltingly.

Maggie crossed from dazzling sunshine into darkest shade under the overarching shadow of the orange grove. The sweet aroma of orange blossoms was everywhere. At closer range now she saw that Melissa was indeed wearing her nightgown, a filmy chiffon thing, almost see-through. "How long have you been wandering out here?" the older woman demanded.

"Not long."

Up close the girl who had been Melissa Agretti looked tired. Circles under her eyes were a bluish-mauve, almost the color of Maggie's tee shirt. "How long?" Maggie persisted. This girl was about the age of her own daughter, Vickie, a fact which freed Maggie of any inhibitions about asking embarrassing questions.

Melissa's face went stone-dead. "All night," she managed to say.

"My dear!"

"All night," Melissa repeated. She began to sob.

Maggie reached out for her. She could feel the

slim young body buckle with the force of her sobbing. "What's the matter, Melissa? You can tell me."

"N-nothing." Melissa drew back and wiped at her eyes with the back of her hand.

In an inbred, closed-off enclave like Falcon Crest, Maggie needed very few clues to Melissa's unhappiness. The source could be summed up in a word: Lance.

Melissa Agretti, whose father, Carlo, owned the second-largest vineyard in the valley, had only recently married Lance, Angela Channing's grandson. Her reasons for the unholy union were perhaps as clouded as his. It was not a marriage made in heaven. But then, few things concocted by Angie Channing were even remotely heavenly, and most had about them the stench of brimstone.

"He doesn't seem to know I exist," Melissa said then, as if reading Maggie's thoughts.

"Lance has never been what you'd call a very sensitive person."

"Sensitive?" Melissa's eyes welled up again. "I don't even ask for that. I certainly don't ask for love. All I need is this much understanding." She indicated a tiny space between her thumb and forefinger. "A half inch of understanding, Maggie. Of what I'm going through. My situation. This hasn't been an easy pregnancy and Dr. Ruzza tells me it will probably grow even harder."

The two women surveyed each other for a long moment. A breeze filtered through the dense greenish shadow under the orange trees. A wisp of Melissa's long dark hair lifted and fell across her smooth young forehead. Unconsciously, she had folded her hands across her stomach, as if protecting her infant from a suddenly hostile world.

Maggie found herself wondering about the marriage and the baby growing inside this young woman. Angie's reason for promoting the marriage was

obvious: a merger between Falcon Crest and the
great Agretti vineyards would give her control of
perhaps the largest and most powerful winery anywhere in the world.

But what had Lance's reasons been? What was he,
a ne'er-do-well, ruthless opportunist, doing playing a
pawn in his grandmother's chess game? And the
baby? Considering that it had been conceived before
the marriage, perhaps that was the clue to forcing
Lance into wedded bliss.

Whatever the tangled vines that had produced
such fruit, Maggie thought, they had created the
deepest kind of misery as well. Melissa had everything:
beauty, a pleasant personality and a family fortune.
She was also possibly the most depressed and unhappy person Maggie had seen in many a year.

"Sometimes," Maggie reasoned, "a young man who's
played around the way Lance has takes a while to
settle into matrimony."

"He's already talking of a divorce." The words
came from Melissa almost unwillingly. "He's already
telling me it's not his baby and he'll have the marriage annulled."

Maggie took a step back. She was used to the
frankness of young people's talk these days—she heard
enough of it in her own family—but telling it like it
was, letting it all hang out, didn't seem to solve any
more problems than the old-fashioned discretion with
which Maggie had grown up.

"Why would he think the baby wasn't his?" she
asked then.

Melissa's dark eyes flashed in the greenish gloom
beneath the oranges. "Because," she said, "it isn't."

"Melissa!"

"No," the young woman insisted, "not his. Never
his."

"Do you . . . ?" Maggie paused. "That is, uh . . ."

"Oh, yes," Melissa assured her. "I know the father."

"But surely . . . ?"

"No." Melissa's long hair swung sideways as she shook her head. "No one knows. No one *will* know. Not even him."

"Not even the real father?"

"Especially not him."

"But why?" Maggie asked.

For a long moment Melissa's dark glance was fixed on the clear blue eyes of the older woman. "That," she said at last, "you will never know either."

Maggie listened to the sound of her words as much as to the sense of them. There was something peculiar about the emphasis she had put on her words. *You* will never know, she had seemed to say. Why me? Maggie wondered. But then, perhaps, she was imagining the whole thing.

In the middle distance, perched on a lower limb of an orange tree, a mockingbird lifted its head and sent a long trill of laughter into the still, scented air.

*Chapter Four*_____

"That's peculiar," Julia said. She was standing in the doorway of her sister Emma's bedroom. Though it was morning, both women still wore their nightdresses. "Chase *didn't* phone you?"

Emma's small, pert face was half buried in her pillows, her tousled hair spreading out around her like an aura. She seemed perfectly at rest, perfectly still. Only her wide-set eyes looked alive.

They darted this way and that around the room, resting for an instant on her sister, then flicking sideways to the morning sunlight in the windows, then across the room to the ornate doors of her great armoire, cream-colored with gold trim in the French Provincial style.

Finally her glance fastened again on her tall, slim sister, standing motionless in the open door, her face still expressing the question she'd asked. But Julia was always that way, Emma thought. Always the factual one, always demanding answers. And what a silly question. Her cousin Chase was Emma's friend, of course, but why wonder that he *hadn't* called her?

"Because he sure as hell woke me up this morning," Julia went on. "The way he was talking, I knew he'd phone you next."

"Nope."

"Emma, think. Your memory lately . . ." Julia's words died out.

There was no need to finish the sentence. Emma knew better than any of them how hazy her grip on reality was these days. Things somehow didn't seem real anymore—at least not at Falcon Crest. She couldn't put her finger on the moment they'd started to turn hazy and dreamlike. It hadn't happened all at once. But it surely was happening now.

"Chase definitely did *not* call me, Julia."

"Then you don't know about the shareholders' meeting."

Emma's eyes blinked once, then again. Something new to cope with? Some new problem? The air at Falcon Crest seemed filled with problems. She inhaled deeply, as if struggling for oxygen. Problems crowded out the oxygen. Problems lurked everywhere. No wonder a person couldn't keep her mind straight, couldn't remember things.

"No," she said at last. "No one told me anything."

Emma could hear the faintly defensive note in her own voice. That was Julia's fault. Her sister and their mother were always *on* her about something. Don't forget this. Did you remember that? Between the two of them they seemed to use up all the available air and light and space at Falcon Crest.

"Well," Julia said in that superior tone of hers, "since the two of us own equal shares in the *Globe*, I imagine Chase would want us both at the meeting."

"Today?"

Again Emma could hear the tone of her voice, retreating. Oh, not today, she seemed to be pleading. Must it be today? Instead she cleared her throat and sat up in bed. "Did you say today?" she demanded. Her voice sounded fake and defensive again.

"In an hour. We're supposed to meet Chase in the

sampling room at the bottling plant. Can you make it?"

"Don't be insulting," Emma snapped. "It doesn't take me an hour to get ready."

"Fine." Julia turned and left, letting the bedroom door slam behind her.

Emma sat up on the edge of her bed and let her feet dangle above the floor. Wonderful start to a day. Julia already angry at her. Chase calling meetings. *Too much* went on at Falcon Crest. Too much for any normal person to bear.

The word "normal" seemed to stick in Emma's mind.

Dr. Ruzza had used the same word, not too long ago. Emma had been to see him about her inability to sleep. He'd given her a mild sedative. "Normally," the doctor had said, "that should do the trick."

"Normally?" Emma picked up, again defensive.

She'd watched Dr. Ruzza's face go red. "I mean . . . you know . . ." He had gestured meaninglessly.

"Implying," she persisted, "that something isn't normal?"

"Not at all."

"Or somebody?"

"Emma," the doctor had said in his fatherly way. "What I used was a perfectly meaningless phrase. Normally, this sedative helps a person sleep. You're reading too much into it."

She'd stared at him the longest time and suddenly she was in tears. Dr. Ruzza had looked acutely uncomfortable, but that was nothing to the way he looked as she began to pour out her troubles to him.

"It isn't just the insomnia," Emma had babbled between sobs. "It isn't just the bad dreams when I do get to sleep, the nightmares that wake me up. It isn't the fact that I keep forgetting things. Simple things. Or that I really can't bear to leave my room in the

morning . . . can't wait to get back to it. Doctor, I'm
not stupid. I can recognize such symptoms as well as
you."

When he had failed to answer at once, when he sat
there thinking for such a long time, Emma's heart
had sunk in despair. Then she *was* going crazy. And
he was trying to find a kind way of telling her. And
there is no kind way.

"Look," Dr. Ruzza had begun slowly. "You've heard
it said nowadays, haven't you, that the world we live
in is getting harder *to* live in?"

"For me, yes."

"For everyone. The quality of life, even here in
Tuscany Valley, is changing. It's getting more strident,
more violent. Even in this pleasant little corner of
the world devoted to good grapes and good wine, we
can feel the mounting tensions, the changes . . . and
none of them seem to be for the better."

"Then it isn't just me?"

"No, it isn't just you, Emma. We cope with all this
through a process called desensitization. You could
call it growing a hard shell. Most of us manage that.
Society more or less hardens our shell for us. But
there are always a few whose skin never does harden.
Such people remain sensitive; in time they grow even
more sensitive. When that happens, life becomes quite
painful for them."

As she got out of bed now, Emma recalled the
doctor's words more clearly than anything else she'd
heard in the past months. His diagnosis had stuck
with her, word for word. Didn't that mean her mind
was still all right?

She bathed quickly and pulled on the handiest
dress, staring at herself in the long mirror. Poor,
dear, kind Dr. Ruzza—how gently he'd let her off
the hook. How diplomatically he'd told her the real
truth. Never mind his talk about society or the world.

In plain English he was saying, *Falcon Crest will drive you insane.*

In a sense she'd always known it. Her mother . . . well . . . Angela Channing's flinty bosom was nowhere for any young girl to lay her head. Her sister, Julia, had never had time for Emma either, once she'd married and given birth to Lance. And Lance himself, the other occupant of this great house, was someone Emma had always been wary of, someone too much out for his own good ever to be a friend in need.

Only Chase had been her friend, Chase and his dear wife, Maggie. But a great chasm, bulldozed by Angela Channing, now divided one side of the family from the other. Angela's idea of loyalty in a daughter was that Emma had to hate her mother's enemies. Chase was one such enemy, but Emma couldn't find it in her heart to hate him or to help her mother play all the tricky little power games that so exhausted the air of Falcon Crest.

Emma combed her hair carefully but put no makeup on her small, delicate face. A leprechaun's face, she told herself now. She looked like no one else in the family. Perhaps she was a changeling? Perhaps the fairies had substituted her for Angela's true younger daughter? She stared at herself in the mirror. She'd always wondered how Angela could have been her real mother. Perhaps she wasn't. Changelings . . . one read of them in the storybooks. Switched in the cradle. Fey folk foisted on human parents and raised as their own flesh and blood. Well, by God, she felt no kinship with Angela Channing nor, truthfully, with her sister or her nephew, Lance. She had always felt out of place here. This was hostile territory for Emma Channing.

She went to the great armoire and opened its doors. Standing back from it, on tiptoe, she craned her neck to see the canvas suitcase on the top shelf. That's what one did, Emma told herself. One fled from hostile territory. One didn't linger. One packed and ran for one's life.

She sat down on the edge of the bed and thought some more. Her mind began to compose a plan. She had to get Desi to take her to the train station or the airport. But it had to be done in such a way that Angela wouldn't know. Although, was it ever possible to do anything at Falcon Crest without Angela knowing?

Emma lay back on the bed and closed her eyes. She vaguely remembered getting dressed. But for what purpose? Had she anything to do, anywhere to go?

Sighing with the oppressive lack of oxygen in her bedroom, she pulled the pillow over her head. In the darkness she tried to remember a time when she had been happy. She made a little tunnel so that the exhausted air got to her. She dreamed without sleeping. It was lovely here in the dark.

And, besides, she had nothing else to do this morning.

Chapter Five

In the distance, San Francisco Bay sparkled under the hard noon sun. Miles beyond, past Sausalito and Tiburon, farther to the east behind a low range of hills, lay the rich, dark fertile soil of Tuscany Valley—out of Richard Channing's sight, but seldom out of his mind.

From this height, the fortieth-floor offices of the *Globe*, Richard Channing might well have stood at one of the great picture windows and faced east toward what he well knew would be his destiny. Instead, he sat with his back to the eastern view, hunched over a great desk on which detailed Corps of Engineers ordnance maps lay. Pencil in hand, Richard traced vineyard boundary lines. And so wrapt was he in this fine-lined work that he failed to hear the knock on his door.

After a moment it opened and Diana Hunter stood on the threshold. "Are you in or out?"

Richard flinched, almost as if she'd slapped him. He looked up. "I thought I left word not to be disturbed."

"That was yesterday." The attractive girl with the piled-up blond hair eyed him for a long moment. "You've done nothing since we got here but pore over maps. They tell me there's a newspaper to run."

"It runs itself," Richard barked. Then he made a face and pushed back from the desk. "Sorry. I'm probably still in jet lag. What's the problem?"

She opened a small notebook and flipped through its pages. "How much time have I got?"

He managed a faint grin. "Sit down. I said I was sorry. Lay it on me."

Diana managed to sit, cross her legs and not notice how far up this caused her dress to ride on her slender thighs. "Item One—your managing editor has wanted a word with you since yesterday morning. Item Two—a man named Chase Gioberti has called you three times. Item Three—I have word from Tuscany Valley that said Gioberti held a shareholders' meeting yesterday with an agenda that remains secret. Item Four—Mr. Denault just called from New York and wants to hear from you as soon as possible. Item Five—the mayor's secretary is trying to set up a meeting. Item Six—your broker has—"

"Stop. Halt. Cease. Desist."

"You told me to lay it on you. There are only twelve more items."

"Thanks." Richard shuffled the maps and rolled them tightly. He slipped them into a metal cylinder and capped it. "Send in the managing editor first." He glanced at his watch. "Get him out of here in fifteen minutes. Then get Mr. Denault on the phone. First things first."

Diana reached across his broad desk to the intercom and pressed a button. "Gladys, send in Mr. Loomis."

"You mean he's been waiting out there for two days?"

"More or less. With time off to run the newspaper." She paused. "You want to speak to him alone?"

"I want him to get the idea that between you and me there are no secrets," Richard told her. "You stay where you are. And pull down that dress an inch or so."

"Demure."

"But devastating," Richard added as the door opened.

Harry Loomis was one of the breed of newsmen who believed, as he soon put it to Richard, that "our main business is getting the facts and printing them."

"There are facts," Richard reminded him, "and . . . there are facts."

The editor paused and scratched the bald spot atop his head. His dark brown jacket didn't match his pale gray trousers, nor had he remembered to fasten the top button of his shirt and neaten the knot of his tie. But to Diana he didn't seem either ill prepared or ill at ease. Just natural, something like an old shoe. And, like an old shoe, he got stepped on.

There couldn't have been a greater contrast between two men, Diana found herself thinking. Harry Loomis was perhaps only five years older than Richard, but the two seemed to have arrived from different planets. Both were lean and rather intense in their own ways, but there the similarity ended.

Richard's good looks alone would have made him different from any other man. But it was what lay beneath the handsome facade that made the real difference. He seemed almost ready to explode with the importance, the sheer global weight of his own mission in life, plus a driven ambition held only loosely in leash.

No such fires possessed Harry Loomis. He had the air of an old-fashioned craftsman who could fix a watch while he listened to your troubles and gave you good advice. He had ambition, but not for himself—rather for some strange entity he called "the truth."

"There's not enough of it in journalism anymore, Mr. Channing."

"Call me Richard."

"Richard. What I'm saying is that in this land of ours there are maybe a handful of real newspapers left. The *Globe* is one. There's another down in L.A. Two on the East Coast. And I'm damned if I can volunteer many more. By and large, Mr. Ch—, Richard, the newspapers of America are mostly advertising giveaway sheets. They're filled with warmed-over public relations garbage, girlie snapshots and casserole recipes. It's no wonder people turn away from newspapers by the million to get their information from TV."

"You may be right, Harry. I know for sure TV can pay its people more than we can." Richard was silent for a moment. "But I keep getting back to the same idea. There's truth, and there's *truth*. The readers of the *Globe* are going to be interested in what you tell them about this new disarmament conference in Geneva. That's why you gave it the number one spot on yesterday's front page. But where did you put that story about the call girl whose body was fished up out of the Bay with two bullets in her heart?"

"Bottom of page three."

"And where's her diary? Where are some sexy photos of her alive? Show me a dead call girl and I'll show you a whole rogue's gallery of people—her pimp, one or more corrupt detectives and a dozen very nervous customers. None of *their* pictures are in the *Globe*."

"Christ, Richard, that isn't the *Globe's* style."

"No? What's style worth if it doesn't give the readers what they want?"

"They can read it in some yellow rag tabloid," Loomis retorted hotly.

"Some rag that's stealing away *our* circulation."

Harry Loomis' normally calm face had grown red. He scratched furiously at his bald spot. "You asking me for a complete turnabout in *Globe* style?"

"No, Harry. I'm not asking you. I'm telling you."

Silence fell over the big room. Outside the picture windows the sun poured in as it began its daily trek across the Pacific Ocean. Diana Hunter shut her notebook and laid it very carefully on the desk in front of her, as if it contained a high explosive, set to detonate at the next outburst.

"Scandal?" the editor demanded. "Nudie shots? Rumors? Innuendo?"

"That's it, Harry. I want the *Globe* moved out of the nineteenth century and into the last decades of the twentieth. I want a *live* paper, not a dead one."

Loomis got to his feet. "No thanks, Richard."

The new owner glanced at his watch. Ten minutes had elapsed. "Then you've got the rest of the day to clear out your desk and leave the premises. Miss Hunter will make arrangements for severance pay."

"Just like that, Richard?"

"Just like that, Harry." Richard smiled slightly. "On your way out, send in that young assistant of yours, Atkins?"

The editor nodded. "Atkins might be just hungry enough to do the job for you. His wife's expecting a new baby."

"Excellent, Harry. Good-bye."

"Do me one favor?" the editor asked.

"Certainly."

"Call me Mr. Loomis?" the man suggested, and walked out of the office.

Richard's mouth, open for a moment in shock, closed at last in a grim smile. He jerked his head sideways at the phone. "Get Denault."

Chapter Six

"Here," Angela Channing said, touching the lined pages of a great bookkeeping ledger. "Right here."

Phillip Erikson, standing behind Angela as she sat at her desk in the wood-paneled winery office, peered over her shoulder at the ledger. Almost carelessly his hand cupped her shoulder, gently massaging. "This is the part of the accounting program that Chase manages?"

Angie nodded thoughtfully. "If you know my nephew at all well, you know he's stretched himself too thin, running around taking care of a million details." She turned her head to stare into her attorney's eyes. "Chase is much too busy to pay any attention to these ledgers, even the part that is his responsibility."

"That's hard to believe. Chase is a businessman, after all."

Angie's laugh was bitter. "He's a poor excuse for one. My father, now *there* was a businessman. It's my impression that somebody could cook this part of the books without Chase ever knowing what had happened."

Outside the office's locked door, the work of the winery went on in an unending flow. At this time of the year, before the harvest of new grapes in October, the men were at work testing last year's wine under Julia's supervision, blending it with other strains and adjusting its alcoholic content to conform to the law. Each day a batch of new wine would be ready for the bottling and labeling plant down the road. Each day anywhere from a thousand to ten thousand bottles were filled, sealed, crated and shipped.

"Angie," Phillip said then, "you're forgetting the EDS."

"I forget nothing," she snapped. "Our electronic data system is the best, the latest in state-of-the-art computer control. Anything in this ledger is accessed into our electronic data bank."

"And *that's* what Chase consults. Not this ledger book."

Angie's smile managed to be both scornful and triumphant. "Sometimes, Phillip, your naïveté surprises me."

Erikson was silent for a moment. "You mean you could cook the computer?"

"I mean I already have. My grandson, Lance, may be hell on wheels with the women, but he did pick up a few useful bits of expertise in school. He knows computers."

"And he *is* your faithful grandson."

"He's already opened a duplicate channel in our EDS that appears to be the true set of accounts for Chase's part of the operation. When Chase switches on a computer terminal, that's what feeds him information over the video screen. But the original channel, with the true data, is now sealed off. There's an electronic lock on it that only Lance and I can open." Angela's voice seemed matter-of-fact, almost bored. But her face revealed a smug content.

The lawyer whistled softly. "My, my, my."

"Which gives me," Angie went on then, "the ability

to dip into Chase's side of the business without his knowledge."

Erikson's other hand cupped her other shoulder. "Angela, you're not only sexy, you're formidable. I'm glad I'm on your side."

"Are you?" Her glance held his. "But am I glad you're on mine?"

"Angela!" Phillip said in a shocked tone.

"A man like you . . ." Angie got out of her chair and strode to the window that overlooked the vast expanse of winery production. Vats stood in long rows receding into the distance, miles of vats, endless arrays held to a strict temperature in a warehouse of controlled humidity.

"Any man except a total leech," she went on then, more to herself than to her attorney, "when he works *for* a woman eventually ends up working against her. It's in the male genes. It has nothing to do with whether he feels she's attractive, or even that he loves her. It's got to do with male independence. And for the best, most sincere reasons in the world, he *will* end up doing her in." She swung on him. "You're no different."

"You flatter me, Angela. I'd have to be a lot smarter than I am to match some of the capers you pull."

"I can't say my marriage to Douglas was a happy one," she went on in an almost reminiscent tone, "but it was an educational one. I learned a lot about men from him, things I would never have learned from my father."

Phillip laughed. "I should hope so."

"Not sexual things. No, from Douglas I learned . . . treachery . . . deceit . . . betrayal . . . humiliation . . ." Her voice died out.

In the silence that followed, Erikson shifted uneasily from one leg to the other. Then: "I'm sorry, Angela. I know he made you unhappy."

"Is that the right word?" she asked him. "Somehow it doesn't seem evil enough."

Someone knocked at the locked office door. Angela Channing ignored the intrusion. "And his evil wasn't buried with him, was it?" she went on. "No, it has returned here to California in the form of his bastard son."

The pounding grew louder. Angie's great eyes swung sideways to the door. "What is it?" Beyond the glass she could see the foreman's unhappy face. He was shouting something but the soundproof door muffled his words.

Phillip unlocked the door and opened it. "Mrs. Channing!" the foreman burst out, "please call the big house right away. Miss Julia's been ringing for fifteen minutes but you had the phone shut off in here."

"Very well." Angie watched him back out of the room. "Lock the door again, Phillip."

She glanced at the small private switch box on the desk, punched a button and dialed a three-digit number that rang in the big house. It rang three times. Then:

"Channing residence," Chao-Li murmured.

"Chao-Li, did Miss Julia want me?"

"Miss Julia has driven to the airport."

"In heaven's name why?"

"Looking for Miss Emma."

"What?"

"Miss Emma took one of the Jeeps. We think she went about two hours ago," the Chinese explained.

"Why should that be the occasion for such panic?"

"Her suitcase. Gone."

"What?" Angie thundered. "Spit it out, Chao-Li!"

"Miss Julia says Miss Emma packed some clothes and left. Left Falcon Crest. Left Tuscany Valley."

"How can she be sure?"

"Miss Emma left a note."

"Saying?"

"Ah . . ." The Chinese faltered for a moment. "I do not have the note in front of me, Mrs. Channing. But—"

"I said spit it out!"

"The note said something about . . . ah . . . well, about Miss Emma's sanity. She said to protect . . ." Again Chao-Li paused. "Mrs. Channing, she said that to save her sanity she had to leave Falcon Crest."

"Oh, did she." Angela's voice sizzled with venom.

"Something to that effect."

"Then good riddance," she snapped. "And may she stay away . . . forever."

Chapter Seven

Like Falcon Crest, Bellavista was a roomy mansion in the typical California Gothic style, cedar-shingled, verandaed and decorated with spires. It sat almost in the geographical center of Carlo Agretti's expanse of vineyards, and, like Falcon Crest, Bellavista was the nerve center of a major enterprise.

Not that Agretti made wine. He had chosen long ago to concentrate only on the grapes, selling his produce each October to the highest bidder. And the Agretti harvest never brought anything but top dollar. Generations of Agrettis had contributed their toil and experience to producing some of the best merlot, sirah, gamay and other varieties grown anywhere in the world.

Perhaps, jealous neighbors hinted, Agretti's success was only a matter of luck, the chemical richness of the vineyard's soil, the way the sunlight warmed his slopes. It may also have been because the Agretti rootstocks, originally brought here in the late 1880s from Europe, had escaped the withering rot that had blighted the best vines in France and Italy after World War One.

When the wine-making countries of Europe sought to replace their blasted rootstocks with new, healthy ones, they had been forced to turn to California vineyards like Agretti's to buy new vines. It was literally true that the best of Europe's wine grapes grew on roots imported from California.

Melissa, Carlo's only daughter, had read all this in the family records. Her father had told her the old stories time and again. She missed this strong link of family tradition now that she lived at Falcon Crest. This evening, feeling faint and vaguely nauseated, she had begged the Channings' chauffeur to drive her "home."

Oh, yes, she told herself, Bellavista is home.

She dismissed Desi and walked slowly, almost painfully up the steps of the veranda. From a distance she seemed to move like an elderly woman carrying a load too great for her, not the vibrant young bride who had only recently married Lance. But no one expected her arrival tonight, so no one saw the painful homecoming.

She found her father in his den, smoking one of the stubby black cigars he still imported from the old country. "I knew it," Melissa said, forcing a smile, "all I had to do was follow that horrible smell and I'd find you."

They embraced. Where Melissa was tall and slim, Carlo Agretti was squat, a true son of the soil who never wanted to stand too tall above it. After a moment he held his daughter at arm's length. "I haven't seen you in . . . nearly a week, is it?"

"Two."

"And you look . . ." Her father stopped. "You're not well, Lissa?"

"I'm fine. Really."

"This time of year," he apologized, "this is our busiest, when the grapes need all our time. I've neglected you, *tesora*."

"I have a husband for that."

"Yes. I haven't forgotten." Carlo glanced behind her. "Is he here with you?" When she shook her head, Carlo sat her down in the easy chair across from him. The room was filled with the mementos of a long and productive life, the walls covered with awards, certificates of merit, photographs of ceremonies and gala harvest picnics.

"Tell me, Lissa. How is my grandson?"

She patted her abdomen. "He's fine. We're both doing well, Papa."

"Dr. Ruzza tells me we have to be caref—"

"Dr. Ruzza is a nervous old maid," the young woman interrupted. She glanced around her. "Somebody ought to take a good feather duster to this place."

"Never mind all that." Carlo eyed her for a long moment. Then: "What brings you here tonight?"

Melissa sat back and boldly returned the questioning glance. There was no way she could ever pull the wool over her father's eyes. Man of the soil he might be, but the emotional bond between them was too strong for her ever to fool him. Besides, there were no secrets in Tuscany Valley. He might not know the precise reason his daughter was unhappy but he could sense her misery and make some accurate guesses as to its cause.

"Lance," she said then, "is not really cut out for marriage."

"No?" Carlo bristled. "Maybe he needs a little pruning, then."

His daughter's laugh sounded hollow. "He's not one of your vines, Papa."

"That I know. He's one of the rootless kind, that kid. He's too vain to think he belongs here among us. He's too careful of himself to take a chance on sinking roots. So, instead, he runs wild. And you know what happens to a weed in this part of the world?"

There's no answer to that, Melissa thought. You don't prune a person the way you prune a vineyard. She hadn't come here to measure her father's anger. She wanted his comfort, his reassurance. She wanted to recapture her sense of belonging, here in Bellavista . . . home.

The telephone rang and she was spared the need to speak. "Yes, this is Agretti. Who?" Her father's glance shifted sideways to Melissa and his eyebrows went up. "Richard Channing? *The* Richard Channing?"

Melissa sat forward, watching her father more closely. She had heard the illegitimate son of Douglas Channing had returned. But what did he want of her father?

"Not now," Agretti was saying into the telephone. "I don't leave my vines for the next three months. What? Yes, I know San Francisco's only an hour's drive. But in that hour anything could happen, a hailstorm, a flood, high winds. Till October, we live here at the mercy of Mother Nature."

Carlo Agretti sat back in his chair. It creaked comfortably as he listened. Now and then he would turn an amazed face at Melissa, as if what he was listening to was either the funniest or the most insane conversation in the world.

"No way. It's precisely five thousand acres. And all under intensive cultivation. I'm not like the people at Falcon Crest. I use every inch of my land for grapes."

He listened again. This time, to Melissa, he rolled his eyes and touched his forehead with one finger. Then: "Mr. Channing, it's crazy. Don't waste your time, Mr. Ch—. All right, Richard. I tell you, Richard, this land is my life. I wouldn't sell either."

He shook his head slowly several times. "No. Absolutely final. Good night, Mr. Chan—, ah, Richard."

Slowly he replaced the telephone receiver and took a long, steadying breath. "Now that," he told his daughter, "is what you kids would call a gigantic ego trip."

"For Richard Channing?"

"Yes. But even more for me. You know what he was asking?"

"It sounded as if he wanted to buy Bellavista."

"That's it. And my, oh, my, did he try. He wanted to buy the land. Then he wanted to sign an exclusive contract for the grapes. Then he suggested me selling him half the land. Then . . . I lost track of the offers."

"Where would he get that kind of money?"

"He claimed he had it, and to spare," Carlo Agretti said. "He said he'd just bought up his father's shares in the *Globe* and there was plenty more cash where that came from."

"And you said no?" Melissa asked.

"Naturally."

"No to any part of it?"

"No to *every* part of it," her father corrected her. "Lissa, you know me. I'm a simple man. What I know, I know better than anybody. And what I know is grapes. Take that away from me and I'm no better than the lowest tramp on Skid Row. Give me a bunch of money in place of my grapes and what have I got? Piles and piles of dirty green paper. Where's the fun in that? Where's the challenge? Where's the life?"

"So that's what you meant, that it was an ego trip for you, too, saying no to that much money. Did he offer a lot?"

"Baby," her father told her, "it's numbers with a lot of zeros added on. A barrel of nothing, Lissa. They say every man has his price? Okay, every man but one. And you're looking at him."

Melissa jumped up and hugged the squat little

man. "You make me proud, Papa," she said. "You make me proud to be an Agretti."

"Thank you," he said in a humble voice. "Now that you're up with the swells there at Falcon Crest, it's good to know you still have me in your heart."

"I always will," she said quietly.

"And you in mine," he promised her. "And after you, Lissa, the grapes. My heart can hold all that. And no more."

"Good."

"Ask me to sell Bellavista . . ." Carlo Agretti fumed. "The nerve of the man. Before I sell Bellavista," he added, taking Melissa's chin in his hand and looking her straight in the eye, "before that, I would die!"

*Chapter Eight*_____

The small chartered four-seater airplane had long since disappeared along the darkening southern horizon. Chase Gioberti sat without moving behind the wheel of the Jeep Emma had used to make her escape. He still wondered why she'd involved him in her plan, but, as he stared at the thick envelope she'd left in his hands, he knew the answer lay inside.

Poor Emma, Chase thought. She never did things except in a dramatic hurry. Tearing off alone in the Jeep, finding him at the nearby general store, begging him to drive the vehicle while she crouched down beneath the dashboard. It was like a Nancy Drew girl's adventure book.

Chase grinned and rubbed his trim beard. It had been his idea, once he knew what Emma wanted, to drive to the smaller airstrip used by the tiny crop-dusting planes and ultralight flying enthusiasts. Nobody at Falcon Crest would think of Emma making her escape from there. They'd be watching the railroad station and the big airport.

And now she was gone. She'd promised to phone Chase and let him know where she ended up on the money she was carrying. That way he could send her more as she needed it.

"But, oh, Chase, if you value my life, please, *please* don't tell a soul where I am," she had pleaded.

"Not even Maggie?"

"It's my secret, in your hands," Emma had reminded him. "Please don't let me down. Please!"

And now her envelope was in his hands. Before he opened it, Chase made sure no one was watching. The airstrip seemed deserted this time of evening, but he could never be sure. He glanced carefully around him—at the tied-down small planes, the rickety hangar building, dark inside, the parking lot with nothing parked but the Jeep itself.

Typical Chase Gioberti behavior, he told himself. Mr. Careful. Mr. Look-Both-Ways.

Well, it hadn't hurt the other day, when he'd called that *Globe* shareholders' meeting, to come on as Mr. Cautious. The trouble with the tangled ownership of the *Globe* was that the entire game had just been stood on its head.

For years the shares had been evenly parceled out to the grandchildren of Jasper Gioberti, meaning Emma, Julia and Chase himself. And there had hung over them the purchase options Douglas Channing had left to his illegitimate son. But for decades now it had been a fact of life that Richard Channing had no money to exercise the options.

At the meeting Chase had called, which Emma had forgotten to attend, he and Julia had reluctantly sat down to figure out where they stood as far as the newspaper was concerned. It became clear that the mysterious Richard owned precisely as much of the *Globe* as did the three of them put together. Richard owned half and Julia, Emma and Chase each owned sixteen and two-thirds percent, totaling the other 50 percent. Plus a few shares owned by the general public.

"In other words," Julia had complained, "he has us beat."

"Separately," Chase had reminded her. "But not if we vote together."

"If we vote together," Julia had retorted, her mind as sharp with figures as her mother Angela's, "what we've got is a fifty-fifty head-on collision. Nobody wins."

"Not quite. Some outstanding shares are held by the public. Anybody who bought those would be able to deal himself into the game."

As he sat in the growing darkness behind the wheel of the Jeep, Chase ran again through the mental arithmetic of the thing and decided there were too many unknown quantities. Until he knew what Richard had in mind for the *Globe* he couldn't reach any valid conclusions. But Richard wasn't returning his telephone calls.

Typical, Chase thought. The man had lived most of his life abroad or in New York. He was a completely unknown quantity. None of them even remembered him as a boy. It was doubtful that any of them had ever seen him in those bygone days for more than a fleeting glance. He'd been treated as a pariah, a guilty secret, something to be hidden, spirited away.

Chase could remember asking his own parents about the missing boy. His father, Jason, had been no help. Chase's mother, who had been Jacqueline Perrault before she married Jason Gioberti, had been even less forthcoming. And now that she spent most of her time in Europe, Chase had almost no access to her. Even on the few occasions when she came back to the Valley to see how her grandchildren, Cole and Vickie, had grown, Jacqueline remained her usual taciturn, private, mysterious self.

"I don't mind that about her," Maggie once told

Chase. "I prefer an aloof grandmother to the smothering kind. Cole and Vickie have a lot more respect
for your mother that way, Chase. They're a little in
awe of her. So am I, to tell the truth."

So was he, Chase reminded himself. Having Jacqueline Perrault as your mother was a little like being
the son of one of the ice sculptures they trotted out
at formal dinners. The workmanship was terrific, all
smooth and glittering, but you didn't dare put your
arms around her and give her a bear hug. You
would freeze to death.

He hefted the thick envelope Emma had left with
him. It was too dark now to read its contents. Chase
switched on the Jeep's headlights and climbed down
onto the dusty roadway. He stood in front of the
Jeep and ripped the envelope open.

Inside . . . what? Chase pawed through the contents,
heavy wads of engraved stock certificates decorated
with gold seals. Good Lord! These were Emma's
voting shares in the *Globe*!

With them came a handwritten note on Falcon
Crest letterhead. "Know all men by these present,"
Emma had written in her awkward, backhand script,
"that all certificated shares in the San Francisco *Globe*
held in the name of Emma Marie Channing are hereby
devised and transferred for proxy purposes to Chase
Gioberti for a period of one year from today, together with my power of attorney to vote these shares
in my interest as he deems best."

She'd signed and dated the document. It might
not stand up in court, Chase thought, but it would
give an opponent quite a headache to try and
break.

By the light of the Jeep's headlamps, Chase stood
there, rubbing his beard and doing his Mr. Cautious
mental arithmetic. Richard Channing had half the

votes. Julia had sixteen-plus percent. And he, Chase Gioberti, now controlled slightly more than a third.

Okay, Richard Channing, man of mystery, your move.

Chapter Nine_____

The Honda 500 emitted a blast of noise like a bull elephant on the rampage. Cole Gioberti twisted the handlebar throttle and forced more exhaust through the twin tailpipes. This hog revved like a jet, he thought. It was the fastest thing on two wheels in the whole Tuscany Valley.

He slammed into gear and did a half-wheelie as he roared off along the dirt road that led from the migrant workers' quarters back to his own home. His mother, Maggie, would have had dinner ready for some time now. Cole was an hour late and fervently hoped the family had eaten without him. Otherwise he'd never hear the end of it.

What the hell, a man of nineteen was entitled to a little fun. And some of the cute Mexican girls among the migrant workers were ready, willing and able to supply as much fun as Cole could absorb.

Chuckling to himself, the young man rocketed along the bumpy road, leaving an immense plume of dust in his wake. But now that the sun was down and night had settled in, who would know he was polluting the good, clean air of Tuscany Valley?

If he used the cutoff through the Bellavista property, he'd be home half an hour sooner. The problem was, Carlo Agretti had ordered him off his property, hadn't liked the fact that Melissa used to see a lot of Cole before she got married. But at night there *are* no problems, Cole told himself. Just as long as old Carlo can't hear the noise this 500 makes, I'm safe.

He eased up on the throttle and ghosted along in the darkness, nearing the Agretti cutoff. But just as he reached the corner he saw a long, low-slung Jaguar coupe rumble smoothly in through the main driveway, headed toward the Agretti house. Too risky, Cole thought. With visitors on the premises, and a noisy hog like this Honda between his knees, he'd be sure to be spotted, even at night.

Reluctantly, Cole wheeled his cycle onto the main road and headed home like an arrow. He was in enough trouble with his family for being late. He didn't have to complicate it by getting old Agretti's dander up as well.

The Jaguar was a taupe color, just a shade darker than the hue of Diana Hunter's nylons as she swung her legs from behind the wheel of the powerful car and stood in front of Bellavista. Alerted by her arrival, the veranda suddenly blazed with light and a chunky Chinese guard came outside, a 12-gauge double-barreled shotgun cradled in his arms.

"Yes, miss?"

"I'm here to see Mr. Agretti. Tell him it's Diana Hunter, from the San Francisco *Globe*."

"Just hold it there a second, miss."

The guard went inside. A moment later he came out, shotgun leveled at the new arrival. Behind him the squat form of Carlo Agretti moved warily, a black cigar clamped in one corner of his mouth.

"You from that Channing fella?" he demanded.

"I am, Mr. Agretti. I'm asking for ten minutes of

your time." Diana started up the stairs. "I think
you'll find the proposition attractive."

"Hold it." The twin muzzles of the Chinese guard's
gun watched her with the intensity of two feral eyes.

Agretti looked her up and down, from her high-
heeled black patent-leather pumps up her sleek, taupe
legs to her brief navy suit and flimsy blouse tied with
a colorful man's foulard. "You don't look like you
could hurt me too much," he said then.

The guard cackled. "Depends on what you call
hurt."

The men chuckled as Diana moved onto the
veranda. "Ten minutes, Mr. Agretti," she repeated.

"What's the hurry?" He led her back to his den,
the same room where he and Melissa had talked
earlier in the evening before she'd gone back to
Falcon Crest. "Have a seat." He set out two big,
sparkling clean red-wine glasses. "Would you like a
glass of wine? It's some I make for myself. I don't
sell it."

"That would be lovely."

Putting out his cigar, he poured the two glasses
half full from an unlabeled bottle, held his glass to
the light, swirled the bright ruby liquid, then inhaled
its aroma before taking a careful sip.

"Not too many people have ever tasted this wine,
Miss, ah, what was your name again?"

"Diana Hunter." She sipped daintily. "Excellent. A
full nose and a really terrific finish. You can be
proud of this wine."

"So tell me, what's Mr. Channing up to this time?"

Diana carefully put down her glass. "You see, over
the phone, he was at a disadvantage. There are fine
points to the bargaining process that can be best
accomplished face-to-face."

"Without anybody tapping the line," Carlo Agretti
finished for her. He winked. "So Mr. Channing sends

out a pretty woman to soften up the old *paisano*, that it? Face-to-face, as you say."

"What he could mention on the telephone was money, Mr. Agretti. You turned him down cold. And Mr. Channing isn't used to that. So he asked me to try to change your mind."

"He isn't used to being turned down?" Agretti's voice had thinned to a sneer. "That's too bad. Lemme tell you something—it gave me a great deal of pleasure to turn down Mr. Channing."

"No need to antagonize him. He can be a very valuable friend if you let him." Her voice held a note of caution.

"Yeah?" the old man's voice had gone up a tone or two as anger began to creep in. "What if I don't want him as a friend? Tell me that? What if I don't want any part of him *or* his cartel."

In the sudden silence Diana Hunter glanced around the room at the pictures, the awards, the certificates. Richard had sent her into a booby trap. This was no simple-minded peasant. This man knew a lot more than any of them dreamed.

"Cartel?" she asked then in her coolest voice.

"Hey, Miss Hunter, when I let somebody taste my wine, I don't want to play funny games with them. I'm a guy who levels, you understand. So don't you play funny games with me."

"But I don't understand you."

Agretti finished the rest of his wine in one furious gulp. "The cartel? You never heard of it? And next you're gonna tell me you never heard of Henri Denault. Or the idea that Channing comes out here to try and buy up the whole West Coast wine industry for Denault's cartel."

"This is amazing," Diana countered. "The man makes an offer for one vineyard and he stands accused of masterminding some mysterious statewide takeover."

"Bellavista first, then the rest. You gotta start somewhere. Channing and Denault want to start with me. Now, finish your wine and get out of here. I took a look at you and thought, here's a pretty woman. What's wrong with a glass of wine and ten minutes talk? But you don't talk. You play games."

Diana glanced at her wine. It was tempting to finish the lovely, velvety liquid, but she wanted to maintain her cool stance with Agretti. "Money isn't all that Mr. Channing could offer you for Bellavista," she said then. "That's why I'm here in person."

"Offering what?"

"How about . . . ? Let's call it freedom," she said airily.

"What?"

"In the agricultural businesses, record-keeping can't be as precise as in manufacturing. So a lot of agribusinesses may not report quite accurately to the IRS. Corners are cut now and then. Sometimes a vintner doesn't even realize he's cut a corner till it's too late. When I say freedom, I mean freedom from someone informing on you to the IRS."

Carlo Agretti sat there in stunned silence. Then: "I'll . . . be . . . damned. Here's a prtty woman, I tell myself. How can she hurt me? Five minutes of talk and you already got a knife on my jugular?"

"It's just a suggestion," Diana retorted coldly. "You'd be the best judge of how you stand with your taxes. But you might find Mr. Channing's offer a welcome escape hatch. Liquidate your property and stop worrying about the IRS."

Agretti was on his feet. "Out!"

Diana got up. "No need to make a decision now."

"Out of here!"

"Just give it some thought," she added, moving toward the doorway of the den.

"Get out of here! Fong! Bring the shotgun!"

"I'm going."

Breathing heavily, Carlo Agretti watched her leave the house. He could hear her sharp heel taps as she descended the veranda steps. A moment later the sleek car purred into life. With a screech of tires, it swung around in the driveway and headed off the property. Some moments later Fong returned to the den.

"She's cleared the property, boss."

"Okay. Shut down the gates and go to sleep."

"Check."

Agretti felt his breathing ease off. The pounding in his head came to an end. He sat at his desk and shook his head slowly, sadly. So that's what he got for letting a pretty woman in the house!

That Channing and his rotten cartel. They were all snakes. Taking him for a fool, some brainless *contadino* who had no idea of the world outside Tuscany Valley. Well, he'd shown her, shown them. Shown Henri Denault. God, how the man seemed to haunt him all these years. Wasn't it ever possible to get rid of such memories once and for all?

"Carlo," a voice said.

He glanced up into the shadows beyond his desk. He knew that voice. It was not Fong, his night watchman, nor was it the silky voice of Miss Hunter.

He was staring into an eye of steel, the muzzle of a .9-mm Browning automatic pistol. It fired the kind of slug that went small into your chest and came out the size of a grapefruit. A great tightness seized Carlo Agretti by the throat.

"Who's there?" he wheezed.

"Carlo," the voice said, "pick up the phone."

*   *   *

Cole Gioberti coasted down the driveway to his parents' home. Only the porch light was on. He let himself into the house and soon realized no one had waited dinner for him. In his excitement over the Mexican girls, he had completely forgotten that the four of them, Mom, Dad, Vickie and he, were supposed to have dinner in town at the steak restaurant.

While he cursed himself for missing a great meal, the phone began ringing. It would be Dad, wondering what the hell had happened to him. "Yeah, I know," he said as he picked up the phone. "I goofed."

"Cole?" a strange voice asked.

"Who is this?"

"Carlo Agretti."

"What did I do now?"

"Can you come over here?"

"No way. The last time I even got near your property you read me the riot act."

"I've changed my mind. Melissa asked me to."

"Huh?"

"Cole, it's Melissa." The voice hesitated. "She's here. She wants to talk to you. Right now."

"You gotta be kidding, Mr. Agretti."

"Please. Right now." The line went dead.

Cole stood there in the darkened living room and tried to figure out this change of heart. Half an hour ago he was carefully avoiding the Agretti property because he was as welcome there as a coyote in a pack of sheep. Now the old guy himself was issuing an engraved invitation—in Melissa's name?

But why not? Maybe there was still something there between Melissa and him, Cole thought. And, anyway, dinner was shot. He got back on his cycle and roared off into the night.

The main house at Bellavista lay in darkness. Cole dismounted from the Honda and pulled his emer-

gency flashlight out of his saddlebag. He flashed it
over the veranda. The front door was wide open.

By the light of the flash, Cole picked his way
inside. He'd spent enough time here as a kid—and
later when he and Melissa were dating—to know his
way around the darkened house.

"Mr. Agretti?"

The house lay still. Not a board creaked. Not a
curtain whispered in the breeze.

"Melissa?"

Cole moved forward in the direction of the room
Mr. Agretti used most, his beloved den. "Mr. Agretti?
It's Cole."

He was standing in the doorway, flashing the light
from side to side. At first it missed Carlo Agretti.
Then it landed full beam on his face, wreathed in
blood. The desk brimmed with blood. A bronze statue
lay on its side, soaked in red. Cole picked it up, then
hastily put it down.

Flashlight wavering, he dialed the telephone.

He could hear the ringing on the line. He reached
over to feel Carlo Agretti's pulse. There was none.
With blood on both hands now, Cole waited. Ring.
Ring. Ri—

"Sheriff's office. Can I help you?"

"This is Cole Gioberti. I'm at Bellavista. You'd
better send an ambulance."

"What's the problem, Cole?"

"It's Mr. Agretti. He's dead."

"What?"

"Murdered."

"What makes you say that?"

"Come and see for yourself."

"Right. And, listen, don't touch anything!"

Hanging up the telephone, Cole got blood on the
instrument. He switched on the room's overhead
light and caught a glimpse of himself in a wall mirror.

Blood stained his shirt in three places. Both his hands dripped red.

Don't touch anything, he repeated dully. Oh . . . my . . . God . . .

Part Two

Chapter Ten

Here in the Valley, Julia thought as she pulled on dark panty hose and stepped into a black simple dress, we take our public occasions very seriously.

She gave herself a grim smile in the mirror as she adjusted the hang of the dress and fastened its front buttons. Black was not her color, never had been. She was too light a blond to carry it off; the black seemed to drain her face and arms. But she had the height and the figure for black, she decided as she surveyed herself.

Where was that small black straw hat? She so rarely wore a hat except as a sunshade that she had quite forgotten when last she'd worn the petite black one. Had it been at her son Lance's wedding to Melissa Agretti? Probably.

That was the Valley social calendar for you, Julia told herself: weddings and funerals. The occasional christening. The Founder's Day outing. Serious events, nothing frivolous. Black would be the usual color in most cases. And especially today, the funeral of her daughter-in-law's father, Carlo Agretti.

Again she checked her image in the mirror and, again, her lips flattened in that peculiarly grave smile.

Well, she could guarantee the behavior of at least

one of them at today's sad occasion: she, Julia Channing Cumson, would play the proper mourner.

About Lance Cumson she wasn't so sure. He'd been treating Melissa to a full dose of his "cool": never there for meals, often out all night, a nightmare distortion of what an expectant father should be.

Julia knew she should have spoken about it more often and more sharply to Lance. He was behaving inhumanly. It hurt her to watch the way he ignored his bride. But Julia knew that Lance's grandmother had already begun to pressure the boy about the same thing, if for perhaps different reasons. And when someone lived under Angela Channing's pressure, he didn't need an extra load coming his way.

She turned to leave her room and descend to join the rest of the mourners gathering at Falcon Crest. But once more she came back to the mirror and subjected herself to a merciless scrutiny. Hat . . . gloves . . . dress . . . the look on her face. Yes, that, too, Julia reminded herself. Expressionless was not the right look. Concerned. Sad. Understanding.

Almost like an actress rehearsing a role, Julia moved her face slowly through several expressions. Refined grief. Utter compassion.

Good. Picking up a small black leather bag, she left the room and descended the stairs at a rapid pace, her long legs flashing. Then, abruptly, she slowed her progress. The rest of the curving marble staircase she took slowly, almost regally, one sad stair at a time.

Three steps from the bottom she paused. In the library, by the fireplace, she saw her son and his bride standing together. Well, not quite, but within a foot or two of each other. They were talking and, for a wonder, Lance's expression was almost . . . yes! . . .

almost a replica of his mother's face. Julia grasped
the balustrade for support. Lance compassionate?

As she watched, her son actually started to put his
arm around Melissa's shoulder. It was a slow, almost
reluctant gesture. And, just as slowly, Melissa took a
step backward, out of his reach. She smiled sadly.
Lance leaned over and kissed her cheek.

Would wonders never cease? Julia asked herself as
she descended the remaining stairs and walked directly into the library toward the young couple. Lance
looked up guiltily, as if caught in an indiscretion.

"You . . ." He paused and seemed at a loss for
words. Then: "Melissa's okay, Mother. She's going to
be all right."

Julia's answer was to go directly to the young woman
and take her in her arms. "Of course she will," she
said soothingly. There was no responsive hug from
Melissa. Over her shoulder, Julia could see her mother
and Phillip Erikson in the far corner of the library,
well out of earshot.

That explained it. Lance had put on this performance for his grandmother.

Kissing Melissa on the cheek, Julia scanned the
long room. As she arrived a curious thing happened.
In quite the same manner as Lance—almost guiltily,
as if caught in something they didn't want witnessed—
Angela and Phillip instantly stopped talking.

"Mother?"

"Oh, it's you." Angie's black dress was, if anything,
cut even more severely than her daughter's. Phillip's
dark gray suit neatly set off the small black armband
he wore. Without further ado, they resumed their
conversation as if Julia weren't there.

"It can't be tied up completely in land," Angie
said.

"But it is," the lawyer assured her. "I made it my

business some months ago—you remember why—to do a full financial check on Carlo Agretti."

He lowered his voice to make sure it didn't carry across the long library to the dead man's daughter. "He wasn't the simple farmer he seemed to be," Phillip went on. "We all knew that. But what we didn't know was that he'd mortgaged so much of his land to make investments outside the Valley."

"A mistake," Angie announced in a crisp tone. "You don't build an empire that way. You make the land pay its way. But you never give anyone an ounce of control over it, especially not a bank."

"What are you saying?" Julia asked. "What's Melissa inheriting? Mortgaged land and a load of bank debt?"

"Keep your voice down," Angela hissed. "That's exactly what he's saying. The question is, does Melissa know it too?"

"I doubt it," the lawyer responded. "Carlo played his cards very close to the vest. He wouldn't have told his daughter a word of this."

To Julia's ears a faint note of discontent sounded in her mother's words. "Have you told Lance?" she asked very quietly.

"I'd have to be insane," Angela retorted. "It's taken all my efforts to get him just to treat the girl decently on the day of her father's funeral."

"Then how do *you* feel about it," Julia persisted.

Angela Channing's wide eyes narrowed slightly as she stared into her daughter's face. "What kind of question is that, Julia?" Her voice seemed to grow even more venomous for being low-pitched. "A man has been murdered. His estate may be in disarray. How do you expect me to feel on the day we bury him? It's a sad occasion. Period."

"So sad," Julia said with sweetly fake politeness, "that all you and Phillip can talk about is mortgages."

Angie's mouth opened in shock. And that was the way Julia left her as she collected Lance and Melissa and headed for the limousine.

"Of course I'm going," Cole said in a mulish voice. "I don't know why not," his father Chase agreed. "Maggie," he turned to his wife, "Cole's done nothing but what any good citizen would do—report a murder."

Maggie wrapped her arms around herself and seemed to be hugging her body for warmth. "I can't explain why I feel this way, Chase. But I'm his mother and if I can't speak my mind, who can?"

"Mom," Vickie begged her, "we all get these . . . uh, feelings."

"Premonitions," Maggie added. "Strong ones."

"About what?" her son demanded. "Look, Mom, I don't put on a suit and a tie—"

"And black socks and shoes," his father added.

"And comb your hair," Vickie put in.

"—just for nothing," Cole concluded. "I didn't like the guy. He didn't like me. But he was Melissa's dad and the fact that I'm the one who found him doesn't mean I shouldn't be at the funeral."

Maggie glanced around at her family. "So I'm outvoted."

"It's not a vote, sweetheart," Chase told her. "This is a decision a man makes for himself. And Cole's made it."

Maggie's hand reached out as if to touch Cole's face. There were a thousand things she could have said, a thousand fears. Couldn't any of them see the incriminating position Cole was in? she wondered. Couldn't they picture, as she had with her writer's mind, that scene last night when the sheriff had found Cole covered with Carlo Agretti's blood? Couldn't any of them realize that Cole had given

no coherent reason for being at Bellavista last night?
Of course he was innocent. Of course he'd merely
been a good citizen. But Maggie had seen enough of
official justice in this world to know that sheriffs and
district attorneys rarely saw things the way one's own
family did.

"A man," she heard herself say in a choked voice,
"has made a decision. That's right. Cole is a man,
now. It's hard . . . it isn't . . ." She turned directly to
her son. "I keep picturing you as a little boy. You're
not. I know that"—she touched her forehead—"up
here. But not"—she touched her stomach—"down
here. Never mind. The decision's been made."

She took a long, shuddering breath. "Let's go."

If it had been up to Diana Hunter, she would have
suggested that she and Richard Channing remain in
the background at the funeral. Or perhaps not even
attend. But here they were, virtually at graveside
now, as the coffin was slowly lowered on its heavy
tapes, inch by inch into the freshly dug ground.

Across the entire Valley sunlight poured down its
richness. Endless rows of vines baked in the brilliant
heat. The service at the church had been the briefest
of funeral masses and the cortege to the cemetery
had been on foot. Now, heads bared to the sun,
several hundred people stood in silent prayer as the
last remains of Carlo Agretti were returned to the
soil he had tilled so well.

Diana's glance shifted subtly from Richard's taut,
handsome face, nearest her, to the face of the woman
on the other side of the grave, whom Diana had
never met. But there was no mistaking the aura of
power about Angela Channing, her great eyes glittering behind her veil, her glance fixed—not on the
coffin or the grave—but upon Richard.

To one side stood the people Richard had identified as Chase Gioberti and his family. It was hard to tell what Chase really looked like because his trim beard defeated Diana's powers of concentration. But there was an odd similarity about the two men, Chase and Richard, their height and build and the conformation of their heads.

Chase's son, Cole, shared his mother's fair good looks, but where Maggie Gioberti seemed lost in thought, Cole glanced from one face to the next, as if forever engraving in his memory the mourners who had gathered to pay their last respects.

Odd, defiant boy, Diana thought. She watched the priest sprinkle holy water over the coffin. Then a tall, slender girl, heavily veiled, stepped forward, accompanied by a young man whose face was set in an almost frozen look of compassion.

The daughter, Diana told herself. And the man must be Lance Cumson, her husband. Peculiar, the way they stood, not touching, a great deal of space between them as Melissa Agretti Cumson bent down and picked up a small bit of the rich Valley soil.

She paused and seemed to steel herself. Then she dropped the handful of earth into the grave. It made a hollow sound as it hit the coffin lid, now hidden from view. The priest intoned his final phrases and for a long moment everyone stood in complete silence.

Far away a flight of small birds swooped over the vines, chattering and shrilling as they skimmed the great fields. Nearer at hand a tractor engine started with the iron clatter of a heavy diesel. Tuscany Valley had returned to its labors.

The crowd of mourners began to break up. Diana could see Chase Gioberti heading in her direction. Richard started to move away, but Chase was too fast for him.

The two men, so similar in build and height, faced

each other. "Richard Channing?" the bearded man said. It was hardly phrased as a question.

"And you're Chase," Richard replied.

They looked each other over for an instant. "You don't believe in returning telephone calls, do you?" Chase said then. "I'll be in San Francisco tomorrow. Are you free in the late morning?"

Richard half-turned to Diana. "I'm calling a shareholders' meeting in the near future. That's the time for you to have your say."

"They tell me you've fired Harry Loomis. That you're changing the newspaper's style," Chase persisted. "You haven't the legal power to do that, not without consulting the other owners."

"Minority shareholders," Richard said coldly, "will have to wait in line."

"Minorities have a way of sticking together. Then it's called a majority."

"Meaning?"

Chase started to say something, then checked himself. "Perhaps you're right, Richard. Perhaps that meeting you intend to call is a better time for you to find out."

"Find out what?"

The bearded man smiled slightly. "But that," he said softly, "would spoil the surprise. Wouldn't it?" He turned and walked away.

Angela Channing had taken Melissa's arm as they walked slowly along the gravel path of the cemetery. "I'm so terribly sorry about this, my dear," she murmured.

"Are you, Mrs. Channing?"

"I know how difficult it all must be with the baby on the way. There is no good time," Angela purred, "to lose one's beloved father. But this could hardly have been worse."

Cole came up on the other side of Melissa. "Hi," he said.

"Cole," the bereaved young woman responded. "I'm glad you came." She took his hand and pressed it softly.

"I'd like a private moment with my grandson's wife," Angela snapped.

"You've got all the time in the world, back at Falcon Crest," Cole spoke up. "Lissa, it was a terrible shock. I know that. I just wanted you to know that if there's anything I can do . . . any help . . . whatever . . . I'm here for you."

"That's sweet of you, Cole."

"The way you were there the night her father died?" Angie asked, her voice brittle with innuendo. She swept back the veil covering her face and glared at the young man. "You're a fine one to offer help. It seems to most of us that you've already helped . . . too much."

"What's that supposed to mean?" Cole demanded.

"Ask the sheriff," Angie retorted.

They had stopped in the shade of a great fir tree, the ground beneath their feet carpeted with long brown needles cast off in previous years. As the older woman and Cole stared into each other's eyes, Richard Channing appeared.

"Miss Agretti," he said. "I'm sorry, I meant Mrs. Cumson, may I introduce myself? I'm a distant relative of yours called Richard Channing." He put out his hand and took hers.

The fury in Angela Channing's face distorted her features into a demon's mask. "You're no part of anybody's family," she growled.

"Easy now," Richard said smoothly. "You'll pop a vein."

"Melissa, let's go. Neither of these people is someone with whom you should associate."

"What a lovely name," Richard murmured. "Melissa. It has something to do with honey, doesn't it? A sweet name, perfect for you." He was still holding her hand. "I didn't know your father very well, Melissa. But he may have told you I wanted to do business with him."

"He mentioned it."

"Bellavista is such a wonderful place. I come from here, you know," Richard went on. "And I want to sink roots back here where I belong."

"You come from nowhere," Angela said in a gritty voice. "You're illegitimate in every sense of the word. And the sooner you go back to nowhere, the sooner we'll have peace in the Valley again."

"*Arrivederci*, Melissa," Richard said. He picked up her hand and kissed it, his eyes holding hers. "Till we meet again."

Angela took the younger woman's arm and marched her off toward the waiting limousines. Richard's handsome face cracked in a broad smile as he watched them go. Then he turned to Cole. "How did you get up there next to me on Angela's hit list?"

Cole had a stubborn look in his eyes. "What's it to you?"

"People with the same enemies often become friends."

"Name's Cole. Cole Gioberti."

"The lad who found Agretti's body?"

Cole's face went white. "That's not . . ." He stopped. "And I'm not a lad," he finished lamely.

"But you are a prime suspect," Richard informed him. "My reporters have been working over the story pretty thoroughly. You may be as innocent as a newborn lamb, my lad, but in the absence of anybody more likely, the sheriff could decide you're his best bet."

Cole glanced around him. "How would you like to say that out of a new hole in your face?"

"Put there by you, laddy-boy?"

Cole's right arm cocked back. His fist started in an upward arc aimed at Richard Channing's strong chin.

The older man sidestepped and, almost as an afterthought, drove his stiff fingers into Cole's rib cage. Cole gasped and doubled over. Suddenly Diana Hunter appeared at Richard's side.

They propped Cole up against the trunk of a tree and watched him for a second trying to catch his breath. Then, silently, they left together, moving toward where Diana had parked the taupe Jaguar.

"Was that necessary? He's only a boy."

Richard grinned at her. "But don't you dare call him one. Did anyone notice?"

"Hard to tell." She walked along in silence awhile. "Did *you* notice Emma Channing?" she asked then.

"Where was she?"

"That's the point. She wasn't." Diana glanced at him out of the corner of her eye. "Odd."

"Very. Can you look into it?"

"Grist for your mill?" Diana asked.

"Diana, there is nothing in this Valley but grist. Buried secrets. Hidden relationships. Clandestine scandals. The new *Globe* is going to have a field day."

"Sounds more like a bloodletting."

Richard nodded as they got into the car. "And that young lad—only you mustn't ever call him that—he's going to be my first lamb led to slaughter."

"Seems too young to have accumulated much scandal."

"Don't let his callowness fool you," Richard declared. "He's a big, hulking, self-destructive, hotheaded, accident-prone meathead. Intimately connected with Falcon Crest. And I'm about to plaster him all over tomorrow's front page."

Chapter Eleven _____

Maggie sat at her typewriter in the small room off the kitchen that had once been a pantry and was now her office. Writing this last part of her film script had become much harder. Lately her mind had filled with new problems that crowded out her thoughts about "Tangled Vines" and how she could bring it to a conclusion.

And now, this new distraction. It had arrived with the morning mail, delivered by the postman with a special flourish: "ARRIVING TODAY SFAP NONSTOP PARIS FLIGHT. JACQUELINE."

Maggie reread the radiogram and, by accident, started to roll it into her typewriter, as if it were a blank sheet of paper. Laughing at her own distracted behavior, she rolled it out, got up and left her office. There would be no more writing today.

Chase's mother, Jacqueline Perrault Gioberti, was arriving at San Francisco Airport this morning on the transpolar flight from Paris, and at this moment Chase and Cole were driving to San Francisco to pick her up. This wasted at least half a day for each of them. But Jacqueline Perrault was a great consumer of other people's lives.

Maggie opened her big refrigerator-freezer and

wondered what she might pull together for a special "Welcome Grandmother" dinner tonight. It would have to be the full treatment: four courses, three wines, candlelight, the best china and silver. And Vickie and Cole on their best behavior.

For a woman who had married a California vintner, Jacqueline remained forever and remorselessly French. Always a petite, pretty woman with a thick head of curly blond hair, she was, Maggie thought, the epitome of European chic, that special look that American women, no matter how much they spent on clothes and makeup, never achieved.

Maggie wondered, not for the first time, what this mysterious quality of chicness might be. She decided, as she sat down now and scribbled notes for a menu, that the chic was in the mystery itself. American women were a known quantity to themselves, to each other, to their men and to the world at large. American beauty had an open look. There might be secrets, but the look didn't depend on them. It depended on being open.

Jacqueline's French chic depended on an aura of mystery. What was this impossibly well-turned-out woman really like beneath the Chanel suit, the Ferragamo shoes, the St. Laurent coat, the Dior hat? The veil of mystery was a trick, of course, but a lasting one.

In Jacqueline's case, however, it was more than a trick. As often as she had conversed with her mother-in-law, as frequently as Chase had reminisced about her, Maggie knew almost nothing of this petite bundle of Gallic charm and reserve.

As the widow of Jason Gioberti, she had money but no more than had been left to Chase. Yet her life-style must cost her dearly, Maggie knew. Nominally based in Paris, Jacqueline could surface almost anywhere in the civilized world, sending postcards to

Vickie and Cole from exotic ports of call like Macao,
Antofagasta, the Seychelles, Leningrad and Chad.

She seemed constantly on the go, and not with the
traditional wanderer's backpack, either. When Jacqueline Perrault traveled, a minimum of eight matched
Louis Vuitton cases moved with her, everything from
the odd gold-clasped vanity case to the immense
steamer trunk in which, as children, both Vickie and
Cole would often hide . . . together.

As if she had summoned up this very apparition,
Cole drove the Jeep into their front driveway loaded
to the rim with matched Vuitton. Behind him, Chase
turned the Olds into its parking space and, quite like
a chauffeur, came around to the passenger's door
and ushered his mother onto the soil of Falcon Crest.

I suppose, Maggie thought, I ought to feel jealous.
Chase and Cole never showered such attendance on
Maggie, nor would she ever think of asking for it
unless she was too sick to handle matters for herself.
A nice example of French versus American style, she
thought as she walked through the house to the
front porch to welcome her mother-in-law.

"Such a surprise!" she said as they embraced. The
older woman's thin, almost wiry arms encircled her.
For an instant, Maggie fought off the mental image
of a spider embracing a fly.

"You look marvelous," she went on.

"You lie charmingly," Jacqueline responded, smiling.
Her accent seemed to get more French with the
passing years. Maggie could remember, when she'd
first married Chase, that her mother-in-law spoke
rather plain American English with only a slight
back-of-the-throat roll to her r's.

"But it is you who are *très jolie, très charmante*,"
Jacqueline was enthusing. "And where is my beautiful granddaughter?"

"She's at school. But she's got the afternoon off."

"My grandson has gained several centimeters in height, *n'est-ce pas?*"

"Several kilos in weight," Chase volunteered. "He's turning into solid suet, this kid. I have to find more muscle-building work for him than romancing the señoritas."

"That's it," Cole urged sarcastically. "Everybody on my back at the same time. Sock it to me."

They settled down in the living room and sipped glasses of Maggie's lemonade. "I was most sorry to hear the sad news about Carlo," Jacqueline said then.

"You really didn't know him that well, did you?" Chase asked.

Maggie watched several expressions cross that mobile face with its carefully outlined mouth and cleverly rouged cheeks. "*Un peu,*" Jacqueline said at last with almost no expression at all. "A little, as I knew most of the other grape growers. Through your father, Chase, secondhand, so to speak. But Carlo Agretti, I have . . ." She stopped and slowly sipped her lemonade. When she finished and spoke again, it was on a completely different subject.

"Maggie, how does the film script progress?"

"It doesn't, I'm afraid."

"This family has to learn to give you more time for your writing."

Maggie glanced at her husband. "You heard what your mother said?" They grinned at each other. "No, Jacqueline. I have the time. It isn't that. In fact, I'm within ten pages of finishing it. But . . ."

"But too many distractions," the older woman surmised. "I know the feeling well. The world is never fully prepared to give to the working woman the kind of mental privacy it willingly gives a man. There are always the needs of the children. The dinner to be prepared."

Her eyes widened stagily in their neatly crafted

beds of mascara and mauve shadow. "By the way, I am taking all of us to dinner this evening. That's understood, *non*?"

Maggie smiled appreciatively at the gift of free time Jacqueline had just made. But she couldn't help wondering where her mother-in-law got her insights into the spare time available to a woman who pursued a career other than homemaker.

Had she ever had to face such time problems? Surely not here in the Valley. Perhaps now, as a much-traveled widow? It was always vaguely understood that Jacqueline did something rather unspecific, some sort of charitable or other fund-raising work. But would that have given her an insight into Maggie's problems of time? Not likely. The older woman had all the time that money could buy.

"I am not without friends in the film colony," she was saying in her thickening French accent in which "friends" came out "fwonz."

"Anybody crazy enough to take a look at my script?"

"*Bien sûr.* I will give you some names and addresses, Maggie."

Jacqueline searched the boxes on the cocktail table for cigarettes. Finding none, she opened her own pack. Both Chase and Cole sprang forward to light it and Maggie couldn't help bursting into laughter.

"My cavaliers," Jacqueline said, joining in the mirth.

She puffed happily away for a moment. "What other news in the Valley? I understand the Agretti girl has married that odious Lance, whose baby will be born, ah, how do you put it delicately, perhaps a few months early?"

"Mother," Chase put in, "that's about as delicate as a meat cleaver. But it is the current news. Oh, and the change in *Globe* ownership."

"Of this I have not heard."

"You knew that when he died Douglas Channing left a great many stock options available for purchase."

"Did I?" The petite woman seemed to be sparring with her son. "It's so long ago."

Maggie's ear caught something false in the older woman's voice. She began to listen more closely. Usually the flood of Gallic compliments and enthusiasms washed over Maggie without effect. But now she was paying rather close attention to her mother-in-law.

"You must remember," Chase persisted. "It's been hanging over all our heads for so long. That one day those options would be exercised. Well, they have been."

"I beg your pardon?"

"The man they were left to has found the money and bought the stock."

"The man . . . ?" Jacqueline's cool voice seemed to falter.

"Richard Channing. You remember, the son Angela never seemed able to give Douglas? Well, Richard's back in San Francisco running the *Globe* and coming on bold as brass. He even showed up at Carlo Agretti's funeral."

"And took a punch at me," Cole groused.

"What?"

"That's all right," the young man explained. "I took one at him first."

"My word!" Jacqueline exclaimed.

Maggie watched the cigarette drop from her fingers. She dived forward to rescue it before it burned the sofa or floor. She managed to snatch up the cigarette and drop it in a bowl.

"Maggie! I am so sorry, *ma chère*."

"That's perfectly all right."

She could see the fine tremor shaking Jacqueline's hands, the tremor that like an internal earthquake had caused that smooth facade to crack for an instant.

Now she could see the woman hiding her hands. They were shaking badly. No wonder she'd been unable to hold her cigarette.

"Are you all right, Jacqueline?"

"Fine. Just fine." Her lips moved silently, as if rehearsing her next line. "Richard Channing," she said then in a voice that almost, but not quite, shook as badly as her hands. "Richard Channing in San Francisco," she said more strongly, as if mastering the tremors. "Well, well, well."

Chapter Twelve_____

Lance hadn't visited his falcon in thirty-six hours. The bird grew restless when it didn't hear its master's voice. Eyes covered by a leather hood, it shifted uneasily from claw to claw, producing a faint rasping noise in the back of its throat. Its legs were gyved together loosely and its wings were similarly restrained, a prisoner until Lance released it.

Lance stood in the doorway of the bird's lonely cell. If he didn't come to feed it, no one would go near the bird, not even Chao-Li, who was normally as fearless as they came. Lance couldn't blame them for not wanting to go near the falcon.

Trained for great, sweeping flights, conditioned to see sharply for miles, by heredity able to plummet like a stone and grasp its prey in steellike talons, the falcon was a true predator, a killer on the wing. Tied and blinded as it was now, its fury could be homicidal, or so everyone thought. Only Lance knew better. The bird had been trained to his hand and his voice. Tired, hungry, inflamed by imprisonment, it would still bow to his will.

And so, one day, would this whole empire, Falcon Crest, of which the bird was only a symbol.

Lance smiled, almost pleasantly. Things were turning his way at last. He watched the bird, careful to remain utterly silent, his breathing muffled, so that even the falcon, with its keen sense of hearing, couldn't detect his presence.

Yes, things were breaking nicely for him. He hated to admit it, but Grandmother's idea of marrying that wimp, Melissa, hadn't been a bad one. She wasn't, after all, hard to look at, even now that she was starting to show her pregnancy. And Lance didn't mind that it was a difficult pregnancy. He rather liked the idea that her bouts with pain and nausea, her constant need to lie down, pretty much kept her out of his hair.

He had all the advantages of bachelorhood and, as a husband, he pretty well had the Agretti property sewed up in his hot little hand. Once the old man's will was probated—he had no heir but Melissa—the whole thing would drop into Lance's lap. It would need only a formality of signing a few papers. In Melissa's poor shape at the moment, she'd probably sign anything just to keep him off her back.

Even the disappearance of Emma was working for Lance, he decided now. It made his grandmother more dependent on him. She'd given him the job of helping Phillip Erikson find Emma. And she'd also added the confidential assignment of cooking the computer channels of the EDS to keep Chase Gioberti ignorant of his own financial condition.

What the hell, Lance told himself, he deserved every bit of luck that was coming his way lately. He'd been his grandmother's houseboy for long enough, taking her lectures, her tricks, her schemes, her threats. Now that she found him useful, now that he was an essential part of her plot to add the Bellavista grape fields to Falcon Crest, now he cut some ice with her.

This business of doing people favors worked two

ways. Grandmother needed undercover help with
her schemes? Fine. But secrets bind people to each
other. The more he did for her, the more power he
could wield over her.

Up until now, Lance thought, he'd been like this
falcon: pinioned and hooded. Now Lance would be
free to fly, to pounce, to claw and to kill. That was
the way the world went and he wanted his part of it
. . . now!

He reached carefully for the strings that tied the
hood to the falcon's head. With one hand, he pulled
off the blinders. With the other he threw a dead
mouse to the predator. Its cruelly curved beak
snapped shut like a shears around the furry body of
the mouse.

"Good boy!" Lance said. "Sensational reflexes."

Greedily, blood spurting from its beak, the falcon
chewed and swallowed, gorging itself in a crimson
orgy of gluttony. Lance grinned with sheer pleasure.
If he was close to one thing in this world, it would be
this bird of prey.

The swallowing sounds, disgusting to anyone else,
pleased Lance. Finally the bird had finished his meal.
A weird, choking gurgle sounded at the back of its
throat. Its eyes, bright as stars, seemed to concentrate their power on the face of his master.

A great, deafening shriek came from the bird. Its
beak yawned wide, as if to swallow the whole world.

Chapter Thirteen_____

Sheriff Robbins was basically capable at his job, although at times he had a tendency to sound incredibly stupid. Physically he was right—tall, strong, square-jawed. He'd been middleweight boxing champ in high school and—although no one knew this—was already a Brown Belt in karate.

Behind his back, several of Sheriff Robbins' men referred to him as "the prince," not meant with affection or respect. He was a martinet, curt, petty about details, much given to shouting orders rather than simply speaking them. But it was also true that Sheriff Robbins had a tough job on his hands maintaining his authority in Tuscany Valley. Not that the Valley was a lawless place. Far from it. Give or take a few Saturday-night brawls among the winery hands when they'd sampled a bit too much of the new vintage, and give or take the odd break-in burglary, crime was well under control.

No, the toughness of the job, and of Sheriff Robbins' style, too, was the result of the fact that in Tuscany Valley every major grower and vintner thought he was a law unto himself.

"They figure," he explained to his deputy, Sid Rawls, "the law stops at their fences. Inside, they're the boss, the judge, the jury, the whole works. You take somebody like Angela Channing, now."

"Naw, *you* take 'er, Sheriff."

Robbins guffawed. An instant later all laughter had wiped off his face as he said, "This is our first murder in three years, Sid. We have to come down hard. All these owners are going to want it handled nice and soft. You watch."

"Meaning the Channings and the Giobertis?" Rawls suggested.

"Them especially. Because, let's face it, the only suspect we got happens to be one of their family."

"Come on," the deputy joshed him. "You don't seriously figure Cole Gioberti for the killer."

"He's a hair-trigger kid," the sheriff insisted. "Remember when we had him up on that assault charge last year? The only reason we couldn't make it stick is because the guy he beat up wouldn't prefer charges. And the only reason for that was somebody bought him off."

"Punching a guy in a fair fight is one thing," Rawls mused. "Battering Carlo Gioberti's head into a pulp is another."

Sheriff Robbins was silent for a long moment. "Yeah, that's the real hitch. Forensics says it wasn't one hard blow that did the old guy in. It stunned him, but then the killer went to work like a maniac, like a machine. It took him twenty blows to make sure he'd done the job."

"Cole's a husky kid," the deputy said. "He could brain a guy in one."

Neither man spoke. Outside, in the squad room, someone was shouting. "See what the ruckus is, Sid."

Rawls went to the door and peered outside. "Reporter and a photographer."

Sheriff Robbins' shoes slammed down off the desk to the floor. He reached for his khaki tie and tightened it neatly in place. Then he glanced at himself in a mirror on the far wall, noting his receding hairline. "Let 'em in."

"Sheriff," the reporter began. "Thanks a lot. I'm Dolan, from the *Globe*. This is my photographer, Klein. Can we take five minutes of your time?"

"Always glad to help the press, gents. Sit."

Diana Hunter put down the telephone, picked up her notes and entered Richard Channing's office by a private door. "I just finished talking to Forbush," she said. "He's got names, dates, places, signed statements and photos."

"Fast worker. Make sure he gets a bonus next week."

"He had help, Richard. If you include Dolan and Klein, we've got seven people out there in Tuscany Valley digging up dirt."

"Bonuses for all of them."

"First let's see what the lawyers tell us about printing the stories."

Richard made a disparaging clucking noise. "I'm surprised at you, Diana. We don't have to bother the lawyers with this one. We've got Falcon Crest dead to rights."

"Yes," she agreed, "on this migrant labor thing we do. Forbush says he's rarely seen such poor housing. The hovels have no electricity or water. And up to a dozen people are living in each shack."

"Lovely."

"But as far as the Agretti murder's concerned, there hasn't even been an arrest."

"Wait till Dolan gets through with that sheriff."

Maggie was grateful for the fact that Vickie and her grandmother had gone into San Francisco for shopping. Jacqueline's presence was too distracting for her to work. But this afternoon Maggie had finally finished "Tangled Vines." She stared at the last page, still in her typewriter, and allowed herself the luxury of a triumphant grin.

"Freeze frame," she read aloud. "Fade out."

In script parlance that meant "The End." And never in her life had she been happier to type those words. "Tangled Vines" had given her a lot of trouble, mostly because Maggie wanted it to ring true to the life of the vineyards and their people. She'd managed to catch the full flavor of the scene with colorful characters and a plot that held great interest. What more could a prospective movie producer ask?

The telephone rang. Maggie reached for the extension on the office desk. "Hello?"

"Mrs. Gioberti?"

"Speaking."

"Uh, is your husband there, ma'am?"

"He's in the field now."

"And your son?"

"Who is this, please?"

"Mrs. Gioberti, it's Sid Rawls at the sheriff's office. We have a few more questions we need answered, I'm afraid."

Maggie sat back. She could feel something cold squeeze at her heart. "Haven't you gotten enough statements from Cole?"

"This is routine, ma'am. Just routine," Rawls said nervously.

The grip on her heart hardened until it was almost painful. Maggie's career as a writer had begun years ago when she worked as a newspaper reporter. She was always wary when a policeman used that word "routine." All police work was routine and the end of it was always to put someone behind bars.

"Can I have him call you when he gets in?" she suggested.

"If you could give us a guess as to where he might be about now."

"I have no idea, Mr. Rawls."

"Well. Then ask him to call. Many thanks."

When she hung up, Maggie got to her feet, massaging her breast where the icy pain had been. She had lied, of course. She knew precisely where Cole and Chase were, in the laboratory, checking a new fungus that had appeared in the southern quadrant last week. She frowned as she paged through the Falcon Crest internal telephone directory, found the lab's three-digit number and dialed it.

"Chase?"

"Hi, darling."

"Is Cole with you?"

"Right here. Why?"

"Deputy Rawls just called. They have more questions. Just a matter of routine, he says. Chase, I'm frightened."

"I can't imagine what new questions they'd have." Concern crept into his voice.

"Nor can I."

"Damn them," Chase burst out, "with their routine. They think nothing of destroying someone else's routine."

"I said Cole would phone them when he got home."

"What's that?"

Over the line Maggie could hear loud background noise. "I didn't tell them where you were. I said . . . Chase? Can you hear me?"

"Maggie, there's a helicopter overhead. It's deafening."

"One of yours?"

"No." There was a long pause while the phone filled with chopper noise. "No," Chase said then, "it's from the sheriff's office."

*   *   *

Flashguns flared. Camera shutters snapped. Two husky deputies hustled Cole into the sheriff's office, his arms handcuffed behind him. Chase followed.

"There was no need for this!" he shouted. "It's outrageous."

Sheriff Robbins came to the door of his inner office. "Sit him down right there," he barked. The deputies shoved Cole into a chair.

"You've been watching too many Nazi movies on late TV, Robbins. This is how the Gestapo stages a raid, not the way you pick up someone for questioning."

"I had my boys in the chopper look for your Jeep. When they found it they made the arrest. Just routine."

"Arrest!" Cole shouted.

Chase jumped forward so quickly that he had the sheriff by his khaki tie before anyone knew it.

"What kind of farce is this, Robbins?" Chase demanded. "You want to question Cole or throw him in jail?"

"Ease off," the sheriff croaked, grabbing at Chase's hand. "Or they'll be two of you behind bars."

Chase relaxed his hold on the man. Flashguns set off bright blue explosions of light. Shutters whirred.

"Cole Gioberti," Sheriff Robbins said then, "I hereby arrest you on suspicion of murder. You are hereby warned that anything you say may be taken down in evidence and used against you at your trial. You are hereby further advised that you have the right to notify an attorney of your choice."

"Cole," his father burst out. "I'm calling a lawyer right now. You have cooperated fully with these maniacs. Now you have the right to stand mute until advised by your lawyer. You understand?"

"Yeah." The young man looked dazed.

"We'll have you bailed out by dinnertime."

Sheriff Robbins straightened his khaki tie. "Now, look," he said in a softer voice, "you don't want to be putting any wild ideas in your boy's head, Mr. Gioberti. We don't intend to rush our routine"—he glanced at the reporters to make sure they were taking notes—"just because Cole is the son of the county supervisor."

"You've got nothing, Robbins," Chase said, trying to match his calm tone. "You're in a panic, trying to dig up anything you can. We'll have Cole bailed by dinner."

He turned to the press. "Now, then, gentlemen, would you like the story of the Gestapo's daring daylight helicopter raid?"

Chapter Fourteen

Julia had been meaning to do this for some weeks now. Driven by guilt at Lance's unfeeling behavior toward Melissa, she had finally made the move. Despite the young woman's acute bouts of morning sickness, Julia had cajoled her into spending a working day with her.

"I don't promise a picnic," Julia had explained. "But it'll be a novelty. And it beats sitting around the house feeling rotten."

Which was why the two women were in a Jeep jolting along one of the many dirt roads that crisscrossed the vast Falcon Crest lands. Julia had shifted down to low gear in four-wheel drive to make sure the uneven road didn't upset Melissa's queasy stomach.

"We're zipping along at four miles an hour, dear," she told her daughter-in-law cheerily. "Let me know if it bothers you."

She glanced sideways at the tall, dark young woman, who held tightly to the Jeep's side. Sick she might be, Julia judged, but she had courage and, perhaps, something more. Melissa had the land in her blood, as did Julia. For both of them, the well-being of the vines was a paramount fact of life.

"Just another minute and we'll be at the winery," Julia promised.

Ahead of them the long, low sheds, in which the fermenting vats stood, formed a pleasant whitewashed contrast to the endless rows of twisting vines with their curling green leaves and fragile tendrils of grapes. Only recently had the grapes bloomed from the size of an orange pip to something more than half an inch in diameter. Soon, as the late summer sun did its work, the clusters would grow huge, bursting with sugary fluids.

Julia found herself comparing the condition of the grapes with that of Melissa. Both bore burgeoning life. Both would come to fruition at about the same time, mid-autumn.

"When I was pregnant with Lance," she said suddenly, without thinking, "I felt just like a grape cluster. Getting bigger and heavier every second."

Melissa's dark eyes regarded her with grave attention. "Did you?" she asked. Behind the eyes a flicker of pain showed. "Funny."

"Funny?"

"Just . . ." Melissa looked away. "Just funny."

Carefully, Julia braked the Jeep to a gentle halt, hopped out and came around to Melissa's side to help her down. But the younger woman was already standing on the ground. "I'm really all right," she assured her mother-in-law. "Are we going to the lab?"

"I have to check some of the older vats. This way."

The two women walked to the far end of the winery, Julia carrying a small leather bag with her, the kind of Gladstone old-fashioned doctors used to use. It had been her grandfather's bag before her.

Most of the instruments inside dated back to Jasper Gioberti's era, nickel-steel thermometers, oddly shaped glass beakers, pipettes and the long tubes with rubber bulbs on top that tested the ferment for specific gravity and alcohol content.

Of all Julia's possessions, her jewels, her antique cabinets and tables, she prized this battered old leather bag and its contents the highest of all. It formed a direct link between her grandfather, who had founded Falcon Crest, and Julia, who had recently assumed daily technical control of its vast creative capacity.

"These three here," she said as they entered the cool shade of the winery. Julia could feel the instant change from outside heat and dryness to the controlled atmosphere within the building.

The two women rolled a ladder-table to the side of the first great fiberglass vat. It dwarfed them with its immense white bulk. Melissa steadied the table and Julia climbed the ladder to unscrew a circular porthole near the top of the vat.

"Mm," she said, inhaling. "A few more whiffs of that and I'd be staggering. Hand me the gravity tester, will you?"

When they had finished all three vats, Melissa helped Julia wash up the instruments. "Be very careful with that one," Julia cautioned her. "It's a real antique. Made in Prague some time in the 1870s and used by Alsatian vintners. It's marked in Réaumur, not Fahrenheit or centigrade."

"This belonged to your grandfather?"

"Yes."

Melissa seemed to cradle the great thermometer as if it were a baby. She held it to her breast as she carefully polished it dry with a bit of cheesecloth.

"Julia," she said then, "I appreciate what you're doing."

"Me? Just getting on with my work."

"I appreciate your bringing me along. I don't really know the wine business, just the growing of grapes. But now that Lance and I are . . ." She faltered. "Well, you understand."

"We're one family now," Julia told her. "All this will be yours. Or his," she added, gently touching Melissa's abdomen.

The two women stood in silence for a moment. Then, suddenly, Melissa turned violently aside, sobbing. "Melissa, what is it?"

The young woman's head shook violently from side to side as she tried to master her tears. "You can't . . ." She stopped. "I mustn't . . ."

"There, there." Julia smoothed her long dark hair slowly, softly. "It isn't easy, this pregnancy."

By a great effort, Melissa calmed herself. "That's it," she said at last in an easier voice. "It's the pregnancy." She shivered and turned toward the outer doors. "It's too cool in here."

"Right. Let's get some sun."

Outside, at the loading platform, one of the foremen was sitting on the edge of the dock reading a newspaper. Several winery hands were reading over his shoulder. "Miss Julia?" he asked when the two women came out into the sunlight. "Seen this?"

Julia took the newspaper from him, that morning's edition of the *Globe*.

Across the top of the front page, in large white type on a blue band, were blazoned the words:

HOW WINERY EXPLOITS MIGRANT SERFS

And under it, in a boxed-off area, appeared these words in black:

"Appalling living conditions for Falcon Crest 'Slaves'; See Page Three."

Julia whipped open the newspaper to the third page and was confronted with a layout of photographs. Undernourished children dressed in rags crawled in the dust before squalid hutlike cabins. Family groups of eight or ten posed in front of even meaner-looking hovels.

"Just because we are migrants," Jose Muñoz had said, speaking slowly in English to a *Globe* reporter, "doesn't mean we're not human beings with rights. Here in Falcon Crest we have no heat, no light, no fresh water, no toilets. They don't treat animals in the zoo that bad."

Julia looked up from the paper. "Where did they get these pictures?"

The foreman jerked his thumb in an easterly direction. "Over to Shantytown, I guess. You ever been there?"

Julia shook her head. "Lance is supposed to supervise labor conditions," she said. "I can't be responsible for everything around here." Her tone was sharp.

"Hey, look, Miss Julia," the foreman reminded her. "It's not *me* making the fuss. It's the newspaper. You . . . uh . . . you sort of missed something else, back on page one."

Julia flipped back the pages of the newspaper. "Where?" she demanded. Then, abruptly, she saw it: a three-column photo of Chase Gioberti grabbing Sheriff Robbins by the tie while Cole sat to one side, shackled in handcuffs:

SHERIFF NABS AGRETTI MURDER SUSPECT;
IRATE DAD NABS SHERIFF

Julia's glance lifted quickly to Melissa. She had seen the picture and the headline. The color seemed to drain from the younger woman's face.

"Melissa!"

Her dark eyes rolled upward into her head as her slender body began to buckle at the waist. The foreman jumped up and lunged for her. He managed to catch her before she slumped to the ground.

Gently, he and Julia carried her under the shadow of the loading-dock roof. Julia wet her handkerchief in cool water and dabbed Melissa's forehead.

"Cole," the girl murmured.

"Wha'd she say?" the foreman asked.

Melissa's lips moved silently. But she said nothing more.

Chapter Fifteen

Angela Channing's face was a study in contrasts as she read the morning paper. Normally she was a woman given to hiding her emotions until it suited her to vent them. Now a series of expressions crossed her face quite like alternating shadow and sunlight passing across fields of vines. The contrast was muted, as it always was in the presence of another person, by Angie's innate need to hide her thoughts.

But Phillip Erikson had over many years learned enough of her character to be able to decipher some of these fleeting changes on her face. This morning he shared the big round table in the coffee room with her, both of them basking in late-morning sunlight.

"The cat," he said at last, "has swallowed the canary."

Angela's wide eyes glanced up at him. "I beg your pardon?"

"Don't give me that, Angela. I find your reaction to this morning's *Globe* most educational." He grinned mischievously at her.

"Perhaps." She put the paper to one side. "What do you make of it, other than that Douglas' bastard son has declared war."

"Oh, I wouldn't put it that way."

"Which tells me you still don't understand the situation." Angela poured herself a bit more coffee. "I can't imagine what the man hopes to do, churning up all this hullabaloo about migrant workers. They've always lived that way, here and at every other winery. There's no news in that. It's simply a stick to hit me with."

"And the way he's crucified your nephew, Cole?"

Another fleeting expression passed over Angela's face. "Gutter journalism," she said then, but in a tone that indicated she hadn't made her mind up yet whether to condemn or applaud it.

"My guess," the lawyer mused, "is that when he saw how much publicity the *Globe* was going to give this, the sheriff reached out for the first suspect he could think of."

"Possibly." Angela put on an innocent look. "But I'm quite sure that if Cole is guilty of anything, it was done in self-defense."

Phillip stared at her, astounded. Then: "Mee-oww," he drawled.

"I don't find that funny."

Erikson removed the sly smile. "Quite so, Angela," he said in a deceptively mild tone. "Tell me, would you like me to offer my legal services to Cole?"

"Oh, I wouldn't go that far," she responded. "Chase can come up with an attorney of his own. This is *his* mess. Let *him* clean it up."

The lawyer watched her for a while. "I am lost in admiration," he said at last. "You understand better than any of us how hostile Richard Channing's attack is. But you're not willing to—you know, to pull the family wagons in a circle and repel the common enemy."

"Common's the right word for Douglas' bastard."

"Illegitimate or not, he owns half of the *Globe*."

"Not quite." Angela got up and adjusted the blinds

so that the sun no longer fell so strongly on the table. "Julia and Emma and Chase, together, own as much as he. And there's a sizable number of shares in the hands of the general public."

"Not that much. Say ten or twelve percent."

She stood silhouetted against the blinds. Phillip had to squint to see her properly. She had chosen the posture of an interrogator with a suspect. "So what do we have, then, my accomplished legal counsel? We have some forty-five percent in Richard's possession and another forty-five with the other three. Does that suggest anything to you?"

Erikson's smile grew slowly. "It suggests that if someone could buy up the remaining ten percent, he could control the whole game." He paused. "Or should I say she?" he asked then.

"But it has to be done very privately," Angela replied. She sat down next to the lawyer and her voice dropped to a conspiratorial level. "You have to do your buying on an eastern stock exchange—Chicago, New York, London. And it has to be done in the name of a dummy corporation. It must never be traced back to me."

"So far, so good," Phillip agreed. "But what do you suggest I use for money?"

"There we're in luck."

Angela's voice grew softer. She moved closer to the attorney until she was speaking only a few inches from his ear. "That part of the Falcon Crest accounts under Chase's supervision happen to be showing a tidy profit at the moment. In fact, quite a cash surplus."

"You don't think Chase would object to you using his funds for this?"

"He'd have no objection," Angie murmured, "because he'd have no idea we were using his cash. You do remember what I told you about the EDS channels?

The one he taps into to get a computer readout is a cooked set of books. The one we tap into for cash is under electronic lock and key."

"Dear me," Erikson sighed and took his employer's hand. "Such sweet, soft, tiny hands. But how they can grab."

"Does that surprise you?"

"Not in the least," he said. "I'm beginning to wonder why Lance is in charge of the falcon. When it comes to being a predator, my dear, you could give that bird lessons."

A frown crossed Angie's face. She drew back her hand and lightly slapped the lawyer across the cheek. "You're not paid for your moral opinions, Phillip. Just your legal services."

He blinked and grasped her hand. "Morals? When was the last time anyone around here worried about morals?"

She withdrew her hand and stood up. "How soon can you start buying stock?"

"As soon as I set up a dummy corporation."

"Use one of my European ones."

"In that case," the lawyer said, "I can start today."

"Richard Channing may be my enemy, but he's not stupid. He's done his arithmetic just as I have. At the moment he's a bit short of cash, having bought up all his father's options. But as soon as he can lay hands on more, he'll be after the same outstanding shares I am. So speed is important."

"And what about Emma's shares?"

"Find Emma first. I'll get a proxy out of her soon enough."

"Poor Emma."

"Don't waste your sympathy on Emma. Think about poor Phillip Erikson, if he doesn't pull this off."

Phillip got to his feet. "Is that a threat, Angela?"

"Would I say a thing like that?" Angie purred. "As

long as I keep paying your exorbitant legal fees, you'll do your usual job. Fast, silent, secret, no loose strings."

"For that kind of money, my dear, you'll not only get your ten percent in *Globe* shares, but I'll throw in Emma for free."

Chapter Sixteen

"I don't care about a front-page photo of me choking the sheriff," Chase shouted into the telephone. "What angers me is those downright *lies* about our migrant workers."

"Lies?" Richard retorted at the other end of the phone conversation. "That's a pretty strong word for something that's been going on right under your nose. What angers you is that the *Globe* won't let you get away with it."

Richard glanced at Diana Hunter as she listened in on an extension line. She had already triggered a tape recorder to make sure every word of Chase's could be verified later.

"Your photographer and reporter are pretty slick when no one's watching," Chase said. "Those photos could have been taken anywhere from here five hundred miles south to the border."

"Nevertheless," Richard insisted, "they were taken at Falcon Crest in the Western Quadrant near the intersection of Road 22 and Road 17. Care to meet me there after lunch?"

"I sure as hell would!" Chase snapped. "Three P.M. On the dot!"

Richard smiled coldly as he hung up, then dialed

an inside number at the *Globe*'s office. "Sam Klein? We're taking a ride out to Falcon Crest this afternoon. Bring plenty of film."

The four men—Chase, Richard, his reporter and photographer—walked slowly from the road intersection under the hot afternoon sun toward a cluster of what looked from a distance to be chicken coops or dilapidated farm structures left to molder of old age. Several dozen of these hovels filled an area in a slight valley watered by a small stream. By an odd trick of perspective, as they neared the shanties, behind them on a distant hill rose the ornate pile of veranda and spires called Falcon Crest. Chase felt as if he had stepped into a nightmare over which he had no control.

"Surely people don't actually live in these huts?" he asked.

Richard's mouth set in a thin smile. "Ask them."

Chase walked up to a small group who stood beside their shack and eyed the four men apprehensively. "Afternoon," he said to the man who stepped forward a bit defensively. "I'm Supervisor Gioberti. Do all you folks live in this one . . . uh . . . house?"

The man's glance darkened with suspicion. "Supervisor of what? You from the Board of Health?"

"I'm supervisor of the county," Chase explained.

"What'd we do wrong?" the man countered. "We pay our rent."

"Rent?" Chase sounded shocked. "For this place you pay rent?" He started to circle the hovel. "No electricity. I don't see any water pipes. What do you folks do f—"

"We got the stream. It's good water."

"And for toilets?"

"The same."

"And someone charges you rent for this?" Chase demanded.

"It's an absentee landlord," Richard told him. "Some corporation back East administers these buildings for the owner."

"Which is?" Chase persisted.

"Don't you ever read your own maps?" Richard asked quietly.

"You're saying this is Falcon Crest property?" Chase asked. He glanced about him, orienting himself to the directions of the compass. The image of Falcon Crest house itself hovered in the air like a mirage, contrasting splendor with squalor. "Well," he said at last, "I guess it is."

He turned to the man who lived in the hut. "This your family?"

"Yeah. We *all* work for Falcon Crest."

Chase eyed the group and counted eight adults and children. "All eight of you? Then surely you earn enough to afford something better than this."

"We're part-timers. We get the minimum wage."

"And no health benefits," a woman piped up.

"You're telling me," Chase began, his anger rising, "that Falcon Crest cheats you on wages and cheats you on housing." He whirled on Richard as camera shutters clicked. "You've got to believe this is the first I've heard of all this. Labor isn't part of my responsibility."

"Whose is it, then?" Richard asked calmly.

Chase felt his anger rising, heightened by the surprise of what he was seeing and the frustration of realizing where it should be focused. It was Lance, protected by his grandmother Angie and taking his orders from her, who was supposed to administer labor relations here. But Chase knew better than to tell any newspaper that much—especially one that had his worst interests at heart.

"Never mind whose," Chase said. The photographer kept snapping pictures. "As of this moment, I'm *taking* responsibility for this disgrace. I'll get to the bottom of it and that'll be the end of your little exposé. Will you give me as much publicity when I set this straight?"

"What law says I have to?" Richard asked.

"No law. Just common decency and the public interest. You pillorize me and Falcon Crest for disgraceful labor practices. It happens, unfortunately, that you're dead right. Now I'm going to set matters straight. I want the same amount of publicity—a front-page banner headline and a page of photos inside."

"We'll see."

"Otherwise you really are a rat in journalism's gutters."

Richard's smile was carefully crafted to look genuine. "We'll see."

"What a nasty little rag you've made of the *Globe*."

"Are you speaking as an owner?" Richard demanded in a challenging tone.

It was Chase's turn to smile. "We'll see," he mimicked.

It was after four when Chase located Lance at the bottling plant, checking the new labels of the Cabernet Sauvignon wine. He strode over to the young man.

"I want our payroll records for the last three years," he demanded.

Lance looked up with insulting slowness from his clipboard. "Ask my grandmother."

"I'm asking you. Get them. Right now."

Lance frowned. "Look, if it's about those migrant workers the *Globe*'s so excited over, it's all legal. We do exactly what every other winery in the Valley does."

"Get the books!"

"Chase, these are unskilled workers. By hiring them part-time we protect ourselves from having to pay full wages and health and pension benefits to people who might not even be here next year. We're saving tens of thousands of dollars."

Chase took him by the shoulders. "Talk sense. Our costs are factored into our per-bottle price, the same as everybody else's. I'm talking about the practice of underpaying help and overcharging them for substandard housing."

"Nobody's forcing them to work for us." Lance's tone was pure arrogance.

"Nobody," Chase retorted, "but hunger."

"They're free to move on, work somewhere else. It's always been that way."

Chase started to shake the younger man slowly, rocking him back and forth. "That may be the way it's always been, Lance. But not anymore."

Lance's face grew dark with anger. "I take my orders from my grandmother."

"And from me. Don't forget it! Now . . . get the books."

Chapter Seventeen_____

The County Jail, which adjoined the sheriff's office,
was a concrete building that might be mistaken for a
three-car garage, except for the bars on its windows.
Steve Barton, the lawyer Chase had gotten for his
son, had picked up Maggie and brought her to the
jail.

They stood just inside the door, glancing around
at the spartan anteroom where Sheriff Robbins and
the jailer were busily handing each other legal-sized
pieces of paper to sign.

"Right," the sheriff said at last. "Bring him out."

The jailer disappeared inside, jangling a small ring
of keys.

Sheriff Robbins eyed Maggie and the lawyer.
"Where's Chase?"

"Busy," Barton responded. "This is not a juvenile
remand, Sheriff. Cole is of age. He's being bailed
into his own safekeeping. Maggie's just here for moral
support."

"Such as I have," Maggie added. She watched the
sheriff closely. "You've given us all a bad time,
Sheriff."

"A bad time? I took a suspect into custody, Mrs.
Gioberti."

"Overnight?"

"Not my fault if it took this long for you to bail him."

Maggie glanced at the lawyer, who spoke up, "It's not the easiest thing in the world to pull together collateral for a bond in the middle of the night, Sheriff. As you very well know."

"Hey, you hear that tone you're using?" Sheriff Robbins started to sidle up to Barton, then decided he was too tall to stand beside. "I'm just doing what the law says I have to do. You make bail, I release him. No dawdling. I don't take sides, you know that."

"Except for the big question," the attorney retorted. "Why you decided Cole was a suspect in the first place."

At this moment the suspect himself, unshaven but not much the worse for wear, walked out into the anteroom, the jailer behind him carrying a plastic bag. "Don't forget your personal effects," he said, offering Cole the bag. "Check 'em out first."

Cole opened the bag and removed his wallet. He leafed through it and seemed satisfied. Then he saw that he had visitors. "Mom." They embraced. "Sure glad to see you."

"Have you had breakfast?" Maggie asked.

"Of course he has," the sheriff cut in. "We don't run a hotel here, but we try to treat a prisoner like a human being."

Cole glanced blankly at him. "Coffee and a baloney sandwich is breakfast?"

"S'what I eat," Sheriff Robbins assured him.

The nonsense of this exchange got to the jailer, who began to giggle. Robbins glared at him. "Shut up, Clint."

"Hard not to laugh, Sheriff," the lawyer suggested. "Cole, all your things in the bag?"

"Yeah."

"Then let's go."

"Hold it," Sheriff Robbins interrupted. "Cole, you'll be notified of any hearings. If you fail to appear you'll forfeit your bail. Get that? If that happened we could issue a felony warrant and rearrest you. Got that?"

"I'll apprise him of his rights," Barton told the sheriff.

"These aren't rights. These are duties. So long." He stuck out his hand to Cole. "No hard feelings."

"Who said?" Cole countered and, ignoring the hand, walked out of the jail. He was silent on the ride back to his home. Finally Maggie could bear the silence no longer.

"Did they mistreat you in jail?" she burst out.

Cole sighed heavily. "They treated me okay. That's not my beef."

"I know your beef," Barton assured him. "Why did they pick you up in the first place."

"I know why." Cole sighed again, an even heavier sound. "They asked me enough questions. Here's a guy gets into the Agretti house in the dark. He's got a flashlight. His fingerprints are all over the place. Also on the bronze statuette that killed Carlo Agretti. Also he's got blood on his hands and shirt. Also, what the hell was he doing there to begin with? You find a fella like that, you lock him up."

"But I understood Agretti telephoned you," the lawyer said. "Isn't that what you told Robbins?"

"He didn't believe it."

"It's too goofy to be a lie," Maggie put in.

Barton laughed. "Your mother's right. Of all the alibis for being there, that's so bad it's got to be true. What did Agretti tell you?"

"He asked me to come over."

"Just like that?"

Cole's face tensed. "Just like that."

Maggie shook her head at the lawyer. "No more cross-examination."

"Cole," Barton told him, "I'm on your side. But sooner or later you're going to have to answer that question."

"Let it be later."

Once home, Cole's grandmother clucked like a French hen, fussing over him. Earlier Jacqueline Perrault Gioberti had announced that she had business elsewhere—some far corner of the globe—and would be leaving today or tomorrow. "But I am so happy you are out of that horrible jail," she told her grandson. She perched on the sofa beside him, and patted his hand.

"Maggie," she said, "this boy should go away to school. Now."

"That's called jumping bail, Jacqueline."

"Then as soon as possible. He is too full of life to stay out of trouble for long in this Valley. I know the symptoms. It's a combination of male hormones and good looks. He must be sent away."

"To a monastery?" Cole asked with mock innocence.

"Don't make fun of your poor old grandmother," Jacqueline said, waving her finger under his nose. "To a desert island inhabited by spider crabs, perhaps."

"Good eating, anyway."

She shook her head. "Incorrigible, this one." Her voice had a tinge of pride to it. "Whatever this lawyer Barton charges you, I want the bill sent to me, Maggie."

"We can certainly afford to—"

"No arguments. I want to make sure my grandson gets free of this ridiculous charge, once and for all."

"I appreciate the interest you take in us," Maggie countered. "But really, Jacqueline, a busy woman like you has other matters on her mind."

"None more important than my family. Which

reminds me." She began pawing through her tiny patent-leather clutch bag. "Where'd I put it?"

"Put what?"

"His card. At my bank in San Francisco yesterday I was introduced to a film director. I told him all about your script, Maggie. He got very excited."

"Really?"

"Here it is." The older woman squinted at the card. Maggie knew her mother-in-law's eyes were ruined for close reading but she refused to use her thick reading glasses unless absolutely forced to. "Darryl Clayton," she said, reading off the card. "Here. He's in town till tomorrow. Call him at the St. Mark."

"What, cold turkey like that? I should use an agent."

"*I* am your agent," Jacqueline assured her. She glanced around her. "Where is the telephone? Call at once."

Cole watched his mother with some curiosity. "But you haven't finished the script yet, have you, Mom?"

"It's as finished as it'll ever be." Maggie stared at the card her mother-in-law had given her. "I should wait to call. The poor man's just gotten out of bed," she protested.

"Call him now," Jacqueline commanded. "He was very excited, that one. I told him who you were. I said you had written an insider's undercover exposé of the Valley. I told him you—"

"He's going to be terribly disappointed. The script's nothing like that."

Jacqueline laughed, a silvery note Maggie had heard before. It was a studied laugh, neither spontaneous nor totally fake—but terribly French. "But, *ma chère* Maggie, nothing in life is ever what we expect."

"I suppose you're right"—spoken with a sigh of resignation.

"To the sheriff, Cole seems guilty. To us, we know he's innocent," Jacqueline said. "To Darryl Clayton I seem like a rich, slightly eccentric lady. To me he looks like a hungry director. To him you sound like a terrific script for a movie. To Cole the pair of us seem like prize lunatics, nattering on about a film scenario when he's just spent the night in jail."

"Go ahead, natter," Cole assured her. "It beats jail."

"You see? Nothing in life is what we expect. To Cole, our chitchat is refreshing. It was ever thus."

Maggie smiled and nodded, thinking that of all the people she knew, Jacqueline ranked first as an expert in how things were different from what they seemed. The word for what she was describing was deception. And on that subject, Jacqueline had written the book.

This whole grandmotherly act, the cozy visits, the postcards to Cole and Vickie, the offers to pay this or that expense, even getting her the name of a film director—none of it was the real Jacqueline Perrault Gioberti. Deep down, Maggie knew this about her mother-in-law. But if you asked her who the woman really was under the grandmother act, Maggie would have come up with a complete blank.

Chapter Eighteen_____

Melissa sat on the comfortable chaise longue Angela Channing had given her as her own. "A girl should have one during the second half of any pregnancy," the older woman had explained, having it moved from her own room to Melissa's.

She was resting comfortably on the chaise as Lance passed along the outside corridor. He paused in the doorway. "Off to San Francisco."

"Lance, are you free this evening?"

There was a long pause followed by a sigh. "I have plans," her husband told her.

"I see." An instant later Lance's grandmother appeared behind him. "Good morning, Angela," she called.

"Morning. Nice to see you two lovebirds together."

"I'm following up that suggestion of yours," Melissa told her. "You know, those natural childbirth classes?"

"Good for you. They're very helpful, even if you decide not to have the baby that way."

"And Lance is going to attend them with me, of course," Melissa added. "The first one's tonight."

With his grandmother behind him and his wife in

front of him, Lance sensed he was surrounded and in danger of being outmaneuvered. "Look, Melissa—"

"Isn't that wonderful?" Angie enthused. "Because these classes are just as much for the father as the mother."

"I'm not sure I can get free to—" Lance began.

"Oh, I'm sure you can," his grandmother told him. She smiled past his sullen face to Melissa. "I'm really glad you two are finally working things out."

"Yeah?" Lance grunted. "What time is the class?"

"Eight in the evening. It's only an hour."

He sighed unhappily. "If you really have to go, I guess it's up to me to take you," he said ungraciously.

"You see," Angela Channing remarked, "you're having such a positive effect on him, my dear."

"Oh," Melissa assured her, "I knew fatherhood would bring out the best in him."

The two women smiled sweetly at each other and Angie swept off along the corridor. The moment she was out of earshot Lance turned on Melissa. "I never knew before what a real hypocrite was. The two of you have taught me a lesson."

"Bitter. Bitter."

"Fatherhood? Me?" Lance insisted. "You of all people know better than that. The one guy who *isn't* the father is the guy you're married to."

"How nicely you put things." A mocking tone crept into Melissa's voice.

"So why should *I* take you to classes to learn how to give birth to somebody else's kid?" he growled.

"Because Grandmother likes it that way," Melissa responded sweetly.

"So what?"

"And Lance doesn't do anything to upset Lance's grandmother," Melissa said in a voice as falsely saccharine as her smile.

*   *   *

Later, in San Francisco, Lance waited at a restaurant for his lunch date, an old girlfriend named Lori Stevens. He hadn't seen her since long before his wedding, and when he'd phoned the other day she had seemed almost reluctant to meet him, even for lunch.

Now he wondered if she intended to stand him up. Lance didn't pretend to know the inner workings of a woman's mind. The outer surfaces were more to his tastes. But he had begun to realize that the marriage his grandmother had forced him to make was turning him into some kind of celibate monk, a situation for which there was only one quick cure.

The cure he envisioned walked into the restaurant at that point—Lori, the attractive girl his grandmother had driven out of his life to ensure his marriage to Melissa. She paused in the entrance and looked around, suddenly shy and uncertain. Lance stood up and waved to her. Slowly, she came to the table.

"I'm sorry to be late," she said, formally, as if to a stranger. "But I had a hard time making myself come here at all."

"But you did come."

"I spent six months getting you out of my mind," she said, her unhappy glance raking across his face. "I went abroad, started up with another man. Lance," she added, still making no move to sit at the table with him, "I'm really here to make sure I'm over you."

He grinned. "Lori, we're only having lunch. This is a restaurant, not a motel."

She tried to relax. They sat and read the menu. She looked up at him slowly and he could see she hadn't read a word on the page. Nor had he. The tension between them was too great.

"That girl," Lori said then. "The one your grand-mother wanted you to marry. Still seeing her?"

Lance took a long breath for courage. "We're married."

"Dear God."

"It wasn't love," he hastened to tell her. "I married her because of Falcon Crest."

"Isn't there anything in your life but that winery?"

"I was hoping there'd be you."

She had no ready reply. They stared wordlessly into each other's eyes.

Chapter Nineteen

The noon sun didn't penetrate far through the windows of Angela Channing's study. She was checking inventory lists from one of the warehouses when Chao-Li entered.

"Mr. Gioberti is here to s—"

"Angie," Chase called, coming in behind the servant. "I've just checked our employment records. We hire a third of our people on a part-time—"

"Thank you, Chao-Li," Angie remarked, maintaining her formal pose and ignoring Chase's obvious agitation.

Her majordomo nodded and left the room. "And pay the minimum wage with no benefits," Chase concluded.

She stared up at him "I believe that's the law, Mr. County Supervisor."

"Angie, these people deserve equal pay for equal work. You should see the kind of shanties we charge them to live in."

"No, thanks."

"You owe yourself that much. Come over with me now and take a look at how a third of our people have to live."

"I'm a businesswoman, Chase, not a philanthropist."

"These are human beings!" He eyed her for a long moment. "You're really afraid of human contact, aren't you? You're afraid you might appear to be human, too."

A slow flush suffused Angela Channing's face. Almost without knowing it, Chase had touched the one nerve she was most sensitive to. "That's how much you know me," she said in a low voice. She pressed a button on her desk phone. A moment later Chao-Li appeared again.

"Chao-Li," she ordered, "please have Desi bring the car around."

Once again, as he had yesterday, Chase was struck by the terrifying contrast of the way he and Angie lived and the way the migrant workers had to exist. The long Mercedes 600 moved smoothly down the rutted lane into the hollow where the hovels lay scattered along a bank of the creek. This time of the year, only a trickle of water moved sluggishly through the bed of the stream, yet it had to provide for dozens of families.

In the distance, like a feverish nightmare image distorted by heat waves under a broiling sun, the spired and turreted image of Falcon Crest house loomed over this scene of desolation. Chase ushered Angie from the limousine.

"Not quite the cottages we provide our regular workers."

Angela Channing stood gazing at the hovels. "Nobody said life was fair."

"That's no excuse for not paying a living wage. And for charging these people rent on a miserable collection of huts."

"It can't be any other way." There was no hint of emotion in her voice.

He watched her glance swing slowly from side to side, not missing a thing, from the half-naked babies in the dust to the rags of washing hung on makeshift clotheslines, from the eight-year-old girl toiling up-hill with a lard can of water to the buzz of flies gathered over the garbage heap.

"Paying part-time help what we pay our regulars," she said simply, "is bad business. Falcon Crest isn't a charity."

"It isn't charity to pay for what you get."

"And it isn't good business," Angie shot back, "to pay more than you have to. More than any other winery in the Valley."

"That's no excuse, either." Chase escorted her back to the limousine. "Here's what's going to happen, Angie. At four P.M. today, right here, I've scheduled a press conference."

"You what!"

"Press, TV, everybody. I don't expect your stepson at the *Globe* will send anybody. But the rest will."

"He's not my steps—"

"We're going to build new cottages here, Angie. Real ones with electricity and running water. And we're going to pay these people full-time, plus benefits."

"You do and you'll pay for it yourself."

"It'd look a lot better if you were with me on this, Angie."

"Do you think I care how it looks?" she hissed. "Thanks to my father's generosity, you control half of Falcon Crest. If he'd known you'd run your half into the ground, he'd never have left it to you. You're not a Gioberti. You're a disgrace!"

"Think about it," Chase persisted. "Because I'm doing this with or without you."

The only reply was the slam of the Mercedes door as Angela Channing left.

Chapter Twenty

Diana Hunter's bedroom was not of her own design. It was simply part of one of the hotel's most expensive suites. Now, at a few minutes before six in the evening, it lay in darkness. The blinds were down, the curtains drawn. Little of the late-afternoon sun penetrated the room.

Lying on the king-sized bed with Richard, Diana stared up at the ceiling. This relationship was not something new between them. The affair had gone on sporadically in New York, but there Richard had had other women. His lovemaking had a rather distracted quality to it, as if it were a pleasant pastime, not a dedicated effort.

Here in San Francisco—so far, at least—she'd had him to herself, and it made a difference. Here she wasn't one of several women he saw, she was his right-hand mainstay, his closest support—his fellow conspirator. And this new intimacy had a wonderfully concentrating effect on Richard, especially in bed.

He slept now, his face in repose freed of many of the lines that could make it look hard—driven by ambition. Exhausted by their lovemaking, he had dropped off into a deep sleep, but Diana knew better than to think it would last for long.

For one thing, she'd set the timer on her TV set so that it would turn on automatically for the "Six O'Clock News"—at Richard's request. For another, he still had a full list of evening calls to make. And then there were the final pages of the *Globe* to check in proof form before the great presses began to run at midnight.

Relaxing in the half-darkness, Diana stared at Richard's face. Even in sleep he had the look of someone special, someone marked by destiny and his own ambition for greatness. Diana wondered what he really thought of her. Surely it must cross his mind, especially here in San Francisco, to try to understand her motives.

It was a complex relationship, originally based on their mutual intelligence and their dedication to the Cartel and its projects. But eventually it had become more than that, much more.

Diana didn't fool herself into thinking that the lovemaking meant as much to Richard as it did to her. It never did with the man, she thought. But some new element had changed the quality of it lately. A certain excitement, a taut sensual tension, seemed to elevate these moments in bed to a different, higher level.

Ultimately these emotions could present a big problem, Diana told herself, because her primary loyalty could never be to Richard Channing. It had to remain what it had always been—a fierce concentration on her role in the Cartel. It was to this end she had dedicated herself, and it was this conflict that would give her the most trouble.

Across the room, the TV set went on in the middle of a margarine commercial. A moment later the fast, staccato tempo of music announced the evening news.

Richard stirred beside her, coming awake in one smooth movement.

"Turn up the volume," he said.

They watched the announcer skim the top headlines of the day, including a transport strike, a fire in Oakland, the arrival of a French navy ship on a goodwill mission . . . and a startling announcement from Tuscany Valley.

Richard sat up in bed. Impatiently he waited while the first news items flashed across the screen. Then the announcer reappeared:

"Meanwhile, at a news conference this afternoon, labor relations history was being made among the vineyards and wineries of Tuscany Valley. County Supervisor Chase Gioberti, half owner of the immense Falcon Crest holdings, told the story this way."

The screen showed Chase on a small platform, Maggie in the background. Microphones had been shoved randomly under his nose as he explained what was happening and pointed to the scattering of shanties behind him.

The camera lens shifted slightly and zoomed in on scenes of desolation and poverty while Chase's voice went on: "These changes will take time, as does anything worthwhile. Today I'm making sure Falcon Crest starts treating its part-time workers as fairly as we treat our regular people. And I urge other vineyards in the Valley to do the same."

"Mr. Gioberti," a reporter asked, off-screen, "do you speak for your co-owner, too? Mrs. Angela Channing?"

"You'll have to ask her," Chase parried.

"Then this was not a joint decision?"

Once again the camera lens shifted from Chase. In the distance a huge Mercedes rolled toward the camera, stopped and Angela got out. She walked confidently toward the lens.

"Mrs. Channing," a reporter asked, "are you aware of the statement Mr. Gioberti has just—"

"I'm sorry he started without me," Angie told the camera. "He's acting on my suggestion. I'm glad to have his support."

"Then this is a joint statement?" the reporter persisted.

"Of course," Angie said smoothly. "Falcon Crest has always led the way in matters of reform. When history's made, Falcon Crest makes it."

The screen's picture changed back to the studio announcer. "In Beirut today, Phalangist guerrilla troops shelled government positions for the third straight day."

Richard was out of bed, snapping off the TV set. "Damn the woman."

"Tricky."

"I'd hoped to split the two of them wider apart this way." He sat down in one of the glove-leather arm chairs. "What do you think of Chase Gioberti? For an essentially ordinary man, he does have a bit of charisma."

"Umm." Diana's glance traced the muscles in Richard's legs. "Not compared to your stepmother."

"Don't ever call her that," Richard said coldly.

"Sorry."

"I'll tell you this one time, Diana, and then we'll both forget it." He was staring at her across the darkened room with a gaze so intense that Diana could almost feel it. "She had her chance to treat me as a human being. When I was a baby, she could have agreed to adopt me, as my father wanted. But she voted me out of her life. Forever. And that's the way it's going to stay."

"Except that you're about to blow up her way of life."

The intense look on his face softened slightly, settling in a cruel smile. "How well you put it." He glanced at the table clock, its green numerals glowing in the dark. "Time to be up and doing."

Diana stretched languorously, half under and half out of the bed linen. She thought of half a dozen remarks, but rejected them. Richard would appreciate none, since each would obviously be designed to get him back in bed. It was too late now, and Diana knew it. That particular compartment of Richard's brain had snapped shut. The TV press conference, and Angela Channing's hijacking of Chase's idea, had shifted Richard back into fighting mode again.

"Either you fight," she murmured, "or you make love. You're wise to keep the compartments separated."

"Get me our man in Arizona, the one who's keeping an eye on Emma Channing. She can't keep running forever. The minute she comes to rest, I want to know it."

Diana got up slowly, stretching, smoothing her body, hoping the sight of her would remind Richard that life wasn't all work. "And put on a dressing gown while you're at it," he added.

"You find the sight of me disturbing?"

He grinned maliciously at her. "Always testing, eh, Diana?"

"I'll put on a gown if you put on a robe."

"I'll do better than that as soon as I talk to Arizona. I'm going back to the office."

"Because the sight of you can be disturbing, too."

He eyed her for a moment. "I'm taking that as a compliment," he said at length. "Tell me, my resident expert on men. Tell me how you react to Chase Gioberti. If it hadn't been for that damnable Channing woman, I could have used him and the migrant workers exposé to gash a major hole in Falcon Crest. As it is, she's outmaneuvered me. But it's only the opening battle."

"Chase?" Diana slipped into her gown. "Chase is family oriented. You saw him on TV. He wouldn't say anything incriminating about Angela even though his jaws ached."

"Then my first instinct was right. The way to knock him off center is through that idiot son of his."

Richard got up and, still nude, strode to the phone. He dialed an outside line and stood there for a moment. "Dolan? It's Channing. Are you still monitoring the Gioberti kid? Good. Now step it up. I want twenty-four-hour coverage. I want to know every move he makes. Photographs. If you need more men, assign them. If you want a private eye, hire him. If you have to bribe a deputy sheriff, bribe him. I want this kid nailed to the cross."

Diana watched him hang up the phone and stride to the window. He yanked open the curtains and blinds to stare down at the San Francisco evening. Dusk had turned the sky faintly mauve. Beneath them, streets were beginning to light up. The illumination reflected from below gave Richard's face sinister beauty.

"You've gone about as far as you can with Cole Gioberti," Diana reminded him. "After all, it was our reporters who got him arrested in the first place."

"Arrested?" He whirled on her. Anger turned his face dead white. "I don't want him arrested," he said harshly, "I want him *convicted*!"

*Chapter Twenty-One*_____

Cole quietly wheeled the Honda 500 away from his family's house and out onto the road. He had no idea where he was going this bright morning. He only knew that the atmosphere in his home—in the whole Valley, for that matter—was the worst. No, there was one thing worse, he thought as he settled into the saddle of the powerful cycle—being in jail.

The trouble was, getting bailed out was almost as bad. Aside from his own family, did anybody believe he was innocent? Thanks to the *Globe*'s strident campaign of half-truths and sly suggestions, Cole felt certain he already stood convicted in the minds of most people.

He tramped on the starter and the engine roared into life. Cole sent the cycle roaring forward along the road to . . . ? Anywhere, he supposed. Anywhere but where he was.

He was zooming along a small paved road fifteen minutes later when he spotted a figure teetering precariously on the roof of a house. He knew the place, as he did most in the Valley. The Demery winery was one of those small holdings that produced very little wine, hardly enough to keep the family going.

He braked to a halt in a cloud of dust. A woman
had climbed a rickety two-story stepladder and was
half stretched across the roof shingles, holding on
for dear life. "You okay?" Cole called out.

She craned around to see him and promptly lost
her hold, sliding a heart-stopping extra yard down
the roof, breaking her fall only by grabbing desperately at the fragile aluminum gutter that hung from
the eaves. "Help!" she screamed.

Cole lay the cycle on its side and ran for the house.
Looking up, all he could see was a long, slim tanned
pair of legs dangling just above his head.

He started to move the ladder toward her, then
stopped when he noticed the gutter start to sag.

"That gutter won't hold!" he shouted. "You've got
to turn loose. It's not far. Don't worry. I'll catch
you."

"Do I have a choice?" the woman's voice called.
"Here I come!"

Suddenly there was a flash of skin and a swirl of
skirts and long hair. Cole braced himself and held
out his arms.

"Gotcha!"

She was beautiful. Her face, flushed with exertion,
was one of the prettiest Cole had ever seen. Her eyes
were wide with fright. She clung to him and he
could feel her young, firm body pressing against
him.

For a moment they stood glued to each other.
Then slowly Cole lowered her to the ground. She
straightened her skirt and fluffed out her auburn
hair. It fell in big, careless curls to her neck. Her
face was still flushed, but Cole had the feeling she
was more embarrassed now than frightened.

"What were you doing up there?" he asked.

"I've got a leaky roof. I thought . . ." She stopped

and held out her hand, her bare arm as tanned as her legs and face. "Katharine Demery."

They shook hands. "Cole Gioberti."

He watched her face for a sign that she'd heard of the celebrated murderer, but her wide eyes remained clear of suspicion. "Cole, you saved my life."

"Maybe just a broken leg or two."

"How can I ever thank you?" She stared around her almost desperately, as if hoping to find some precious reward worthy of her savior. "Not much to look at, this place," she said then in a graver voice. "It's got me licked, I don't mind admitting."

Cole's glance followed hers. The Demery spread was small, all right, and run-down, to boot. Its vines looked as if they needed a good weeding and its winery shed sagged precariously to the right, as if ready to give up the ghost.

"What kind of help do you have here?"

She shrugged. Cole liked all of her gestures. They were open, concealing nothing. He liked the way she looked him straight in the eye when she spoke. "Since Jim died, not much. I sign on a few migratory people at harvest time. In between, well, you're looking at the full, complete staff of Demery Wines."

"Just you?"

She nodded. "Not quite up to your Falcon Crest standards."

So she did know who he was, Cole thought. And she hadn't treated him like some kind of leper; but then maybe she didn't read the papers? "I sort of give my dad odd-job help at Falcon Crest," he said then, "when the cops aren't on my case, breathing hard."

She nodded again. "I read all about it in the *Globe*. Can't you sue those people? As far as I can see, you just happened to be at the wrong place at the wrong time."

Cole could hardly believe his ears. He cracked the first smile he'd been able to spare in some time now. "My lawyer's concentrating on bigger things, like getting me permanently out of trouble."

"And, in between, you're just sort of marking time?"

They stood without speaking for a long moment. There was nothing uneasy about the silence, Cole realized. It was as if the two of them didn't need to keep talking. And yet they were communicating, of that he was sure.

"Looks like you could use an odd-job man around here," he said then.

"You? I'm sure your dad needs you."

"He's got dozens of people to help," Cole insisted.

"I couldn't pay you what he does."

"Oh, I don't know," Cole said, dead-pan. "What I'm getting, basically, is room and board."

"I could manage that," Katharine Demery said. There was another of those easy pauses between them. "But at a time like this, you're better off with your own folks. There's no substitute for T.L.C."

"Is that what I'm getting?" Cole asked. He stared off across the Demery vineyard.

When she said nothing, he found himself wondering about the nature of Tender Loving Care, the T.L.C. she thought he was getting at home. What it came down to was sympathy from his sister, Vickie, and his grandmother, Jacqueline, when she came out from the city now and then. But from Maggie and Chase what he was getting was tension, their own anguish, their own sense of helplessness, their own anger at the sheriff and the *Globe*. He would hardly call that T.L.C.

"Listen, Mrs. Demery," Cole said at last, "real all-around odd-job men don't come down the pike every day in the week. Do we have a deal?"

Her smile was beautiful as it spread slowly across

her face, brightening the air like a separate sunrise. Cole found himself wondering about her: he knew that she had been widowed for nearly two years, but she couldn't be that much older than he was. Early twenties? Mid-twenties? When she smiled she looked like a kid.

"You can weed?" she said then.

"With the best of 'em."

"And handle the vats? Cleaning, vinifying, bottling?"

"Sure."

"But can you fix a leaky roof?"

"Hey, Mrs. Demery, that was my major in school. I have a diploma in Roof Fixing." They burst into laughter. She put out her strong hand again.

"Cole, let's give it a whirl. On one condition."

"Name it."

"I don't care what you call me—Katharine, Kate, Katie or hey-you—but if you're working for me, no more Mrs. Demery. Understand?"

Cole shook her hand. Neither of them seemed anxious to let go. "Kate," he said then. "I like Kate best, I think. Okay, Kate. We have a deal."

Chapter Twenty-Two_____

Melissa sat quietly on the chaise longue Angela Channing had given her. If she sat very still she could feel the baby kick inside her. But if she moved around at all, nausea seemed to well up around her, a feeling she tried to ignore. Pretending it didn't exist, however, only led to worse problems—dull, aching pains that frightened her far more than the feeling of sickness did.

Chao-Li arrived at her bedroom door with a small tray on which sat a pot of coffee, toast and a tall glass of iced tea, decorated with lemon and mint leaves.

"You ... ah ... might prefer something more bland than coffee?" he suggested.

"Chao-Li, you're a mind reader. Take the rest away, including the toast."

"Miss Melissa needs her energy."

"Miss Melissa needs a lot of things."

The Chinese bowed solemnly and left. Melissa slowly sipped the tea. It stayed down. If she hadn't glanced up at that moment, she would have missed Lance walking by her door.

"Hardworking husband," she called.

He peered in the doorway. "I like to keep busy."

"Day and night. Not many wives would put up with such a busy husband."

He smiled coldly. "Not many wives have painted themselves into the corner you have."

She returned the smile. They did seem to delight in taking swipes at each other, didn't they, she thought. "Getting out of tight spots," she told him, "is one of my specialties. Will you be home for dinner?"

"Don't hold your breath." He was gone.

She waited until his footsteps faded away. Then, stifling a moan, she got up and went to her dressing table. She started to pick up a lipstick, then thought better of it. The wan, pained look was much more effective.

When she made her way downstairs to the breakfast room, Angie and Julia were already there. "The new batch of Zinfandel is going off," Julia was saying. "It's loaded with tartaric acid crystals. I'm not sure what caused it."

"How much is spoiled?" her mother wanted to know.

"One vat."

"Can you filter out the crystals and convert it to vinegar?"

"That's not the point. I have to . . ." Julia stopped, staring at Melissa as she entered the room. "Good morning, dear. Are you all right?"

"I didn't sleep."

She sat down with her back to the brilliant sunlight filtering through the windows. Her face looked even more drawn in the half-shadow. Julia reached across to take her hand. "It's all too soon after your father's death, Melissa. Grief takes time to pass."

"I never sleep well when Lance has to work all night," the younger woman said in a small voice.

"What?" Angie thundered. "*All* night?"

"But wasn't last night another natural childbirth class?" Julia chimed in.

"Oh, yes. Lance took me there."

"But . . . ?"

"He doesn't attend the class. He never has." Melissa's eyes were downcast. "One of the other women gives me a lift home. Lance is too busy working."

Julia glanced angrily at her mother. "Night work," she said. "And it isn't even harvesttime yet. I think . . ." She stopped, took a final sip of coffee and got to her feet. "I think I'll speak to Lance. He's working much too hard."

This corner of the warehouse was reserved for special wines, the more expensive types—some of them selling for as much as thirty or forty dollars a bottle—and the champagnes. Lance was slowly checking over the contents of a great rack when his mother arrived. For a long moment she watched him, wondering how to begin her little speech. They had never been close enough for straight talk in an atmosphere of relaxed give and take. There was a hardness to Lance that made him almost impossible to mother properly.

"Must be a special occasion."

Lance whirled. "What? Oh, the wine. Yes, something to go with Dungeness crab."

Julia went to another rack. "This might be just the thing."

"Not bad." He took a bottle of the Chardonnay

"Tonight we're having Chao-Li's boeuf bourguignon. So you must be eating out . . . again."

The silence hung between them, growing heavier the longer it lasted. Finally, Lance smiled, somewhat crookedly. "I'm having Dungeness crab."

"This is most upsetting. You—"

"It doesn't upset Grandmother," he countered. "We

have a deal. As long as I come home to roost now
and then, she doesn't worry about any birdwatching
I manage to do."

"You have no such deal with me, Lance. Your
wife's having a baby. She needs you."

"Melissa can take care of herself," Lance said
matter-of-factly.

"What choice does she have? You even leave her
stranded alone at her childbirth classes."

"She doesn't keep many secrets, does she?"

"I want you to go with her from now on," Julia
insisted.

"No way."

"Lance, she's the mother of your child."

With a certain light sarcasm, Lance asked, almost
to himself, "Now why do I keep forgetting that?" He
paused, as if in thought. "You know something?"

"What?"

"On second thought, I'm taking two bottles of
Chardonnay." He lifted a second one from the rack
and left the warehouse.

Julia stood there in despair. What she had always
feared she knew to be true, that Lance could be
influenced only by his grandmother, certainly not by
his mother. It was an unnatural state of affairs, Julia
told herself, but given her mother's strong personality,
it wasn't surprising.

The two of them. Both headstrong. Both wrapped
up in their own egos. They were a match for each
other, Julia knew. Certainly she was no match for
her own son. He had turned out to be—

The telephone rang and she answered it quickly.
"Yes."

"Julia Cumson, please?" a man's voice asked. It
had a pleasingly taut quality to it, as if the single
thing on his mind was to find her and her alone.

"Speaking."

"Julia! It's Richard Channing."

"What?"

"Your half brother, Julia."

"I . . . I knew you were in t—" She paused, realizing she was babbling. "Yes," she managed to go on more smoothly. "I thought I caught sight of you at Carlo Agretti's funeral. That *was* you with the knockout blonde?"

"With Miss Hunter, my associate. Julia," Richard surged on, "we've remained strangers too long. I'd like to see you for lunch today."

"Out of the question."

"Come on, Sis," he teased. "I won't bite."

"There's too much for me to do here, Richard."

"Don't you lead the life of leisure?"

"I'm head oenologist for Falcon Crest. This time of year—"

"This time of year," he cut in, "you can't be all that busy. The grapes are doing all the work. What about that nice new French restaurant at the head of the Valley. Say one o'clock?"

"Not possible."

"Then tomorrow."

"Can't be done." Julia took a long, steadying breath. "Let's leave it till later, Richard. When I've got some free time, I'll call you."

"Don't call me, I'll call you?" Richard quoted sarcastically. He laughed. "Then you don't want to be rich, is that it?"

"I have all the money I need."

"I mean independently wealthy for the rest of your life."

"I am already, Richard."

He sighed. "You have no notion of how rich you could be in your own name. If you won't have lunch with me, I'll just have to drop in on you."

"What? When?"

"One of these days."

"I *am* quite busy," she protested.

"One of these days." Richard laughed softly. "When you least expect me. When you're totally off guard. When you're distracted with work. That's when I'll strike, little half sister. That's when I'll strike."

The line went dead.

Part Three

Chapter Twenty-Three _____

Chase was running late. His day had been completely filled with minor detail, the kind of nit-picking
problems his co-owner Angela Channing felt herself
above handling. Complicating Chase's day was the
complete absence of Cole. He seemed to have vanished,
and only the fact that his Honda 500 was gone too
gave Chase any clue that this was a self-imposed
disappearance.

Not that he blamed the poor guy. Thanks to the
Globe's nasty innuendoes, Cole was already wearing a
"guilty" label. Chase realized that as the boy's father
he was spending too much time with his own work
and not enough reinforcing Cole in a moment of
stress.

Unfortunately, this was not the time to do anything about it. He was late for a trip into San
Francisco, where his mother was giving herself what
she called her "really big" family dinner. As Chase
got out of the shower and toweled himself dry, he
realized he would be at least half an hour late. He
was heading for the telephone to relay this message
when the phone rang.

"Maggie?" Chase asked as he picked it up.

"Wrong!" a woman's voice responded, chuckling. "Try Emma."

"Emma!" Chase half-shouted. "Where are you calling from?"

"East of Oklahoma, Chase. I'm on the lam and your line's probably tapped." She sounded stronger, more confident than the time he had last seen her.

"Who'd tap my line?"

"The same people who've been shadowing me all the way from California. They picked me up in New Mexico and I've had company ever since."

Chase frowned. "Can I help you? Do you need money?"

"Chase, I'm looking for . . ." She paused. "I need help of the therapeutic kind. I don't need to feel like a hunted woman. Can you call them off, whoever they are?"

"Meaning Angie?" Chase surmised. "If she's having you followed, I'll speak to her. Since when did she ever listen, though?"

"That's why I gave you my *Globe* stock proxy," Emma reminded him. "That gives you leverage with Angie. Call off her hounds, will you?"

"I promise. You okay otherwise?"

"I will be, Chase," she said in a determined voice. "I sure as hell *will* be. 'Bye!" The line went dead.

Mentally reviewing all that had happened in the last few days, Chase finished dressing and got in the big family car. As he drove into San Francisco, he tried to picture Emma "on the lam." She had always been the vulnerable one, too sensitive for the rough-and-tumble life of Falcon Crest. But she was still a cross between Gioberti and Channing genes, so underneath she had to be as tough as old rawhide. Chase smiled grimly. Emma would have to be as tough if she expected to win back her sanity and her

purpose in life in the teeth of her own mother's
disdain.

Jacqueline Perrault Gioberti had booked what
amounted to a private room at one of the city's most
expensive eating places. It was a corner table, surrounded on two sides by plate-glass windows overlook-
ing San Francisco and shielded on its other side by
potted plants and palms. Four waiters danced attendance, one for each person at Jacqueline's table.

"Sorry I'm late," Chase said. He blew a kiss to
Maggie, pecked the top of Vickie's head, embraced
his mother and turned to the fourth person at the
table, a compact, slim man in a pale beige suit of shot
silk over an open-at-the-neck voile shirt the color of
blanc-de-blanc chenin grapes in late August, a kind of
yellowy green the French called chartreuse.

"And this is Darryl Clayton," Chase's mother said.
"He's going to direct Maggie's film."

"That's news to him," Maggie put in. "Darryl must
think he's fallen in with a family of con artists,
Jacqueline. He hasn't even read the script."

Chase shook the newcomer's hand and found it
rather hard and firm, the kind of hand Chase associ-
ated with physical labor, not with directing movies.
"Heard from Cole?" he asked Maggie as he sat down
beside her.

"Not a word, the naughty boy," Jacqueline answered for her. "I have seen so little of him this
visit."

"Any idea where he was today?" Chase asked his
daughter.

"None of us knows," Jacqueline responded.

A furrow of irritation appeared between Chase's
eyebrows. "Mother," he said in a soft, patient voice,
"will you let them answer for themselves?"

"*Oui, bien sûr,*" she said with equal softness. "I
must be very careful with my nearest and dearest,

M'sieur Clayton. They consider me *de trop*." She made a small wrist gesture. "What you call 'too much,' eh?"

"You bowled me over and I don't bowl easy." The director turned to Chase as if trying to reestablish some modicum of male-female balance in the conversation. "It runs in the family, I guess. I've only read the first few pages of Maggie's script but it bowled me over, too. There is no substitute for absolute authority. And your wife really knows the vineyard scene."

Chase grinned at Maggie. "Someday when we have time, will you explain it to me?" He got a warm, answering smile. Then his glance moved past his wife's head to a tumble of shiny boxes lined up along the bottom of the window. The names of half a dozen of San Francisco's finest stores and specialty shops graced the wrappings.

"Who's been buying out the town?" Chase asked.

Vickie blushed. "Grandmother . . . for me."

"But it's not necessary," Maggie cut in, talking to Jacqueline. "Vickie has a perfectly good wardrobe. When she needs new things, she can buy them herself. And she certainly doesn't need . . ." Maggie gestured grandiosely. "Well, really, Italian boots at five hundred dollars a pair?"

"But the leather," Vickie pointed out enthusiastically, "it's so soft."

"It's a simple economy," Jacqueline purred. "Expensive clothes are the cheapest in the end because they last the longest."

"Mother," Chase told her, "in the case of five-hundred-dollar boots, I would call it overkill."

"What else should one spend one's money on but one's family?"

Chase was about to reply, pointing out that the co-owner of Falcon Crest could easily afford to keep his own family in boots, when his mother began delving in her tiny handbag. *"Alors,"* she said at last, removing a folded bit of paper. "Take this, Chase. It is for Cole's defense. I want you to hire Marvin Perlmutter. He's the top defense attorney in the entire West."

"We've got a perfectly good local man for Cole."

"Perlmutter will get Cole off."

"Cole is innocent. He doesn't need Perlmutter. Again, Mother, it's overkill."

"Don't argue, silly boy." Beyond Jacqueline in a palm count, a quartet began playing for dancing. Couples appeared on the small parquet floor. *"Très charmant,"* Jacqueline cooed. "M'sieur Clayton? Shall we?"

For a long moment, while the band played a medley of old Gershwin songs, Chase, Maggie and Vickie watched the director pilot Jacqueline flawlessly around the floor. He wasn't extravagant in his movement, merely firm and knowing. This allowed Jacqueline to spread her wings so to speak, and grace the dancing floor like a vivid butterfly.

"Très charmant?" Maggie muttered. *"Trop charmant."*

"Meaning 'too much'?" Chase suggested.

"She thinks she can buy all of us. Vickie with the most outrageously expensive wardrobe a girl her age ever had. You with a check for Cole's—" Maggie reached across and opened the folded check. "Will you look at that number, Chase?"

He pursed his lips and silently whistled. "I could buy Perlmutter five times over for that much money."

"You see how she buys us?"

They watched Clayton and Jacqueline finish the set and, applauding, move slowly back toward the corner table.

"Nicely packaged fella," Chase said in a dry voice. "When you talk about Jacqueline buying us, let's don't leave out her pet director for your script."

Chapter Twenty-Four _____

If anyone had had the inclination, they could have stared down through the glass picture windows of the rooftop restaurant and, as the twilight lingered over the harbor area, might have seen Lance Cumson's car pull to a halt at a rickety old fisherman's wharf not far from the Embarcadero.

Instead the growing dusk hid Lance's arrival from everyone but the young woman sitting cross-legged at the far end of the pier, a fishing line in her hand, a bucket of seawater by her side.

Lance moved softly along the shaky wharf so as not to disturb Lori at what she was doing. He'd often gone crabbing this way himself when younger. You got a bit of raw liver, threaded a hook through it, added a sinker or two and lowered it to the bottom, which was quite deep hereabouts, often as much as two hundred feet. The big beasts roamed the bay floor, the killer crabs that made such good eating because they fed so indiscriminately themselves. Like most seafood lovers, Lance had no use for crabs, lobsters, crayfish and the like that were raised in the quiet backwaters of hatcheries and other artificial environments supervised by man.

It was the lone-wolf crab who roved the bay bottom for his own dinner that attracted someone like Lance. And, obviously, Lori.

"Quiet, Cumson," she breathed. "I've got the sucker hooked."

Lance froze in his tracks. Slowly Lori was pulling in whatever had taken her bait. In the bucket beside her lurked a huge crab fully a foot across, with great, cruel pincers as deadly as Lance's own falcon's beak and talons.

Gradually the end of the line came into view. "Hi'ya, Killer," Lori murmured softly. "Be a good boy and hang in there just long enough . . ."

She swung the line up over the edge of the wharf. With one swift, complex movement she grabbed a short length of iron pipe, let the crab drop to the desk of the pier and rapped it sharply on its mottled carapace.

"Careful," Lance cautioned. "He's only stunned."

"That's perfect." She let the crab drop into the bucket beside her previous catch. "Okay, Killer," she told it, "sleep it off awhile. The two of you have dined well all these months. Now it's our turn."

Lance hoisted the bucket and slid his arm around Lori's slender waist as she got to her feet. "I've got a couple of bottles to go with these fellas."

"They ought to taste scrumptious. The waters here are polluted enough to give them a real gourmet flavor."

Lance laughed out loud. "God, you think like me, you know that?"

She took a grip on his waist. "Counting the crabs," she said in a reckless voice, "that makes four of us."

"Four of us what?"

"Four of us killers."

Chapter Twenty-Five_____

This was only Cole's third day at the Demery place, and it was shaping up as a disaster—not because of Kate, but because of his own family. Cole supposed he had handled the situation all wrong, but that didn't excuse the scene this morning.

"What's all this?" his mother, Maggie, had started, right before breakfast.

She'd found Cole loading a duffel bag full of his clothes on the pillion seat of the Honda. "Laundry?" she asked.

"N-no. Look, Mom, it's like this. This is a real, permanent job. I mean, I'm not just dropping by to help out now and then. It's a firm job offer from Ka—, from Mrs. Demery. And it's room and board. So . . ." He moistened his lips nervously. "So I'm moving my stuff over to the Demery place."

Maggie's eyes snapped dangerously. "How big a bed has she got?"

"Mom! I'm bunking in my own room off the winery."

"Just hold it right there," Maggie warned him. "Chase," she called, "come out here, will you?"

Towel in hand, Cole's father appeared on the front porch still drying his bearded face. "What's up?"

"He's going to live with Katharine Demery."

"Look, you two—" Cole began.

"What?" Chase asked. "What's wrong with the job you have with me?"

"This is a *real* job," Cole said. He could hear the stubborn mulish note in his own voice, but he didn't care. "Working for your own family isn't real work. Besides, Kate needs me."

"Kate, huh?"

"She told me not to call her Mrs. Demery. I mean, after all, she's practically my age."

"Cole," Maggie told him, trying to soften the shock of her words, "Katharine Demery is precisely ten years older than you. And ten years younger than me. Does that straighten out your head a little?"

He gave the elastic cord a final yank and secured it to the rear seat of the cycle. "Thanks for the rundown," he said, stamping on the starter pedal. "You know where to find me. So long!"

Plume of dust. Hideous roar. Good-bye home. Good-bye parents. It didn't have to be that way, Cole told himself now as he unpacked his duffel and made up his bunk with sheets and a light blanket.

Kate stood in the doorway. "You need help with that?"

"It's all done. Figured I'd start weeding the back vines near the trees."

She eyed him a long while. "You okay today, Cole?"

"Never better."

"Your folks had something to say about your moving over here," she suggested. "It's only natural."

"What's natural," Cole told her, "is that when a guy gets to a certain age, his folks let go of him."

"Easier said than done."

She plucked at the bed sheets and neatened them, then plumped up the pillow. "You know you're welcome here, Cole. But if it'd be easier on you to stay at home . . ."

"And blow a half hour each day to and from work?" He grinned at her. "Lady, you got too much work here to waste time getting *to* it."

"Still, nothing's worth having a bust-up with your folks."

"This isn't a bust-up," he assured her. In the half-dark of his bunkroom her lovely face seemed almost incandescent. Cole found himself wondering why, all these years, he had never *seen* just how beautiful she was.

"No," he said, finding his voice at last and trying to sound casual. "It's just something I have to do. Be on my own. Sort things out."

"There never was a better time than now."

"That's for sure . . ." He paused. "Why did you say that?"

She laughed. "Because what you're going through is a test, Cole. Somehow, by being in the wrong place, you've got yourself stuck in a crack and life is really squeezing you. That's when you have to know who you really are. Otherwise you can't stand up to the pressure."

He thought for a long moment. "You sound like you've been there yourself."

"Oh, yes," she assured him. "Two years ago, when Jim was taken from me, I panicked. He'd done all the thinking for both of us. He'd done the planning, everything. And, suddenly . . ." She stopped. "It was like being cut in two when Jim died. I felt like half a person. And it's taken me all this time to grow whole again."

Cole wanted to reach out and touch her tanned hand, hold it, kiss it. He knew she could read what he was thinking because after a moment she straightened up from the bed and turned to leave.

"Lunch is twelve noon sharp. Nothing fancy. Just you and me and the kitchen table." She waved as she left.

The weeds hadn't been touched in at least two years. Cole sweated and snipped and dug and carted trash until he'd managed to free eight rows of vine from the smothering embrace of the unwanted plant life that stole nourishment from the same soil and growth from the same sun.

He had raked the green cuttings into a pile and set fire to them when he saw Kate waving to him from the main house. As soon as he had the fire smoldering without flaming, he joined her in the kitchen.

"I warned you," she said, passing a plate heaped with thick peanut butter and jelly sandwiches. "Nothing fancy. I generally save my breathtaking gourmet cookery for dinner."

"What does the chef recommend for tonight?"

"Tonight," Kate said in a fake French accent, "we 'ave ze *coq au vin* wiz se *petite quenelles.* In other words, chicken stew with dumplings."

"You sound like my grandmother," Cole remarked, reaching for another sandwich.

Kate took his hand. "What happened to your thumb?"

"A scratch."

"Deep. And dirty." She pulled him to his feet and led him to the sink. Carefully, she washed out the cut.

"You're going to love this next part," she said, dabbing red liquid on his thumb. A searing pain shot up his arm, then died away. "Hold still." She applied a big adhesive bandage and taped the edges shut to keep out dust. "There." But she didn't release his hand just yet. "Did you ever play the violin?" she asked in mock innocence.

"Nope."

"Well, you never will again," she added mischievously. "Back to the peanut butter."

They munched in silence for a while, sipping cold milk from tall glasses. Seeing her across the table, Cole couldn't believe what his mother had said about her age. Ten years older? Impossible.

"I know how important it is to clear out the weeds so the grapes can do their thing," Kate was saying, "but I'd really appreciate it if you could look at my roof. There's a hole in it the size of a baseball."

"Right after the weeds."

Someone was knocking on the front door. Kate got to her feet and disappeared toward the front of the house. After a moment Cole could hear her talking. The answering voice had a French accent. He jumped to his feet just as Kate led Jacqueline Perrault Gioberti and Maggie into the kitchen.

"I wish I could offer you something more than this," Kate was saying.

"But how charming," Jacqueline enthused. "Cole must be in seventh heaven. Peanut butter, jelly and milk. Perfect."

Her big, dark eyes darted this way and that about the small, clean kitchen. "You must forgive our intrusion, Mrs. Demery," she went on, accenting Kate's name on the last syllable as if it were French. "I prevailed upon Maggie to show me where my grandson is living."

"And working," Cole put in.

"*Naturellement,*" his grandmother said in an indulgent voice, as if it didn't much matter to her what Cole was up to here. "This will do you very well, Cole. Mark my words, it can only make a man of you."

The extravagance of her statement was in sharp contrast to Maggie's utter silence, her stare riveted to Kate's pretty face. After too much of this unblinking regard, the atmosphere had become uncomfortable, at least to Cole. But he didn't know how to cope with his mother's cold anger.

"Mrs. Gioberti," Kate said then, "you don't approve of Cole working here."

"Or living here," Maggie added in an echo of the earlier conversation.

"But that's foolishness," Jacqueline burst in. "You don't understand Cole, my dear."

"Don't I?" Maggie's ironic tone made her son feel incredibly uneasy.

"His reasons for breaking away," her mother-in-law continued, "for being here."

"Those reasons," Maggie said, staring Kate Demery full in the face, "I understand with absolute clarity, now that I've met his new employer."

"Mom. This is insane."

Maggie nodded slowly, but when she spoke it was to Jacqueline. "Think, Jacqueline," she said. "Think if Vickie went to work and live in the home of a single man. How carefree would your attitude be then?"

"But that's just it," her mother-in-law said, letting loose that silvery cascade of careful laughter she did so naturally. "We're talking about Cole, not Vickie."

"And Mrs. Demery isn't just anybody," Cole spoke up then.

"I beg your pardon?" his mother asked.

"She's had a lot of trouble herself," Cole went on in a strong voice. "If anybody ever needed a helping hand before it's too late, she does."

The silence began to crystallize around those last words. Finally Maggie stirred. "Is that how you see yourself, Cole? As someone in trouble who needs a helping hand?"

"You tell me," he said challengingly.

The tension seemed to evaporate on the silence that followed Cole's remark. Maggie sighed and shook her head slowly; she seemed to pull herself together, as if remembering her manners in the nick of time. "Mrs. Demery, I think I may have been out of line. I apologize."

"Please, it's Kate. Neighbors are neighbors, not strangers."

As the two Gioberti women left, Jacqueline could not resist glancing back at Kate, then winking at her grandson. It was a conspiratorial gesture, something along the lines of "Don't do anything I wouldn't do. On the other hand, there's very little I'd stop at."

Silently, Kate and Cole sat back down and returned to their lunch. "Your grandmother is quite something," Kate said at last. "But your mother is a real lady, Cole. No wonder you're such a good kid."

"Kid? How old do you think I am?"

"Nineteen? Twenty?"

Cole's face fell. "Not many secrets in Tuscany Valley."

"Your mother senses some sort of attraction between us," Kate went on in that direct, no-nonsense manner of hers. "And there *is* one. But it's not the kind she thinks."

"No? What kinds have you got?"

Her smile was a thing of perfect, balanced pleasure. "A friendly attraction. We're good friends, Cole, because we're on the same side in life."

"And that's all?"

"It's more than enough."

By the time Cole got around to looking at the roof, the afternoon sun was headed toward the western horizon and the air had cooled considerably. He set the rickety ladder against the side of the two-story house, but dug the bottom of the uprights a good two inches into the gravel. Then he climbed to the top and secured the ladder with twists of haywire.

He went down and up many times, carrying

shingles, nails and tools until, by five o'clock, he had most of the leaky roof redone. Between the climbing and the hot sun, he had worked up a terrific thirst.

"Cold apple juice?" Kate asked.

She had climbed the ladder and was holding out a tall glass of amber liquid to Cole. He took it gratefully. "You're saving my life, Kate."

"But this is where you saved mine, remember?"

He drained the glass and edged down the slope of the roof to hand it back to her. "It must be the magnificent view from up here," he wisecracked.

"The view of the vast Demery estates, known throughout the world wherever fine wines are appreciated," Kate remarked kiddingly.

"Someday," Cole promised.

"You're sweet to say that." Their faces almost touched. Both their hands were on the empty glass. An instant later Cole had suddenly closed the gap and kissed her on the lips.

There was dead silence on the rooftop. Even so, neither of them heard the velvety whirr-click a Nikon shutter makes when the photographer presses the button. In this case the Nikon was resting in the fork of a tree nearly a thousand feet away from the Demery house. But its 400-mm telephoto lens had an unobstructed view of the roof.

Greedily, the shutter snapped again. And again.

Chapter Twenty-Six

In the late afternoon, the atmosphere inside the huge Falcon Crest winery grew chilly. The great white vats seemed to stretch out into infinity. Julia moved here and there with her old-fashioned doctor's bag, testing, evaluating, using the antique instruments her grandfather had brought from Europe.

When she returned to her office she closed the door, checked her notebook, switched on the computer terminal and began keying data into the EDS. So wrapt was she in this that she failed to hear the door behind her open. Finally the creak of the floor caught her attention.

She whirled in her chair. A handsome man was smiling down at her. Richard Channing!

"You fool," Julia said, not unkindly. "Trying to sneak up on me." She held out her hand as she got to her feet. "How are you, Richard?"

"Just fine, Sis." Ignoring her hand, he locked her in a tight embrace, kissing her firmly on both cheeks, as close to the corners of her mouth as he dared.

Julia's face flushed crimson. "You've got to watch those half-brotherly smooches, Richard," she said tartly. "Is this the surprise call you warned me about?"

"Nice layout here," he said, by way of not replying

to the question. "These old instruments," he remarked, fondling a nickel-steel thermometer. "These were Jasper's, weren't they?"

"Yes. Still accurate to a tenth of a degree."

"He certainly wouldn't know Falcon Crest anymore," Richard said, sitting down across the desk from her. "Stainless-steel vats, air-bag presses that gentle the juice out of the grapes. More varietals than Jasper ever knew possible. And now I finally get to meet the scientific brain who's responsible."

"Hardly."

"You've built it up and you're content to hang in here," Richard went on as if she hadn't spoken, "tied to the land, to the grapes, to the wine. If I know you, Julia, your idea of investing your money wisely is to buy some new books on wine-making."

"Not a bad idea. We're always learning."

"That's the trouble with you people. Basically you're farmers land-rich and cash-poor."

"It's never given me a sleepless night," Julia parried.

"You've never had the sheer socko thrill of being cash-rich," her half brother told her flatly. "You've never had that kind of power in your own hands. Ask your mother about it sometime."

"I can do without her input," Julia assured him. "Is this the same bait you were dangling on the phone? Quick riches?"

Richard captured her hand and held it in his. Julia could feel an odd tingle run up her wrist. "Here's the offer—I'll buy your shares of *Globe* stock at forty dollars each. Do I have to do the math for you?"

Julia released her hand, cleared the computer video and tapped in a computation. A number with a lot of zeros showed on the screen. "Last I heard those shares were worth twenty each."

"My half sister gets a premium price."

"Try it for yourself," she said, moving to one side to let him get at the terminal.

"I . . . don't trust those things," Richard said, reaching in his jacket pocket. He pulled out a small ebony and teak abacus, its beads strung on shiny brass wires. Effortlessly he flicked a few beads up and down with the tip of his finger. "With your shares, I'd own over sixty percent of the *Globe.*"

"Which should be worth a lot more to you than forty dollars a share."

"Spoken like a true Channing," he said. "Financial modesty was never our strong point. Forty-five?"

Julia swiveled back to the terminal and touched its keyboard. A number with more zeros showed up on the video. "Try fifty dollars a share," she suggested.

"If we can conclude the deal today. Right now."

Julia's smile went impish. "Just putting you on, Richard. Just testing. My shares aren't for sale. I may be cash-poor. But I'm not exactly starving to death."

For a moment Richard's attractive features seemed to harden into a steel mask. Then, with an effort, he forced himself to smile. "I don't take kindly to teasing, dear sister," he said then. "The moment you want to talk deal, seriously, don't waste time in telling me. But I can't guarantee it'll be as sweet for you as the deal you nearly had just now."

Beyond the laboratory doors they could hear voices. They got to their feet and peered out into the winery. In the distance a smallish party of people was moving from vat to vat. In the gloom Julia could recognize Chase by his beard. The rest were women.

". . . Cabernet Sauvignon," Chase was saying. "It should be ready this fall, but the final word on that always comes from Julia."

"She is Angela's oldest daughter?" a woman with an accent asked.

"She's also our head oenologist."

"I thought you knew such things, too," the woman persisted.

"As a practical matter, yes," Chase agreed. "But Julia's college-trained. You can't trust the output of Falcon Crest to anybody except an expert like her."

"There she is," Maggie said. "Julia, are your ears red?"

Richard escorted her down a long flight of stairs until all of them were standing in a group together. "Julia, you remember my mother, Jacqueline Gioberti," Chase said. He eyed Richard with distaste and seemed reluctant to mention his name. "What're you doing here? Digging up more dirt?"

"Just a friendly chat with Julia."

"If this guy bothers you," Chase told Julia, "let me know. We'll have him off the premises in no time flat."

"My goodness, Chase," his mother said. "Who is this handsome young man?"

Chase frowned. "A large pain in the neck," he muttered.

Jacqueline was smiling directly at Richard. The aura that surrounded this attractive woman was always strong, but never more so than when she met a good-looking man. The eyes brightened. The smile widened. The face glowed.

"This is Richard Channing," Julia said. "Douglas Channing's son."

In the great echoing vault of the winery, the words seemed to reverberate endlessly. For a long moment, no one spoke, certainly not Jacqueline, who stood like a statue, smile frozen in place.

"How do you do?" Richard said then.

"Yes." The woman's voice sounded weak for a moment. Then, more strongly: "How do you do."

"I feel as if we've met," Richard went on, producing a smile with even more voltage than hers. "My associates in Zurich speak of you."

"You have the advantage of me," Jacqueline replied.

"Richard is publishing the *Globe* now," Maggie explained.

"Unfortunately," Chase added, "he's just leaving."

Richard laughed easily. "Always a welcome mat here at Falcon Crest, eh, Chase? Don't worry, I am going."

As he walked out through a side door, Jacqueline's stare seemed to follow him, not merely after he was out of sight, but as if with X-ray vision she could follow his progress to the ends of the earth. A clouded look came over her lovely face.

"Mother?"

When Jacqueline didn't speak, Julia suddenly stirred to life. "I left my terminal open back at the office. Nice to see you again, Mrs. Gioberti."

Chase waited until Julia had left. Now only he and Maggie attended his mother. "Mother?"

Jacqueline shivered. "It's too cold in here."

"Yes. Time to leave."

"For me, too," she said. "I heard from René in Zurich today. I am needed there tomorrow at the latest. A matter of some signatures."

"Jacqueline," Maggie objected. "You can't just drop everything and run off."

"You don't keep Swiss bankers waiting, my dear. There's a night flight over the pole that leaves this evening. I've got ..." She peered nearsightedly at her wristwatch.

"It's nearly six o'clock," Chase told her.

"I've got two hours before the flight leaves. *Alors, tout de suite.* We must hurry."

"You're not serious," Chase demanded.

His mother's face had a haunted look to it. "Oh," she said, "but I am."

Chapter Twenty-Seven

Maggie Gioberti propped up the note on the kitchen table: "Case, Vickie & Co.," it read. "Lunch is on bottom shelf of fridge. I'll be back no later than 4 P.M. Where am I going? To lunch with " 'my' " director!!!"

She smiled as she drove out of Tuscany Valley for the highway into San Francisco. Jacqueline was gone only one day; already life seemed much simpler. The fact of the matter was, Chase's mother spooked Maggie. She was, to put it simply, too chic, too sophisticated and too rich for comfort.

Not that Maggie wasn't grateful for the introduction to Darryl Clayton. But the nagging thought remained, just as Chase had voiced it: Jacqueline could find a way to buy even Maggie's friendship.

Of course, if she could believe Darryl, the script had sold itself. "I'm serious," he'd enthused over the phone this morning. "Please let's have lunch. I want some sort of handshake agreement before I leave for L.A."

She parked near one of the better-known seafood restaurants along the waterfront and found him, still in his ecru shot-silk suit, but set off this time by an open-necked shirt in orangey rose. His slim, compact body rose from the chair as she approached his table.

"I'm so glad you could make it," he said, ordering planter's punches for both of them. "I'm due back in L.A. for a dinner meeting with a couple of potential investors."

"Jacqueline mentioned you'd been looking for money-men up here."

"That's a director's full-time job these days," he explained. Maggie studied him as he spoke: he had a small head and a rather square face, crowned by short-cropped light brown hair. If he'd dressed in more conventional clothing, Maggie realized, he would have been hard to distinguish in a crowd.

"Sometimes," he explained, "you take three years to get financing for a movie that takes less than six months to shoot. It's frustrating."

They sipped their drinks slowly, cautiously sizing each other up while maintaining a steady flow of light chitchat. Maggie found him refreshingly candid about the glamorous life of the Hollywood director. She began to warm to him.

"The property I was trying to get backing for," Darryl was saying, "is an old F. Scott Fitzgerald story. It's not easy. People in the business still remember him as controversial. But with a script like " 'Tangled Vines' " I've got a known quantity, the wine business. I've got an easy location schedule, right here in California. And I've got characters that stars will be willing to fight to play."

"I can't believe it doesn't need revisions."

"Sure it does," the director told her. "But wait till I get a few bankable actors interested. Then it can be tailored to them."

"You honestly think so?"

"Maggie, in this business there are no guarantees. I like it. But I may not find anyone to agree with me.

Here's what I need from you." He pulled a small notebook out of his breast pocket. "I want to take a six-month option. That's a common arrangement. But I can't pay for the option. That's where we have to trust each other."

"How so?"

"You'll sell me a conditional option, for, say, one dollar. But the condition is that the moment I start to get financing, I pay you a five-thousand advance against the full price."

"Not hard to take."

"But the moment I do, you've got to start the rewrite."

"I understand."

"No, you don't," he corrected her. "I'm the kind of director who takes an active interest in the script. The revisions will be done by you, but in consultation with me."

Maggie sat back in her chair as the waiter brought their order. They'd both chosen Coho salmon poached in bouillon. It arrived in a long copper *bain-marie*, together with side dishes of vegetables and a pale green chive mayonnaise.

"Mm," she said. "I like this deal already."

He looked at her and she realized that he had a very warm, reassuring smile, the kind that managed to make everything seem just fine. "I hope you keep that attitude," he said then. "It won't be easy. You'll be living in a rented apartment somewhere in L.A., punching the typewriter day and night."

Maggie looked up at him. "I thought—"

"You thought we could do this by mail?" Darryl asked.

"I'm not sure I could leave my fam—"

"You'd have to," the director cut in. "Not for long, just a few weeks at a time. But, after all, you'd be only an hour's plane ride from them."

"Y-es," she said doubtfully, "but—"

"Let's do justice to this salmon before it cools," he interrupted again. Expertly, he transferred fish to her plate, then helped himself. Maggie looked down, then up at him. She giggled.

"What's funny?"

"It's the same color as your shirt."

He compared the two. "Well," he said at last, "let's start with the fish. We could always have the shirt for dessert."

She ate in silence, enjoying the delicate texture of the salmon, the unusual flavor given it by the broth, the tang of the special mayonnaise. As she ate, Maggie turned the idea over and over in her mind. She was taking a chance, giving him a free option. But, oddly enough for someone she'd met only recently, she trusted this man. And, besides, who else did she know in the film business?

As for leaving the Valley to work on revisions, that was out of the question now, with Cole in deep trouble and Chase needing as much help as possible from her. But revisions wouldn't begin for some time. At least six months? By then peace might have descended on the Valley and maybe she could run off to L.A. now and then.

"I find this whole thing very exciting," she said then.

"The fish? Or me?"

When she glanced up at him she caught an expression in his eyes that hadn't been there before. She knew the look. Every attractive woman does, even when she's been a faithful wife for twenty years. By rights, the look in Darryl Clayton's eyes should have been a warning.

For some reason, it suddenly wasn't.

Chapter Twenty-Eight_____

For some hours the pain had grown steadily worse. Melissa prepared herself for sleep, haunted by the sure knowledge that the baby inside her would give her no rest. She lay down in bed and tried to find a position of comfort. There was none. What had begun as a dull ache had now built up to short, sharp stabs of agonizing pain.

Lance had been dawdling in their bathroom. She had half-expected him to come out in pajamas, but it was no real surprise when he appeared fully clothed, although it was nine o'clock at night.

Masking the pain, Melissa affected a calm, slightly ironic tone of voice. "Working the night shift again . . . in San Francisco?"

Lance watched her warily. Then, in a cool tone: "Yep."

"Your nerve is improving. You didn't even flinch."

"What do I care?" he snapped. "We've got a modern marriage, remember?"

"Does that mean it's out of the question for you to stay home even one night?"

As he glared at her, she felt an acute stab of pain. Her face contorted, but she managed to remain silent.

"Why?" Lance asked. "So we can keep taking pot-shots at each other?"

"How about a cease-fire? Just for tonight?"

"Too late." He turned and started for the door.

The pain suddenly rocketed up inside Melissa like the thrust of a sword. She screamed. Lance stopped and looked back at her.

"Hey, give me a break."

She could feel perspiration on her forehead as the pain kept growing. She had bitten down on her lip in an effort to remain silent. Now a low moan escaped. She writhed sideways on the bed.

Lance frowned. "What is it?"

Her face white with effort, Melissa managed to whisper, "Dr. Ruzza. Call him."

There was a knock at the door. Angela Channing swung it open. "Melissa? Are you all right?"

"Help me," the younger woman moaned. "Please?"

"What's wrong?" Angie rushed to the bed. "Are you in pain?" She glanced at Lance. "What's been going on here?"

"I don't know what happened. She was just lying th—"

"It hurts," Melissa managed to say. "Sharp pain. Call Dr. Ruzza."

"Lance, get on the phone. Now!"

"The baby's not due for another two months," he said. "She just went ape. I didn't do anything."

His grandmother turned her wrath on him. "Do something now!" she thundered. "Get on that phone. Fast!"

He began dialing a number. Angie bent over Melissa. "Did something happen to bring this on?" she asked her.

Biting her lip, Melissa shook her head from side to side. "But he mustn't talk to me like that," she managed to say.

Angie's eyes flicked sideways to her grandson. "Tell him to get over here on the double. Wait." She snatched the phone out of Lance's hand. "Doctor? This is an emergency. Break every speed record." She slammed down the phone and whirled on her grandson. "What sort of tricks have you been up to?"

"Nothing. This isn't my fault," Lance protested.

Angela Channing began pacing back and forth across the carpeted floor. From Melissa to the phone, from the phone to Melissa. "I've been entirely too lenient with you," she told Lance. "You haven't the slightest idea of proper behavior. Well, young man, you're going to shape up, and fast."

She stopped and stared at him. "What're you dressed for this time of evening? Another night on the town? Your wife and your baby are in trouble. Your place is here. And, by God, here is where you're going to stay!"

"Grandmother," Lance pleaded, "none of this is my fault."

He was still defending himself when the doctor arrived and shooed them both from the bedroom. He stayed for some time with Melissa while Lance and his grandmother waited downstairs, surrounded by a heavy silence broken only by the steady ticking of the hall clock. Finally Dr. Ruzza could be heard descending the curved marble staircase. They moved toward him.

"She's resting," he began. He was a short, squat man with a shiny bald head fringed by curly gray hair the consistency of steel wool.

"The baby?" Angela demanded.

"I've sedated Melissa. She should be more comfortable."

"The baby?" she insisted.

"She hasn't lost it."

"Thank God," Angie breathed.

"But there are complications," the doctor went on. "The baby's in a breech position. This could change in the next few days. But if labor began prematurely . . ." He paused.

"Can it?" Angie demanded.

"The possibility is always there." Dr. Ruzza started for the door, but stopped and turned directly to Lance. "I have to tell you, Lance, if she goes into labor prematurely we have a dangerous situation. It could—" He paused and his face grew very still. "It could endanger your wife's life . . . as well as your child's."

The three of them stood without speaking for a long moment. Then Angela Channing looked the doctor directly in the eye. "Tell us exactly what to do."

"She must remain in bed for the full term," he explained. "She must avoid anything that upsets her, physically or emotionally. I'll drop by tomorrow morning. Good night, Mrs. Channing . . . Lance."

"Thank you, Doctor." Angie held the door open for him and, after he left, closed it very slowly. "You heard?" she asked Lance.

"Yeah, I heard. Look, Grandmother, this isn't my—"

"Melissa is to have whatever she needs," Angie cut him off. "That includes the loving care of a husband. On hand. At any hour. At *every* hour."

"Look—"

"Lance," his grandmother said in a voice so strong it hit him almost as if she had hurled a javelin at his breast.

"Yes?"

"This baby," she said in that same tone, "*must* live!"

Chapter Twenty-Nine

It was one of those rare occasions when the two owners of Falcon Crest were forced by circumstances to sit down at the same table together. Both had contracts that needed the other's signature. It was typical that Chase Gioberti arrived alone, while Angela Channing made her appearance on the arm of her attorney, Phillip Erikson.

The meeting was set on neutral ground, quite like a truce parley between warring nations. The small French restaurant that overlooked Tuscany Valley had put aside a private room for them and supplied a small snack lunch.

Again, it was typical of Chase to begin at once spreading various contracts and other legal documents on the table. But before the attorney would start the meeting he first toured the room, peering under tables and behind pictures on the wall.

"Looking for eavesdropping bugs?" Chase suggested. "Nervous?"

"That's what I pay him for," Angie snapped.

Phillip grinned. "Chase, these days any school kid knows how to record a conversation secretly. You'd do well to pay more attention to security problems yourself."

Chase shrugged. "What's the point? My closest and dearest enemy is right here in the room with me."

Angela Channing produced a laugh that sounded more like a snort. "Don't kid yourself, Chase. There isn't a winery in the Valley that wouldn't love to eavesdrop on Falcon Crest's inner workings."

"This is routine stuff," Chase countered. "Here, this is simply a contract with our new Canadian distributor. You sign here."

Angie picked up the weighty sheaf of papers, donned her reading glasses and paged quickly through the contract. "Have you read it?" she asked Erikson.

"It's okay to sign."

"That's not what I asked you."

"Angela," the lawyer said in an exasperated tone, "darling Angela. Try to control your natural tendency to treat me as a first-year law student."

"Mm." She unscrewed her pen and began signing on various lines. The meeting continued slowly but smoothly for another half hour until all business had been attended to.

"What are these supposed to be?" Angela asked then, picking up a canapé from a platter and examining it as if it might, indeed, contain a miniaturized listening device. "Is this their idea of lunch?"

"*Nouvelle cuisine*," Phillip suggested. "It's supposed to be slimming."

Angela munched suspiciously. "More like an alfalfa fritter."

"Angela," Chase said then, "I've heard from Emma."

A glance darted between Angie and Erikson. "Where is she?" her mother demanded.

"That's not the point. She wants you to stop having her followed."

"What makes her think I'm having her followed?"

"Someone's trailed her halfway across the continent."

Erikson frowned. "Where did she call from?"

Chase paused for a moment. "I guess it can't hurt to tell you because she's far away from there by now. She said she was east of Oklahoma."

Once again Angie glanced sideways at her attorney. "That could be anywhere."

"Let's assume Louisiana," Chase replied.

The frown on Erikson's brow deepened considerably. "Angela," he said at last, "I think we'd better pool information with Chase."

"I don't."

"Be sensible, Angela."

A frustrated look settled on Angie's face. She picked up another canapé and tentatively nibbled at it. "Watercress soufflé. Tell him."

"Chase," Phillip went on, "Emma's right. We've had a man trying to locate her."

"You can't blame a mother for wanting to know her daughter's safe," Angie cut in.

"But the problem is, our man lost her somewhere in Arizona. That's a hell of a long way from Louisiana."

Chase thought for a moment. "I got the feeling there was someone on her tail at that moment," he said at last. "I got the distinct idea she was still under surveillance."

"Then it wasn't our man," Erikson concluded.

"Then whose?" Angie burst out.

"Someone with the same interest in Emma that you have," Chase said with a faintly malicious smile.

"Nonsense. I'm her mother. Nobody has a mother's interest but me."

"Your interest in Emma," Chase told her flatly, "is summed up in one succinct phrase—her share of *Globe* stock."

"Don't be insulting."

"And that sums up the interest of whoever else is having her shadowed," Chase finished. "So we really don't have to spend too much time figuring out his identity."

"Richard Channing," Angela spat out. "That miserable, shrewd, nasty bast—"

"Your opinion of Richard isn't any lower than mine," Chase interrupted. "In any event, I want him to call off his dogs."

"How do you propose to do that?"

"By showing him he's barking up the wrong tree." Chase's smile grew broader as he reached in his jacket pocket and produced a handwritten letter. He smoothed it out on the table, but made sure he protected it with both hands from being snatched away. "You recognize Emma's handwriting?"

Phillip Erikson bent over the letter, as did Angie. After a moment they both looked up, startled. "She's given *you* her proxy?"

"That's what it says." Chase folded and pocketed the letter.

A long silence ensued. Chase carefully packed away in a briefcase the various papers he had brought to the meeting. Phillip did the same. Only Angie seemed thoroughly lost in thought. She stared at the tray of snacks but her glance was unfocused, faraway.

Finally Chase got to his feet. "Good-bye. Enjoy your rabbit-food lunch."

Angela's vacant stare followed his figure out the door. Then she returned to her own thoughts.

"Bit of a shock," her lawyer said then. "This gives Chase the second-largest control in the *Globe*, after Richard."

"It makes it imperative you keep buying up shares."

"They're not cheap, Angela," Phillip cautioned her. "Since Richard has been running the *Globe* the share price has started to rise."

"I don't care what they cost. Keep buying."

"And charge it to Chase's part of the Falcon Crest accounts?"

"Yes," Angela said. For the first time that day she smiled and picked up another canapé, which she tasted. "*Pâté* of dandelion," she pronounced. "Rabbit food indeed."

"What do you care, my dear?" her attorney remarked. "You're already eating Chase Gioberti alive."

Chapter Thirty

From her bedroom window, Melissa had a magnificent view of the valley. The vineyards of Falcon Crest swept down and then up, forming a fertile valley that ended, to the north, in the vineyards of her father—now *hers*. To the west, much closer but hidden by a clump of trees, were a series of much smaller holdings, the Carloni vineyards and those belonging to Katharine Demery.

Although she was supposed to stay in bed, Melissa felt too restless this afternoon. She had carefully gotten up and walked to the window. The exertion had produced no bad effects. Thanks to the gentle sedation Dr. Ruzza had given her, she no longer felt any sharp, stabbing pains. An occasional ache was the only reminder of that horrible night a week ago.

Melissa looked at the sky to the north. A towering buildup of dark clouds signaled the threat of a thunderstorm. She knew that this late in the summer a really heavy rain could hurt the grapes, and certainly a month from now, rich with September fullness and weight, the grapes could be torn from the vines by too violent a storm.

She stared westward into the setting sun. Its rays touched the leaden heights of the incoming cloud bank and for a moment turned them to gold. This house at Falcon Crest, Melissa thought, really dominated the Valley, the view, everything. And one day it would belong to her child.

She tried to catch a glimpse of the Demery house. Gossip had it that Cole was working there. A few weeks back she'd seen someone who might have been him on the roof, laying shingles. The house was only a ten-minute walk from here, but now, in her present condition, she didn't dare attempt to make it.

As she peered through the window, she wondered about Cole, how he was weathering his ordeal. The *Globe* hadn't printed one of its nasty little rumor-mongering articles for a while. Strange to think that only through the pages of the newspaper could Melissa keep up with the news of the Valley. She was a prisoner here, thanks to the baby growing inside her.

Straining her eyes, she thought she could make out a tall man working in the Demery vineyard. A woman seemed to be nearby. Melissa sighed unhappily. The baby was due in six weeks. Till then, she knew she would be virtually bedridden, only an onlooker to the events of the Valley.

The only bright spot was that Lance had stopped going out nights. Melissa's face went blank. Bright spot? She returned to her bed and sat down on the edge of it. She had wanted Lance with her. But his presence hadn't been as bright a spot as she'd hoped for. She was beginning to realize that a falcon caged against his will is not a particularly responsive pet.

Downstairs in Falcon Crest mansion, Angela Channing and her daughter Julia had met in the library. Chao-Li served them chilled glasses of the new Pinot Noir. They sat in opposite wing-back chairs and silently sipped the straw-pale wine.

"A touch too fruity?" Angie suggested.

"Not after it breathes." Julia held the glass up to the sunlight streaming in from the west. "Give it five minutes in the glass. Then try it again. But what about the color? Too pale?"

"Not for my taste."

"Mine either. Oh, I called the weather bureau."

"What's the verdict?"

Julia made a face. "Does the weather bureau ever give you a straight answer? There's a heavy buildup of cumulo-nimbus heading this way, but there's been no sharp temperature change to trigger off any precip. Can you translate into English?"

"Sure. It's a definite, positive maybe." Angela laughed.

"I've told all the foremen to stand by in case we need to cover the new gamay vines. They're too vulnerable."

Angie sipped her wine again. "Better. But do most people let wine stand in the glass for five minutes? You've got to improve the next batch, Julia."

"Come on, Mother. If a person knows anything about wine, he knows it needs to breathe a little."

"Reds, yes. This is a white."

Julia laughed bitterly. "Don't you ever let up?"

"Not when it comes to wine." An uneasy silence fell between them. Angie continued sipping the Pinot Noir. Her glance shifted first to the north windows, where the sky was a bruised gray, then to the west, where the sun still shone brightly. She saw a copy of the *Globe* crumpled in the wastebasket.

"Did you throw the paper away?"

"It's trash, Mother."

"I agree," Angie admitted. "But that son of Douglas' seems to have upped the circulation and advertising. Shares in the *Globe* keep rising in price. Apparently he knows what he's doing."

Julia said nothing, thinking of the offer Richard had made recently for her own shares. The profit would be even higher now.

"Of course," her mother went on, "if the public wants trash, anybody who sells it to them ends up making a profit. In Douglas' day the *Globe* managed to make money and still be a decent newspaper."

When Julia remained silent, Angie got up and went to the wastebasket. She retrieved the paper and sat back down in her chair, pouring herself another half glass of the Pinot Noir.

"Don't tell me you really like the new wine," Julia said then. "I'd faint if I ever got a compliment."

"It's . . . adequate," her mother confessed grudgingly. "In fact, it's . . . pleasant."

She began reading the *Globe*. "In fact," she mused aloud, "you might even say the wine was . . . hell and damnation!"

"What?"

"You were hiding this from me, weren't you?" Angie's eyes blazed at her daughter. "You didn't want me to see this?"

"I said it was trash."

"FALCON CREST MURDER SUSPECT DALLIES WITH WIDOW," Angie read aloud from the newspaper headlines. "And here's a picture of them kissing. How in God's name do they get these photos?"

Her eyes raced furiously from one column to the next. "How can they print this kind of innuendo?" she demanded. "Listen to this. 'While Sheriff Robbins continues collecting evidence, his chief murder suspect, temporarily at large, seems to have established an illicit liaison with an older widow. Cole Gioberti, 19, of the Falcon Crest clan, has apparently become the live-in companion of Katharine Demery, 29, despite the fact that a deep pall of suspicion

concerning the Agretti murder hangs over him.'
Julia, the target of this isn't Cole. It's Falcon Crest."

"No one believes it."

"They believe photographs," Angie stormed. "The
difference in their ages makes the gossip even
smuttier. It's a smear campaign against Falcon Crest.
We're not just a place, Julia. We're a trade name. It's
on every one of our bottles. Richard Channing is
making sure that when someone sees the name, he
associates it with illicit sexual gossip, accusations of
murder—. Chao-Li!" she shouted.

"Calm yourself," Julia advised.

"I'm calm. Don't worry about that," Angela snapped.

The Chinese majordomo appeared in the doorway.
"You called?"

"Where is Mr. Erikson? Can he be reached?"

"I will try, Mrs. Channing."

"Get him on the phone for me as soon as possible.
Here!" She shoved the newspaper at him. "Take this
out and burn it!"

The *Globe* tucked under his arm, Chao-Li retired
to the pantry and dialed several numbers. He left
urgent messages. The call light in the butler's area
glowed red for Melissa's room. He hurried up the
curved stairs. In the distance, thunder rumbled.

"Yes, Miss Melissa?"

"I seem to have run out of water, Chao-Li. Could
you fill my carafe? I have to take my six o'clock
capsule."

"Certainly, Miss Melissa."

Thunder rolled closer. "Isn't it odd?" Melissa asked.
"Here in the west the sun's shining. And to the north
it's starting to rain. Is that the *Globe*?"

"When that happens," Chao-Li said gravely, "sunshine and rain together, the farmers have a saying,
'The Devil is beating his wife.' Curious."

Melissa reached for the newspaper under his arm.

"My father used to say that, but in Italian, *'Il Demonio'* . . . I can't remember." She opened the *Globe.*

"I'll get your water."

Melissa's glance skipped here and there across the front page of the newspaper but her mind was still on what her father had said. She had never been able to speak Italian, nor had Carlo Agretti attempted to teach her. In his generation, one was proud of being an American. But in her generation, Melissa knew, there was a great feeling for getting back to one's roots. A few phrases of Italian had remained with her. But . . .

Il Demonio batta . . .

Outside the north windows, rain rattled now, a gentle sound at first. Chao-Li reappeared with the filled thermos carafe, poured a glass of cool water and helped her take her sedative.

"I don't really need it anymore," Melissa remarked. "I'm really fine."

"Still . . ."

The Chinese went to the north windows and closed them until only an inch of open space remained at the bottom. "You will nap now?"

"Probably."

She watched him leave. *Il Demonio batta su . . .*

She relaxed with a sigh. A moment later, one arm folded over the unread newspaper, she fell asleep.

A bolt of lightning cracked down on the mansion and hit one of the bronze-bound cupolas with a sizzling crash. The explosion seemed to fill the world with noise. Melissa jumped awake.

A full storm was beating against the house now. She had been asleep for some time. Someone had come in and closed the west windows against the rain. The small bedside clock showed the time to be after 9 P.M.

Melissa got out of bed and padded on bare feet to the nearest window. Wind lashed the trees. The rain was hard, beating down with a kind of fury. In the distance lightning flashed again. She shivered and pulled on a thin dressing gown. As she returned to the bed, another flash of lightning burst nearby and she saw the newspaper on the coverlet. She switched on her bedlamp, and the moment she did, the headlines seemed to leap out at her:

FALCON CREST MURDER SUSPECT DALLIES WITH WINDOW

Eyes wide, Melissa scanned the photograph. It was Cole, no mistaking him. And the caption said the woman was Mrs. Demery, who was much older than . . .

Melissa jumped out of bed. She strode to the west windows and stared out into the night at the storm ravaging the land.

Somewhere over there, about a mile away, Cole and that woman . . .

Thunder filled her ears. She winced, twisted away from the window and fell on one knee. Abruptly, a pain like a lightning bolt seemed to slice through her midriff. It burned. She gritted her teeth. It struck again. "Lance?" she called.

Grasping the bedpost, she got to her feet. She pushed the bell, waited. Where was everyone? She kept pushing the bell. "Lance?"

After what seemed like an age, she stepped into her slippers and made her way to the door. The pain seemed to fill her whole body. It cut at her brain. She staggered out into the hallway.

"Lance?" she called. "Help! Somebody!"

Thunder drowned out her cry. Holding onto the

curved railing with both hands, Melissa made her way down the staircase, lightning flashing, thunder roaring in her ears. *Il Demonio* . . .

She couldn't get it out of her head. The pain was blanking out her ability to think. *Il Demonio batta su . . . moglie!* That was it!

She half-fell against the front door of the mansion, wrenched at the knob and pulled it open. Rain sluiced down over her.

All the lights were off in the Demery house. But Cole had built a roaring fire in the living-room hearth. He and Katharine had finished a small bottle of wine. Arms around each other, they stared into the flames.

"Nothing better on a rainy night," Cole murmured in her ear.

"Romantic," she responded, snuggling closer to him. "Far from the sweat and strain of trying to grow grapes."

"We'll make out just fine," Cole assured her. "The vines are clear of weeds. We'll have a full harvest if this storm lets us alone."

"I like that youthful confidence," Kate told him. "We'll make out just fine," she quoted. "No doubts whatsoever."

He turned her face to his and kissed her slowly and lovingly. After a moment he could feel both her arms encircle him. They clung to each other as lightning split the sky and thunder crashed.

"No doubts at all," Cole said then. "Do you have any?"

"About the grapes? Or us?"

"Do I look like a grape? About us, you and me."

She sighed happily. "I can pretty well imagine what people will say about you and me." Her pretty face broke into a grin. "And I don't give a hoot. Do you?"

By way of answer he grabbed for her and they rolled over onto the threadbare carpet. The fire crackled reassuringly. He pulled down one shoulder of Kate's blouse and kissed the tanned skin there. "Freckles."

"Not just there," she admitted.

"Other places?" Cole asked. "I have to make a full inventory."

Someone was pounding on the front door. Cole had pulled the blouse farther down, but Kate suddenly sat up. "On a night like this? Visitors?"

The pounding grew louder. She got to her feet and opened the door. There on the porch, dripping wet, stood Melissa. She reached out for Kate and would have pitched forward if the older woman hadn't caught her.

"Cole! Help me carry her in."

They got her in front of the fire and Kate put a bath towel around Melissa's shoulders. "I have to talk to Cole," she was babbling.

"I'm right here, Lissa."

"I have to talk to Cole," she kept insisting.

He knelt in front of her. "Lissa, it's me."

Her eyes widened. She clutched at her abdomen. "The pain!"

"Lissa, what is it?"

"It's *all* wrong, Cole. The marriage. The baby. The Devil is beating his wife."

Cole glanced up at Kate. "She's off her rocker. We'd better get—"

"I need to talk to you," Melissa said, grasping Cole's arm.

"Why me?"

"Because . . . all the good times we had . . . the picnics . . . doesn't that mean something to you?"

Cole's face had gone white. "You're married to Lance now."

"The pain!" She seemed to crumple forward.

Kate bent over her. "Easy. Is it labor?"

"This baby," Melissa managed to say in a tight, gritty voice. "Someday this baby will . . ." Agony twisted her face. "Will inherit all of Falcon Crest!" she screamed.

"Relax, Melissa," Kate said in a soothing voice. "We're going to get you back to Falcon Crest as soon as this storm's over."

The pain seemed to shake Melissa's slender frame. Then it subsided for a moment. "Cole," she said then in a small voice.

"Yes?"

"I've never made love with anyone but you."

A great bolt of lightning slammed into the earth and the house rocked with the violent crash of thunder.

"This baby," she gasped, "is yours."

Part Four

Chapter Thirty-One _____

All night long, Julia, Lance, Chase and the Falcon Crest foremen and workers had been coping with the downpour, shielding and covering the vines wherever possible. Dressed in a slicker and rain hat, even Angela Channing had been out on the land with Chao-Li, protecting the rich grapes from early destruction.

When they returned to the mansion, dawn was breaking in a clear sky to the east. Underfoot, paths were already dry. There had been amazingly little damage. Angie and Chase compared notes as they sipped coffee and decided that, on the whole, Falcon Crest had gotten off lucky.

"She's gone!" Lance burst in. "Melissa's not in her room."

At that moment the telephone rang and Angela snatched it up. "Mrs. Channing, it's Dr. Ruzza."

"Melissa's—"

"She's here at the hospital. May I tell you? You're a great-grandmother."

"What! But, wasn't this much too early?" Angie looked up at Lance.

"It was an emergency procedure. What I'd feared would happen, did. Premature labor. But if we're careful—and lucky—I think we can breathe a sigh of relief."

"Boy or girl?"

"A little boy. Just under four pounds. But that's not bad for a premie. We'll fatten him up."

"Lance," Angie said, "you're the father of a boy." She started to hang up the telephone with the look of a cat that has just finished a delicious saucer of milk. Then, remembering: "How's Melissa, Doctor?"

"Neither of them is in top shape. But, as I said, with a little luck and a lot of care—"

"Yes. We'll be right over." She hung up the phone, then turned slowly to Chase. "Well!"

"Well!" he echoed back. "Got what you wanted after all, eh, Angela?"

The smile on her face broadened to a grin. "Falcon Crest and the Agretti vineyards, all wrapped up in one little baby boy."

"How'd she get to the hospital?" Lance asked then.

"Probably—" His grandmother frowned. "Nobody was here at home last night. I suppose she had enough sense to call the doctor and an ambulance." She got to her feet and went to the cupboard, where she brought out a bottle of brandy produced at the turn of the century by her own grandfather, Joseph Gioberti. "Julia!" she called. "Chao-Li!"

As they arrived, tired but alert, she poured five glasses of the amber liquid. "We're drinking a toast," she said, "to your first grandson, Julia. To Lance's first son. To my first great-grandchild. May he inherit the earth!" She raised her glass.

Julia looked radiant. "To my grandson."

Chase yawned. "To one more cousin."

Angela's grin went lopsided. "Nobody makes good wine from sour grapes, Chase."

He thought a moment. "You're right, Angela. To the new member of the family." He raised his glass.

Everyone sipped their brandy. "Well, Lance," he went on, "how's it feel to be a father?"

The young man stood silently for a long moment. "I don't know," he said at last. "You tell me."

The fire that had blazed so brilliantly in Katharine Demery's hearth now lay cold in ashes. She stared down at it, standing in the center of her small, neat living room. Cole sat in a straight-backed chair and watched, not the hearth, but Kate.

"That was close," he said at last. "If we hadn't gotten her to the hospital, she would have had the baby right here."

Kate nodded, but said nothing. She stared deeply into the cold ashes.

"Still," Cole went on more slowly, "she sure didn't look good after delivery."

"How was she supposed to look?" Kate asked.

"Huh?"

She whirled on him. "How is a woman supposed to look, having an emergency premature delivery of a baby that isn't her husband's?"

Cole's mouth opened, then closed. He got to his feet.

She turned back to the fireplace. "Cole," she said after a moment, "I know what Melissa told you about her baby was almost as big a surprise to you as it was to me. I want you to understand that there is no judgment or blame in what I'm going to say."

"Uh-oh."

"But you have to see it from my angle," Kate went on. "It hit me out of the blue. You, at least, if you could remember back that far, might have been a little less surprised at the news."

"Back that far?" Cole responded. "It was only last winter."

"I'm surprised a man would keep track of such a

thing." She glanced at him. "Women do, as you know. We have to."

"Look, Melissa swore she had—you know—taken precautions."

"Spare me the details."

"I'm getting really bad vibes, Kate."

"Then you're not quite as insensitive as I thought." She turned to face him fully now. "Cole, much as I need you here . . . much as I think *you* need me . . . I'm asking you to leave."

"What?"

"I thank you sincerely for the tremendous job you've done getting the place in shape. I thank you for your love and"— she faltered—"and the warmth of our . . ." Her eyes had gone damp. But she remained face-to-face with Cole. "I am seeing us in a new light and it's . . . you're right, it's bad vibes."

"Just because Melissa—"

"That has less to do with it than you think," Kate interrupted him. "It shook me up, I'll say that. Here's this bright, handsome young fella who's the light of my life and, oh yes, he's sired a baby on somebody else's wife."

"She wasn't married then."

"Cole, grow up!"

She took him by both shoulders and gently shook him. "There's a saying that goes, 'People who don't learn from their mistakes are doomed to keep repeating them.' I don't want you to go that road, Cole. I want you to learn from this."

"Learn what?" Cole demanded.

"Learn relationships. Learn who you are."

"How did I get to be the heavy in all this?" Cole inquired. "You go on about Melissa as if she was some sort of innocent child. Let me tell you, Kate she is no—"

"I asked you to spare me the details," Kate cut him

off. "I suppose what I'm really asking is that you take responsibility for what you are and have done. Don't tell me it takes two to tango. I know that."

He stood in silence. Now it was his glance that seemed riveted to the dead ashes in the hearth. Only a few hours ago it had blazed so warmingly.

"So that's called growing up," he said at last.

"That's the biggest part of it. Taking responsibility."

"And that's it?" he asked in a pained voice. "Who'll you get to do the odd jobs here? Can't I still do them for you?"

Her head had started shaking even as he spoke. "A clean break," Kate said at last. "Surgical. No lingering infections." She gave him a rueful smile. "Cold turkey, you might say."

"God, Kate."

"Better start packing your duffel bag. Come on. I'll help you."

Lance stood by Melissa's bed. The rest of the family had paid their respects and had retired to let the new father and mother have a moment of quiet togetherness.

"You feeling okay?" Lance asked.

"Not sensational." Melissa's face had been washed completely clean of makeup. She looked younger but, at the same time, intensely tired.

"But Dr. Ruzza says—"

"I know what he says," Melissa interrupted him. "I've been hearing it for hours. It's his job to stay cheerful, Lance. But the baby is so . . . so frail. So tiny. I'm not even allowed to handle him."

Lance looked thoughtful for a moment. "Still holding the line on that kid, huh?"

"He's your child, Lance."

"We both know that's a lot of hot air. Anytime I

want to blow this fantasy of yours out of the water I just have to take a paternity test."

"But you wouldn't."

"What's in it for me, pretending to be his father?"

"Future control of Falcon Crest."

"I've got that already."

"Plus the Agretti vineyards."

"That's always been your ace in the hole, Melissa. My grandmother's idea of heaven is joining Falcon Crest and your dad's vineyards. But, baby, it's not my idea of anything worth playing poppa for."

Melissa was silent for a long moment. "You could still . . ." She paused. "Once Joseph grew older you could still . . . you know, overnight in San Francisco."

"Her name's Lori Stevens."

"Again?" Melissa taunted him. "Don't you ever attract anything new?"

"And who's this Joseph character? Is that what you're calling the kid?"

"Joseph Carlo Cumson," she told him. "He's named for your great-grandfather and my father."

"Sounds more like the title of a corporate merger," Lance said. He grinned maliciously. "And not a very permanent one, either."

Angela Channing sat across the desk from Dr. Ruzza in the small examining room he used as an office. "I've seen the baby," she said. "They showed him to me through two layers of plate glass. I have never seen anything so scrawny. But you insist he's a typical, healthy premature baby?"

The doctor puffed his cheeks and let out a sigh. "Mrs. Channing, you're probably the only one in the family I can tell this to. He's running a slight fever. That in itself isn't anything alarming . . . yet. But it could be the symptom of something more dangerous. You've had two children of your own, Mrs. Channing.

You know that in a normal delivery of a normal child, there is a natural built-in immunity to whatever infectious bacteria are in the environment. Without that autoimmune system, the newborn wouldn't have a chance, even in the sterile atmsophere of a hospital."

"I'm aware of that," Angie said in a cautious tone.

"Then perhaps you know that some babies are born without that natural immunity. Or with only a partial amount. This can be true of premies, which is why we protect them so carefully from untrained handling and contact with nonsterile individuals."

"That's a curious way to describe a baby's own family."

Dr. Ruzza smiled slightly. He rubbed his bald spot for a moment, as if in thought. "It's a medical description. Here's my point, Mrs. Channing—we may have such a situation with your great-grandchild. I sincerely hope I'm mistaken. We won't know for a few more days."

"You're saying . . ." Angie's throat seemed to close over. She got to her feet and stared down at the doctor in horror.

"I'm saying we may have trouble."

"You're saying he may die!" Angie barked.

The doctor was silent. Then: "That's one way of putting it."

"Now you listen to this, Doctor," Angela Channing told him. Her finger moved like a gun barrel until it was pointing directly at his heart. "I'm saying he *won't* die! I'm saying he'll *live* and grow strong! Do you hear me?"

"Certainly."

"If anything happens to that child," she added, her finger prodding his chest, "I'm holding you personally responsible. Do you understand?"

The silence in the tiny room stretched itself thin and taut. It seemed to last forever. Finally Dr. Ruzza stood up and opened the door:

"Good-bye, Mrs. Channing."

Chapter Thirty-Two_____

The dinner party had been a good one because Richard Channing had kept it small. He and Diana Hunter had been host to three other couples in one of the attractive private dining rooms in the hotel where each maintained separate suits. Now the two of them were enjoying a nightcap liqueur together in Richard's rooms and idly reviewing half a dozen topics of conversation as each of them wound down from a long, strenuous day and evening.

"The mayor's wife was wondering why you didn't find yourself a nice bachelor apartment on Nob Hill," Diana was recounting. "What she was really probing for was some sign that you and I are living together."

Richard's strong, handsome face looked tired. "Working together," he mused, "thinking together, eating together, sleeping together. What would the mayor's wife call that?"

"A lot more than she has with His Honor the Mayor."

Diana laughed softly and undid the long kapiz-shell pins that held her hair up over her head. Her dark blond tresses fell in thick, attractive curls.

"By the way," she went on more thoughtfully, "the

fellow from the bank who was sitting on my left, Jim Pearson? He's a close friend of Chase Gioberti."

"How marvelous for him," Richard replied.

"He doesn't take kindly to the *Globe*'s stories about Cole Gioberti."

Richard sipped his Grand Marnier. "Did he put it more strongly than that?"

"He didn't come right out and say 'Stop printing that stuff or we'll call in your loan for collection.' He merely registered an opinion."

"Fine. Remember, Diana,"—Richard paused a moment—"as we originally discussed in New York with Henri Denault, this is a hit-and-run operation. Adverse opinions we can risk because we're not married to this project forever. If a bank should start to threaten us, however, that's different."

Diana let a moment of silence go by. "Richard," she said then, deciding to risk being absolutely frank with him. "It can't have escaped your eagle eye that while this may be a hit-and-run operation, the target persists in getting up every time it's hit."

His face went cold. But when he spoke his voice sounded calm enough. "Translated into plain English you're telling me we've been here three months and we've gotten nowhere."

"Nothing of the kind."

"Well," his face softened, "you're not far wrong. We've managed to turn the *Globe* around and almost double the price of its stock. But that's peanuts to what the Cartel expects."

"Which you promised Denault you'd deliver," she reminded him.

Richard got up and, carrying his liqueur glass, went to his desk to bring back one of the many large-scale ordnance maps of Tuscany Valley that he studied constantly. This one he smoothed out on the long glass cocktail table.

"I want to show you something," he said then. "So far I've been using the *Globe* to harass the enemy. And, as you say, each time I hit him he manages to get up again. I've been trying to split families apart. It's a long-term effort. I don't expect quick results. But there is another way we've got to try. We have to split the land."

"I don't understand. Split Falcon Crest?"

Richard's face grew somber as he studied the map. "This triangle here." He tapped it with his finger.

Diana peered down at a place on the map colored faintly green. "Is it a park?"

"It's one of those triangular pieces of land left over when the great holdings were carved out. The county owns it as parkland, but it's really five acres of weeds."

"It doesn't adjoin Falcon Crest. How do you pl—"

"It doesn't have to. I'm going to make a formal proposal to the county to buy that parkland as a public memorial to the man who made the *Globe* a great paper, one of Tuscany Valley's most famous sons, whose name is now permanently intertwined with the history of the Valley." He glanced up at her mischievously. "Got a clue?"

"Your father?"

"Bingo!" He tapped the green triangle on the map. "A memorial to Douglas Channing. Nothing grandiose, a small statue, maybe, I'm not sure. Right here at the apex of the parkland."

"And that is supposed to split the land asunder?" Diana queried.

Richard's lips twisted into a small, off-center smile, one corner of his mouth up, the other flat. "The memorial leaves unused four and a half acres of perfectly good land. I will have bought it all for the memorial. On the rest of it I build . . . ?" He glanced at her again. "Got a clue?"

"Richard, you're kidding. A winery?"

"Bingo again. No vines. Just some vats, a small press and bottling facilities."

"This is crazy."

"Think." Richard reached over and cupped his hand under her chin. Gently he shook her head from side to side.

"Think about being a winery with roots struck deep in the Valley. Of being able to bid against the other wineries for the grape harvest. Of bidding against Angela Channing. And of having the resources of the Cartel behind me so that I can bid up the harvest price until it bankrupts her!"

Diana Hunter watched his face, the way it lit up with a kind of unholy glee. Something inside her responded fully to that feeling. She wondered if theirs was—ever would be—more than a working relationship. But career came first. Playing Richard's games was pleasant enough, but falling in love with him would be a major mistake.

"The strategy of it is impeccable," she said then in an admiring tone. "But the tactics aren't too clear. How do you get the county to sell public parkland to an outsider like you?"

"First of all, nobody will object to the reason for the memorial. I daresay even Angela will agree to it. Secondly, the building of the winery needn't attract a lot of attention. There are prefab units one can buy. Trucks converge on a place and in twenty-four hours it's a winery. Presented with a *fait accompli* like that, the county can't possibly revoke its sale."

"But what makes you think they'll even entertain your original offer?"

"It goes first to someone in a tight spot, on whom

a lot of pressure is being placed, with a lot more to come . . . the county supervisor."

"Whose name," Diana added, smiling, "is Chase Gioberti."

Chapter Thirty-Three————————

Steve Barton reread the page of the *Globe* Chase had torn off and brought to him. The lawyer's face set in grim lines as he reread the collection of rumors and rehash the newspaper was serving up in the wake of its sensational "DALLIES WITH WIDOW" story.

"No," Barton told Chase, "this follow-up stuff is weak. The real libel is in the first story. Except that, in conjunction with the photograph of the two of them kissing, I wouldn't have a chance of making a libel charge stick."

Chase Gioberti sat back in his chair, his mouth pressed in such a tight line that it practically disappeared against the background of his neatly trimmed beard.

"This stuff is killing Maggie," he said then. "She was against this move of Cole's from the beginning. I guess I didn't come down hard enough on her side. Anyway, Cole's of age. We couldn't stop him. But what's it doing to his chances of a fair trial?"

Barton shoved the newspaper aside. "At this point, do we even know he'll stand trial?"

"What d'y'mean?"

"We have go to into this with a positive attitude, Chase. We know Cole's innocent, so we have to work on the assumption they'll find a more likely suspect soon enough."

"Not when the *Globe* keeps shoving Cole down their throats every day."

"There is that," the attorney admitted. The springs of his chair creaked as he sat back in it. "Chase, are you much of a gambler?"

"What's that got to do with it?"

"I want to suggest taking a gamble with this case. You willing?"

"Not when it affects Cole's life," Chase responded firmly. "What're you suggesting?"

"I'm giving away a few secrets of the law when I explain this," Steve Barton began. "But the law is not a precise concept. As a layman you think, well, the law is written down in regulations and codes. It must be precise. In fact, the law changes every hour of the day. What we're talking about is *how the thing looks.*"

"You're telling me the law is like the rest of life," Chase said. "Appearances are everything."

"Right." The lawyer smiled slightly. "The moves I would make in a courtroom for instance. Some are made only because they *look* right. In Cole's case, we have moves we haven't used yet. One of them is to demand a second autopsy on Carlo Agretti."

"What would that prove?"

"Search me," Barton admitted. "But it'd *look* good. Cole Gioberti's lawyer is so confident of his innocence that he requests a second autopsy. Would a guilty man take that chance? Never. So, whatever the autopsy finds, even if it finds nothing, it *looks* good."

Chase made a disgusted face. "I hate this kind of malarkey, Steve."

"I do too," the attorney assured him. "But will you let me try it?"

"You're the lawyer."

"I'll need an authorization from the next of kin,"
Barton said. "That may not be easy. I understand
Melissa had a tough time with the new baby. She
may not want her father's grave disturbed."

Chase sat in silence for a long moment. "I wouldn't
blame her. Steve, let's drop the whole thing."

"It could help."

"It's just a trick. Isn't that what you said?"

"But what if a second autopsy finds new evidence?"

"You're suggesting that the first time around the
coroner was careless? Or stupid?"

The lawyer grinned nervously at him. "I never
thought I'd get arguments from the father of a client.
But, Chase, if you want a good reason I'll give
you one—nobody's perfect. Even coroners overlook
things."

"Something that might help Cole?"

"Maybe."

"And on the strength of that one 'maybe,' you
want to open up the Agretti grave?"

"It's a lawful procedure, Chase. Stop acting as if
we were body snatchers. It's done where there's some
doubt in a case."

"*If* Melissa gives her okay," Chase grudgingly agreed
after a long pause.

"That's it."

Chase got to his feet. "Okay, Steve. You want to
ask Melissa? Or shall I?"

"No need for you to appear in this yet."

"Is there a way of asking her so it doesn't get back
to Angela Channing?" Chase said then. "Because the
minute Angela gets wind of this . . ."

"Then keep your fingers crossed, Chase. And
mum's the word."

Chapter Thirty-Four_____

Angela Channing gave Melissa a peck on the cheek and left the hospital. As she got into her limousine, she saw her daughter Julia drive up in one of the Falcon Crest Jeeps. She paused.

"Mother, how's Baby Joseph?"

"Not any better," Angie said grimly. "Instead of gaining weight, he's losing. Where's Lance?"

"I had to leave him on duty. He'll be by this afternoon."

"See that he is," her mother snapped. "Drive on," she ordered the chauffeur.

"Where are you going?" Julia called after her.

"San Francisco. Back this afternoon."

The big Mercedes purred off along the highway and was soon lost to sight.

"You didn't need to come all the way back to San Francisco," Maggie Gioberti told the director.

Darryl Clayton had a worried look as he took her by the hand and led her into the oasis of potted plants and palms where the hotel served lunch. In the background a trio played light jazz.

He sat her at a tiny table, then took a chair opposite her. He was dressed informally in a sports jacket and chino trousers, but his plain light-blue shirt had a tie. Eating places like this one tried to preserve a certain formality.

"This isn't something I could tell you over the phone or in a letter," he said. He hadn't yet given her back her hand. Now, as they sat across from each other, he held her fingers lightly but firmly.

"So this is bad news," Maggie surmised. "You showed the script to your money people and they got sick to their stomach."

Darryl laughed. "As a matter of fact they liked it. But they think it's controversial."

"What?"

"Too close to home, Maggie. Right in their own backyard."

"I'm not saying anything really bad about the wine business," Maggie said, trying not to sound defensive.

Darryl nodded. "My money people think it's too sensitive. They suggested we move it to France." He tried to laugh again but the proper mirth wasn't forthcoming. "Can you imagine? We've got the blockbuster idea of all time and they want to rob it of its biggest plus. Who wants to see a movie about French vineyards?"

"Not when you can see 'Tangled Vines' in all its glory," Maggie kidded him. "Darryl, you have no idea how this news hits me."

"Hard?"

"Like a drop of dew. I've got real problems back home. Heavy stuff." She squeezed the hand by which he was holding hers. "I've got a son involved with an older woman while the sheriff tries to convict him of murder. I've got a local newspaper trumpeting scandal to the skies. You tell me my script's too controversial? Compared to real life, that script's a pussycat."

Quickly, he lifted her hand and kissed her fingers.

"I'm sorry," he said then. "I had no idea what you were going through."

Maggie had had her hand kissed before. In fact, there had been a time years ago when Chase had often kissed her hand. So, by rights, she should have been immune to any reaction to such treatment. Instead, the place where his lips had pressed against her fingers seemed now to be charged with a strange electricity. Her whole hand tingled softly. She stared across the table at him.

"Darryl," she said. "No more of that, please."

"I couldn't help myself."

"You certainly can help yourself." She smiled at him and pulled her hand free. "Now, let's finish off this business lunch in a businesslike way."

Behind her, Angela Channing arrived on the arm of her attorney, Phillip Erikson. Without either woman realizing it, they were now seated back to back at adjoining tables, but with a high, almost hedgelike, row of potted plants between them. The trio's soft jazz filled the silences of the room.

"I can't think of a more intimate place to have lunch with an attractive woman," the attorney murmured in Angie's ear as he settled her in her chair.

"It's about as private as a football field."

"But a hotel," Phillip corrected her. "There's always an erotic atmosphere in a hotel. You lunch. You have some wine. You fall in love. And, meanwhile, upstairs there are soft, fresh beds just waiting for new arrivals."

Angela stared at him. "Phillip, have you gone off the deep end? If I wanted to resume a relationship with you I would certainly not pick a hotel room for it. Act your age."

"Then where are we going to have it?" he persisted.

"Are you going to keep this up? I arranged this lunch because I want to stop Richard Channing from ruining the Falcon Crest name. I do not want his photographers snapping blackmail photos of two middle-aged lovers mussing up a hotel bed."

"You now own ten percent of all outstanding *Globe* stock," Erikson told her, getting down to business. "It cost an arm and a leg, but you're in a position now to demand a shareholders' meeting and move a vote of 'censure' or 'no confidence' or whatever will stop Richard fastest. You'll be able to count on Chase's votes. He's also got Emma's. You merely have to convince Julia to vote your way and you can not only stop Richard, you can have him canned."

A sweet smile appeared for a moment on Angie's lips. "You make it sound so easy, Phillip. I hope you're right."

With their coffee, Darryl Clayton tried to interest Maggie in the script again. "I don't want it touched," he said. "I certainly don't want it shifted to France. But perhaps you could sort of de-fuse some of the more sensational scenes."

Maggie was silent a long time.

"What do you say?" Darryl asked.

"I'm sorry. I was a million miles away. You said . . . ?"

"Some of the seamier scenes. You could tone them down."

"Would that make it easier to find backing?"

"No guarantees."

"Darryl," she said. "I think we've come to the parting of the ways. You were a great shot in the arm for me. I do appreciate your flying up here just to tell me the bad news in person. But I'm not about to go back to writing, not till I get some of my other problems straightened out."

The look on his face was a mixture of anguish and longing. "You're paying me back for that kiss on the hand, is that it?"

"Don't be ridic—"

"I told you, I couldn't help it. The truth is I'd do it again."

"Darryl, cut it out."

Behind her, Angela Channing laid her finger over her lip. Phillip Erikson stopped talk in mid-sentence. Both of them listened. It wasn't easy to hear the conversation behind her, but Angela was certain she recognized the woman's voice.

"I know one thing," Darryl was saying. "Once your family affairs are in order again, you'll wish you'd hung in with me on this. Because without your interest in the project, I'm forced to go back to that Fitzgerald property. If that takes off, it'll be years before I can get back to your script."

"You go on with your other projects. Forget about 'Tangled Vines.' "

"I hate the idea of dropping it."

"It's your money people who're dropping it."

"A little development money would be all I needed. I could start paying you for revisions. Together we'd solve the problems in the script and I'd find a backer."

Maggie wanted to explain to him, again, that it wasn't a matter of money. She simply hadn't the heart for her writing now. Cole's problems were too much with her.

"It isn't to be," she said softly. "But thanks for thinking of me and encouraging me. That was worth a lot more than money."

At the table behind her, Angela Channing's face set in strong lines, not grim but purposeful. She signaled Erikson to get the check. Then, as he was paying it, Angie left the table and positioned herself beyond the doorway of the eating area, where people would pass on their way out of the hotel. After a while, standing behind an especially large palm tree, she saw Maggie Gioberti shaking hands with a man in a sports jacket.

"My car's parked in the garage downstairs. Goodbye, Darryl."

He lifted her hand to his lips. "Watch this," he said. "A man's heart is breaking, but does he let on? Does he rant and rave? Just a quiet kiss, Maggie. You don't begrudge that to a heartbroken man."

Maggie turned and went down an escalator. Just before she descended out of sight, she waved to the director. He waved back, turned and almost walked into Angela Channing as she emerged from behind the palm.

"Aren't you Darryl Clayton?" Angie asked.

"Why, yes."

"I'm Mrs. Channing of Falcon Crest. My chauffeur's waiting outside. Let me drive you to the airport, Mr. Clayton, while I suggest something you may find interesting."

"An idea for a film?"

"No-no," Angie said. "An idea for . . . shall we say . . . an idea for your personal happiness?"

Chapter Thirty-Five_____

Chase Gioberti tugged at his beard as he stared into the video screen of the EDS computer terminal in his office. He tapped a command onto the keyboard and the screen showed an outline map of the entire land mass of Falcon Crest. Chase keyed in a second command and the map enlarged to show only the western quadrant of the land, this time in a curious blend of colors.

Chase sat back and dug his fingertips into his beard, rubbing slowly, reflectively, as he studied the video screen. He found it difficult to concentrate. When he'd awakened this morning he'd found his son Cole sleeping on the long couch in the living room, his duffel bag beside him.

"This a visit or only a pit stop?" he'd asked

Cole had had the good grace to look sheepish. "Kate kicked me out," he admitted.

"Then do I take it we have the immense honor of your presence in the family again?" Chase asked with some sarcasm. "At least until you find another attractive lady somewhere in the Valley?"

"Lay off, Dad."

Chase massaged his beard as he watched Cole rub his unshaven chin. Involuntarily, Chase grinned. All their life together he and his son had reflected each other's movements. Cole being left-handed, his gestures exactly matched what Chase would see in a mirror. He tried to mask his grin of pleasure at having his son home again.

"Why not move back up into your room," he suggested then. "Your mother and I don't really appreciate dirty boots on the couch."

"You mean—?"

"Go on," Chase ordered good-naturedly. "Home is the one place they can't kick you out of." Grinning, he had left for his office, happy to have his son at home again.

Now he wasn't quite as happy. Cole's return was a good thing, in that it would put a stop to the newspaper gossip. But there remained the problem of finding useful work for a young man bursting with such energy. Of course, Cole could fall back into his usual routine, backing up Chase as a kind of right-hand man. But he was getting too independent for that sort of thing. He needed work he could call his own, his own area of responsibility. He needed to be out of the shadow of his father, doing his own thing. The way he'd shaped up the Demery vineyards on his own had proved to Chase that his son was ready for major work.

Thus, the computer survey Chase was trying to set up now on EDS. From the colors on the tube, he could analyze the land lying fallow to the far west of Falcon Crest. It represented unused, and thus unwasted, opportunity.

New strains of rootstocks could be planted there. Falcon Crest could profitably branch out into producing some of the new varietals that other wineries were creating. Already they had established a demand for them in the market. It took money, of course, but, more than money, it took time—years of time, years that only a young man like Cole could devote to such a long-range operation.

Chase keyed another command into the computer and got a figure of nearly two hundred acres, which translated into thousands of rootstocks, months of trenching and planting, thousands of gallons of fertilizer, millions of gallons of water, stakes, wiring, windbreaks, sunshades.

And that was only the beginning. Years of pruning and weeding, perhaps as much time in grafting, would be needed before the first growth arrived, the new grapes whose potential for making good wine could only be guessed at until the moment the first harvest was taken, perhaps five years hence.

It was an ideal project for a young man. It would also be a major expenditure for Falcon Crest. Angela Channing would be against it, not because it cost a lot of money, but because Chase would put Cole in charge of it. True, Julia would be on hand to supervise the technical aspects of the work. But the new vines would be Cole's responsibility. They would be the making of him.

Chase's fingers dug almost savagely into his beard as he switched the computer to another area of EDS memory and summoned up a financial statement. The cash position was never very strong in any vintner's books. Too much money was permanently tied up in land, vines, ferment and unshipped bottles. But EDS now told him there was certainly enough cash to make a beginning. So be it.

Chase closed down the computer and got to his feet. As co-owner of Falcon Crest, he had to clear his decision with Angela. The discussion would not be an easy one.

"You're insane," Angela Channing told him. They were sitting across from each other at her desk in the mansion house. She was still dressed in the cheongsam dressing gown she often wore until late morning. But there was never anything sleepy about Angie at any hour of the day or night.

"To want to renew old land?" Chase countered. "I don't think that's insane. To want to lay in some of the newer varietals? That's only good forward planning."

"To put a boy under suspicion of murder in charge of a five-year start-up," Angela blasted back. "That's rational?" She took a breath and seemed to gather more power. "Moreoever a boy who hasn't any idea of how to lay down a new vineyard? Whose only expertise to date has been with lonely young widow-ladies?"

"Knock it off, Angela," Chase retorted. "Cole's back home. He's no longer living with Katharine Demery. Speaking of which, he did one hell of a job shaping up that place of hers. It's not expertise we need for this. It's youth and a good strong back."

"And then there's the money," the mistress of Falcon Crest went on. "Do you have any idea of the start-up costs alone?"

"Half a million, before we get Grape One." Chase nodded. "I do my homework, Angela. I wish to God you did yours. The market's crying out for these new, lighter whites and reds. Falcon Crest can't even begin to supply demand for five years. The sooner we start, the better."

Angie's lips moved, as if about to speak. Instead, she dialed an inside number on her desk phone. "Lance," she said, "get me a printout on the Gioberti cash position." She frowned. "That's right. I want it on paper. What Chase's cash holdings in Falcon Crest are worth. Also their liquidity. How fast he can get them. And I want it here in ten minutes." She hung up.

"Why only mine?" Chase demanded. "Why not the full picture that includes your cash as well?"

"Because," Angela Channing said with a small smile, "if you want to finance a make-work project for that unstable son of yours, it'll have to come out of your pocket."

"This development benefits all of Falcon Crest," Chase retorted hotly.

"That's as it may be." The smile widened. "But for at least five years it will be a dead drain on finances—yours, not mine."

"Now who's insane?"

"A five-year project that depends on Cole staying out of jail?" Angela asked with a broad grin. "It's so crazy, the only person who could think of it would be Cole's father. And he," she added, getting up from the desk, "is going to pay the full bill for his lunacy."

Chapter Thirty-Six

Melissa had carefully packed away her nightclothes. Chao-Li had taken the small suitcase out to the waiting limousine.

Dressed in her street clothes, Melissa stood at the double plate-glass window of the hospital's nursery room where newborn infants were kept. She knew Joseph's plastic-bubble crib's location by heart. Second from the left, one row back, the small cart stood, encased in a transparent shell that effectively insulated Joseph Carlo Cumson from an environment that was still, to him, hostile.

Melissa tried to catch a glimpse of the tiny form beneath the bubble. He was so small! He seemed even smaller than she remembered from her last visit early this morning. And now she was going home while Joseph remained a prisoner within his glass cage.

Something hard seemed to grip Melissa's heart and wrench at it, an unknown tug as implacable as a bolt of lightning. She hadn't wanted this child, not at first. But everyone else had urged her to have it. She could remember the look on her father's face when she'd told him:

"*Bene! Benissime!*" he'd cried out. "I don't care who

the father is, Lissa. Nothing matters to me. Only that you are healthy and the boy is born healthy."

Now her father was dead and her son was dying.

Oh, yes, Melissa remembered with bitterness. Everybody had wanted the child, even coldhearted Angela Channing. It was a conspiracy. Never mind who the father was, deliver up to us your baby, everyone seemed to be saying, hinting, urging.

To me the pain, Melissa thought. *To them the—the what?—honor, glory . . . what exactly do they want?*

She thought she saw the tiny, sickly form of her son stir slightly. He lay on his stomach, tubes connected to his arm, bubble tightly closed and linked by a thick hose to some sort of machinery. The conspiracy continues, Melissa thought. And now they don't even let me see my own baby, my own flesh and blood.

She gestured to one of the nurses and pointed toward Joseph's crib. This was the part of the farce she hated most. The nurse would move the crib, examine the chart attached to it, return to the plate-glass window and make shrugs and placating gestures as if to say, "Not yet. Too delicate. You understand."

Melissa pointed to the door at the end and walked toward it. On the other side of the glass the nurse mirrored her movement. She opened the door a thin crack. "Mrs. Cumson," she began without an instant's hesitation, "we have to keep these doors tight shut, you know."

"But I'm leaving the hospital."

"You're welcome here any time during visiting hours."

"Nurse, you don't underst—"

"Any time, Mrs. Cumson," the nurse said and firmly shut the door.

Tears welled up in Melissa's eyes. She had made

such a mess of this thing. The joy of motherhood tantalized her because she was denied it. The pleasure of holding her own baby, of feeding him, of playing with him. All sacrificed to the wasting illness that seemed every day to diminish the poor little thing and leave him even weaker.

It felt to Melissa as if the cord that had once bound Joseph to her had in some mysterious way continued to exist long after it had been cut on delivery. As if a kind of psychic bond still linked her to this frail infant, a bond *that meant life to him*. Once let her leave this place, once give him over completely to strangers, and he would . . .

The floor seemed to come up under her. It slammed against the side of her face. Darkness. She could hear shouts. Someone was lifting her head. So dark . . .

She was sitting in Dr. Ruzza's office. He removed a cool, damp towel from her forehead. "That's better," he said. "Here." He held a glass of water for her and she gulped greedily at it. The coolness of the liquid coursing down her throat seemed to bring her back to reality.

"Did I pass out?"

"For a moment. The nurse said you tried to see Joseph again. You know it's out of the question, at least for now."

Melissa stared up into his face, trying to find a clue as to what the doctor was thinking. She stared deep into his eyes, willing him to speak. After a moment his glance wavered. He sat down across from her and took her hand in his.

"Melissa," he said then, "you and I go back a long way."

"You delivered me," she said with a nod of her head.

He smiled gently. "So I did. And a healthier, pret-

tier infant I have yet to see since." His face darkened.
"With Joseph, we have quite a different situation."

"I know."

"As you're going home today, I guess I can't put
this off any longer." He rubbed at the monk's ton-
sure of hair around his bald spot. "He's not responding properly, Melissa. We're doing everything to build
him up to a weight at which he can sustain himself,
but his body simply refuses our best efforts. It's got a
separate problem it can't solve. At this point, we're
not able to do much to help."

"The business of natural immunity?"

"Joseph is a sitting duck for bacteria and viruses
that a normal newborn would laugh off. It's a situation medical science has no fast answers for. A lot of
the research in this field is being done back East and
in Europe. I've combed through the recent literature.
Whatever I've found, we've tried. It isn't working."

"If it's a matter of money, I—"

"Don't you think I know that?" Dr. Ruzza cut in.
"I'm well aware of the tremendous forces and power
concentrated in this one unfortunate baby. Believe
me, Melissa, if money could do it, I'd yell for help."

"Then what can we do?"

"Wait. And hope. And keep on doing what we can
for him."

"In other words," Melissa's breathing quickened,
"my baby's life is up for grabs."

"We're in an area of great risk-taking," Dr. Ruzza
said quietly.

"Gambling!" she burst out. "Gambling with his
life!"

The doctor recoiled from her words. He sat back
and paused, searching for a way to calm the young
woman. "All life's a gamble, Melissa. I could walk out
that door and be run over by a truck."

"Or have your head beaten to a pulp while you sat

at your desk," Melissa added, her voice thick with
the memory of her dead father.

Dr. Ruzza nodded. She could feel her knees start
to buckle and she stiffened her muscles in an effort
to stand straight. "Thanks for all the reassurance,"
she said then in a bitter voice. "Good-bye."

"Melissa?" he called after her.

She walked down the corridor and out into the
brilliant daylight, her eyes fixed on the Falcon Crest
limousine, Chao-Li standing at the door holding it
open for her.

Beyond, baking in the sun, stood the long sleek
taupe mass of a Jaguar car, and beside it, a young
woman with dark blond hair piled high on her head.
Where had she seen this woman before? Melissa
wondered.

"Mrs. Cumson?" Diana Hunter asked.

"Excuse me, miss," Chao-Li interposed smoothly.
"If you have business with Mrs. Cumson, please call
for an appointment."

"We met at your father's funeral," Diana continued,
unabashed. "I work with Richard Channing. Remember?"

Melissa blinked. "I really have to get home."

"I quite understand," Diana said quickly, reaching
Melissa's side before Chao-Li could and helping her
down the stairs to the waiting Mercedes 600 limousine.
"I won't bother you at a time like this," she murmured in Melissa's ear.

"Thank you."

Melissa felt herself being helped into the soft,
shaded interior of the automobile. Diana still stood
outside, smiling down at her as Chao-Li prepared to
close the door.

"Mr. Channing has some important medical con-
nections back East," she heard Diana say. "There

might well be a doctor who could help with Joseph's prob—"

The door slammed. An instant later the limousine surged forward. Melissa turned around to gaze through the rear window at the attractive blonde.

"A doctor who could help with Joseph's problem . . ."

The words reverberated in her ears like a great curling wave of surf. "Stop the car," she called weakly.

But Chao-Li and Desi, the chauffeur, didn't seem to have heard her cry.

Chapter Thirty-Seven

"Not too much that isn't routine," Dee Merriam said. She handed a slim file folder to Chase Gioberti as he sat at his desk in the county office, trying to clear up matters here before going into San Francisco for a meeting with his banker. It was typical of Chase to put county matters ahead of his own, but he counted on Dee to speed things up by separating the routine from the important.

"These permit applications are all in order," she told him.

"Then sign them for me."

"And this water-rights quarrel has finally sorted itself out," Dee went on. "Each side gave a little. We can okay it now, I think."

"Fine. Do so." Chase frowned at the next item, a thick wad of legal-sized papers attached to a sheaf of maps and architect's drawings. "What now? The Encyclopaedia Britannica?"

"Oh, that." Dee sat down across his desk from him. "There's no rush on that one. And it's too complicated for you to make a decision quickly."

"Give me the rundown."

"Richard Channing wants to erect a memorial to the memory of Douglas Channing."

Chase snorted. "Better late than never, eh? What does it have to do with us?"

"He wants to buy lots 485 through 490. They're zoned for parkland. He needs a variance from us and if we say yes then we have to set a price."

Chase pawed quickly through the maps. "Hmph. What's his idea of a memorial?"

"A small statue. The rest of the acreage planted with shrubs and trees. Flowers. Grass. A few benches. The usual."

"Dee, nothing Richard Channing does is 'usual.'" Chase frowned as he stared at the various sheets of paper. "You're right. It's too complicated for a quick answer." He shoved the papers to one side. "Anything else?"

Dee smiled in slight embarrassment. "We have to issue demolition permits to tear down those migrant-worker shacks at Falcon Crest. And a set of building permits to erect new cottages."

Chase's face reflected her embarrassment. "It's been delayed too long, but I can't just sign out of hand. Hold it for the Improvement Committee meeting on Thursday. We'll call a vote. I'll abstain. Otherwise it would be a conflict of interest."

She nodded. "I figured you'd be too straight-arrow to sign the forms yourself."

"You figured right." He got to his feet and started for the door. As he swung it open he paused. "A *memorial*? To his *father*?"

His assistant laughed. "That's what the man says."

Jim Pearson turned at right angles to his desk and switched on his bank's computer terminal. "Just your own cash?" he repeated.

"Unfortunately, yes," Chase told him.

"You can't budge Angela on this?"

"Can anybody budge her when it comes to money?"

Pearson's fingers touched the keyboard here and there. "I've noticed that our illustrious, crusading newspaper, the *Globe*, hasn't had anything nasty to say about Cole for nearly a week," he remarked as he waited for the computer's response. "I hope I can take some credit for that."

"How so?"

"I aired a piece of my mind about it to that lovely blond vixen Channing keeps by his side."

"Diana Hunter. You spoke to her?"

"A group of us high-ranking San Francisco yokels were the recipients of lavish *Globe* hospitality the other night." He frowned at the video screen. "Here it comes. Not really wonderful."

"What would a banker call wonderful? A billion dollars in nickels and dimes?"

"How about an overdraft of five grand?"

Chase gasped. "Overdraft? You've got to be kidding."

Pearson tapped the keyboard. "Here it comes again. Repeat. Five thousand overdraft."

"Jim, the computer's gone nuts. What about the money market account? What about those ninety-day Treasury bills? What about the six-month CD's?"

"What about 'em?" the banker asked.

"When I ran a check yesterday they showed me a cash position, or at least a highly liquid one, of over a hundred grand."

"You checked yesterday?" Jim Pearson's frown had turned into a scowl. "But the money market was closed out weeks ago. So were the Treasury bills. And you sold the CD's at a slight loss for early redemption. That happened, uh, let's see. That happened last month."

Chase got to his feet, came around the desk and stared at the video screen. "That's got to be wrong, Jim. And how did it get into overdraft?"

"Your normal check writing. Instead of drawing on

the money account, you were writing checks against overdraft."

Chase stood motionless for a long moment. "Is there some way you can have this checked by your computer people?"

"Immediately." The banker tapped several commands on the keyboard and closed it down. He swung back to stare at Chase. "We may have stumbled onto something here," he said, concern in his voice. "Somebody may be looting your account."

Chase sat back down. "I'm relieved you don't believe I did it to myself."

"Mr. Cautious?" Pearson grinned. "But why wouldn't it show up yesterday when you checked your own terminal?"

"Wait a second." Chase got a closed look on his face, as if his thoughts were miles away. "How does somebody beside me issue orders to my account? By knowing the proper access code. Who knows it here at the bank?"

"You're looking at him. Me and nobody else."

"S'what I thought." Chase sat in silence a long time.

"But you have just thought of someone else who knows the code?" Pearson suggested at last.

"You mean besides Maggie?" Chase shook his head. "Nobody knows, Jim. Just the three of us. But I've had another thought. A whiz-kid could set his own computer to work going through an infinite range of variations until it came up with the right code. How long would it take a computer to do that?"

"Hours? Minutes? Depends how lucky it got."

"But eventually it would get it."

"Eventually. Of course, such a thing is a felony."

"That wouldn't bother a computer whiz kid."

"Whiz *kid*?" the banker picked up. "You keep saying whiz *kid*."

"Do I?" There was a vote of sarcasm in Chase's voice.

"As if some kid had planned this caper."

"This kid," Chase agreed, his voice growing far-away with thought, "or someone who does the kid's thinking for him."

"Oh, dear."

Chapter Thirty-Eight_____

The only thing more distracting than having her son living with his lover, Maggie Gioberti thought on this morning, was having him back home.

The telephone had been ringing steadily for two days, mostly Vickie's friends, but some calls for Cole. His duffel bag had proved to contain perhaps the most heavily compacted mass of dirty laundry ever assembled west of the Mississippi River. The Crown Prince himself had promptly undone his neatly arranged room, returning it to its usual state of chaos. All the while, he and Vickie had been closeted, trading secrets. Breakfast had been trebled to take care of Cole's seemingly insatiable hunger and his apparent desire to consume his own weight in pancakes with butter and syrup. Now, having turned the house upside down, he was asleep in his room, leaving word that he was "out of it" for the rest of the day.

The telephone rang.

Wearily, Maggie picked it up. "It's Steve Barton, Maggie," the lawyer said. "Is there somewhere I can reach Chase?"

"He's in San Francisco."

"Did he mention we were going to request a new autopsy in the Agretti case?"

"Something about getting Melissa's permission?"

"I've got the go-ahead from the coroner's office," Barton explained. "But I've been reluctant to see Melissa at the hospital."

"She came home today."

"Ah! Well, then . . ."

Maggie waited. When nothing further was said she asked, "Well, then what?"

"I'm still reluctant." The attorney's voice took on a baffled tone. "I guess I'm being chicken about this. I know Chase wasn't too happy with the idea of opening the Agretti grave."

Maggie was silent for a moment. There were a million good things about being married to Mr. Nice Guy, she reflected silently, but there were some drawbacks, too. "So you're diffident about asking her?" she prompted.

"Very."

"I'm not," Maggie informed him. "One of the things about being a mother is that you do anything if it might help your child."

"And, anyway, you're sort of close to Melissa, aren't you?" Barton suggested.

This time Maggie's silence was more prolonged. She realized Barton was laying off a sticky job on her. She didn't mind doing it, but she resented being manipulated.

"Steve," she said then, "just come right out and ask me. As for being close to Melissa, nobody's that close, certainly not since the murder of her father."

"But you'll give it a try?" the lawyer prompted.

"Yes," Maggie agreed in a weary voice. "It's probably good for my character. Is there something she has to sign?"

"I'll messenger it over to you."

"In fact," Maggie said wryly, "you probably have

the boy on his motorbike right now. Thanks, Steve."
She hung up.

Men. She'd married a good one, but it didn't pre-
vent Maggie from knowing that when faced with a
thoroughly unpleasant and complicated problem in
human relations, most men had to turn to a woman
to get the job done. "You're a woman," they all
seemed to say. "You can deal with it better than I
can." This left men only a few major chores in life,
like fixing flat tires and removing wasps' nests.

Maggie's ironic smile turned grim. And a wasp's
nest might well be what she was walking into with
Melissa. To have lost a father and produced a sickly
child in mortal danger—and then to be asked to sign
an order to violate her father's grave—might produce a situation with Melissa that made even a wasp's
nest look peaceful by comparison.

Nevertheless, Maggie told herself sternly, I've done
little enough for Cole these past weeks. This was her
chance to accomplish something important. It might
be worth nothing but Brownie points, but she *would*
do it.

Pale, wan almost to a wraithlike pallor, Melissa lay
beneath the thick shade of a tall juniper on the west
lawn of the mansion. She had donned a brief white
tennis dress and halter and had arranged for Chao-Li
to bring a small lawn table, on which sat a tray with a
pitcher of lemonade, two tall glasses and a telephone.

"Please," she said, still lying back in a canvas deck
chair. "I'm not too steady yet. Forgive me for not
getting up."

Maggie kissed her cheek and sat down in another
deck chair. "You might be better in the sun than the
shade," she remarked. "A good tan will do wonders
for you, Melissa."

Behind the girl, something flickered in the bow

window of the mansion. When it came to spying, Angela Channing did her own dirty work. Maggie couldn't see the older woman behind the voile sun curtains, but she could absolutely feel her malign presence there.

"They tell me your baby's having problems," Maggie went on, hoping by mentioning what was uppermost in Melissa's mind to clear the air for other matters.

"What's your opinion of Dr. Ruzza?" The younger woman asked bluntly. "In fact, don't you think the whole Valley Hospital and staff are way behind the times?"

"It's a very well-equipped facility."

"Not for what Joseph has." Melissa's slender arm moved languidly to indicate the extension telephone Chao-Li had brought out from the house on a long cord. "I've put in a call for some advice. Specialized treatment."

"I see. Perhaps, in San Francisco . . .?"

"Exactly." Melissa's eyes sought hers. "How's Cole?"

"Back home with us."

Melissa nodded. "I knew that couldn't last. It wasn't for him."

"Surprisingly, Mrs. Demery asked him to leave."

"Oh?"

"Cole hasn't explained why." Maggie paused a polite instant. "It's about Cole that I've come, Melissa. If we're to defend him against this murder charge, there's something you can do to help."

"Anything. I know he's innocent."

"Thank you. But you won't like what I'm asking."

"Ask it."

"The coroner has agreed to perform a second autopsy." Maggie stopped. The look on Melissa's face was absolutely unreadable, deadpan, but abruptly wary. "He needs your authorization."

"What?"

"I won't play games with you on something this serious," Maggie told her. "Before they can open your father's grave and do a new examination, you have to sign this paper." Maggie opened her bag and produced the form her lawyer had sent over.

"Open his . . . grave?" Melissa's voice was soft, vulnerable, trembling.

"Yes."

"I can't . . ." Melissa's throat seemed to close with an audible click. "I won't do . . ." She gasped for air. "Maggie, do you realize what you're . . . ?"

The two women stared intensely into each other's eyes. At that moment the telephone on the folding table rang shrilly. Both of them jumped. Maggie reached for the instrument and lifted it across to Melissa's lap.

She let it ring three more times. Then, biting her lip, she picked up the receiver. "Hello?"

She listened. "Lunch tomorrow?" Another pause. "I only wanted to ask about what Miss Hunter told . . ." This time her caller seemed to go on for a much longer time. As she listened, Melissa's cheeks suddenly grew pink. The wan look seemed to fade away. Maggie sat back in her deck chair and sipped lemonade.

"Dr. Edsen?" Melissa asked then. Another pause. "But what makes you think he can fly here from Sweden?"

Once more, Melissa's caller continued talking for some time. "In that case," Melissa said at last, "let's make it as late as possible. One? One thirty?" She nodded twice. "See you then."

She hung up the phone and for a long while stared down at it in her lap. There was a faint smile on her lips. There had been an almost miraculous change in Melissa, Maggie noticed. Suddenly her color had vastly improved; she no longer looked wan and forlorn. Whoever she had been talking to had apparently come up with the name of another doctor for the baby. Or was it more than that? Something that could only be discussed over lunch tomorrow?

"Good news?" Maggie asked at last.

Melissa's faint, remembering smile faded. She returned the phone to the table and, with the same gesture, reached out to Maggie. "Give me the paper to sign."

"Just like that?"

Melissa nodded. "Just like that."

Women, Maggie thought as she drove back to her home.

No wonder her sex seemed confusing to men. Women were confusing even to each other. After appearing to hate the idea of the exhumation order, one mysterious phone call and Melissa's objections had vanished. Whoever had placed that call was something of a miracle worker.

Her own telephone was ringing as she entered the house, and she raced to get it. "Maggie Gioberti."

"Thank the Lord I got you!" a man exclaimed.

"Who is this?"

"It's Darryl," he explained. "I've got terrific news!"

Maggie sank down on the bench beside the phone. She wasn't in the mood for any more eventful happenings. The day was already overfull. "You're making my movie?"

"Not quite. But, listen to this—I have development money!"

"What does that mean, Darryl?"

"It means that 'Tangled Vines' stays alive as a project. It means I can pay you to do revisions. It means I can start finding a star or two with bankable reputations."

Maggie's heart sank. "I'm in no mood for revisions."

"Hey, Maggie, I'm not asking for much. One week of your time. I'll book you a Beverly Hills hotel suite and turn you loose on a typewriter. And pay for your time. Fair enough?"

"Now? I can't just drop everything, Darryl."

"What's hanging fire in Tuscany Valley that can't wait a week?"

"For one thing, we've just got an order for a second autopsy in the murder case in which my son has been charged. It could be important to him."

"You're talking about at least a week's waiting while the coroner gets his act together." The director's voice sounded young, boyish with enthusiasm. "During that week all you can do is chew your nails waiting for the result to be announced. I'm offering you an escape hatch. A week of hard, honest work. Take your mind off everything but your script. Then back to the Valley in time to—"

"I don't need a scenario, Darryl. I get the picture. Let me think."

She sat there, tormenting herself. Cole had just returned. He needed her. Chase and Vickie depended on her. Still, what Cole needed most, she had just delivered. Melissa's signature.

"You owe it to yourself, Maggie," the director was saying. "You're too housebound. You have to get out and see the world. And be seen. That's the nature of this business. If you don't hit hard when you're hot, you can cool off overnight and never get a second chance."

"Darryl, that's nonsense," Maggie retorted. "If I go down to L.A. for a week, it's strictly to work."

"Naturally. What else?"

"Nothing else," she said firmly. Maggie told herself she really believed this.

Chapter Thirty-Nine_____

"Slowly, Chao-Li."

Angela Channing's voice had dropped almost to a whisper as she sat in the back seat of the pale-gray station wagon normally used by the winery foremen. It was typical of her, when on a mission of this kind, to use her Chinese majordomo instead of Desi, the chauffeur. Both could be trusted to keep their mouths shut, but only Chao-Li, Angie felt, would keep silent even under torture.

"Behind this grove of trees," she murmured softly.

The long gray vehicle eased quietly out of sight. Chao-Li switched off the engine and twisted in the driver's seat to look at his employer. His impassive face remained absolutely expressionless as he surveyed the woman in the back seat, uncharacteristically dressed in faded denims and a broad-brimmed straw hat.

Angie eased out of the station wagon and peered through the tree branches to the kitchen entrance of the French restaurant that stood at the head of the valley. She glanced at her watch: half-past one.

"And now, Mrs. Channing?" Chao-Li asked in a quiet voice.

"And now . . . we wait."

                    *   *   *

"Do you really think you can get him out here?" Melissa asked Richard Channing. "This Dr. Karl Edsen must be much too busy to leave his clinic in Stockholm."

"He is."

Richard's strong, handsome face looked solemn for a moment as he stared at her. He had picked a table well back from the great picture windows that gave the clientele of the restaurant a superb view of Tuscany Valley. And he hadn't let his glance waver from Melissa's face during any part of the meal.

"But he happens to owe me a favor," Richard went on smoothly. "Money couldn't budge him from Sweden. But I can."

He watched the young woman's face even more closely, reading there the urge to ask questions, piercing ones. But the hope he was offering her was too great, and he could sense that she hesitated to distract him with details. It was just as well. Karl Edsen owed no favors to Richard Channing, but his research center for newborn diseases did owe a lot to the charitable gifts of some of the other higher-ups in the Cartel. Dedicated to making money, the organization nevertheless knew the publicity value of a few well-placed donations to popular causes. Besides, such contributions were tax deductible.

"Believe me, Melissa," Richard was saying, "if anyone in the world can save Joseph, it's this man."

"And if he can't?"

He took her hand in a discreet, friendly manner, sheltering the gesture so that it would be difficult to notice from any of the other tables at the restaurant. "I know what Joseph means to you," he said in a low voice that seemed to throb with understanding. "So the word 'can't' has no place in this. Edsen's the best. He's the only man I'd trust to save Joseph. I have every confidence in him."

He watched Melissa's great dark eyes widen with hope as he talked. But Richard Channing was too wise in the ways of human nature to think that a promise made today would keep this lovely girl forever in his debt. So he took the risk of bringing up the question that undoubtedly troubled her already and that she would someday ask.

"If you're wondering what's in this for me," he continued smoothly, his grin strong and broad, "I'm not going to tell you that for a woman as lovely and exciting as you, I'd do anything."

"What?"

"I'm not going to tell you that," Richard insisted, "even though it's true. You're too smart and too attractive to be conned by flattery."

Melissa's grin matched his. "But don't stop trying."

"No, seriously," Richard went on. "We're both worldly enough to recognize the attraction between us. I can see it in your eyes and I know you can read it in mine. But that kind of emotional and sensual bond between a man and a woman is on another plane from saving the life of an infant in danger. We don't want one to color the other. I'm sure you agree."

Melissa was silent for a long moment. "Richard," she said then, "I was there when you called my father and made offers for the Agretti grapes."

He nodded calmly. "I appreciate your frankness."

"If you know me at all—and I think you do—you know I would never go against my father's wishes."

"I agree. But, Melissa, in the aftermath of his tragic death, who's to know what his final wishes were? Not even you." He gently caressed her hand. "The world moves on. You have a young son to protect and there's no one to help you. Don't," he added abruptly, "tell me you can rely on Lance. Or anyone at Falcon Crest. We both know better than that."

Melissa's cheeks flushed. Her eyes darted across Richard's face, as if searching for truths. Finally: "What are you suggesting?"

He gave her hand a squeeze. "At the moment, only one thing—saving Joseph."

"And after that?"

He smiled softly with that same boundless air of understanding that could be so reassuring. "You may have heard that I have a pretty hard head for business," he said then. "It's true. I discipline my mind. I plan quite thoroughly, even to wanting your father's property. But I've never been any good at disciplining my heart."

The silence that fell over the two of them lasted for a long time. Richard's gaze never left Melissa's face. It had a hypnotic power that compelled her glance to match his. Like a high-tension wire, the aura between them crackled with leashed energy, a tension that promised explosive excitement if released.

"Richard, I'm no match for you," Melissa said in a small voice. "I'm way out of my depth and you know it."

"I don't think so." He caressed her hand again, very lightly so that her skin tingled. "I think you've been languishing in a small pond. The people around you are no match for the real Melissa. They haven't even begun to touch the real you."

"You're putting ideas into my head." Her voice had suddenly grown almost breathless.

"I'm telling you there's a great big world outside Tuscany Valley. I can show it to you. And you'd match it perfectly."

Something turned behind Melissa's eyes. Her lips took on an ironic twist. "Would I match it as well as, oh, Diana Hunter?"

Richard threw back his head and laughed, but not loudly enough to attract attention. "You're very good," he said then. "You're even better than I dreamed." His face grew solemn. "Diana's my employee, Melissa. She has her career to think of and I assure you it comes first. But I'm not offering you a job. I'm offering you . . . the world."

The woman in the denims and broad-brimmed straw hat paused in the door of the ladies' room as Richard Channing helped Melissa to her feet. Still holding her hand, he led her between the other tables to the entrance, where the proprietor, all bows, bid them a fulsome farewell. At no time during this passage did Melissa's glance leave Richard's face.

Well and truly hooked, Angela told herself.

Her mouth hardened into a bitter line as she turned and left the restaurant by the kitchen. Pausing in the shadow of the doorway, she watched as Richard opened the door of his rakish sports car, waiting for Melissa. She paused before sliding into the front seat. They were sheltered by the shade of a huge overbranching oak. No one else was in sight.

Slowly, Richard bent over her. They kissed, briefly. Then once again. Angela Channing's lips pressed into an even grimmer line. She watched the couple drive off, but waited for a moment in the shadows before returning to her station wagon.

Whatever else he was, she admitted to herself, Richard Channing was a consummate charmer. And a fast worker. All that she'd witnessed would have to be used in her war against this man. She could fashion it into a weapon. But, like a sword, it could cut two ways. She had to be careful.

First, therefore, she would try out its sharpness on her grandson, Lance.

Chapter Forty

For the first time in many weeks, Maggie noted, all four Giobertis were home for dinner. It should have been an occasion for celebration, or at least of good feeling. Instead it had the depressing feel of a wake.

Chase, at the head of the table, idly formed patterns with his fork in his uneaten mashed potatoes, a trick Cole in the opposite chair seemed to pick up and mirror without even realizing what he was doing. Vickie caught her mother's eyes and indicated with her own glance what the two men were up to, their usual unconscious game of what Vickie referred to as "monkey see, monkey do."

"Maybe we ought to try it, too," the girl remarked.

By way of reply, Maggie raised her eyebrows. Vickie mimicked the movement. Maggie frowned. Vickie frowned. "Okay," Chase said at last, "bring on the clowns."

Cole looked up. "Huh?"

"The atmosphere around here," his mother said, "is about as cheerful as a broken leg. I know," she went on, turning to Chase, "tomorrow's Cole's pretrial hearing. It's a crucial day for us. But tonight doesn't have to be this gloomy, does it?"

Cole gave Maggie a rueful look. "Slip me some good news and watch me smile."

Maggie's glance swept the table. "Okay," she said then. "I'm not sure this is good news or just hard work. But I've heard from the director who wants to do 'Tangled Vines.' He's got what he calls development money. He can pay me for revisions."

Cole's face broke into a grin. "Terrific!"

"Wonderful," Chase enthused. Maggie watched him work up a head of enthusiasm for something so distant from Cole's trial. "That's *great* news, Maggie," her husband continued. "Really great."

"Mom, you're on your way," Vickie added.

"To premature old age," Maggie finished. She hesitated for a moment. "I know you had a call from Steve Barton," she told Chase. "Anything remotely like good news?"

Chase shrugged. "You know lawyers. He's had the second autopsy, thanks to you, and we'll get the results before the pretrial hearing, but that's all he—"

"Second autopsy?" Cole cut in. "You mean Melissa said yes?"

"After your mother talked to her."

Cole sat back in his chair and beamed at Maggie. "Who needs lawyers? All you need is a mother."

Attorney Barton arrived early in the morning, before Chase had left for his office. The two men conferred briefly on the veranda, then went inside the house to join Maggie in the kitchen.

The three sat around the table staring at a thick sheaf of papers Barton had brought with him. "I had no idea post-mortem medical examinations were that lengthy," Maggie commented.

"This one is," the lawyer assured her. "The coroner's reputation is on the line. So, to some extent, is the district attorney's. After all, the charges they've filed against Cole depend to a great extent on the autopsy being correct."

"Then what chance do we have that they'll change their minds with the second?" Chase demanded. "If anything could produce a cover-up, this would."

"Well . . ." Barton looked uncertain. "I've been up most of the night reading this thing. It mainly reinforces the findings of the first examination. All the same points are made for a second time. But you have to remember that the coroner is on the spot in more ways than one. I'm pressing him hard. Also, this is a capital offense. The trial will get maximum press coverage. He's got to leave no stone unturned."

"Or lay on a whitewash so thick nobody can see through it," Chase added.

"Not as easy as it sounds," the attorney remarked. "Anyway, here are the findings. I'd like to go over a few points with you because . . . well, frankly, I'm clutching at straws. There isn't much for me to get my teeth into. Or is there? You tell me."

He leafed through the report transcribed from the coroner's dictated statement.

"Cole should be down here," Chase said. "Let me roust him out of bed. It's time he was up anyway."

"No, Chase," Maggie cautioned him. "Let's keep this among the three of us. Cole may look like a big strong kid to you, but he's teetering on a knife edge."

"Let me read you this section," the lawyer suggested. "I'm quoting now. 'Death was produced by a crushing blow to the left tempula of the skull, producing perforation of the frontal cortex resulting in massive hemorrhaging. Positional plotting of the trajectory indicates the blow was delivered face-to-face by the perpetrator's right hand.'" He looked up. "This is really the only new thing in the findings."

"I understood the killer had landed a series of blows."

"But they were all identical in trajectory," Barton said.

"Which makes it even clearer that the killer was right-handed," Maggie spoke up.

The attorney frowned. "That's right."

Maggie glanced at her husband before she spoke again. "Do you think the coroner will stand by this second report? No chance of him reneging on any of it?"

"On the contrary, he *has* to swear to it. It's all his baby."

"So at the pretrial hearing this afternoon," Maggie persisted, "this is what he'll state under oath before the judge?"

"No question of it."

"Maggie," Chase asked, "what are you getting at? I know that ex-reporter's look in your eye. You're onto something."

"Can't you guess what?"

Vickie paced the airless halls of the county courthouse. Maggie huddled in a bench along one wall and followed her daughter's progress for a while before tiring of it. She glanced at her watch. "It's going on too long," she murmured.

"But, Mom, isn't that a good sign?"

"I suppose so. The more doubt Steve Barton can create, the longer it would take the judge and the D.A. to reach some kind of agreement."

"I don't think it's fair that we aren't in there."

"I chose not to. I think Cole . . ." She stopped. "If something went wrong. If they decided to go ahead and put Cole on trial despite . . ." She paused again. "This is hard to explain, Vickie, because it has to do with male psychology."

"Don't tell *me* about males," the girl retorted. "They're all weird."

Maggie couldn't hide a smile. "Not any weirder than females. It's just that the male, when in trouble, prefers to work it out with other males. The presence of a female, especially a mother or a sister, isn't such a wonderful idea because—"

The courtroom doors slammed open. Chase came out at a brisk pace. Maggie stood up, her face pale. "Chase?"

"He heard us out," her husband said in a grave voice. "The whole analysis of the autopsy report."

"And?"

"Well, my dear, a little bit of history was made in there just now. The D.A. had to admit he didn't have sufficient evidence to pursue the state's case against Cole."

"Chase! How marvelous!"

"Judge Barclay had no choice. He threw the indictment out of court."

"Dad!"

"So it looks like the sheriff's going to have to put his bloodhounds to work sleuthing up some new suspects. Vickie," Chase nearly shouted, "your brother's free as a bird!"

All three of them embraced each other, hugging for dear life as Cole came out of the courtroom with Steve Barton. "Hey," Cole called, "is this a private huddle or can anybody get in on the act?"

Vickie launched herself at her brother and jumped halfway up into his bear hug. "Brother dear, you are one lucky duck."

"Not luck," Cole said, winking over her shoulder at his mother. "Sheer genius is what you mean."

"You a genius?"

"Well," said Cole, "I was smart enough to be born left-handed."

Part Five

Chapter Forty-One _____

In Tuscany Valley, and in San Francisco, it was time for councils of war.

The atmosphere in Richard Channing's lofty office at the *Globe*, some forty floors above the city, seemed perversely more appropriate to a diving bell thousands of feet under the sea. "Oppressive" was the word that came to Diana Hunter as she sat across from her boss. The man himself paced steadily along the broad expanse of picture windows, a silhouette that flashed back and forth across Diana's vision with such nervous speed that it seemed to blur.

"Damn them all," Richard spat out, coming to an abrupt stop. "The judge, the district attorney, the whole lot of them." He glanced almost guiltily at Diana. In the Cartel, outbursts of emotion were frowned upon.

"Then it's lucky you've put the Karl Edsen business into the works," she said in a smooth, unaccented tone, as if they were simply discussing the weather.

"But until Edsen gets back to us," Richard pointed out, "the Melissa project hangs by a thread."

"Oh, I wouldn't be that pessimistic."

"Meaning?"

"You've got her in your pocket, Edsen or no Edsen." Diana's cool voice continued in its unexcited way. "You do have a way with the fair sex, Richard."

He stared at her for a moment. "You're not developing symptoms of a female complaint . . . like jealousy?"

"Not I." Diana flipped open her morocco-bound notebook and ticked off something written there. "As for the memorial to your father, I'm informed it's been put on the county board's agenda for the next meeting. What are we prepared to pay for the land, if we get a permit?"

"A thousand an acre would be too much."

"That's not what I asked," she persisted.

Richard's face went grim. "You know the answer as well as I," he replied angrily. "We pay whatever we have to pay. But not so much that it stirs up suspicions."

"That's what I like," she mused in an ironic tone. "Clear-cut, no-nonsense instructions. You're leaving the negotiations to me?"

"I don't want to appear in this just yet."

"Then I'll attend the board meeting." She checked off another item in her notebook. Then she looked up at him.

"The other day you said that the strategy of splitting apart families was a long, drawn-out process." She paused and patted her upswept hair, smoothing a few stray hairs. "I presume the Melissa project, as you call it, is part of the same strategy."

Richard nodded curtly. "Before it's finished, I'll have the whole Agretti thing in the palm of my hand, as land or as contracts to buy the grapes. Either way, it checks Angela Channing. It may even checkmate her completely." He paused and a sigh escaped him. "Long and drawn-out. I know it better than you. And even though the one thing the Cartel teaches us is patience, I'm beginning to lose mine."

"But not just yet," Diana suggested with a smile.

"No, not just yet. Not just yet." Richard went on with a burst of new energy, "We want a little dynamite. The *Globe* shareholders' meeting is long overdue. I think I'll blow the lot of them sky-high."

Diana closed her notebook. She got to her feet and joined Richard at the picture window. "You read your broker's report," she said then in that same even, almost soothing tone. "Someone has been buying up outstanding shares of *Globe* stock, no matter how high the price has gone."

"It's not hard to identify the buyer."

"Oh? My understanding is that the shares were bought by Account Bravo Tango Two-Four, Swiss Credit Bank, Basel."

"Meaningless."

"The Swiss banking secrecy makes it impossible for us to know who owns Account Bravo-Tango Two-Four," she pointed out.

"Not necessary. It's Angela Channing. Or it's her attorney, Phil Erikson, in her name. These layers of gauze and camouflage work only when you haven't a clue to your opponent. But I *know* my enemy, whatever name she operates under."

Diana was standing next to him now. She reached out with the back of her fingers to smooth his cheek where it rose from his cheekbone, across the corner of his eye to his temple. "Richard," she said in a low voice, "it may be time for a short break. You've been at this hot and heavy. It may be time to relax for a few days."

He shook his head. "No. It's time for a shareholders' massacre."

"With Angela owning ten percent of the stock? And her children and Chase Gioberti holding the

rest? It's a standoff, Richard. You haven't the votes
to blow them sky-high. They may even have the
votes to turn you out."

His smile was a wonderful and frightening thing
to see. Diana watched it with conflicting emotions of
pleasure and fear. Yes, it signified humor, that oddly
curving smile like the complex twist of a scimitar
blade. But it spelled something wild and dangerous
as well.

"No," he said in a surprisingly mild voice. "I'll not
only have a majority of the votes but, in the process
of beating them, I'll set one against the other so
neatly they'll knife each other to death before my
very eyes."

"They'll do your work for you?"

"And quickly, too. By the time the meeting is end-
ing the floor will be awash in blood."

Diana involuntarily took a step back from that
horrifying smile. She recovered her poise at once. "I
liked you better when you were busy saving Joseph
Cumson's life."

"Oh, that'll happen, too."

The telephone rang and Diana answered. "Yes,
Dr. Edsen. He's right here." She handed the telephone to Richard and whispered faintly, "I'm impressed."

A purposeful grin split Richard's handsome face.
"Karl? Good to hear your voice. When can you be
here?" A pause. Richard's eyes flashed victory.
"Wednesday will be fine, Karl. We'll meet your plane."

When he hung up the phone he reached for Diana and lifted her high in the air, his powerful
hands clasping her waist in a tight grip. "You see?"
he crowed. "You see?"

"I see," she said breathlessly.

"And now . . . the massacre."

                    *   *   *

The second council of war started off on such a peaceful note that at first Lance had no idea of what he was in for. Nor did his mother, Julia. She and Lance were in her laboratory classifying the results of two new vinifications. One would provide a table wine to be sold in half-gallon jugs. The other had turned out so markedly better that it required special bottling at a much higher price.

"I'd put it away for a few years," Lance suggested. "I've got space in the West Warehouse. The longer we keep that red under wraps, the more we can charge for it."

Julia shook her head slowly, thoughtfully. "That's not the nature of the merlot grape," she told her son. "When it's this good now it doesn't get much better over the years. And those were merlots from the Agretti vineyards, the best money can buy."

"Everybody around here sure puts a lot of faith in Agretti grapes."

Julia eyed her son for a long moment. "You and Melissa still at it?"

"Look, I've told you, just because I was silly enough to let Grandmother pick out a bride for me doesn't mean I have to be madly in love with the girl."

"But now, with Joseph . . ."

"Who may not live," Lance added coldly. "And it's just as well."

"Lance! You're not to say such things."

"No? It's time for some plain speaking about dear little Joseph."

Julia's face grew white. She shook her hands in front of her face as if to ward off, choke off, her son's next words. "I don't want to hear about this, Lance," she implored. "Your grandmother may have forced that marriage on you, but she's been incredibly generous to Joseph. She's made him her chief residual beneficiary."

"Huh?"

"Her holdings at Falcon Crest go to you, in trust for Joseph. It's a bequest worth millions."

"What about you and Aunt Emma?"

"We're already provided for by Grandpa Jasper. But you're my mother's chief heir—for Joseph. So I don't want to hear any of your cynical sarcasm about the poor little thing. Do you hear me?"

"*I* hear you," Angela Channing said in a deadly voice.

Julia and Lance looked up to see her in the doorway of the lab. She remained motionless for a long moment. Then, when she spoke again, it was with the same deadly calm as that of a cobra coolly circling its prey.

"But I want to hear more," she went on, her eyes flashing. "Particularly about you and Melissa, Lance."

"You already know whatever there is to know." His tone had grown stubborn.

"I know you've treated her abominably," Angie snapped. "I know she's had a very hard time with the baby and part of it is your fault. I know that we're going to be lucky to keep Joseph with us. And I know something else."

"Yeah?" he asked in a surly voice. "Like what?"

His grandmother advanced slowly into the room, her stride smooth and almost slinky, as if measuring her victim before striking. "You know, in the jungle, the animals have it all worked out. The strong eat the weak. With all the education I've paid for you to have, I trust that bit of wisdom hasn't escaped your attention?"

"So?"

"So when an animal weakens, no matter how strong it once was, it becomes fair game for a stronger predator. Am I going too fast for you, Lance?"

"Keep talking."

"Your wife, Melissa, is such an animal. She was strong. Now she's in a particularly weak position. Her health . . . well, it'll improve. But her mind is at risk. She worries over Joseph. She worries about you. She's vulnerable. She's fair game for a stronger animal, Lance. Are you still with me?"

"Get to the point."

"Somebody got there before me." Angela Channing was standing in front of her grandson now. Although Lance towered over her, for some reason he looked small and ineffective confronted by Angela's cold, angry stance.

"Somebody?" he faltered. "What's that supposed to mean?"

"It means someone's making a play for your wife, Lance." The words cracked like a whip in the quiet atmosphere of the laboratory. "It means someone's using her feelings for Joseph to get her hooked into an adulterous affair."

She stared up at Lance's face, but whatever she was expecting to see there didn't materialize. Instead a slightly off-center, reckless grin appeared on the young man's face. "Is that all you can do? Grin?" she snapped.

Lance shrugged. "Sauce for goose is sauce for the gander."

Angie whirled on her daughter. "You hear this, Julia? This son of yours is having affairs all over the place. So he doesn't at all mind that the mother of his child may be about to take the plunge. Is this the kind of animal we've raised? Is this the person wh will inherit Falcon Crest?"

"Mother, I'm sure he meant noth—"

"That's exactly what I mean," Lance assur

"You people kill me. To you Melissa is innocent child. Well, she's

this little mother. It's about time you realized who
you're dealing with."

Again, Julia's hands went up as if to protect herself.
"Don't start that again, Lance. You can't solve your
problems by blackening Melissa's reputation."

"No? Then how about a paternity test?"

The two women looked shocked. They stared in
utter silence at Lance, whose face was a mask of
sneering superiority.

Julia was the first to regain her composure. "What
are you saying?" she asked her son. Her hands still
seemed to shield her from his reply, but her eyes
were wide with pain.

"He's saying Joseph isn't his," Angela Channing
remarked in a dry tone. "If he's right . . ." She paused.
Then she shook her head. "He can't be right."

"I'd know a bit more about it than you, Grandmother."

"Would you?" Angie's tone was almost too sweet.
"Then, of course, you'd know the ramifications of
what you're saying. You'd know that if you really
wanted to ruin this family and Falcon Crest *and* any
chance you ever had of inheriting it, you'd just go
right ahead and have your paternity test."

"Boy, when you lay down a threat, you don't spare
the horses."

For some reason this brought a wry grin to Angela's
                          ind of grudging admiration
                          e, you're a total scoundrel,
                          oitome of selfish, male ego."
                          e Falcon Crest has to go to
                          ave the sheer gall to run it

                          e seemed real enough. "Then
                          Melissa."
                          ve affair with yourself," his

grandmother told him, "you aren't even curious about the animal who's tracking Melissa."

"Couldn't care less."

"That's where we part company." Angela Channing drew herself up to her full height and, once again through some trick of sheer personality, she seemed to dwarf Lance. "I'm only going to say this once," she commanded. "Listen hard. The man who's got Melissa on the hook is Richard Channing. He is *my* enemy. He is *your* enemy. He must not be allowed to win her away from us. That means no paternity tests. No more dalliances with that Lori Stevens girl. That means, my dear grandson, that you stay home, stay available, stay sweet and stay by Melissa's side. Got it?"

"I heard it," he said grudgingly, after a long pause.

"And you'll do it," Angie snapped. "Oh, yes, you'll play the part. Because the alternative, Lance, is too horrible for even you to dare."

Chapter Forty-Two

When the telephone rang in the Gioberti house at 6 A.M., Chase was in the kitchen making coffee. He grabbed the phone off the hook after its first ring to spare waking the rest of the family.

He already knew the call would be for him.

It would be well after lunchtime in France or Switzerland at that hour. Just about the time when Jacqueline Perrault Gioberti, having finished the heaviest part of her business day, would turn her thoughts either to her family or her plans for the evening. Did it never occur to her that the hour she chose to place her calls w̲a̲s̲ ̲ ̲ ̲ ̲tirely inconvenient for California? But, eq̲ ̲ ̲ ̲ ̲ ̲ ̲it never occur to Chase that his moth̲ ̲ ̲ ̲ ̲ ̲ ̲ ̲this hour, made sure she spoke t̲ ̲

her," he began.

se. I didn't wake you?"

noncommittal tone as he

anyway."

aid, knowing the hu-

queline seemed to

ur telegram was

magnificent news. I am so happy Cole is free. But now we must make plans for him. He needs a strict regimen, this young man, or else he gets himself in trouble all over again."

"I already have plans for him."

Chase wondered how much of this new project he should divulge to his mother. She had a disconcerting habit of jumping into his life with unsettling results. Still, nobody had a better business head than she did—except maybe Angela Channing.

"I'm thinking of replanting some fallow acreage," he went on then, telling her briefly of his plans, but neglecting to mention that in some sinister way, the money for the project was missing. He needn't have bothered to conceal that important point from Jacqueline. Her mind went directly to it.

"And the financing?" she asked. "You will need cash."

With Jacqueline it was nearly always impossible to hide things. She had her own spy network, Chase knew, and it was nowhere stronger than here in California. "There's a problem," he said then.

"But surely there is a start-up funding?"

"Angela refuses to come in on it."

"That woman . . ." She stopped herself. "But if it is a matter of a bit of money, Chase, you have only to ask me. My grandson's future is dear to my heart."

"That's not the problem." Chase's tone sounded irritated and he knew it. "There's a shortage. Someone's gotten into my side of the accounts. Jim Pearson is looking into it. I haven't had the time to follow up because of this business with Cole. But now I'm going to get to the bottom of it."

"Shortage?" Jacqueline's voice rose. "In a computerized system? Have you considered asking Lance Cumson?"

Chase sat down on a kitchen stool and shook his

head slowly. There was no way you could ever get
ahead of his mother in business matters. From halfway around the world, her mind could get right to
the core of the problem. "I don't want to *ask* Lance,"
he told her. "I want to *confront* Lance and call in the
cops unless he pays me back immediately."

"*D'accord*," she agreed. "Give him that chance, for
the good of the Falcon Crest name, to keep the
matter private. But, of course, he is merely that
woman's cat's-paw. It is she who must be confronted."

Something clicked in Chase's head. He stared for a
long moment at the coffeemaker, as if deriving vital
information from it. "That's it," he said at last. "Lance
wouldn't dare do this on his own. Angela's looted the
cash. But for what purpose?"

"Does she need one?" his mother demanded. "Sheer
greed."

"No. This was a high risk she took. It had to be for
something very important to her."

"Find the reason," Jacqueline suggested, "and you
will find the evidence you need to confront her.
What?" she asked, evidently addressing someone on
her end of the transatlantic line. She switched rapidly into German, telling that someone off in no
uncertain terms. "*Alors*," she continued more calmly
to her son. "May I make a small investigation of my
own in this matter?"

"From eight thousand miles away?"

"I know Angela," Jacqueline assured her son. "She
has as many uses for Swiss banking secrecy as the
rest of us. Any investigation should begin here, in
Zurich."

"From what I hear of Swiss banks, you won't get
far. I mean, even the FBI and the SEC can't seem to
break down their secrecy."

"We . . ." His mother paused an instant, hardly

more than a second. "I have my ways," she went on smoothly. "I have my contacts."

"Madame Mysterious," Chase kidded her.

"There is no reason for the whole world to know my personal life," she retorted. "How I had a son like you, so open, so honest, so trusting, I shall never know. Chase, leave this matter with your 'mysterious' mother. Mystery has its uses."

"Am I that much of a disappointment to you?" Chase went on in the same joshing vein. "Would you have preferred a more devious son?"

There was a long pause at the other end. "Is that the right word?" Jacqueline said at last. "Devious? It has an ugly sound to it. Clever? Ambitious? Totally dedicated?"

"The word you're searching for," Chase told her, "is ruthless."

Another lengthy silence at Jacqueline's end of the conversation. Then: "Perhaps. Tell me, how is Vickie? Maggie?"

"Both fine. Vickie's taken up running."

"Running? Running where?"

"Anywhere. It's exercise."

"But she is not overweight."

"All her friends are running," Chase explained. "It's a fad, like anything else. First comes the clothing. Everyone dresses in track suits and running shoes. After a while, naturally, they have no choice but to start running."

Again the humor was lost on Jacqueline. "And Maggie? Her film script?"

"Good news there. At first the director couldn't get any backing. Maggie was relieved, really, because she wanted to devote her energy to Cole. Believe me, and without going into details, if it hadn't been for Maggie, Cole might not be free today. But now there's very good news. The director has found development money."

"Wonderful."

"So he's paying Maggie to do some revisions for him. She goes down to L.A. for a week of hard work."

"Yes?" His mother's voice sounded vaguely doubtful. "Ah, well, that is also wonderful," she added quickly.

"So, you see, except for a few monetary problems, we're all in good shape, Mother."

"Yes?" Again that slight hesitation. "Chase, I will get back to you soon about the money. If it passed through Zurich, rest assured I can pick up its trail."

"Right." Chase glanced at his watch. "It's been good talking to you, Mother. And, as always, educational."

"What was that word?"

"What word?"

"The one you said. This mythical son of mine. Not devious."

"Ruthless."

"*Bien sûr.* Ruthless," she repeated. "This I must remember."

"I'm afraid it's too late for me to develop in that direction," Chase admitted.

Jacqueline produced one of her perfectly sculpted peals of tinkly French laughter, moving expertly up the scale like a trained musician. "For you, my dear, it's entirely too late," she agreed. "Somehow, at an early age, you turned toward painful honesty the way a flower turns toward the sun."

"Poetry this early in the morning?"

"Where," she wondered out loud, "did I go wrong?"

Chapter Forty-Three

"Okay, it's a setback. I admit it," Sheriff Robbins said. As always he remained seated, heavy boots propped up on his desk. His deputy, Sid Rawls, sat across from him, reducing a kitchen match to the proper thinness from which to create a toothpick.

"One of us shoulda spotted the kid was a leftie," Rawls mused. "But the first autopsy report didn't mention the right-handed thing."

"I thought the D.A. could've fought a little harder on that," the sheriff said. "I mean, where is it written a leftie can't deliberately pick up a weapon with his right hand, just to confuse us?"

Rawl's wrinkled his nose. "Nah, makes no sense."

"I know." Robbins sighed. "I know."

Slowly, with the care of a trained dental hygienist, the deputy began removing traces of lunch from between his teeth.

"In a way," the sheriff confessed, "I'm kind of glad Cole Gioberti didn't go to trial."

"Because of the family."

"That much money buys a lot of high-powered legal talent. Some of these hot-shot defense attorneys have a way of getting you on the stand and making a monkey out of you."

Sid Rawls produced a sigh reminiscent of Robbins'. "I know," he said in the same tone, "I know."

Neither man spoke for a long time. Outside the sheriff's office, a heavy truck trundled slowly past. Both men looked out the window to see one of the Falcon Crest diesels, crammed with crates, move by.

Robbins made a face. "So where do I go from here?"

"Search me."

"If it wasn't Cole, I've wasted a helluva lotta time collecting evidence it was. Now I have to start from scratch."

"It'd sure help if we had a second suspect handy."

"Second? We have a dozen. I mean it," the sheriff went on excitedly. "If you look at motivation, there are lots of people who might want Carlo Agretti dead. The trick . . ." He sighed again. "The trick is to figure out which of them wanted it enough to kill."

"The trick," Rawls said in a ponderous voice, "is how they got in the house to do it."

"You crazy? Anybody coulda got in."

"Not anybody. Cole got in through the front door. We've established that. But Agretti was already dead. Freshly dead. Still bleeding, in fact."

"I get you," Robbins responded. "How come Cole didn't run head on into the killer. There had to be a way in and out that had nothing to do with the front door."

"Lots of ways," the deputy mused. "Back door. Side door."

"No way. We dusted them all for prints. They were locked solid from the inside and the only prints on them were either Agretti's or his houseman, Fong's."

"Remember what Cole kept insisting? I mean, the kid is a hothead, but he may have had something."

"That he was set up?" the sheriff asked. "Every suspect claims he was set up."

"Suppose the killer wore gloves. Say he left the front door open to lead Cole into the trap. Cole claims Agretti phoned him to come over. Say the killer forced him to make that call."

"Okay. Say all that. Now say the name of the killer."

Rawls laughed without mirth. "One thing."

His boss eyed him sourly. "Yeah?"

"We never did sweat Fong properly."

"Why sweat him? His story made sense."

"I know. I know."

They lapsed into brooding silence again. "What the hell," Sheriff Robbins said at last. "Why not sweat him? He's the nearest thing we have to a witness."

"Waste of time."

"Got any better ideas?"

A long black Fleetwood limousine surged past the window. Both men turned in time to see two men ride by the chauffeured vehicle. One they recognized as Richard Channing. The other, an older man with bright blond crew-cut hair, was a stranger to them. They watched the heavy automobile until it was out of sight.

"Heading toward the hospital," Sid Rawls volunteered. "What's Channing going there for?"

"No idea." The sheriff frowned and his gaze unfocused. "You know what my old man used to tell me? He used to say, 'Kid, for the rich, life is sweet. And the poor even get a taste of it.' Driving around in air-conditioned limos. That's the life."

"I know." Rawls sighed. "I know."

Chapter Forty-Four_____

The hotel was a city within a city. Surrounded by the leafy streets of Beverly Hills, swathed in lush green lawns and shrubbery, the place was laid out like a resort, buildings spread in several directions, immense swimming pool, several lounges and restaurants and shops.

So far, on her first day, Maggie Gioberti had had the time to investigate only the suite in which Darryl had installed her. Its huge living-room picture window faced onto a broad expanse of flowers and greenery. Inside, lounges, chairs, tables, a private bar and an immense TV set invited one to relax and enjoy life. A second television served the huge bedroom with its king-sized bed and separate dressing room. All this, Maggie thought, and the only thing that really matters is the electric typewriter with a ream of blank typing paper beside it and six sharpened pencils.

Farewell swimming pool. Farewell lush lounges with their long iced drinks under colorful umbrellas. She sat at the desk, riffled once more through a script of "Tangled Vines" and came again to the first scene that needed rewriting.

Darryl's penciled instructions were precise. "Tone

down language here. Develop more action. What about moving scene into a car? Could they be going on a picnic? This changes Scene 17 too. Make it an exterior under some trees. What about weather? We could use a storm here to heighten tension."

Maggie stared at the script and found herself wondering what Cole was doing. Chase had told her of his plans for the fallow vineyards, but there appeared to be some holdup on funds that he hadn't seen fit to explain.

She glanced at her watch. Darryl would be coming by for lunch at any moment. All she'd done this morning was to have croissants and coffee in the breakfast lounge and leaf through her script, reading his revision suggestions. An entire morning had passed without a line of new script being written.

What a difference this was from her normal work habits. She longed for her little cubbyhole behind the kitchen, her beat-up portable typewriter and the hours stolen from household routine. There she was in charge. There she set her own schedule, and if a day passed without writing, so be it.

Here she was being paid, like a girl operating a sewing machine in a dress factory, to produce. Everything was wrong. Even the typewriter scared her. She had switched it on and idly touched the keyboard, only to have it go berserk and print out an angry line of x's, like someone cursing.

There was a knock at her door. "Come in."

Darryl appeared, carrying a kind of garment bag. "I brought my swim suit. How about a dip before lunch?"

"I didn't bring mine."

"I figured." He grinned boyishly at her. "Brought you the latest in the hotel shop. Here."

He handed over what turned out to be the briefest bikini Maggie had ever seen. Vickie had wanted to buy one like that some months back and gotten a flat "no" from Maggie. And my figure, Maggie thought, is quite a bit lusher than Vickie's.

"This?" she asked, holding up the two dots and a dash that constituted the entire swim ensemble. "No way."

"Have you seen what's parading around the pool out there?" he countered. "Have you caught a glimpse of the solid sag being displayed? You'd be a knock-out in that, Maggie. I'd have to fight off the talent scouts looking to sign you up."

"As what? The 'before' picture in a reducing-pill ad?"

His smile faded. "Maggie," he said then. "Maggie." He sat down on the sofa. "It's time for a lecture."

"Spare me."

"A pep talk, then. For a woman as attractive and talented as you, who has made such a success of her life, you suffer from chronic lack of self-confidence."

"And I have reason to."

"Nonsense." He patted the sofa next to him. "Listen to Uncle Darryl. In this town of fake facades and phony fronts you stand out like a diamond in a pile of broken glass. There are people in Hollywood with a tenth of your looks and a twentieth of your talent who are brilliant successes because they believed in themselves."

"That's not my style."

Carefully, she sat down some distance from him on the sofa. "I'm from a different world, Darryl. Two different worlds—first newspaper work and then plain, honest farming. Appearances mean nothing in those worlds. Results are what count."

"Here appearances *produce* results. Your own opinion of yourself, your own image of how good you are, comes first. If your image is strong enough, everyone has to believe it. That's true anywhere, Maggie, not just in Tinsel Town."

Maggie sat holding the scraps of bikini in her hands. She tried to keep her glance from the director, but his eagerness and the obvious fact that he believed in her made it hard not to look at him.

"You deliver a pretty fair pep talk," she said at last. "But let's skip the pool and go for the lunch."

He was silent quite a while. "I'm not getting through to you, is that it?"

"That's exactly not it."

He swung around on the couch to establish direct eye contact. "Hear me out. You've got a good life, but nothing is forever. I don't mean some horrible disaster is lurking in the wings. I mean nothing stays the same. Your kids grow up, move away. Your husband changes slightly in character as he gets older. So do you."

"I'm prepared for that. It won't be a surprise to me."

"But it will," Darryl pointed out. "Subtle changes. You get out of breath climbing the stairs. You start putting on weight. Your looks change. Your memory. Your attitudes. It's called aging."

"Listen to the expert."

"I'm about your age, Maggie. I know what I'm talking about. Life is a one-way trip. Once you've passed a place, you don't return. It's not a merry-go-round. It's a rollercoaster."

"With a long downhill slide, is that what you're saying?"

"You read me loud and clear."

"And never again," Maggie suggested somewhat mischievously, "will I be offered the chance to display my charms in a bikini."

He stifled a smile. "Never again," he assured her with mock solemnity.

"In that case." She got to her feet and left the room.

In her dressing room she stripped quickly and pulled on the tiny bikini. To her the effect was shocking, indecent. Her breasts seemed huge, her thighs ... her waist ... her hips ... too much! Hurriedly she reached for a sheer chiffon dressing gown and quickly shrugged into it, fastening it at the waist.

Better, she thought. At poolside, it gets whipped off and into the water I plunge. No striptease. Let the water cover me. She felt light-headed. Vickie had described the way she felt when she had run five miles. "It's a high, Mom. The oxygen in your blood ... it's like bubbles in champagne."

She strode back into the living room, her head singing with bubbles.

Chapter Forty-Five

Richard Channing's suite at the hotel consisted of a large living room and bedroom, both with magnificent views of San Francisco. As he ushered Melissa in, he closed and locked the door behind them, fastening the chain as well. Then he went to the private bar and mixed them each a drink. The air-conditioned atmosphere was refreshing, since throughout the day the sun had beat down with uncharacteristic intensity. Now dusk drew near.

"Relax," Richard said, sitting on the sofa and patting the place beside him. "It's been a long, hard day."

Melissa took her vodka-and-tonic from him and sat at the far end of the sofa. She sipped briefly. "What do you think?" she asked then.

"About Karl Edsen? Why take my word for it? Your Dr. Ruzza said it all." Richard eyed her for a moment. "You remember what he said?"

Melissa shook her head. "I'm afraid I was out of it, Richard. Just the sight of that poor little wasted body put me in a state of shock. And the way the two of them handled the baby. As though it were a . . . I don't know . . . a bag of vegetables."

"They do know what they're doing," Richard assured her. "Ruzza told me privately that he'd been at his wit's end with Joseph. Well, you and I knew that, didn't we? But then he said, 'Thank God for a specialist like Edsen. I'm only guessing. This man *knows*.' You were standing right there."

Melissa nodded tiredly. "I know. I just can't take the waiting. This new course of treatment Edsen's prescribed. It may take weeks before—"

"More like days. I've asked him to stay on through tomorrow. He feels we'll know what the hormone does by then."

Melissa smiled sincerely. "I do thank you, Richard, from the bottom of my heart. I know none of this would be possible without you."

"I don't want thanks. I want Joseph to get better." He lifted his glass. "Here's to the little guy. He looks pretty game to me."

He watched her sip her drink. A few minutes later, when the glass was only half full, he discreetly topped it up again with vodka. Melissa began to relax somewhat. She glanced around the suite.

"I had no idea they treated you so well here. It's quite like a private apartment."

"Not like mine in New York." Richard freshened her drink again. "Wait till you see it. I've got all my paintings there. It's my one weakness, buying art. I miss my collection when I'm away from it."

"But surely you plan to be out here for a while."

"Maybe permanently. In which case I'll have it all crated and shipped to California," Richard explained very plausibly. "Of course, whether I stay or not depends on a lot of things."

"The *Globe* seems to be doing well."

Richard gestured impatiently. "A newspaper's all right. But it isn't what I want from California. Either I put down roots here, or I leave."

"Roots? I had the idea you were in love with travel,"

Melissa said. She watched him move to freshen her drink, put out her hand to stop him, then decided not to. "What's stopping you from taking root?"

Another impatient gesture. "It's not something you do mechanically, like digging a hole for a post. It's a matter of the feel of a place and the people who go with it. Take Bellavista, for instance."

"My father's place?" Melissa sounded surprised. "It's pretty old-fashioned."

"Oh, it would need refurbishing. I'd have to spend quite a bit sprucing it up. But I wouldn't change the line of it."

"I had no idea you liked Bellavista that much."

He nodded. "The place . . . and the people who go with it."

"The workers?"

"The woman who owns Bellavista."

Melissa sat without speaking. She started to sip her drink out of sheer nervousness, thought better of it, then decided to take a sip anyway. "You mean that married woman, Melissa Cumson."

"I mean that exciting woman, Melissa Agretti."

Melissa laughed almost helplessly. "I love the way you ignore my marriage."

"Doesn't Lance?"

Her face darkened for a moment. "Let's leave him out of it."

"Let's." Richard got to his feet and went to the large expanse of window. "There's that great big outside world I was telling you about, Melissa."

She joined him at the window. Dusk was falling over San Francisco. Varicolored lights sprang up here and there. "It does look wonderful."

"And it's yours."

"Through you?"

"This kind of life is no fun alone. It may look

glamorous, but if you have no one to share it with
. . ." He let the thought echo unspoken.

Melissa shook her head as if to clear it. "Things
are happening too fast for me, Richard. Edsen's just
arrived. Joseph isn't out of danger. And you're coming on as if I were a free woman."

"Aren't you? Isn't freedom a matter of will?" he
asked.

"Will?"

"We are what we want to be," he told her forcefully.
"Look at me. You know my history. I don't have to
tell you what it was like growing up a virtual orphan.
But I had the will to overcome that. I had the will to
change my life, to make it what I wanted. So do
you."

Outside, the city of night was coming to life. Headlights flared. Buildings lighted up. Melissa felt almost breathless with longing for . . . for something
she couldn't put a name to.

"You make it sound so easy."

"It gets harder the longer you put it off. Melissa,"
he went on, putting his arm around her waist,
"nothing is forever. Do you know what I mean?"

"Things change."

"Constantly. You're very young and the young fail
to realize what I'm saying. But nothing stays the
same. Everything changes. The woman you are today will be quite a different person in twenty years.
You have a chance to decide what she's going to be.
How she's going to live her life."

He tilted her head up. Their lips were inches apart.
As it had once before, his gaze seemed to thrust with
almost physical force, compelling her eyes to meet
his head on. Something electrical charged the air
around them. When they kissed, her lips felt almost
scalded.

In the darkened bedroom, as he undressed her,

Richard could hear a key inserted in the outer lock of his suite. He paused and listened. Diana's key made almost no sound. Nor did the chain when it barred her opening the door. After a moment, he could hear the door shut and the faint sound of the key being withdrawn.

He smiled a secret grin, one of half joy, half disaster, as he buried his face between Melissa's breasts.

Chapter Forty-Six

Bellavista stood in the growing darkness. Once it had bustled with life, but now the old house was empty, bereft of its master. The trees around it seemed to have grown closer, almost touching its shingled walls as if to enfold it and bring it back to nature, to reclaim it.

The sheriff's car paused at the locked gate. Robbins honked his horn loudly for a long time before he and Deputy Rawls saw sign of life inside the old Agretti compound. Someone shined a powerful flashlight in their direction.

"Wha'chu want?" a man called. "Go 'way!"

"Fong? It's the sheriff," Rawls shouted. "Open up."

There was a pause as the darkness seemed to gather almost palpably around them. Then the ghost figure trudged toward them, a shotgun cradled in its arms. Fong appeared, blinking in the headlights of the car. "Wha'chu want, Sheriff?"

"Put down that shotgun and open this gate."

"Wha' for?"

"It's real simple, Fong," the deputy explained. "Either you do what the sheriff says or you get arrested for obstructing justice. That's thirty days in the slam with no time off for good behavior."

"Shees! Only doin' my duty," the Chinese complained. "You don' have t'take my head off. Here."

He leaned the weapon against the fence and searched through a huge ring of keys until he found one that unlocked the heavy gate. "What's up this late?" he asked, swinging the gate open.

"Just routine," Sheriff Robbins assured him. "Only I like it a whole lot better when nobody's pointing a twelve-gauge shotgun down my throat."

"Sorry about that. Now the old man's gone, we get kids looking to break in."

"That I doubt," Rawls told him. "You're too good a watchman."

The husky Chinaman appeared almost as wide as he was tall. His chest puffed out a bit and he grinned in the headlights. "You damned straight Fong's a good watchman. What can I do for you gen'mum?"

"Like I said, just routine. We have to go over the house again."

"At night?"

"Day, night, what's it to you?" the sheriff said, a who-cares tone creeping into his voice. "Open up the front door and stick with us."

The three men plodded up the path and entered by the broad veranda. In a moment the old house was ablaze with light. Robbins and Rawls paced here and there, doing things with a tape measure. The deputy made copious notes, responding affably to Fong's questions while the sheriff rudely ignored them. Although the watchman had no way of knowing this, the two officers were already setting up the ground rules for their interrogation. Each had a role to play. They were called, in police slang, Mr. Hard and Mr. Soft.

"You prepared to testify *in* court *under* oath," the sheriff growled, "that these three doors are the *only* way into Bellavista?"

"In court?" Fong quavered.

"*On* the stand, *with* your hand on the Bible, you take the oath and then you talk. You tell everything. We catch you in one lie, you're a gone goose."

"Hey, boss," Rawls suggested quietly, "Fong's okay. No need to come down hard on him."

"Remains to be seen. You notice he ain't answered me?"

"Yes!" Fong burst out. "I testify. Only three ways in or out."

"Says you," the sheriff sniffed.

They were in Carlo Agretti's den, the room in which the murder had taken place. In the absence now of a suspect charged and ready to stand trial, Robbins had ordered the room to remain untouched. The desk was covered with a cloth. He whipped it off. All three men stared down at the blackish layer of caked blood that had dried there.

"Sit!" Sheriff Robbins ordered.

"Not in that chair," Fong demurred.

"In that chair!"

"The blood . . ."

"Makes you a little sick to your stomach, huh, Fong? Sit!"

Gingerly, he lowered his stocky frame into the chair where Carlo Agretti's body had been found.

"You want to start?" the sheriff asked Rawls.

"Sure. Fong, the thing is, we're starting this whole case from scratch again. It's routine, like the sheriff says, but we got to set up a whole new roster of suspects."

"And guess who leads the list?" the sheriff demanded.

"Now, we're not saying you killed the old guy," the deputy said softly as Fong started at him in horror. "We're just saying we have to include you in the list. It's just routine police procedure. Now, tell us again how it happened. From when you heard Cole Gioberti call out. And you came running?"

"I c-came running," Fong stammered. "Yes, fast. And there is Cole, covered in blood. Him, the telephone, Mr. Agretti, everything." His eyes got wider.

"Is that how you found him?" Robbins suggested. "Or is that how Cole found you?"

"Sheriff, I swear I—"

"The old guy's will's being probated, Fong. Did you know he left you five thousand bucks?" the sheriff snapped. "I've seen a guy killed for a helluva lot less than that."

"Please, Sheriff. I didn't know he was—"

"Take it easy," Rawls told him soothingly. "Relax. Tell us the truth and you got no problems, Fong. We're on your side. We want to see you get a fair shake on this."

"And we also want the murderer," Robbins added ominously. "So be careful what you tell us, Fong. One false move and you'll never see daylight again. Once more. Tell me the ways into this house."

"Three. Front. Side door. Kitchen door."

"Baloney. Isn't there a way in through the greenhouse?"

"No."

"Through the garage?"

"No."

"Stop lying. What about the basement? You trying to tell me there isn't a separate cellar door?" Sheriff Robbins bore down. "You see? Already you're caught in a lie."

"No basement d-door," Fong stuttered. "I s-swear it."

"He's telling the truth, Sheriff," the deputy admitted. "This is a straight-arrow guy, boss. Fong don't lie."

Back and forth they whipsawed him. The desper-

ate light in his eyes shifted from despair to hope as
Mr. Hard and Mr. Soft took their turns. But, for
some reason, Robbins kept returning to the cellar
idea.

"Okay, we know there's no basement door. We
know you get to the cellar from the kitchen. But it's
fishy as hell, Fong. It makes no sense. The basement
is where the old guy kept his wine. You're telling me
somebody had to carry that stuff case by case down
those rickety stairs from the kitchen to the cellar?
And carry up the empties. It stinks, Fong."

"Look," Rawls picked up in a reasonable tone. "It
may seem fishy, but it's easy enough to check out.
Whadya say we give Fong a break, huh, boss? Let's
go down to the cellar and see for ourselves."

"Why not?" The sheriff jerked his thumb at the
watchman. "Lead the way, Fong, and no tricks."

They waited. The man seemed to have collapsed;
the bones and spine seemed to have melted from his
husky body. His eyes rolled sideways in his head.

"I said no tricks." Robbins turned to his deputy.
"This monkey faking a fit or something?"

"Fong," Rawls pleaded. "This is your chance. Take
us through the cellar and you're home free. Cooperate,
baby. That's the name of the game. You help us. We
help you."

The Chinaman moaned; it was a choking sound
that seemed to rise from his very bootheels. He struggled to sit erect in the chair. After a moment, grasping the arms of the chair, still coated with blackened,
dried blood, he hoisted his chunky frame erect and
stood, wobbling.

"You guys," he said, out of breath.

"Onward," Robbins ordered.

"Okay," Fong almost gasped, breathing hard.
"Let me get my flashlight. There's no lights in the
basement."

Weaving slightly, he staggered out of the room. "Be right back," he called.

When he seemed out of earshot, Rawls murmured in the sheriff's ear, "Think we sweated him too hard?"

"Never laid a finger on him. Words, Sid, only words."

"Still, he looks shaky as hell."

"Good. Then we're doing our job right."

They stood there for a moment, mentally reviewing the minimal information they'd gained from Fong. After a while, Rawls glanced at his watch. "How long does it take to find a flashlight?"

Sheriff Robbins' eyes flared bright with suspicion. "Damn it! Let's go!"

A quarter of an hour later they had to admit defeat. Fong was nowhere on the premises. An open gate that led to a tract of wooded land at the rear of the house seemed to indicate the escape route he'd taken.

The sheriff and his deputy returned to the house, still ablaze with lights. "We let that sucker back-door us," Robbins muttered.

"How were we to know?" Rawls picked up the phone and dialed a number.

"Nix." The sheriff slammed his hand down on the phone, cutting it off. "Before we call in any of the boys, you and me have a job to do."

"In the basement?"

"In the basement."

Sid Rawls' rather large mouth twisted into a wry smile. "Well, at least we got one thing to show for our trouble."

"Yeah?"

"Yeah. We got us a brand-new suspect."

Chapter Forty-Seven_____

"I'm sorry, Mrs. Cumson," the nurse said. "Visiting hours are long past. Besides, Dr. Edsen has placed the baby in quarantine."

Julia's eyes widened. "Dear God!"

"Don't be alarmed." The nurse looked from Julia to her son, Lance. "It's merely a precaution after the interchange procedure."

"What?" Julia gasped.

"We've managed to change the baby's blood completely." The nurse suddenly stopped, as if she'd said too much. "You'd better let Dr. Ruzza explain it."

"Ruzza? But you mentioned a Dr. . . . someone else."

"Come on," Lance growled. "She's not going to tell us anything."

"There's a phone at the nurses' station near the elevators. You can call Dr. Ruzza from there."

"Forget it," Lance rasped. He led his mother away. "They treat everybody the same in these places. Rotten."

"But, Lance, the baby . . ."

"Melissa was here all afternoon. We'll get the story from her."

Julia's glance shifted sideways as they got in the elevator. "But she hasn't come home. I mean . . ." She stopped. "Perhaps she's still here."

"I said forget it."

Lance led the way out the lobby to their parked car. "Don't you want to know what's happened to your son?"

"Stop calling him my son."

He slammed on the engine and wheeled off in a harsh squeal of rubber on pavement. Night had fallen. The car's headlights bored twin beams through the darkness as Lance steered recklessly around corners.

Julia rocked from side to side, her eyes straight ahead. Finally, she laid a hand on her son's arm. "Slow down, Lance. I mean it."

He grunted, but let up on the accelerator slightly. "You don't understand," Julia said then in a low voice. "You've never . . . I've never had the time to . . ." She stopped and took a long breath. "I'm not very sophisticated, Lance. I've never seen much of the world. After college I went right into the Falcon Crest labs. It's all I know. To me, the appearance of a thing is the truth of it. I see a grape that's infected with fungus, I know what I'm looking at. I see crystals of tartaric acid in a bottle of wine, I know what I'm seeing. I look at Melissa and I see a girl shaken by grief. A girl who loves her husband and her baby. Who's lost a father she loved. Now you tell me it's all a sham? That she isn't what she seems? That your marriage is a . . . a lie?"

"For God's sake, Mother!"

"Tell me," Julia pleaded. "Please tell me."

"You can't be so wrapped up in your work that you don't know what's going on under your nose," Lance pointed out. "It just isn't possible to be that naïve."

"I'm sorry. It is."

"This is ridiculous," he fumed. "It's as if you want me to tell you where babies come from."

"I'm sorry," she repeated with some dignity. "It's this one baby I'm asking about. Where did it come from?"

"Not from me," her son said curtly. "I have an idea who the father is, but no proof."

"Who is he?"

"That's not the point. The point is I'm *not* the father. And I'm not going to be tied down by Grandmother's threats just because she wants the Agretti vineyards welded for life to Falcon Crest."

"But we all want that," Julia burst out.

"Oh, do we?"

"We all want what's best."

"For Falcon Crest!" Lance exclaimed angrily. "But what about me?"

"You?" his mother cried out. "What about me?"

"You're home and safe," Lance told her brusquely. "But my inheritance hangs on the life of that little bastard they've hidden away in the hospital."

"Lance!"

"What else should I call him?"

He slowed down the car until it was crawling along the night roads. "Look at it from my angle, will you? Grandmother controls half of Falcon Crest. I only work for her, the same as you. If this were a normal family, instead of living in the shadow of one greedy woman, I'd have no problem. I'd inherit in my own right, no strings. But I'm not good enough for Grandmother. She only uses me to latch onto the Agretti vines. She makes Melissa's baby the linchpin in her whole crazy plot. Without the baby, I'm just another hired hand. *But it isn't my baby*!"

"Why not say it is? Why stir up trouble for yourself?"

"Because I'm me. Either I'm worth enough to inherit in my own right, or Falcon Crest can get along without me. I'm not wasting my youth in a place where my entire future depends on whether some kid lives or dies."

She patted his arm comfortingly. "I understand, Lance. It's demeaning the way my mother treats people. She can't help it. Her vision of this place takes precedence over everything. She feels she's at war, constantly, if not with Chase then with Richard Channing. If not with them then with the other vineyards. That's the way she is."

"At war? Then she's firing on her own troops."

"Yes. You're right about that." Julia grew silent for a moment. When she spoke again, her voice had grown somber and grave. "She has no idea how much we do for her. And at any moment she can turn on us. What did you say? Firing on her own troops. That's my mother. And don't think she makes empty threats."

"She shot off quite a few at me."

Julia's eyes seemed to go blank as she stared out at the night scene passing by her. "She can be so unthinking. At one stroke, she can undo what I . . ." She stopped. Lance was busy turning a sharp corner. He failed to see the stricken look on his mother's face.

"Blind, obsessed woman," Julia murmured.

"Too bad about her," Lance retorted. "I have my own life to live."

"Do you?" Julia's voice had gone strangely high, like a little girl's. "Do any of us?"

"Don't give me that, Mother."

There was a sharp intake of breath and suddenly Julia's voice had returned to its full power. "Give you?" she demanded. "I've given you everything, Lance. You'll never know how much."

Chapter Forty-Eight

"Scene 59, Exterior," Maggie typed.

She glanced over the original scene in her film script, frowned at Darryl's notes scribbled in the margin and typed a few new lines. The electric typewriter was the kind that first showed you the line you'd typed on a tiny video screen. If you didn't like it, you made changes before letting the typewriter put it on paper. Maggie sighed with exasperation. She jumped up and went to the picture window of her hotel suite.

The faint illumination of garden torches and lights reflected on her nearly naked body. Still wearing the bikini, but without the protective filmy dressing gown, she examined herself in the plate-glass reflection.

She found herself wondering why she'd been so afraid to appear in a bikini. She looked quite good, enough to rivet most men's glances around the pool and to monopolize Darryl's attention until she finally had to get rid of him after lunch in order to resume work.

He was due back soon to take her to "an important dinner." But first, Scene 59. The telephone rang.

"Honey," Chase began, "how's the screenwriting going?"

Holding the phone in one hand, Maggie found herself frantically trying to pull on the dressing gown, as if Chase could actually see her. "Slow work," she heard herself say. "How's everyone? How are you?"

"Coping. Have you got a decent place to work?"

"Not bad. But they've given me this genius typewriter that's much smarter than I am." Maggie gestured meaninglessly, as if giving up the idea of explaining herself to her husband. "What made me think I wanted to be a screenwriter?" she asked abruptly.

"Tough work?"

"Confusing." She knew he had no idea just how confusing the life was here in this little lap of luxury Darryl had provided for her. "But I'll cope, same as you."

"Good. Do you think you'll be home for the weekend?"

"Definitely."

"We have that dinner with the Pearsons on Saturday night."

"I haven't forgotten. What's the news from Jim?"

"We know how to get at the money. It's just a matter of time."

There was a long pause at both ends. Then Maggie asked, "What's the news of Melissa's baby?"

"They've brought in a Swedish miracle man. Everyone sounds very optimistic."

"They? You mean Angela?"

"Uh-uh. Richard Channing."

Another long pause ensued. "I don't understand," Maggie said at last. The affairs of Tuscany Valley seemed strangely remote to her. She even had to think for a moment to remember who Richard Channing was.

"Neither do I," her husband admitted. "And I've

picked up a rumor that he's calling his first share-holders' meeting next week."

"Surely he wouldn't be that foolish."

"My experience with the man tells me he's not only a risk-taker, but a master conspirator as well. I'm prepared for fireworks."

Neither of them spoke again for a long moment. Maggie had the sickening sensation of rapidly increasing distance, as if Chase were not only four hundred miles to the north, but getting farther with each second. "Chase?"

"Yes?"

"Uh . . . you'll be careful, won't you?"

"Need you ask? Anyway, you'll be back by then and I can get your thoughts on the subject. You're not such a bad conspirator yourself."

Maggie almost flinched. A feeling of guilt seemed to flood through her. But how could Chase know? And what was there to know, anyway? Just an afternoon by the pool. "Right," she said at last. "Give my love to Cole and Vickie."

"Will do. Good night, darling."

Maggie glanced at her watch: 9 P.M. But Chase would be asleep in an hour or less. While she . . .

"Good night, darling," she echoed. "Thanks for calling."

As she hung up, there was a knock at her door. She ran to open it. Darryl stood there in what amounted to formal dinner attire, a white tuxedo and black bow tie, a pale gray shirt with ruffles and gold studs. His eyes lighted up as he saw her still in her bikini.

"Still dressed to kill," he said, stepping inside and, in the most natural way in the world, taking her in his arms.

He kissed her lips, lightly but firmly. It still seemed, to Maggie, a most natural thing to do.

*Chapter Forty-Nine*_____

Somewhere in San Francisco a bell tolled nine times.
Melissa gave a soft moan of pleasure as she came
awake in Richard Channing's bed. She reached for
his body, but found herself alone. Sitting up, she
stared through the darkened bedroom toward a light
burning in the living room. She could hear him
talking, but no one answered. She got to her feet
and tiptoed to the doorway, remaining out of sight.

"That's really very provincial of you," Richard was
saying into the telephone. "Quite out of line, too."
He listened for a moment. "Just confine yourself to
your assigned duties and we'll both get along. Do
you understand?"

Melissa's smile in the half-darkness was a peculiar
mixture of pleasure and malice. She stepped into
her panties and quickly pulled her dress down over
her head. A moment later, putting on her shoes, she
went to the mirror and with her fingers pulled her
great dark curls into some semblance of order. Then,
heels cracking loudly, she walked into the living room.

Richard looked up from the telephone. "That's
fine," he was saying, "Make sure it does. Right.
I have to hang up now. Good night." He replaced
the phone.

"Poor Diana," Melissa said with that same sly smile.

Richard laughed softly. "You look superb. Ready for dinner?"

Melissa shook her head. "We married folk have our obligations. Can you get me a cab back to the Valley?"

"I can drive you there much more quickly."

"And much more disastrously. Call a cab."

Dinner at Falcon Crest had been more than usually strained. Only Angela and Julia had eaten the appetizer. Lance had made a pretense of pushing it around on his plate, but Julia knew the weight of his rage was too great for him to continue playacting through the entire meal.

"That Number Seven Vat," she told him as Chao-Li cleared for the main course, "the foreman said it might be building up too much pressure. Can you run over and check it?"

Lance was on his feet before she finished speaking. "Won't take a minute. Don't wait for me." He was gone before his grandmother could say her first word.

"Well!" she managed to gasp.

"The safety valve may be gummed shut," Julia said, spinning out her fiction about Number Seven Vat.

"I've never seen Lance behave quite that rudely," Angie continued as if her daughter hadn't spoken. "But I suppose he's got justification. *Where* is that tramp of his?"

"Mother, Melissa is no tramp."

"Nine o'clock and she's not home yet? And what's all this about some Swedish doctor?"

"I phoned Dr. Ruzza. The new man is an expert of neonatal illnesses. Dr. Karl Edsen. He's supervised a complete blood transfusion for Joseph. They're trying a new hormone therapy program."

"And who called in Dr. Edsen?"

"Melissa. So you see, she *does* take her responsibilities seriously."

"Do you take me for a fool, Julia?" Angie's sharp eyes swung like a pair of sabers to slash at her daughter's face. "We are talking about Melissa Agretti, a grape farmer's daughter. She snaps her fingers and across the world in Sweden some renowned expert answers her bidding like a bellhop?"

Julia spread out her long, powerful hands on the tablecloth. "I wouldn't know about that, Mother. Dr. Ruzza seemed to feel that perhaps Richard Channing had been helpful in this matter."

"More like it." Angela Channing nodded twice, grimly. Then: "Have you spoken to Lance about this paternity-test idea of his?"

"I have. He's promised to drop it."

"Don't lie to me, Julia. To begin with," her mother told her in cold, unemotional tones, "you're very bad at it. And, secondly, what you say makes no sense. The boy is in a self-destructive phase. He gets that way now and then. He tries to bring his whole world down around his shoulders, like Samson."

"Like who?"

"Never mind. Let me tell you about your son, Julia. He responds to only one thing—pressure. You can't reason with him. You can only coerce him. If he whines about not being given more responsibility around here, that's the reason."

"And what," Julia darted back breathlessly, "is the reason you don't delegate more responsibility to me?"

Her mother's eyes widened alarmingly. "Do you really want to know?"

"I asked, didn't I?"

"You have no imagination, Julia. No scope. You're

a drudge. Perhaps a talented one, at least in the laboratory. But to give you more responsibility than that would be disastrous."

"Thanks."

"You asked."

"Then let me tell you about yourself, Mother."

"I don't recall asking for advice."

"But you're getting it," Julia retorted, trying to hold down the fury she felt building inside her. "You have delusions of grandeur, Mother. You blunder along, fighting your private wars, making one mistake after another. The rest of us have to tidy up after your mess. Without us, you'd be a pathetic old woman and Falcon Crest would have fallen apart at the seams."

For a long moment, Angie's face was expressionless. Then she smiled sourly. "Congratulations, Julia. You still don't make any sense. But I'm glad to see that you have at least a spark of gumption. Tidy up after my mess? I wonder what on earth you could mean by that?"

"You wouldn't understand."

"Have you been up to something I don't know about?" Angie persisted. "Because eventually, you know, I'll find you out."

They both heard the sound of a car outside. Angela went to the window. "A cab. It's Melissa, at last. I'm going to give that young wom—" She stopped herself. "Look at her. For a mother whose baby is struggling for life, she certainly carries herself with a jaunty air. I wonder."

Melissa's dark eyes flashed almost wildly as she entered the dining room. "Dinner over?"

"Didn't Mr. Channing give you dinner?" Angela asked in a fake tone of concern. "No gentleman, he."

"I was with Dr. Edsen," Melissa lied fluently. "He really has given me new hope for Joseph."

Angela Channing surveyed her granddaughter-in-law from head to toe. Her lips crisped into a wry line of amusement. "I'll have Chao-Li set a place for you," she said then.

"Not hungry. I'm making an early night of it." Melissa left the room. They could hear her heels as she mounted the curved stairway to the second floor.

"Lance will be so pleased," Angie murmured as she sat down in her chair and rang the bell for the main course to be served. "Melissa's such a good mother."

"Don't talk nonsense." Julia watched the mood change closely, alert to every facet of her mother's strange personality.

"And this Dr. Edsen really is quite a miracle worker," Angela Channing went on unperturbed. "It's fascinating. Somehow, in conference with him, Melissa has neglected to put her stockings on."

Chapter Fifty

Dee Merriam glanced around the county meeting room. Most members of the board seemed to be there, nearly a dozen men and women in all, with Chase Gioberti sitting in the supervisor's seat at the head of the long table. Dee caught his eye and switched on a tape recorder.

"Right," Chase began. "I call to order this meeting of the County Board of Tuscany Valley on the fourteenth of September at two-thirty P.M. The agenda is as follows—minutes of the last meeting, treasurer's report, discussion of applications and new business. Any additions to the agenda?" He waited. "There being none, let's hear from the secretary."

Dee read the last meeting's minutes. The treasurer reported the current balance. Routine applications for water rights and variances were heard, discussed and voted on in order.

"This last application is a bit out of the ordinary," Dee Merriam announced. She then proceeded to read out loud Richard Channing's request for a variance on five acres of parkland as a memorial to Douglas Channing.

When she finished no one spoke. Chase stirred in his chair. "Any comments?"

"Why now?" Phil Mosconi, a vintner, asked. "Douglas has been dead—what is it?—twenty years? More. Why a memorial now?"

"That's easy, Phil," said Mrs. Foran, who owned the agricultural equipment store. "Richard Channing's back and he's got the money. So he's making up for lost time." She glanced around the table, a small, plump woman in her late fifties. "I mean, it's not as if Douglas didn't deserve a memorial."

"No question of that."

"Right."

"It's fine with me."

Chase waited until silence settled over the group. "He's asking to put in a sort of park, a statue or something like that, some benches and shrubbery. The present status of the land wouldn't be altered much."

He sensed that the board was hoping to take its lead from him, since they all knew no love was lost between Chase and his Aunt Angela, Douglas Channing's widow. Chase decided to take the bull by the horns.

"Dee sent a routine notification to Mrs. Channing," he announced. "I have her response." He held out a letter. "She writes, 'I have no objection to the proposed memorial.' Signed, Mrs. Douglas Channing."

"That's all?" someone asked.

"Short and sweet." Chase glanced around him again. "Do I hear a motion to allow a variance?"

"So move," Mrs. Foran said.

"Second," Peter Vermilyea added.

"Moved and seconded," Chase echoed. "All in favor?" He listened to a chorus of "ayes." He glanced up from Angela's brief note. "All those opposed?" Silence. "Variance is granted. There's a Miss Hunter waiting outside. She's empowered to negotiate price. What is the pleasure of the board?"

"You handle it," Phil Mosconi suggested. "We don't need to get in on the haggling. But get a good price, Chase. He can afford it."

"Give me a ball-park figure."

"Last week," Bob Duff said in his wheezy voice, "I had to pay damned near five grand an acre for that orphan lot on my west line. Is that the going rate or was I had?"

"You're suggesting we ask twenty-five thousand?" Chase asked him.

"You handle it," Mosconi repeated. "If you get twenty-five grand, I won't cry. We need double that to fix up the playground and the ball park."

"Right," Chase said. "Dee, let's move the agenda."

Nobody in Tuscany Valley would think of using any doctor but Ruzza, or the new man, Benjamin, although a great many of the vineyard hands traveled into the next county to use a Dr. Aguilar, who spoke Spanish. So it was unusual that Lance had driven all the way to a clinic in San Francisco for his paternity test.

Lori Stevens had suggested this small, out-of-the-way storefront in the area behind Ashbery Avenue. "They're reliable," she had told Lance, "and especially competent in private matters like abortions and herpes and such."

"Sex doctors?" Lance cracked.

"Aftermath-of-sex doctors," she corrected him.

"But they know their business?"

"Absolutely."

"And a written statement from them would carry weight?"

"Certainly."

The storefront looked vaguely dingy. It had once been a supermarket. Now its interior was cut up into cubicles, painted stark white and brilliantly illumi-

nated by blinding fluorescent bulbs. Lance watched
the nurse rub his arm with an alcohol swab and
remove what seemed like a great deal of blood from
his vein.

"Why so much?"

"Technical reasons," she said in a cool voice.

"Come on. It's my blood."

"You guys who want to get out of supporting a
baby," she said, unloading a certain amount of her
own displeasure, "have no business complaining that
we need a lot of your blood."

"Hooh!"

"Basically, we have to test a lot of different factors,"
she went on. "Type, Rh, that sort of thing. Even
then, you know, you still might not get a clear result."

"You mean I'm paying in blood for nothing?"

"I mean the baby's blood and yours might match
or might not, or might show a partial match. This is
the sort of thing you should have thought about
before you and your girlfriend—"

"You're absolutely right," Lance told her with faked
solemnity. "This is a real lesson to me. How soon will
I know?"

"Next week."

"No good."

"In a hurry, are we?" She gave him a disapproving
look as she emptied the hypodermic syringe into
four test tubes and corked each with a puff of cotton.
"You can have the results tomorrow for an extra
twenty bucks."

"Sold."

"Sold?" Diana Hunter asked Chase.

He watched her without speaking. Something about
her reminded him of his own wife, Maggie, her air
of competence, her dark blond beauty. He found
himself missing his wife, and this disturbing young

woman who showed too much of her legs did nothing to ease his mind.

"It looks that way." Chase glanced over at Dee Merriam. "We can draw up the contracts by the end of the week, can't we, Dee?"

"Or certainly by next Monday."

"But they're standard contracts," Diana pointed out. "Surely—"

"This has waited a long time," Chase reminded her. "A little more delay can't hurt."

"I was going to suggest," Diana went on, crossing her legs, "that one of our lawyers could draw the contracts tonight and we could sign them tomorrow. In fact," she added, opening her handbag, "I'm empowered to give you the check right now."

"What's the rush?" Chase asked.

She gave him a wan smile. "You don't know my employer, Mr. Gioberti. When he wants something, he wants it yesterday."

"Isn't that charming?" Chase responded in a lazy drawl. "The rest of us usually wait our turn. It must be lovely getting such prompt service. But it has a drawback."

"Yes?"

"It puts people's backs up." Chase grinned at her. "It kind of gives people the idea that a little normal delay would do Mr. Channing a world of good."

"So you're going to delay the contracts?"

Chase glanced at Dee. "The secretary has a deskful of work waiting for her. That's always the case after a board meeting."

He paused, sensing that this attractive young woman was anxious to say something more, but at the same time struggling not to say it. He found himself fascinated by her apparent conflicting emotions—the urge to use Channing's clout and the knowledge that Chase Gioberti was the wrong man to use it on.

"You said?" he prompted.

"I? I said nothing."

Chase rubbed his beard slowly, thoughtfully. "Tell Mr. Channing he's been such a gentleman in the past. With such a gentlemanly newspaper that prints such factual stories about people. Tell him in honor of all that I'm letting his lawyers do Dee Merriam's work. Got it?"

The dazzling smile on Diana Hunter's face almost knocked him off balance. It seemed to be her first real, unforced, human gesture of the whole interview. "He'll appreciate that message," Diana told him.

"Will he now?"

"Oh, my, yes." Her smile widened to a mischievous grin.

Chapter Fifty-One _____

Sheriff Robbins stood in front of the telex machine and watched the punched tape reel through, printing out for the third time that week an all-points bulletin that went to every law-enforcement office within a two-hundred-mile radius.

"APB," the machine ticked off. "APPREHEND AND RETURN TO TUSCANY VALLEY SHERIFF'S OFFICE THOMAS JOSHUA FONG, ALIAS TOM FONG, ASIATIC, FIVE-FIVE, 180 LBS, BROWN EYES, POWERFUL BUILD, LAST SEEN WEARING LUMBERJACK SHIRT, DUNGAREES. WANTED FOR QUESTIONING IN CONNECTION WITH MURDER CASE. MAY BE ARMED. ROBBINS, SHERIFF."

He switched off the machine and returned to his office, where Rawls and another deputy were putting the finishing touches to an architect's sketch of the ground and cellar floors of Bellavista.

"Starts here, behind the wine racks," Rawls was saying. "Damndest thing. You could look at it a dozen times and still not see the opening."

"But it was wide enough for a guy with Fong's build," the other deputy replied.

"Tight squeeze, if you ask me."

"Even tighter," Robbins put in, "when you remember it leads into a tunnel that hasn't been used in

God knows how long. I mean, it's out of a horror movie, all full of roots and moss and toadstools."

"And tracks?" the other deputy wanted to know.

"I've got Killian working on that," the sheriff said. "He's a full-blooded Kwakiutl Indian from up Oregon way. If anybody can pick up a track, he can."

"And it ends here?" the other deputy asked, touching a place on the drawing with the eraser tip of his pencil.

"That's another weird thing," Rawls told him. "It's an old pump house. I mean old. It's still got a donkey engine in there from the turn of the century. Works on naphtha. Pumps up water from a well. But Agretti's irrigation system is modern stuff, electric-powered from a place a mile away. In other words, nobody's gone near that old pump house in a long time."

"Somebody did," Sheriff Robbins said then.

"That night," Sid Rawls agreed. "And it looks suspiciously like that somebody was guided in by Fong."

"Has to be," his boss assured him. "The way he panicked when I started bearing down hard on that cellar? Remember? He nearly threw a fit."

"And lit out for the tall timber," Rawls reminisced.

"Or maybe he only panicked because he'd forgot to tell you about the tunnel," the other deputy suggested.

"There's panic and then there's panic," Robbins retorted. "This guy had guilty written all over him. If it was only an oversight, he'd have coughed up the truth then and there. Instead he took to his heels."

All three men stared for a long time at the sketch. "Killian's good," Rawls said at length, "but that tunnel isn't going to show much. My hunch is, Indian or no Indian, Killian will come up blank."

"The tunnel might not tell us much . . ." his boss
agreed.

"But?"

"But Fong will."

Chapter Fifty-Two_____

Richard Channing kissed Melissa's ear in the half-darkness of his bedroom. Then, perversely, he nipped at her earlobe and she yelped. "Nasty," she said, rolling over on top of him. "Now you get punished."

Richard laughed as they tussled in the bedclothes. When his alarm went off at nine o'clock in the evening, neither of them heard it over the intensity of their lovemaking. Only later, as she dressed, did Melissa seem to come back to earth again.

"I know you don't like to hear it," she told Richard as he sat in the living room watching her dress. "But I will always be grateful to you, Richard. When I went to the hospital this afternoon, they let me hold him. He's gained a whole pound. His color is so much better. He's active, squirming. I'll never forget what you did."

"You amaze me, my dear."

"With my motherly instincts? Or in bed?"

"Both," he said admiringly. He sipped a glass of mineral water. "You're the new breed, aren't you? You're a responsible mother and you're also a wild, extravagant lover. The way you can be both is what amazes me."

"It's possible only if you call me a cab this instant."

302 · Patrick Mann

He nodded and made the call. "Getting any flak at home?"

"Not from Lance."

"Well, you've got an arrangement there, haven't you?"

"But of course."

"Then it won't worry you to learn that he's gotten himself a paternity test? One of my reporters has an informant in a clinic over on Ashbery."

"Lance is an idiot," Melissa said coolly. "The only thing he can do with a paternity test is cut himself out of his inheritance."

"I would have thought so, too. That doesn't bother you?"

"Lance can do whatever he wants with his life. The Agretti vineyards are mine. Bellavista is mine. And I'm yours."

Richard sipped his drink slowly, watching her over the rim of his glass. She had a lithe, attractive body that was almost more exciting clothed than nude. But he was beginning to tire of these evening sessions. And it was only a matter of time before Diana would be in full revolt, no matter how strong Cartel discipline might be. Besides, he had his shareholders' meeting to mastermind. It would take all his attention.

"Darling," he said then. "You know how miserable I am when we can't be together. But I'm going to be closeted all evening tomorrow with my broker."

"You can't see him during the day?"

"Not on this matter. It's top secret."

"Then the evening after."

"Perfect," Richard agreed. His telephone rang. "Your cab," he said. He escorted her to the door and they kissed for a long moment, clinging together fiercely. "I hate not seeing you tomorrow," he breathed in her ear. "But it makes the night after that much more exciting."

He waited until he heard her footsteps pause at the elevator door down the hotel corridor. When it had opened and closed, he peeked out into the hall and saw that she was truly gone. After a moment he went to the phone and called the front desk. "My guest has gotten her cab?"

"Just took off, Mr. Channing."

Smiling, Richard pushed down the telephone button, got a new dial tone and rang Diana's suite. "Ready," he said when she answered the call.

A moment later, dressed in a bright flame-orange at-home sheath, Diana let herself into Richard's suite. In her wake came a tall, spare man with a nervous, hound-dog look. "Joe!" Richard exclaimed. "I hope Diana's been entertaining you properly."

The thin man worked his busy eyebrows up and down with an exaggerated leer. "Not in the manner to which I'd like to become accustomed." He sank into one of the glove-leather sofas and shook his head as Richard offered a drink. "Diana's been too liberal with me already. If we're going to make sense, I'll pass up any more booze."

Adjusting her slit skirt so that she could sit down, Diana took her place beside Richard. She picked up his glass of mineral water. "Riotous evening, eh, Richard?"

He frowned at her. "Joe, this new stock issue. If all you're going to tell me is how difficult it'll be, I don't need you as my broker."

Diana sipped the water. "On the other hand, you don't need a broker who's a yes-man."

"Thank you." Richard's voice sounded sarcastic. "As far as I can tell from the by-laws of the *Globe* corporation, there is nothing that specifically stops the management from issuing new shares."

"Nothing at all. The hitch comes from the SEC," his broker told him. "You can announce the new

issue but, as an insider, you are barred from purchas-
ing shares before the rest of the stock-buying public
gets a chance."

Richard's frown deepened. "But that's—"

"I know. That's the whole idea. Except that you're
an insider. So your hands are tied."

"Damn!"

"It's a delicate situation," the broker went on. "We
both know a dozen ways you can buy those shares
through a dummy front or street name. But that
works only when nobody's watching you closely. The
moment you announce the new issue your stepmother
and the whole Gioberti clan will be examining everything with a microscope."

"She's not my stepmother," Richard said sharply.

"Sorry." The broker turned his hands palms up.
"In other words, if Angela Channing finds out that
the ZYX Corporation or some other front group has
bought out the new issue before she had a chance at
it, she's going to yell and scream until the SEC pulls
out its great big can opener and gets to the bottom
of it."

Richard nodded slowly. "What about a Euro issue?
Denominated in dollars but sold only in London and
Zurich and Milan?"

"That gives you a bit of lead time. Say twenty-four
hours."

"More than that," Richard contradicted him. "It
gives me immunity from the SEC."

"Not entirely."

"Enough. And in twenty-four hours, half a dozen
of my dummies can snap up the entire issue. It'd
take the SEC years to unravel. But what I have to do
is going to take days, not years. You follow me?"

"Not at all. But it isn't important," his broker said.
"As a Euro issue, the new stock would give you
enough time to play whatever game you have in

mind." He held up his hand like a traffic cop. "No, don't tell me what game it is. I have to have deniability."

He gathered his skinny legs under him and got to his feet. "On that basis, Richard, I can get started tomorrow morning. We could have this in the bag within days."

"Then go for it, Joe."

Richard stood up and ushered him to the door of the suite. "You see how simple life is when you have a whole world of stock markets out there to play with?"

"Richard," his broker said, "I hope you're right."

After he left, Diana went to the private bar and made tinkling noises with ice cubes. "How about something stronger than soda water?"

"Just some scotch on the rocks. A splash."

"The intoxicating Melissa is still coursing through your veins?"

"Cut it out. You're being bush-league."

"To kid the boss?" Diana asked innocently.

"To call Melissa intoxicating." His smile turned evil. "All she can talk about is the miracle of her kid getting better. Can you imagine pillow talk like that?"

Diana sat down beside him, handed Richard his drink and began to stroke his forehead. "Poor Richard. Poor sex object."

"Take off the sex object's shoes, will you?"

"Just the shoes?"

"Is this some sort of test of my recuperative powers?"

"Now . . . there's an idea."

Chapter Fifty-Three_____

The only way she had gotten through the week, Maggie realized now as she finished the last of her script revisions, was to enforce a kind of sexual truce with Darryl.

The odds against it working had been poor. There was the general atmosphere of her lush hotel, with its many implicit invitations to relax and enjoy life. There was the difficulty of the writing itself, which tested her willpower a hundred times a day. And, finally, there was Darryl.

Maggie had grown oddly fond of him. Was that the right word? she wondered as she stared down at her typewriter.

Fond? Not strong enough. Amused with. Dependent upon. Attracted to. Yes, there had always been an attraction and during a week of truce it had only grown stronger.

She tried to clear her head. Relationships had been easy for Maggie because they were of a "standard" kind. She loved her husband, her son and her daughter in a straightforward, normal way. Whatever that meant, she thought now. What is "normal" love? What is the nature of the emotional bonds within a family? And when did the special link with her hus-

band drop back into the general melting pot of the
family itself?

Wasn't that the problem? she asked herself. Hadn't
her love for Chase—which had come first—now become only part of family affection? And wasn't that
what made Darryl's attraction so dangerous?

As she straightened up the typed pages of copy
paper and put them in a folder, Maggie tried to
remember back to the days when she had been a
girl, seeing various men, enjoying brief, innocent
love affairs until she had met Chase.

Perhaps the root of the trouble was that she'd
been a "good" girl? She'd married quite young and
quite without any experience in the sometimes tricky
and always confusing realms of love. Was that why
Darryl had such an effect on her?

It wasn't fair, Maggie reflected now. Her generation had arrived at maturity just as the greatly publi-
cized American sexual revolution had begun. Whatever it actually meant between men and women, this
revolution had arrived five minutes too late for girls
brought up by rather strict parents like Maggie's.
Women the age of Melissa had reaped all the benefits of the new emotional freedom. And the drawbacks too, Maggie reminded herself. Soon it would be
Vickie's turn.

The thought of her own daughter's initiation into
sexual love gave Maggie much more of a jolt than she
realized. She could handle her own life and the
increasingly intricate dance she and Darryl were going
through. But would she be able to handle Vickie's
initiation?

It suddenly struck Maggie that she had no idea of
Vickie's private life. She had made the usual assump-
tions, based on observation of her daughter. Athletic.
Outdoorsy. One or two open friendships with boys
she'd gone to school with. But had Vickie . . . ?

It was impossible. Maggie rose from her desk and
picked up the telephone. She dialed the hotel desk.
"Can you have someone pick up a manuscript for
photocopying, please?"

As she did, she caught sight of herself in one of
the huge wall mirrors with which the living room of
her suite was decorated. The bikini she wore today
was a slightly more modest one she'd bought for
herself at one of the Wilshire Boulevard stores Darryl had taken her to. It still concealed very little, but
it gave Maggie the illusion, at poolside or in her
suite's private garden, that she was not entirely on
display.

She grinned at her own confusion. In some peculiar way the bikini had become a symbol for her of
this whole insane week. It spelled Hollywood, glamour,
the strongly sexual atmosphere of the hotel, the exhi-
bitionist nature of the film business and, more subtly,
her own feelings about her body and Darryl.

She sighed. Darryl was the core of her problem,
always had been. He represented a challenge to
Maggie's own image of herself. She supposed, staring at her body in the mirror, that writers rarely
considered the impression they made on others except through their writing. The words stood for the
person. But in her bikini Maggie was made flesh.
Too much so.

What would happen now, she knew, was that the
truce would come to an end . . . tonight. And tomorrow she would be on the morning flight to Tuscany
Valley Airport. Tonight would be Darryl's big moment.

He'd already laid on promises of an amazing dinner at a new and highly popular beach restaurant,
followed by dancing at a new and highly popular
disco down in the old part of Los Angeles, followed
by . . .

Followed by a good-night kiss and a firmly closed

door, Maggie told herself. She might not know the depth of her feelings for Darryl, but she knew how she would feel the morning after she betrayed Chase with another man. That feeling she would avoid at any cost.

She nodded firmly at her reflection in the mirror. Her intentions were crystal clear and absolutely firm.

Chapter Fifty-Four _____

Chase listened while the hotel switchboard kept ringing Maggie's suite. It was nine-thirty in the evening.
He would go to bed soon. He knew Maggie should
do the same, since she had an early-morning flight
to make. But she wasn't in her room. Unhappily,
Chase hung up.

He stared at the telefaxed papers he'd spread over
the kitchen table. They had arrived over Jim Pearson's
bank's receiver that afternoon, sent by Jacqueline
from Zurich in a scrambler code that made it impossible for anyone else to read the documents.

And what documents they were. Somehow, his
mother had successfully pierced the famed Swiss banking secrecy to obtain—who knew at what cost?
—specific details of deposits and withdrawals over
the past months in Account Bravo Tango Two-Four.

Jim Pearson had done the rest of the work, linking
specific dates to other, less secret events. The day
after someone had invaded Chase's Falcon Crest account and wiped out his Treasury Bond holdings, the
precise amount of dollars represented by that theft
had been deposited in Bravo Tango Two-Four.

Within another twenty-four hours of that deposit,
the same amount had been removed from the Swiss

account by a check made payable to a brokerage
house in Manhattan, which turned around and bought
several thousand shares of *Globe* Corporation common stock. In the name of . . . ? Naturally, in the
name of Brave Tango Two-Four.

Correspondences between the looting of Chase's
funds and the buying of *Globe* shares explained why
the money had been stolen. But the identity of the
thief, like that of the buyer of shares, could never be
determined in this factual, painstaking way. It had to
be forced.

That was why Chase needed to talk to Maggie. He
was now in the realm of human relations. He—with
Jim by his side—would have to call a showdown
meeting with Angela Channing and her cat's-paw,
Lance. They would have to flourish the telefaxed
documents, without actually showing them to the
guilty parties, and indicate dire consequences. They
would have, in other words, to come down so hard
on Angela that she would return the money at once.

Maggie understood Angela Channing far better
than Chase did. The internecine warfare among the
Gioberti clan affected Maggie only as a concerned
bystander. The full emotional charge of family ha-
treds and jealousies hadn't impaired her judgment.
Chase knew it had hurt his. With the proof of Angela's
treachery lying on the table before him, he could
barely control himself. A red, blinding rage seemed
to drop down over him like the scarlet rag shown to
a bull, goading him into battle.

Dear God, he thought, you lead a straight, quiet
life, you try to do the honest, human thing. But it
isn't enough. There is always someone ready to knife
you in the back, trip you up and leave you dying in
some lonely alley. And that someone is *always* Angela
Channing.

Now, when he needed Maggie most, she was out

of touch. Chase had no idea where she might be, but in the more rational part of his brain he was sure she had to be out of her room for a good reason. Yet that rational part was being swamped by crimson waves of fury at Angela. He could hardly think straight about any of this. One moment he mentally accused Maggie of the vilest kind of betrayal. The next he knew he was wrong to doubt her.

He tried to calm himself. She would be back here with him tomorrow. She would be full of her adventure in Hollywood, but she would have to put it to one side while she helped him plan his all-or-nothing bluff of a woman he had tried not to hate, but who constantly renewed the loathing he felt deep down inside his soul.

He got up from the kitchen table and took a turn around the room, putting a stray cup in the sink, locking the rear door, busying himself with routine nothingness. The telephone rang.

He leaped for it. It had to be Maggie. She had sensed his need for her by that wonderful telepathic rapport she had with him. "Hello?"

"Chase," Julia Cumson said. "Sorry to bother you this late."

"Oh, Julia."

"Mother was wondering if you could come over for an early breakfast tomorrow morning?"

Chase's eyes seemed to bug out with rage. Curse the woman! What in the name of God did she want with him now? He was alone. She sensed his weakness without Maggie. "Breakfast?" He tried to sound calm.

Julia's voice took on the same false note of calm. "It's this meeting Richard's called."

"Richard?"

"Richard Channing, my half brother."

A red flare seemed to go off behind Chase's eyes.

Would they never stop persecuting him? "I'm well aware of his identity," he managed to get out. "What meeting has he called?"

"You haven't gotten your letter then? Ours arrived this afternoon. It's the shareholders' meeting we've all been expecting. And it's for Monday noon."

Leave me alone, Chase's mind screamed. He could hear it in his ears, a hoarse howl of anguish. Leave me alone, you vultures, you jackals, you feeders on rotting flesh.

He found himself squeezing the telephone so hard his fingers ached. Slowly, he eased the pressure. He tried a long, steadying breath. It didn't do the job. "Get to the point," he snapped. "What have Angela and I to discuss?"

"Everything."

"Then let *her* call me. Don't be her cat's-paw, Julia. The woman lives by getting others to do her dirty work." He slammed down the phone and instantly felt better.

His breath surged in and out of his lungs like an overworked bellows, but he felt better. He kept telling himself he felt better.

Then he caught sight of the telefaxed documents on the kitchen table and everything he had to do— alone! alone!—flooded over him in one enveloping wave that seemed to lift him up in an angry surf and crash him down on some hostile, alien beach.

Maggie, he thought. *Why aren't you here?*

Chapter Fifty-Five

"It's been a wonderful evening, Maggie." Darryl's enthusiasm seemed as fresh at midnight as it had all evening. Maggie unlocked the door of her suite and swung it open.

"It's been a fascinating week," she said then. "Thank you."

"It's I who has to thank you."

For some reason they found themselves inside the suite now. As Maggie closed the door she watched Darryl go directly to the bar and make two drinks. She felt puzzled. She had intended the evening and the week to have ended outside the door. Somehow the moment had passed for such a farewell scene. It would now have to be staged in the privacy of her suite.

"Hey!" Darryl called across the room. "What kind of look is that?"

"A confused one."

She sat down on the sofa and took her drink from him. They touched glasses and sipped whiskey on ice. "Puzzled," Maggie continued, "because I don't seem to be in my right mind."

"That disco music will do it every time."

"Siren's music."

"What?"

Maggie shook her head. "You remember the sirens in the old Greek myths? They used to lounge around strumming their lyres and singing their siren's song. They lured sailors onto the rocks. Terrible fate." She stared into her drink. "I'm not making much sense."

He sat down beside her, touching her. "Maggie," he said gravely, "I'm not luring you onto any rocks. That song you hear isn't coming from me."

"It's inside my own head," she admitted. "You don't have to tell me. I've been hearing it for days."

He put down his drink and gently kissed her. Then he took away her drink and put his arms around her. They kissed again, longer. Maggie could feel his lips opening against hers. The feelings inside her began to swirl slowly, feelings she hadn't had in years, stirrings she could barely remember. Her skin began to tingle where it touched him. She could feel every part of her begin to tense as she became aroused. She broke away from the embrace.

"Listen," she said. "I mean, I did say I wasn't making much sense."

"Sense?" he repeated. "The only sense is what we feel. The sense." He kissed her again, more roughly.

It was like taking a step closer to a great fire. All of her seemed ready to burst into flame. Her blood as it coursed through her veins felt on fire already, a tangle of ignited fuses. Her arms went around him. Her mouth opened. The telephone rang.

She jumped out of Darryl's arms, got to her feet. Both of them stared at the telephone as it kept ringing.

"Don't answer," he said at last.

"I have to. It's Chase. Nobody else would be c—" The words stuck in her throat. Ring. Ring. Ring.

"Don't panic," Darryl said. "You can always call

him. You're going to see him tomorrow. Stay calm
and don't answer."

Ring. Ring. "Something may be wrong back . . ."
Again her throat closed shut. She didn't want to
answer. That was the truth of it. She reached for the
telephone.

"Please." Darryl's arms went around her thighs. As
he embraced her he stared up into her face. "This is
something very important for the two of us," he
begged. "Please don't let it be wrecked."

The ringing stopped. Helplessly, Maggie stared
down into the adoring face of the man who so obviously worshiped her that he had put off this night all
week, in the hope that the two of them . . .

"Darryl," she said then. "We're all right now. It's
stopped ringing."

His hands moved up her flanks. The sensation of
heat flowed upward through her body in great rip-
pling waves that almost shook her with their intensity.
Below her his face seemed to glow with the same
frantic flame.

"Stay calm?" she asked then. "Is that what you told
me to do?"

She reached for the small white patent handbag
she had been carrying during the evening. "Finish
your drink," she said, breaking out of his embrace
and taking a step toward the bedroom. She realized
she was unsteady on her feet. "Finish your drink.
Give me a few minutes."

She walked toward the bedroom door. As she closed
it behind her, she glanced back at him. Eyes shining,
he sat on the very edge of the sofa and seemed to
want to devour her with his glance.

Inside the bedroom she stared despairingly about
her. She had packed her small bag early in the
evening. Now she picked it up and headed out the
side door that led from the bedroom to the corridor.

Downstairs, under the porte cochere of the hotel, the night man summoned a cab for her. She waited until the cab had moved out of the hotel driveway before she told the driver:

"Take me to the nearest rent-a-car station that's open."

"This time of night? It'd be at the airport, lady."

"See how fast we can make it. I have a very long drive ahead of me." She burst into tears.

Chapter Fifty-Six_____

Cole kicked the Honda cycle into life, revved it a few times and took off along the road that led north into the less-cultivated parts of the valley. The cool air at dawn blew against his face. The sun had not yet appeared on the eastern horizon. He was alone and moving. Nothing else mattered.

Since he'd dropped out of the Agretti murder case as a charged suspect, Cole had had time to think. These early-morning bike rides had helped him clear his head of what he felt was a lot of accumulated trash. In this period, when his family was being careful not to put any burdens on him, he felt he had put the time to good use.

He began to see himself as others—mostly women— saw him. Kate Demery's view of him, for instance, he had at first found impossible to understand. Now he thought he did. Melissa's feelings about him remained a mystery. But that was her fault, not his.

The cycle ate up mileage, sending a tall plume of dust into the clear air as it traversed back roads. In the distance, Cole caught sight of an immense eighteen-wheel semi jackknifed around a corner where two dirt roads intersected. He let up on the gas and

coasted silently forward, braking very slightly. This
maneuver allowed him to approach undetected.

The great truck was trying to negotiate a tight
corner where several vineyard holdings came together,
leaving a small green triangle of land that belonged,
Cole seemed to remember, to the county.

He pulled over to the side of the road, legs still
straddling the Honda, and watched from a distance
as the driver finally made his turn and rolled the semi
up onto the weed-choked triangle. Immediately, a
crew of six men jumped out of the rear of the trailer
and began unloading crates.

As two of them pried open the wooden containers
with claw hammers, the other four quickly set up a
variety of objects. Cole couldn't be sure but he counted
several park benches, public wastebaskets and a deco-
rative picket fence laid out in sections. One man with
a motorized auger began digging postholes, the small
gasoline motor making a machinegunlike sound in
the clear dawn air. Another dragged in posts and
hastily tacked up the sections of redwood fencing.

Meanwhile, with the aid of an overhead gantry
and winch, the rest of the crew got busy unloading
some strange objects. At this distance, Cole found it
hard to identify everything, but they seemed to be
prefab panels for a kind of structure that might,
when bolted together, resemble a warehouse without
windows, but with translucent panels of corrugated
plastic that let in light.

Finally, packed deep within the bowels of the semi,
three immense white objects were slowly winched
into view. Cole recognized them instantly as fiberglass fermentation vats. As if to verify this identifi-
cation, the last item unloaded from the trailer was
another familiar object, a brand-new pneumatic grape
press of modest size.

Frowning, Cole's first reaction was to drive up and

question the men. Then he paused. Wasn't this county land? Maybe his best move would be to turn around, go home and report what he had seen to the county supervisor, who happened to be his father.

Chapter Fifty-Seven_____

On Sunday, many of Tuscany Valley's citizens stayed home and read the newspapers or watched ball games on TV. Others got in cars and visited friends or relatives. And some went to one of the four churches in the Valley.

Only a few attended the simple family ceremony in the cemetery where Carlo Agretti lay buried. The headstone was being set in place, a rather large slab of travertine that replaced the smaller stone that had marked Melissa's mother's grave for so many years.

"Carlo Vincenzo Agretti," the new stone read, with his dates, all carefully incised in the left-hand side. To the right had been chiseled, "Maria Teresa Agretti (Russo)," and her dates. Nothing more.

As Melissa stood there, with Lance on her right and Angela Channing on her left, the sun's rays threw the textured surface of beige and tan travertine into sharp relief. Veins were clear to see, whorls, crevices. For dead stone, the whole surface seemed amazingly alive on this sunny day.

The priest had intoned his simple dedication. He shook hands with the three and with Julia, who stood to one side. Then he left. The masons who had set the stone stood for a moment longer, holding their caps in their hands. Then they, too, left. The family stood alone.

In the distance, a small tractor chugged busily. This late in the year, with the harvest getting nearer each week, Sunday was no longer a full day of rest. Lance looked up, as if to find the source of the noise. Instead he saw Chase Gioberti's automobile moving slowly along the main road outside the cemetery.

When it reached the spot where Desi had parked the long Mercedes 600 limousine, Chase's car seemed to pause for a moment. Then it drove slowly on past where Lance had left his own car. It disappeared from view.

Lance looked back at his wife, mother and grandmother. None had seen the car. He found himself wondering how long they would have to stand here staring at a piece of stone. He had a date in town. Only the combined force of his mother and grandmother had gotten him to attend the ceremony. Now he wanted to be off.

"Well," he said then. "This is it, then."

Melissa glanced at him. "Yes. All right." Her voice sounded draggy, not quite with it. She looked as if her thoughts had been miles away. "Thank you all for coming," she said then.

Angie led the way to the cars. "They do amazingly good work for a country funeral home," she said in a conversational tone to Julia. "I mean, that kind of stonework is almost a lost art these days."

At the limousine, Lance waved and headed for his own car. "See you."

"Lance!" Angie's voice had the ring of a military command.

Her grandson paused in mid-stride, his tall frame motionless. "What now?"

"I know what you've got in mind," she snapped tersely. "It's out."

"What?"

"You're coming back with us. We're spending the day as a family."

No one could mistake the statements for anything but an order. Lance pivoted on one foot and tried to stare his grandmother down. It had never worked before and it didn't this time, either. "I've got other plans," he said in a stubborn voice.

"Canceled."

"Look, Grandma—"

"I told you the other day, Lance. I don't intend to repeat myself. You're to behave . . . or else."

Something twitched in the young man's face, as if he'd been slapped. "I will not be or—"

"Either you're family," Angela interrupted coldly, "or you're no longer part of it. You have a wife and a son to look after. Every day of the week. And especially today."

"I . . ." Lance's lips moved silently. He seemed to be choking on unspoken words. "Listen hard, Grandmother," he said then, his right hand digging into the inside breast pocket of his jacket. "I have no son."

Julia took a step toward him. "Lance," she began.

He pulled a long white envelope out of his pocket and held it in the air. "Any of you want to see my ticket to freedom? It's the results of a paternity test. There is no way on earth I could be that kid's father." He shook the envelope at them. "It's all here in black and white."

"Lance," Melissa said in that same low, almost drugged voice. "Your sense of timing is way out."

"I'd say it was deadly," Chase Gioberti said.

All four of them whirled around. There stood Chase, Maggie two steps behind him, shielding her eyes from the sun. She looked tired, wrung out, but Chase was bursting with energy. He looked larger than life. His close-cropped beard seemed to vibrate in the bright sunlight. His eyes were wide with something Lance had never seen there before. Anger?

"This is a private ceremony," Angela Channing said coldly.

"This isn't a ceremony," Chase corrected her, "it's an execution."

"Chase," Maggie said warningly.

"No time like the present," Chase told her, his voice barely level against the rising flood of rage inside him. "By rights, Angela, Jim Pearson should be here. And a couple of cops. But Maggie's convinced me to keep this in the family. I'm not sure she's right. I'm not even sure it can be kept private even if we want it to. Felony's been committed. Grand larceny, by the size of it. Computer fraud, too. And I'm sure the SEC will have to be told that someone's violated Regulation 13-D by buying more than five percent of a corporation without revealing their identity."

The still air of the cemetery carried no sound to the six people standing by their cars. Shut behind his chauffeur's windows, Desi smoked a cigarette and watched them without quite getting the drift of their talk.

"What are you raving about?" Angie demanded.

"I had no idea I'd run into you today," Chase told her. "Otherwise I'd have brought along all the bank's documents. Pearson has the whole thing tied together by date and transaction. Placed in the hands of the D.A., at least one and possibly three people will spend a lot of time behind bars." He smiled slightly, but the fury within him enlarged the gesture to a grimace. "At your age, Angela, you'll *die* in jail."

Her wide-set eyes flickered sideways a moment,

then zeroed in on her nephew, Chase. "Would you care to explain yourself coherently? Otherwise I don't have all day to listen."

"Fine," Chase retorted. "My lawyers will take the documents to the San Francisco district attorney's office tomorrow morning." He turned away. "Come on, Maggie. I warned you we couldn't keep this in the family." He started to lead her away to their car.

Lance's mouth had turned bone-dry. He watched Chase open the passenger door for Maggie. As she got into the car, Chase closed her door. He started to get behind the steering wheel.

"Lance!" his grandmother's voice cracked like a whip.

He flinched. He could feel his whole body react to the snap of his name through the silent air. "Lance, what's been going on here?"

He opened his mouth to speak, but no words came out. He watched Angela's eyes swivel from his face to Julia's, to Melissa's and then to Chase. "Come back to the house," she called to her nephew. "This is no place to discuss family matters."

"A cemetery's just fine for me." Chase's voice sounded lighter, easier, as if, in some way Lance couldn't understand, he had won a victory.

"What sort of documents do you have?" Angie went on, her voice filled with a kind of finicky disdain, as if discussing some rather ugly disease.

"Enough to prove that you had Lance loot my accounts for more than a hundred thousand. Enough to prove that the money went to buy *Globe* stock in a dummy name. I figure by the time we're through with this, you, Lance and Phil Erikson will have at least fifteen years apiece to mull over where you went wrong."

"Where *we* went wrong!" Angie rasped. "Lance, what have you been up to? Tell the truth!"

Lance could feel his face redden. The scalding nerve of the woman! He had done nothing but what she'd asked. "Look," he began, "if you think you c—"

"A hundred thousand," his grandmother cut in. "Is that what you said, Chase?"

"Plus. Jim Pearson has the exact figure."

There was a long pause. In the distance, as if growing impatient, a woodpecker began to hammer insistently on the trunk of a tree.

"No need," Angela Channing said then in a flat voice, "to bring Jim into this. You'll have a cashier's check for the full amount by the end of the business day tomorrow."

Chase stared hard at her. "Before the banks close tomorrow," he corrected her.

"Yes, all right. Before the banks close."

Chase started his car's engine. He leaned out through the open driver's window. "It's always a pleasure," he said, "doing business with you, Angela."

And drove away.

Angela Channing whirled on her grandson. "You dim-witted little idiot!" she burst out. "You don't have the brains of a third-rate burglar. You told me there was no way anybody would be able t—" She stopped cold, her glance darting to Desi, sitting behind closed windows.

When she spoke again, her voice was much lower, but far more menacing. "You're finished, Lance," she said slowly. "I'm disinheriting you. I'm cutting Joseph out of my will."

"No!" Julia's cry echoed through the cemetery.

"Shut up, Julia," Angela snapped. Lance watched her terrifying glance return to him. "Pack your bags. You have till dinner to clear out." Her merciless gaze shifted to Melissa. "That goes for you, too," she added. "I have been surrounded by cheapness. Cheap minds. Cheap deeds. I'm cleaning house at Falcon Crest and I'm starting this minute."

Lance looked at Melissa, who merely shrugged softly. She walked over to his car and got in. "Home, James," she said. "Wherever that is."

Grinning at her sheer gall, Lance got behind the wheel. "How does it feel to walk out on a zillion bucks in heartaches?" he asked.

"Terrific!"

Julia and her mother watched the car leave in Lance's usual squeal of rubber on pavement. Then Angela strode to her limousine and got in before Desi could run around to open her door. "Coming, Julia?"

"N-no."

"Suit yourself."

Off went the Mercedes. Julia stood for a moment, staring sightlessly around her, as if suddenly blinded. Without warning, her knees seemed to buckle. She fell onto the grass, her arms ahead of her, the palms of her hands taking the brunt of the fall.

Now she crouched on hands and knees like an animal. And from deep in her throat came a moan of pure animal hurt, a wail that filtered through the leafy glades of the cemetery like the howl of a displaced ghost.

Slowly, she collapsed until she was lying facedown in the grass and dirt. And still that eerie moan filled the bright day with a nameless dread.

Part Six

*Chapter Fifty-Eight*_____

Phillip Erikson, his white hair disheveled by a breeze, walked as fast as he could, without running, out of the bank.

Unconsciously, he touched his jacket to reassure himself that the envelope containing the cashier's check for Chase was safely tucked away. A passing pickpocket would have recognized the gesture for what it was and might have had a try at lifting something the fast-walking gentleman seemed so concerned about. As it was, Erikson got safely into a cab and gave the driver the address of the *Globe*. He had five minutes to get there before the shareholders' meeting began.

Erikson sat back in the cab and tried to calm himself. Handling Angela Channing's legal (and less than legal) work was never an easy task. But the turnabout drama of the past twenty-four hours had left the attorney quite fatigued. The job of finding that much money had taken all morning. Only by arranging a second mortgage on some of Angela's Falcon Crest property had it been possible.

That had been difficult, but well within Erikson's capabilities. Now he faced the true unknown, a meeting of *Globe* shareholders in which most were members of the same strife-torn family while some were concealing their ownership behind false fronts. It would be a lot like trying to find a black felt hat in a totally dark room, with your eyes blindfolded.

He sighed unhappily. Not that Angela didn't pay him well, but he would long ago have resigned the account except for his hopes of getting back on a personal basis with his client, perhaps even marrying her. It would not be a restful, or even pleasant, marriage, the lawyer reflected, but with that much money at stake it was worth his time to try and arrange an affluent old age for himself.

Richard Channing had scheduled the meeting for the *Globe*'s executive dining room, relegating his editors and other executives to eat with the rest of the staff in the cafeteria this day. The room was not big, but neither was the group attending the meeting.

Erikson sidled in and took a seat at the rear. He nodded to Angela, seated in the front row, and tapped his chest to indicate that he had the check with him. She sent her glance piercingly from her attorney to Chase, who sat across the room, and nodded her head.

Phillip changed seats to one beside Chase. He handed over the envelope. Chase opened it, glanced inside and put it away in his own inside breast pocket. He then looked to the speaker's dais, where Richard Channing was conferring with his corporate secretary. Neither had seen the transaction. In any event, it was none of their business.

"Ladies and gentlemen," the secretary said then. "The special shareholders' meeting of the *Globe* Corporation is hereby in session. I call on our chief executive officer and editor in chief, Mr. Richard Channing, to chair the proceedings. Mr. Channing."

Richard took the podium and stared out at each of the shareholders in turn. His glance lingered on Chase, on Julia, on Angela and several other people who held small portions of stock. His own broker, the tall, spare man he called Joe, also occupied a seat toward the back of the room.

As Channing's glance roved, so did Erikson's, following his lead. Thus the lawyer came to see the broker, an old acquaintance. The two men nodded politely to each other. Jordan Brink had at various times handled quite a few investment matters for clients of Erikson. He hoped to handle more. The lawyer had handled several legal matters for clients of Brink. He, too, hoped to handle more. It was a fruitful professional association, Erikson knew, and could bear even more fruit if properly cultivated.

"Fellow shareholders," Richard began in his deep, easy voice that nevertheless seemed to crackle with excitement somewhere in the lower bass notes. "There is a skeleton agenda for this meeting, copies of which you have all received. I now call for any additions or suggestions to that agenda."

He waited. Erikson's glance continued around the room and stopped cold when it came to Diana Hunter, seated almost behind him. He wanted to crane around and get a better look at this delectable creature with her high-piled dark blond hair, but the twisted pose would have been a dead giveaway to Angela.

"There being none," Richard continued, "we come to the first item of business, which is the most important one, I'm sure you agree. It has to do with the entire future of the *Globe* as a viable entity in today's extremely risky communications industry. I refer to Proposition One, One A and One-B, copies of which Miss Hunter has placed on each chair. Would you take a moment to reread the propositions before I call for discussion?"

Phillip picked up a typed copy of the proposal and scanned it quickly. Speaking of competition and rising costs, what was being asked for was the shareholders' approval of a special Management Committee with expanded and independent powers.

It was to act on such matters as changing the format of the *Globe* to tabloid size, investigating opportunities to buy a local TV station, the possibility of a move into cable television and into neighborhood shopping giveaway papers.

As far as Erikson could see, the only controversial part of the proposal was that the committee would be chaired by Richard Channing and answerable to no one. In effect, the power of the shareholders to control their own corporation would be eliminated. They were being asked to hand it over to Richard.

"Can we have your comments on Proposition One, One-A and One-B?" Richard asked smoothly, as if he were asking them for a match.

Chase Gioberti raised his hand. "You can't really expect us to—"

"I'm sorry," Richard interrupted coolly. "Please state your name, address and number of shares you represent."

"Ridiculous," Chase retorted.

"It's for the record and the recording secretary."

Chase sighed impatiently. He identified himself and his share holdings. "I also carry the proxy votes for Miss Emma Marie Channing, who owns the same number of shares."

"May I see those proxies?" Richard demanded.

"You may not. When a vote is taken you'll get your chance."

Chase had gotten to his feet now as the two men locked horns for combat. Watching them face off against each other, Erikson was struck by the strange similarity between the two, same height and build, same rather intense manner.

He knew Angela's opinion of her nephew as a man too dangerously softhearted to be trusted. But after yesterday's bloodbath, in which Chase had wrung back every cent she'd taken from him, perhaps Angela had new respect.

"Speaking to the propositions," Chase went on relentlessly, "and without any more harassing interruptions from the chair designed to delay, let me point out that various proposed new ideas may have some merit. But the manner in which the shareholders are deprived of a voice is not only without merit, it is totally unacceptable. I oppose the propositions and I urge my fellow shareholders to oppose them. This represents nothing less than handing over the *Globe*'s future to you, Mr. Channing, and giving you a completely free hand to run it as you wish. Having already seen how you run the newspaper, I don't think any of us are interested in letting you tamper with the corporation's future."

There was a moment of somewhat shocked silence. Then Angela, of all people, applauded vigorously. Taking her cue, so did Julia and several others in the room. Chase sat down. Richard grinned malevolently at him.

"I will, of course, answer all your allegations in due course," he promised. "Those of you who have seen the dollar value of your shares nearly double since I took the helm of the *Globe* will have your own ideas about how competently I've been running things. Any other comment?"

Phillip had been watching Angela Channing's face for a cue. Now she nodded once, almost imperceptibly. The lawyer got to his feet and introduced himself by name as representing shares held by a company based in Liechtenstein called Anstalt Weingut.

"And the ownership of this company?" Richard interrupted him.

"Can be secured," Erikson replied with smooth assurance, "by applying to the company at its headquarters in Vaduz." He cleared his throat. "I'd like to speak against Proposi—."

"Just a second," Richard cut in again. "You know how it is. We've all heard about these dummy corpo-. rations that live in some lawyer's file drawer in Vaduz. Can you be a bit more forthcoming?"

"I cannot, without violating my client-attorney relationship." The lawyer's mouth pursed in a feline smile. "Nor have you the authority to delve any further nor to delay my statement."

He cleared his throat again. "My client is firmly opposed to Propositions One, One-A and One-B as being not simply dangerous, but actively destructive to the very fabric of American stock ownership control by which our nation's great businesses have been answerable to their shareholders for more than two centuries. To put it in other words, I—"

"Are you seriously telling us that corporations take their leadership from their stockholders?" Richard asked in a scornful tone.

"I am saying that such control, whether exercised or not, remains implicit in the very fact of stock ownership. Some corporations may try to disregard their shareholders' wishes. I pray God this one does not!"

The applause this time was even stronger than it had been for Chase. "Thank you," Richard said, as if the approval had been for him. "Perhaps it's time to hear a brief word on this very point from the broker who specializes in our shares. May I call on you, Joe, to comment?"

The broker's face went dull red. Every angle of his lanky body, as it slowly unfolded and he got to his feet, indicated to Erickson that Jordan Brink absolutely did not want to comment on this last point. He was in a tight spot and he knew it.

"I doubt my competence to make a real contribution to this—" he began.

"Please state your name, affiliation, et cetera," Chase broke in. "Sorry."

Brink's face grew, if anything, even redder. "Jordan Brink, executive vice-president, Halsey, Smith and Brink. I am, as Mr. Channing puts it, a specialist in this stock. But as to the point being raised by Mr. Erikson, I am perhaps a bit beyond my depth." He glanced imploringly at Richard with a look that cried out for him to be let off the hook.

"Very well, Joe," Richard said briskly. "But as long as you're on your feet and properly introduced, perhaps you can clear up a matter germane to Mr. Erikson's point. He's talking about stock ownership. Give us a brief summary, will you, of who owns what?"

The broker's face resumed its normal pallor. He delved into his left jacket pocket and brought out a fistful of small file cards. These he riffled through quickly.

"There are, according to the latest figures, somewhat in excess of twelve thousand shares in the hands of private owners. Of these—"

"Hold it," Chase snapped. He was on his feet. "The last annual report we got listed exactly ten thousand shares."

"Yes?" Brink asked. "That was the situation at the time of the annual report. But, of course, the new issue of two thousand shares of common is now on sale and—"

Pandemonium!

Erikson jumped to his feet. Between him and Chase, the volley of questions and cries of outrage from other shareholders began to grow in intensity. Richard Channing rapped the podium with a small wooden gavel. "Order," he said, not loudly. He seemed to want the confusion to last a bit longer. "Order," he said again.

Then, finally, raising his voice, "Order, please!" The room simmered down slightly. "Joe, you have the floor."

"It's my understanding," the broker said, reaching in his right-hand pocket and bringing out a handkerchief, "that the new issue went on sale this morning in London and Hong Kong. It's proved quite popular, according to early reports. Most of it's been bought by institutional investors."

"*What new issue?*" Phillip Erikson thundered.

Brink mopped his face with the handkerchief. "The by-laws of the corporation allow for additional issues of common stock if they don't exceed twenty percent of the original equity. This hasn't been done in many years, of course. But it has made an outstanding start with, as I said, institutional investors."

"*What investors?*" the lawyer yelped.

"Why, ah, it's too early to—"

"The usual investors," Chase suggested coolly. "Small Liechtenstein companies that live in some lawyer's file drawer."

The earlier pandemonium was now dwarfed by a real groundswell of anger as everyone in the room seemed to want to get into the fracas. This time, Richard gaveled the podium with some force. It had no effect. Several minutes elapsed before he could quiet the room, and by then, Erikson was calling out in a loud voice:

"In view of this unprecedented state of affairs," he bellowed, "in which no one in this room any longer knows what percentage of shares he or she owns, I hereby move for a one-week postponement!"

"Second the motion!" Angela Channing snarled. It was her one and only speech of the day.

"Move the question!" Chase called.

The look on Richard's face was, as always, an unholy amalgam of several conflicting emotions. He looked angry, Erikson saw, but he also seemed slightly amused and—or was Erikson wrong?—just a bit scared?

"A motion for a one-week postponement of the special meeting has been made and seconded," he began in a voice that, for him, was slightly unsure of itself.

"Point of information, Mr. Chairman," Jordan Brink said.

"Yes?"

"It will take more than a week to untangle this. May I suggest two weeks?" He glanced at the attorney and again mopped his face. "Will Mr. Erikson accept this amendment to his motion?"

"I will."

"Call the question," Chase repeated in a strong voice.

"You have heard the motion as amended," Richard told the audience. "All in favor please raise their hands." Behind him the corporate secretary counted. "Those opposed?" No one raised a hand.

"Motion carried," Richard intoned. "This special meeting is adjourned until twelve noon two weeks hence. That will be"—he glanced at his calendar watch—"September twenty-eighth." He rapped the podium with his gavel. "Adjourned."

For the third time the room burst into agitated talk as people left their chairs and began milling around in small, argumentative groups.

Phillip Erikson found himself standing beside Angela. Their voices could not be heard above the general hubbub. "Talk about double dealing," the lawyer murmured. "Wait till I get Joe Brink in a corner on this."

"Forget Joe Brink," Angie told him quietly. "It was Chase's help that turned the tide."

"Kind words for the hated nephew?"

"Blood's thicker than water," she mused.

"But not thicker than wine."

She frowned at him. "Not funny. I have to be impressed by Chase. When you think how he had all our heads in a noose . . ."

"Thank God he puts family first, then," Phillip breathed. "But I am going to speak to Brink. He can't get away with this."

"I told you to forget him." Angie's voice got even quieter. "The damage is done, Phillip. Now I want Richard Channing damaged."

"Beg pardon?"

When she spoke again, her voice had the dry hiss of some cold-blooded serpent winding its way across a floor. "Damaged," she repeated, "beyond repair."

Chapter Fifty-Nine

San Francisco's Chinatown, preserved in dozens of novels and movies over the years, is disappointing these days to tourists in search of glamorously evil opium dens, tong wars and the white slave trade. It is a businesslike place, filled with busy people. The only concession it makes to the notorious past is a series of popular restaurants where dishes like shark's-fin soup and ancient eggs are served to discerning gourmets.

Sid Rawls was not one of them. His idea of a Chinese dinner would be egg foo yong, heavy on the sauce, and a side order of fried rice. But this evening the deputy sheriff of Tuscany Valley was not in search of Chinese food. His itinerary led him in and out of more than two dozen Chinese restaurants, however, without even giving him a nibble at an egg roll.

In each he sought out the manager, showed him a picture of Tom Fong and asked the usual questions. Thus he spent from six in the evening until nearly midnight before he found his lucky fortune cookie.

"Hai!" the owner of a rather greasy joint just outside the Chinatown area exclaimed. "You want him? I want, too!"

"He was here?" Rawls asked.

"Work all week, dishwasher. Dishes always dirty. I fire."

"So he left?"

"Him leave with my cash," the owner confessed. "Him thief."

Rawls frowned as he opened a pack of cigarettes and offered one to the restaurant owner. He lit both their cigarettes in a friendly manner. "You always talk that way to cops?" he asked then.

"Wha'?"

"Will you stop?" the deputy pleaded. "Stop that horrible pidgin English."

The owner laughed. "I thought you guys expected it," he said then. "What do you want this creep for? Did he rob some other joint?"

"Just questioning," Rawls said cautiously. "Got a home address on him?"

"If I did, I'd have my money back, wouldn't I?" the restaurateur replied.

"Any notion?"

"I asked all my people. Nobody knew the guy." He thought for a moment. "Money wasn't all he took. He lifted my cook's passport."

The deputy's eyes closed to a squint. "When was this?"

"Noon today."

Rawls pulled over the telephone and dialed the number of a sergeant friend of his on the police department. Speaking urgently, he asked for a water-front search. "It'd probably be a freighter due to pull out tonight. He might try to sign on as crew. Or he might have enough cash to buy passage."

"Where to?" the sergeant asked.

"Anywhere."

"Anywhere's a big place, Sid."

But "anywhere" turned out to be Hawaii. The

Nippon Maru, ten thousand tons, was due to sail at midnight for Honolulu. The assistant cook was brought back in handcuffs to the Embarcadero police station.

"Hi, Tom," Rawls said.

"Oh. It's you."

"Yeah. Sorry."

"No Honolulu, huh?"

"Not right away," the deputy said.

Fong shook his head sadly. "I could almost taste that pineapple."

"Hey," Rawls told him, "I said I was sorry."

Chapter Sixty_____

Diana Hunter glanced at the clock in her office. 6 A.M. It would be 9 A.M. in New York. Henri Denault would have just arrived at his office there. She pulled over her desk phone and had begun to punch in a series of numbers when she frowned and hung up.

Perhaps she was being paranoid. Surely Richard wouldn't have bugged the telephones here in the office? Then why had she suddenly thought better of using this phone for this particular call?

Snatching up her bag, she left the office, took the elevator to the street and walked several blocks until she found the kind of hotel she needed, a big one belonging to a national chain, a place from which dozens of long-distance calls were made every hour to everywhere in the world. She spoke to a young woman at the desk and installed herself in a hotel phone booth. Then she dialed Denault's private New York number again.

"Yes?" The monosyllable was terse, but the voice was unmistakable.

"It's Diana Hunter. Do you have a moment?"

"No, but I assume you wouldn't have called if this weren't important."

She shivered at the impersonal words and the bloodless tone in which they were spoken. All her training in the Cartel flooded back into Diana's mind. This move might well be the mistake of her career but not making it might be an even worse mistake. If she handled it right, it could be the making of her.

"I'm afraid we've had our first real setback here," she said then. Quickly she described the shareholders' meeting. "I'm sure Richard is keeping you in the picture. But I thought I owed you a description from a different viewpoint."

"Dear God, yes," Denault said. "From what you tell me he hasn't split the family apart, he's managed to weld it together."

"That may be temporary."

"There is nothing wrong with your memory, Diana. You will clearly recall me describing this as a hit-and-run operation. It's already gone on much too long without producing any real results."

"There are other parts of it that may work better," she said, rapidly sketching Richard's affair with Melissa.

"This gets worse the more you tell me," Denault growled.

"I don't mean it that way. But his project with the winery will certainly produce results."

"You think so?" His tone was more of a sneer. "It's good for you to be loyal to Richard, but you mustn't let your judgment be warped by such close proximity to him."

Diana smiled very slightly. She *had* handled the call properly, then. Denault thought she was still Richard's loyal handmaiden. "I really called for advice," she said then. "I'm not sure I can be of much help to Richard if he sticks to this course. Tell me what to do."

"You've done precisely the right thing by calling me," Denault assured her.

There was a pause at the New York end. "This is more complex than you realize," Denault said at last in an almost unwilling voice, as if begrudging each word of explanation. "There are complications that go beyond my realm."

"I don't understand."

"None of us in the Cartel is a free agent. Surely you see that I have someone to whom all this must be reported."

Diana nodded but said nothing. The mysterious Number One, was it? Richard's feckless adventures in Tuscany Valley were of interest that high up in the Cartel. "I had no idea," she breathed into the phone.

"Very complex," Denault said. "Very complex." He never repeated himself. He must, Diana realized, be under some strain about this.

"What can I do to help?" she asked then.

"Nothing more at the moment. Give me a number where you can be reached on a secure line."

"I have no such line."

Denault made a sound of exasperation. "Then you must call me from a safe place. Where are you phoning from now?"

She described the hotel. "Better than nothing," Denault admitted. "Tomorrow, this time, call me from that phone again. I'll be at the St. Mark."

"You're coming to San Francisco?"

"As fast as I can."

Chapter Sixty-One _____

The elders of the tribe had gathered, along with a few supporting players. Angela Channing had issued an extremely polite invitation to Chase and Maggie for "drinks and a bit of planning." One of the year's big events was rapidly approaching, Founder's Day. Discussions were in order.

They sat in the great living room at Falcon Crest mansion, its huge bank of windows letting in the afternoon sun in slanting rays of deep yellow. Outside, the sounds of activity were everywhere as vineyard hands prepared for what promised to be the biggest harvest in history.

Maggie had taken a comfortable chair behind a large rosewood desk, which served more as an ornament than a working surface. Across a floor carpeted in glowing Persian rugs sat her husband, Chase, gently rubbing his beard as he stared across at her.

He had been doing a lot of that lately, Maggie knew. Ever since her return from Los Angeles, driving her rented car like a madwoman all night, Chase had seemed to look at her in a new, questioning way, as if he wanted to ask something, but was never able to reach that point.

Julia sat in front of a long, low marble cocktail

table, carefully decanting a pale white wine from an unlabeled bottle into several glasses. Chao-Li stood by her side, impassively watching the movements of the bottle and the unsteady trickle of wine into each glass.

At the far end of the room, in front of a great fireplace fully three yards wide, stood Angela, dressed not for a simple family session but in a neat blue suit with a plain pale green blouse and a huge gold pendant in which was set a cluster of grapes worked in emerald, turquoise and lapis lazuli mosaic.

At the opposite end, near the archway that led into the great room, stood Phillip Erikson, as if not sure of his welcome, although Maggie was certain Angela had insisted on his presence.

The only notable absences were those of Lance and Melissa, Maggie noted. Perhaps they were at the hospital, visiting Joseph. The baby had been making great strides. Within a week he would be big enough and healthy enough to be taken home.

"We're all here," Angela said at last. "Julia, stop fiddling with that wine. Chao-Li, please serve it."

Gravely, the Chinese passed the tray to each of them. "It's a new *blanc de blanc*," Julia announced, her voice shaky. Perhaps that was why she had taken so much time pouring the wine, Maggie thought. But why would she be unsteady?

"All but Emma, of course," Angie amended. "I believe you might be able to fill us in on that, Chase?"

"Not very much. She's in an inst—" He paused and accepted his glass of wine. "Thanks, Chao-Li. She's getting some therapy in a place somewhere in the Midwest. I talked to her last week. She sounded absolutely great."

"Good," Emma's mother enthused in such a saccharine tone that Maggie winced. "We're so glad to hear that." She watched Chao-Li serve the last glass to the attorney. "That'll be all," she called.

The Chinese left and, as he did, slowly swung shut the great oak and wrought iron curved doors that closed off the archway. They clicked shut with an oiled precision and a sense of finality that sent a shiver up Maggie's spine.

"First of all," Angela said, lifting her glass, "a toast to the family. We have our outs and ins. But we're still a family."

Everyone raised his glass. "More or less," Chase commented wryly. He tasted the wine. "Julia . . . superb."

She nearly jumped. "What? Oh. Why . . . uh . . . thank you."

Maggie tasted the smooth, vigorous wine, light but full of flavor. She set down the glass beside a morocco-leather holder on the desk. Idly, she opened it and found herself looking at the three-to-a-page checkbook of Angela Gioberti Channing.

"Secondly," Angela was saying, "without going into the details, I want to thank you, Chase, for doing the decent thing about Lance's defalcation. I must tell you that he and Melissa are no longer welcome here at Falcon Crest."

"Poor Lance," Chase murmured.

Usually, Maggie saw, when he made an ironic comment like that, he glanced at her to make sure she got it and was enjoying the sweet satisfaction of having bested Angela at her own game. But this time he did not. Instead, he concentrated on his glass of wine.

"Thirdly," Angie continued, unperturbed, "I want to express my personal thanks both to you, Chase, and to Phillip, for the way you headed off that stampede at the shareholders' meeting. Phillip, you've got some further news about that?"

The lawyer ran his fingers through his crisp white hair. "I had a talk with Joe Brink. From the beginning he knew he was sailing too close to the wind and might get flak from the SEC. So he began by protecting his flank. All these stock sales for the new issue have been set up as conditional. Richard wasn't told this. In other words, if nobody screamed, the sales would go through. But if we blew the whistle, Joe would be able to cancel the sales because they were conditional to begin with. Am I making sense to you folks?"

"Sure," Chase said, "but what does Richard think of the way Brink diddled him?"

"He doesn't know yet."

Chase pursed his lips and blew a silent whistle. "Brink's got a chance of killing off the whole stock issue?"

"And our *Globe* holdings remain undiluted," Angela added.

"I presume," Chase pounced, "that this Liechtenstein Anstalt Phillip was muttering about yesterday, the one that owns ten percent of *Globe* common, is not totally unknown to some of us here at Falcon Crest?"

"Let's not get bogged down in business," his aunt suggested in a sweet voice. "This is a family gathering. We're ironing out the last details of Founder's Day. I thought this year we ought to take as the theme our harvest. It's a record."

"And," Julia added in her strangely tentative voice, "if the weather's kind, I think we may have our best grapes yet."

"Can we have the firehouse band again?" Angela asked.

"And the fireworks," Maggie suggested. "We can't skip them."

"Very good." Angela positively beamed at her. "And

the usual barbecue. How much of this new *blanc de blanc* can we spare?" she asked her daughter.

"Not this. I'm pricing it at twelve dollars a bottle, retail."

"Then something good."

"Yes, of course." Julia's mind seemed to wander slightly. "Something good chilled. Something . . ." She stopped and picked at a bit of lint on her pale blue skirt. "Something memorable. Something . . ." This time her voice trailed off and she said no more.

Angela strode to the cocktail table and poured herself another glass. As she did, Maggie took advantage of the moment to flip through a few pages of the checkbook stubs.

"I'm curious," Chase said then. "Do you mean you've actually cut Lance out of your will?"

Angie straightened up suddenly, her eyes wide. "That's my business." She paused and tried to shift the features of her face to a less arrogant look. "Surely, Chase, you understand. I mean, I don't ask you the details of your will."

"You see," he persisted, "in a family-run corporation it's everyone's business who inherits what. You've just told me that our plant manager, Lance, is no longer with us, so naturally I'm filled with curiosity. Will we have someone to replace him? And, in the long view, when my share of Falcon Crest goes to Cole and Vickie, who will halve the responsibility with them if Lance doesn't inherit? Your will may be your business, Angela, but we have to know some of it."

She glanced across at her attorney. "What do you think?"

Erikson shrugged. "I'm the sort of fella who gets a quid for his quo. If you want answers, Chase, what're you prepared to swap?"

"Let's not get bogged down in business," Chase

responded, grinning, as he quoted Angela's earlier line. "I've deposited your cashier's check. That part's all right. I'm going to start Cole replanting the fallow acreage. That's okay, too. I sort of have the feeling I'm sitting pretty." His grin widened. "But you're going to spoil that illusion for me, eh, Phillip?"

"There was the mention of some documents."

"Yes. Safely tucked away."

"I'd be happier if they were in our hands. That's not too much to ask," the lawyer said. "We paid dearly for them."

"With my own money," Chase pointed out. He thought for a while. "I've got a lovely quo for your quid. Founder's Day we celebrate our biggest harvest yet. Next years' will begin to be even bigger because of new acreage under cultivation. So let's announce that the new expansion is jointly financed by Angela and me."

The great room echoed with silence for a long moment. All eyes were on them. Maggie turned another page in Angela's checkbook and came across a stub that read, "Darryl Clayton, $5,000." It was dated a week before she had been summoned down to Los Angeles.

"More cash?" Angela burst out. "You're pauperizing me."

"I'm prepared to put up the hundred grand you sto— The money appropriated," Chase corrected himself. "I expect a matching amount from you, Angela. With two hundred thousand to spend, this project will get off the ground much faster. Oh, and the documents will be turned over to you."

"Blackmail," Angela snapped.

"You're so right."

"Phillip?" she demanded.

He laughed helplessly. "It's your decision, my dear. It doesn't sound all that bad."

Angie's mouth firmed into a hard line. "Done!" she said in a voice that would have suited equally well for a curse word.

"I thought we weren't going to get bogged down in business," Maggie asked sarcastically. She could feel a peculiar pressure under her lungs, as if it were impossible to fill them with air. Almost breathlessly, she added, "And when did you start investing in films, Aunt Angela?"

"What?"

Maggie tapped the open checkbook stub. "When did you start paying money to Darryl Clayton?"

"You pawed through my private papers?"

"Fortunately. Otherwise I'd never have known the source of Darryl's development money, the same five thousand he paid me for revisions."

For once in her life, Angela Channing had nothing to say. At least not at first. It was awesome, Maggie thought, to see the way she began to steel herself for combat. Her figure straightened, her shoulder seemed to tense. Her throat pulsed powerfully and her face went totally blank.

"Are you sure that's all you did for your five thousand?" asked Angie.

The sneer in her voice seemed to reverberate around the suddenly silent room, abruptly huge and echoing like a courtroom in which all manner of insinuations could freely be made. Maggie felt herself gasp involuntarily. The sunlight glared blindingly in her eyes.

"My information," Angela went on assuming the tone of a prosecuting attorney, "is that Darryl got a lot more out of you than rewrites."

Maggie's stricken glance shifted to Chase. His new, questioning look seemed suddenly to ignite his eyes, as if knowledge was unwillingly exploding in his brain. "What are you babbling about, Angela?" he demanded.

"You might ask any of the staff at Maggie's hotel in Beverly Hills." Her voice had the silky slipperiness of a well-made noose. "They're used to any sort of carryings-on, I suppose. But the fact that those two were together every night would certainly have raised one or two eyebrows."

"Angela!" Chase's tone was a yelp of pain.

"Or the staff of any of the restaurants, nightclubs or disco joints where those two spent most of their evenings," Angela added. "Precious little revising got done, it appears."

"You're lying," Maggie said. The quivering tension beneath her lungs seemed about to choke her. She could hear her voice shake. "Chase, there is no truth to this. She's up to her old tricks."

"No truth?" Angie's laugh had the dry, scuttling sound of rats in the woodwork. "There are several dozen photos and a sheaf of affidavits on their way up from L.A. We'll see what's true and what isn't."

"Darryl wouldn't—" Maggie stopped herself.

"You're quite right," Angie agreed. "He's a decent enough young man. He wouldn't have done the wooing *and* the spying. That last part was done by private detectives."

"Paid by you." Chase got to his feet. "Tell them to keep their filth, Angela. There's no market for it here."

He strode across the room and took Maggie by her arm. "Let's go. Once again she's managed to turn a family gathering into a bloodbath." He slammed out through the great oak doors.

In Chase's car, they drove off at unusual speed. It was only when he was out of earshot that he slowed down.

"Thank you," Maggie said. "You know she's lying. I appreciate what you did in there."

"I?" Chase asked. "I know nothing of the kind."

"But, Chase—"

"I only know that the one night I needed you—really, desperately needed you—you weren't there. Or you weren't answering your phone. Does it matter which?"

"But it's not what it s—"

"As far as Angela is concerned, I would never let her think I believed her. But between you and me . . ." Chase glanced sideways at his wife. "Between you and me, Maggie, I . . ."

The muscles in his face worked silently. She could see a tear well up in his eye. "Chase, darling. Please believe me. Nothing hap—"

"Save it," he said in a cold voice. "Maggie, as far as I'm concerned, I'll never believe anything you tell me again."

"Chase!"

"I just wouldn't be that stupid."

Chapter Sixty-Two

Melissa was in a happy state of shock. The day before she had given Lance the keys to the small guest-house that sat a few hundred yards from Bellavista, really just a bungalow her father used for grape buyers who'd missed their last plane out and had to stay the night.

"It's probably been taken over by spiders," was her only comment.

So when she arrived this morning with her son, Joseph, and a hired nurse, Miss Cleeve, she had expected almost anything from a total wreck to a sketchily swept-out shambles. "It's not important," she'd warned Miss Cleeve. "You and I will be moving to San Francisco soon."

It was typical of Melissa to have half-invented the story. True, Richard had made noises about installing her and Joseph in a small, pretty apartment on Nob Hill. Now Melissa had escalated this vague promise into firm fact.

Lance stood at the doorway, grinning self-consciously. He pecked Melissa dutifully on the cheek, nodded to the nurse and shocked his wife by taking the small bundled form of Joseph out of Miss Cleeve's arms.

"Hiya, kid," he told the tiny baby. "Welcome to your new home."

Melissa wandered through the four-room house, eyes wide with surprise. With help from the wives of several vineyard hands, Lance had had the place vacuumed, scrubbed, the windows cleaned, furniture dusted, beds made with fresh linen and—the final shock—refrigerator and pantry stocked with food.

"I'm impressed," Melissa told him. "What's the gimmick? New leaf?"

Lance shrugged. "If we have to live here, it might as well be clean. And you can't beat the rent."

Miss Cleeve was busy in the tiny kitchen warming Joseph's formula. "How long does she stay?" Lance asked in a careful undertone.

"A month or more." Melissa looked into his eyes. Now was the time to tell him this place was only a stopover. Now was the time to explain that she had been shown the great world outside Bellavista and she wanted it all, for herself, not Lance.

Now, she thought, is really the moment to tell him I'm filing for a divorce. She realized that, without knowing her plans, Lance had outmaneuvered her by fixing this place up so brilliantly. He might be only a pale shadow of his crafty grandmother, but he'd certainly inherited Angela's knack of getting ahead of other people.

"Look at that," she said then. Joseph's tiny fingers seemed to be groping for Lance's face. The incredibly small fingernails, pale dots of white, touched Lance's cheek. Joseph's mouth turned up in a smile. He produced a gurgle and then belched delicately.

"Alka-Seltzer for this one," Lance commented. "You think he knows me?"

"Seems to."

"That puts me one up on his real father," Lance said, deadpan. Then he winked at the baby. "It's a

big secret from both of us, kid," he told Joseph.
"Let's keep it that way."

Something peculiar happened to Melissa in that
moment. It was as if the room had shifted under her
feet, not the violent wrench of an earth tremor but
the gentle change of a dimension in her heart. It
almost seemed as if Lance liked the baby. As if he
were willing to let bygones be bygones. As if, Melissa
told herself, he had actually turned a new leaf.

She busied herself feeding Joseph his bottle while
the nurse and Lance shifted furniture in what was to
be the nursery. "If you move that cot in here," Miss
Cleeve explained, "I can sleep next to Joseph. It's
the best way, at least for the first few weeks."

Seated in her living room, the late-morning sun
drenching the house with warmth, Melissa and the
baby formed a tight little picture of contentment.
She had the illusion of being able to see that picture,
herself with Joseph in her arms. Without knowing it,
Lance had provided the proper frame for the image.
Did she really want to break camp and move into
town?

Melissa's heart seemed too full of contrasts. She
felt too much at home here to think of leaving almost at once. Perhaps she could put Richard off for
a few weeks. It might be best for Joseph to have a
stable, fixed environment for a while. That would be
the excuse to give Richard.

A shadow fell across the sunny doorway.

Melissa looked up into the wide-set eyes of Angela
Channing. "Isn't that darling," the older woman said
with no trace of sarcasm. "He's really gotten huge,
hasn't he?"

Melissa frowned. "What do you want here, Angela?"

Lance, hearing the voices, came into the room and
stopped cold at the sight of his grandmother. "Now
what?" he demanded.

"Just a plain, ordinary grandma visit," Angie purred.

"Don't give me that."

Angela advanced on Joseph and, without asking, swept him out of Melissa's arms, bottle and all. "That's it," she urged the baby. "Finished it allllll up." He sucked greedily.

Lance and his wife exchanged puzzled glances. "Grandmother, are you going to explain yourself," Lance asked, "or do I just order you off the premises, the way you got rid of us?"

Angela looked up from the baby. "That's all forgotten, Lance."

"Not by me," Melissa countered.

"By all of us," the older woman assured her calmly. "It was a ploy. I had to do it to keep Chase from creating a public scandal. Now he's agreed to treat the defalcation as a loan, which I've repaid. So your little adventure is forgotten, Lance."

"*My* adventure?" he burst out.

"You're welcome back to Falcon Crest anytime."

"No thanks," Melissa told her. "Lance has gone to a lot of trouble to fix up this place. It's our new home. Permanently."

She took Joseph back in her arms to emphasize the point. But it occurred to Melissa that by opposing Angela in this matter she had sealed her own fate. What about her plans to live with Richard in the big city? What about the fabulous travels he had promised her? London, Paris, Rome . . . what of them?

"The future heirs of Falcon Crest," Angela Channing said in a solemn tone, "really can't live permanently in this tiny guesthouse." She glanced around the place. "I've decided to give you the entire West Wing of the big mansion. It's yours."

"In other words, you've changed your will again?" Lance asked.

"I never did cut you out. Do you think I'd do that to little Joseph?"

"And kiss the Agretti grapes good-bye," Lance finished in a bitter tone. "Come to think of it, no. You'd never do that."

Angela went to the doorway and stood silhouetted in the glowing sunlight. "The harvest is on us any day now. So, for a while, you might want to stay here. Let's call this the nursery, eh? But your real home awaits you. Just give Chao-Li twenty-four hours notice. And, Lance, your mother and I expect you back on the job at the winery."

"Oh, do you."

"Tomorrow. Harvesttime, you know."

"I'm considering another job," he said sullenly.

"Falcon Crest has authorized a twenty percent pay increase for you, Lance. It will buy a lot of diapers." Her smile was as sweet as syrup. "See you at the office tomorrow." She turned and left.

Neither Lance nor Melissa spoke for a long moment. Finished with his bottle, Joseph rode over his mother's shoulder as she massaged his tiny back. After a long moment, he produced the expected belch delivered with a great deal of vigor.

"My feelings exactly, kid," Lance said.

Chapter Sixty-Three

"Look, Dad," Cole said, "I know a fermentation vat when I see one. At the rate those guys were working with prefab modules, there has to be a full, working winery by now."

Chase stared at his son. "Why did you wait so long to tell me?"

"You think I didn't try? You've been sort of busy the last few days."

Chase nodded slowly. "So," he said then, "it's not a memorial at all. Channing's tricked us into selling him land for a winery. It directly violates the terms of the sales contract."

"So?"

"So he'll just have to tear it down," Chase said.

"That guy? You'd have to hold a gun to his head."

"The man has finally got his heart's desire," Chase mused out loud. "He's finally sunk roots in the Valley. Too bad he's going to have to rip them up."

"You sound almost sorry for him."

"After what he's done to us?" Chase laughed without mirth. "But I sort of understand him. He's lived all over the world. No family. No place to call his own. Just money, piles of it."

"Is that so hard to take?"

"Only if your heart's set on something else."

Maggie had been preparing a salad at the kitchen counter. She turned now, bowl in her hands. "That's assuming he's got a heart," she said.

Chase seemed to freeze up at the sound of her voice. Cole thought for a moment before replying. "I haven't seen any sign of one." He took the bowl of salad from his mother. "Where's Vickie?"

"Running."

Silently, they sat down to their lunch. For a long time neither Chase nor Maggie spoke. Cole had already sensed the coolness. It was impossible to live in the same house and not see that his mother and father were no longer their usual loving selves.

"I did a circuit of that fallow acreage this morning," he said then, trying to relax the strained air with some semblance of normal conversation. "Before we clear the place we have to bulldoze in some roads. Five or six. The old paths are grown over with weeds."

Chase grunted, but said nothing. Maggie pushed her salad around on her plate, as if trying to find some sort of artistic arragement. "Then it has to be refenced," Cole continued, finding the conversation hard work. "And then we have to do a soil test. My guess is it's gotten a little too acid over the years."

"Mm," his father muttered.

"What?" Cole asked.

"Nothing." Chase looked up almost guiltily. "Sorry, my mind's on that damned winery of Channing's. He must think we're a bunch of country yokels to let him get away with anything that raw."

"You'll have to revoke the sale," Maggie suggested. "That takes time."

Chase resumed eating without comment. More silence. Cole's glance went from him to his mother. "Hey," he said, "I can't stand all this chatter. Don't you guys ever stop talking?"

"The fact . . ." Maggie said and stopped.

"I'm not in . . ." Chase said and stopped.

They had spoken over each other, canceling out the sense of whatever each had been about to say. Another long silence followed. Cole finished his salad and pushed back from the table. "What's the problem?" he asked at last.

"Problem?" Chase looked up from his plate.

"There is a very, very slight air of tension in this household," Cole said with sarcasm. "It's a little like living inside the San Andreas Fault. Is it a private war or should I tune in the six o'clock news for the latest combat bulletins?"

"If you're finished lunch," Chase said, "perhaps you have chores to do."

Cole reacted as if slapped. Maggie put her hand on his arm. "What your father means is that he and I have a difference of opinion that has nothing to do with you or Vickie. So . . ."

"So get out of here while you hash it over." Cole stood up. "Hey, I can take a subtle hint." He winked at her and left the house.

Neither Maggie nor Chase spoke. They could hear Cole start his Honda and roar off. Even then, as silence settled over the house, neither of them spoke. Finally, Maggie got to her feet to clear the table.

"I'd really like to," she said then.

"What? Like to what?"

"Hash it over."

Chase's scowl was magnificent. It seemed to create a large storm cloud in an otherwise sunny kitchen. "Thanks to Angela, we've never been farther apart. You can trust that woman to exploit the slightest sign of weakness."

Maggie listened to the inner surfaces of her husband's words. He was giving her an out, blaming Angela and indicating that, perhaps, if Maggie followed suit, they might find a way of talking to each other again.

But Maggie knew her husband better than he did. Differences papered over in a superficial way would never last with Chase. He might not want them to get down to the bedrock truth, but it was the only way of dealing with him.

"Weakness," she echoed. "She saw my weakness where I didn't."

His face cleared and left puzzlement in its wake. "What are you saying?"

"I had a weakness for Darryl." Maggie looked Chase straight in the eye. "Angela smelled it, the way a shark smells blood a thousand miles away."

"A weakness for Darryl?"

Maggie tried to choose her words carefully. "First of all, there was what he stood for. The glamour, the fame. The idea that he thought my script was good. He represented a kind of door to me. If I opened it, I could get what I've never had before—success as a writer. But that wouldn't have worked with me if Darryl had been a fat little bald fellow with a stutter."

Chase's glance seemed welded to her. "Go on."

"This is the part Angela could smell and I couldn't, Chase. Because she knows what marriage does to people."

"She's been married only once," he pointed out. "If you want an expert, my mother just buried her sixth husband last year."

Maggie shook her head. "You and I . . . we're a perfect example. We fell in love. We got married. We had two nice kids. And all the rest, Chase, all the rest . . ." She could hear the huskiness in her voice and she prayed that she could finish before her voice gave out. "All the rest is laundry lists."

"What?"

"June, moon, swoon. Then it's laundry lists. Do we

owe the Joneses a dinner this week or do they? Did you remember to get the spare tire fixed? Why can't Cole learn algebra? It's all the details, the endless decisions that turn a marriage into a . . . a corporation."

She buried her face in her hands and sobbed. Tears trickled down over her fingers. Her body shook for a moment. Then she tried to calm herself. She pushed the palms of her hands into her eye sockets and tried to press away the tears, but they kept coming.

"Maggie, my God."

She tried to see him through the mist. He looked awful, stricken, his forehead crossed with deep worry lines.

"So along comes a Darryl," Maggie said, sniffing mightily. She sat up straight. "He finds me attractive. He isn't shy about letting me know that. And he also knows how much I want recognition as a writer. He can't swing it. The money isn't there. Then, suddenly, it is, thanks to Angela. He grabs it. She knew he would, just as she knew I'd grab the chance at getting away from the Valley to the lush life of the movie colony."

She was calm now. She could tell that Chase wasn't, but that was the price of getting down to bedrock truth. "Well, it wasn't all nightclubs and discos. That happened one night, just one. But life down there *is* lived around the edge of a swimming pool. I won't pretend I didn't enjoy it. Or that it wasn't flattering to my ego to have a film director courting me. Angela was right. She spotted my weakness. Now she's trying to use it as a wedge between us. But I can't let her do that, Chase, because I'm not the woman she thinks I am. None of her insinuations are true. Nothing happened between Darryl and me. I didn't sleep with him. What I did was hop into a Hertz car and hightail it out of L.A. as fast as I could."

Chase sat back in his chair and seemed lost in thought. "You know," he said then, "I did wonder about that. I knew you had the return half of a plane ticket. So when you showed up that morning, hollow-eyed and dead-tired, I didn't know what to make of it."

He reached across the wide table and took her hand. "So you fled temptation, is that it?" he asked in a kidding tone. "Thank God Hertz was open."

She stared at him. "Then you do believe me?"

"Of course I do."

"But you said you never would again."

"I was hurt. Angela . . . that's her specialty. She got to me and I struck back hard because that same night, when you were out of your hotel-room, I was having a bad time here. I needed you. And I still do."

He got up and came around to her. They embraced, his face half buried in her shoulder. "All that business about laundry lists," he murmured, "about what happens to a love affair when it turns into a marriage. *That* was the convincer. *That* was the real moment of truth. It's no different for the husband, is it? Neither one of us gets much joy out of laundry lists."

"Maybe we can do without them," Maggie suggested.

"We can do without the daily hell of Angela," he said bitterly. "No marriage should be subjected to such unrelenting hostility."

"No, I mean . . ." She sniffed again, trying to erase all her tears. "The children are grown. Maybe we can get back to each other."

She was on her feet now, hugging him. They kissed for a long moment. Cole came in the rear door without them noticing. He stood for a moment, watching, then, very silently, tiptoed out of the house and left them to each other.

Chapter Sixty-Four _____ _____

The late hours were always the best, Sheriff Robbins thought. You could interrogate a prisoner all morning and get nothing from him. But let him sit in his cell all day, staring at nothing, and by nighttime he was vulnerable. This had been his strategy with Fong for the past three days. Only it hadn't worked.

"That's because he doesn't think he's guilty of anything," Sid Rawls told his boss.

"You kidding?"

"Somebody made it worth Fong's while to let him in that tunnel and then clam up. Whatever made Fong do that—threats or just plain cash—he doesn't see himself as a criminal."

"Whad'ya call accessory to murder?"

"You know it. I know it," Rawls continued. Patience was very important in dealing with the sheriff. He had few ideas and they were hard for him to deal with until they'd been planted firmly in his head. "But Fong doesn't admit it to himself. That's why he hasn't cracked."

"Okay," Robbins said. "Now what?"

Rawls sat back in his rickety chair opposite the sheriff's desk. He studied the soles and heels of his boss's boots, displayed on the desk top.

Patrick Mann

"Chinese are family-proud," the deputy said at last. "Fong has no criminal record. A visit from his family would do a lot of good toward getting him to feel guilty."

"What family?"

"We dug up a married sister over in Contra Costa County. And a nephew in Napa Valley."

The family visit took place that evening, after dinner. Both Fong's sister and nephew arrived carrying the same items: small, neatly wrapped parcels of food. They sat with Fong in the locked interrogation room for nearly an hour, while the sheriff paced his office floor, cursing Rawls for not letting him bug the room.

"We could hear everything they say," he fumed.

"They'd talk Chinese," his deputy reminded him.

"Oh."

At 9 P.M. Rawls knocked on the interrogation door, unbuttoned his revolver holster and carefully unlocked the door. "Time's up, folks."

The nephew was first to rise. He bowed to his uncle, turned and left the room. He waited until Fong's sister joined him in the sheriff's outer office.

"I'm sorry about this, folks," Rawls told them. Through the open door to the sheriff's office, he could see Robbins in his usual pose, boots up on his desk.

"It is we who are sorry," the nephew said. "My uncle is . . ." He gestured, as if groping for words.

"Ah," the sister breathed. "He is afraid you believe him to be guilty of the murder."

Rawls shook his head. "We believe he can help us find the murderer."

The nephew nodded. "That," he said, "is wisdom. Good night, sir."

Rawls let them out and went into his boss's office. "Lock me into the cell with him for an hour."

Robbins frowned. "Give me your gun." He took it from his deputy. "This guy could tie a knot in your neck, Sid. He's powerful."

"I won't argue with you there."

Fong's cell had the usual furnishings: a washbasin in one corner and a wooden bunk hinged to the wall. Sid Rawls sat down on the bunk beside the Chinaman. They heard the echoing sound of Sheriff Robbins sliding the bolt shut and locking it. Robbins' bootheels clacked off into the distance. They were alone.

Rawls offered a cigarette, which Fong refused with a shake of his head. Outwardly he appeared as usual—quiet, intractable—but the deputy noted that a fine sheen covered his face. Whatever he and his relatives had discussed, Fong was now in a sweat.

"You see," Rawls began in a plain, conversational tone, "we don't know what you were offered. Did the murderer threaten you or bribe you? If it's a threat, we can protect you. If it's a bribe, you've been diddled. You're hoping this'll blow over and you'll collect. The only thing you can do at this point is win back your freedom and your good name. That I promise you . . . if you start talking."

"My good name." Fong's voice rose barely above a whisper.

"The good name of your family."

"You know I didn't kill the old guy. You know that."

"Do we?" Rawls countered. He smiled lightly. "*I* know it. But until you start talking, I won't be able to convince my boss."

"You promised."

"If you talk."

Fong's tongue moistened his dry lips. He was staring straight ahead at the blank opposite wall of the cell, on which generations of previous prisoners had scratched words and drawings.

"Okay," he said at last. "Here's what happened."

Chapter Sixty-Five

Richard Channing strode briskly up Post Street toward the office of the *Globe*. San Francisco lay before him, smothered under a blanket of early-morning fog. But high in the east a pale disk of white suggested that the sun would soon burn off the mists and the day would be fine.

As he turned a corner only a few doors away from his office, Richard became aware that a long black Fleetwood limousine was pacing his progress along the street. He glanced at it in time to see the auto slow to a halt and the rear door open slightly.

Henri Denault beckoned to him.

Richard stopped in his tracks and stared at the older man as he sat on the rear seat of the limousine. Then he came to the car.

"A pleasant surprise, Henri."

"Get in."

Richard paused only momentarily. There had been a time when any order of Henri Denault's was carried out instantly. For just the briefest of moments, Richard hesitated, then got in. "Ghiradelli Square," Denault told the chauffeur.

"What brings you to San—"

"Later."

Denault's laserlike glance indicated the presence of the driver. The two men in the back seat sat in silence until the huge auto drew up at the bayside area of picturesque wooden buildings, boutiques, eating places and a small park which at this early hour was mostly deserted.

"Stop here," Denault commanded. "Call for me in fifteen minutes."

He and Richard got out and watched the Fleetwood drive off. Denault found a bench in a corner of the landscaped square far from passers-by. He sat down and Richard joined him.

For a moment the older man carefully scanned the surrounding area, shrouded in fog. Aside from a woman walking her terrier, they were alone. "I've read your reports," he began at once without any ceremony. His tone was, as always, steel-cold. "You've managed to dig yourself into an early grave, Richard."

"That's not the case. As a mat—"

"This is not a conversation," Denault cut him off rudely. "You are to listen. When I ask a question, you're to answer. Otherwise, you are to be silent."

Richard could feel an unreasoning anger building up in him. This man, whom he'd known most of his life, his adoptive father, his mentor in the intricate affairs of the Cartel, this man whom he hadn't seen in months, was treating him like some kind of lackey, a stranger—and a hostile one, at that!

"To begin with, your little adventure is over," Denault told him flatly. "You overcame my better judgment and got my backing for this scheme of yours. You've spent hundreds of thousands of the Cartel's money on it. And all you have to show for your maneuvering is that for the first time in history, Angela Channing and Chase Gioberti have formed a solid wall against you."

"Not quite all I—"

"Silence." The older man's cold voice seemed to quiver suddenly with something Richard had never heard in it before—rage.

"Instead of tackling this problem in a businesslike manner," Denault continued brusquely, "you've become as hotheaded and trivial as your opponents. You've flailed out in all directions like a drowning man. You've taken chances no prudent businessman would ever countenance. You've gone from small failures to large ones and now you're so far out on a limb it will cost hundreds of thousands more just to buy your escape in one piece. I'm tempted to let you sink in the quicksand of your own making. But I don't have the final say in the matter, as you know."

"So Number One doesn't agree w—"

"Richard!" The older man's voice had dropped very low, but it projected like a dagger. "You are still under Cartel discipline. The order is silence. You will obey."

He sat for a moment as if to calm himself. His face grew extremely grave. "I have been persuaded that to leave you to your own devices would be far too expensive a solution. Somehow the Cartel must buy your way out of the convoluted insanity you have created here. It will, of course, do so. But without you. Your connection with us is at an end, Richard. I have brought with me a very simple letter of agreement which you are to sign, by which another corporation assumes the liabilities of the *Globe*, the mad scheme for watering down its equity ownership, the so-called Douglas Channing Memorial Winery and any other projects you may have begun without consulting us."

He reached into his breast pocket and brought out a long, legal form enclosed in a gray paper cover and bound with a red ribbon. "Sign here," he said, opening it to its last page.

"Ridiculous."

"Sign here. Sign now," Denault ordered him.

"You're bluffing," Richard told him. "This paper wouldn't hold up in court and you know it. What you're trying to do is cash in on my hard work. I've nearly doubled the per-share price of *Globe* stock. You think I'd sign that away? I've become a Tuscany Valley vintner, able to bid on Valley grapes. Would I sign that away, too? And soon, very soon, I'll be able to take over the Agretti holdings in my own name."

"By marriage," Denault finished for him. "You're a rash young man. Your commitment to Agretti's daughter is one mistake from which the Cartel can't extricate you."

The anger in Richard flared almost beyond control. "You're not my *real* father," he said in a sharp, bitter voice. "I'll handle my own affairs, thank you."

The morning fog drew closer around the two men. Out in the Bay a boat horn hooted mournfully. They seemed to be entirely alone in the universe. Richard felt the chill in his bones, but steeled himself against it. He watched the older man carefully because Denault's face, always impassive, had shown a quick flicker of emotion.

"Yes," he said at length. "That is at the bottom of it."

"What?"

"Your . . ." Denault paused. His tone was somber, as if reading a funeral eulogy. "Your heritage," he said finally. "Your true identity." He sighed, something Richard had never heard him do before. "Oh," he said then, "how well I knew this adventure would end in disaster."

Across the invisible waters of the Bay another fog-horn moaned. Denault seemed to square his shoulders. "Enough. You're finished, Richard, and so is this ill-fated idea of yours." He stood up.

"Hold it," the younger man snapped. "You don't pull that on me, Henri. Not without hearing my side of this. I don't know who's been telling y—" Richard cut himself off. That was it, he realized; he had an informer inside his organization and, with abrupt clarity, he knew her name.

"Good-bye, Richard," Denault said. He strode off into the fog, and in a moment had disappeared.

Richard jumped to his feet. "Henri!"

Iron-hard arms circled him from behind. He struggled to free himself. Out of the fog someone reached for his pinioned arm, pulled up the cuff of his coat and shirt. He felt a sharp sting as the needle entered his wrist. He twisted with all his strength. A moment later, he felt nothing, saw nothing.

Foghorns howled. But the fog closed over like a thick, impenetrable blanket of forgetfulness.

Chapter Sixty-Six

The West Wing of the mansion at Falcon Crest got the afternoon sun in great blinding sheets of warmth. Melissa tucked the baby into his crib and left him in Miss Cleeve's care. She wandered along the second-floor corridor to her bedroom and found Lance moving out an easy chair to make way for a great, comfortable chaise longue she had enjoyed using before.

"Isn't that Angela's?" Melissa asked.

"Nothing's too good for us, baby." Lance straightened up and grinned at her. "Isn't it weird the way Grandmother keeps readmitting us to the human race?"

"On her terms, of course."

"Not that hard to take," her husband countered. "I get a raise. We get this whole West Wing setup. She pays the tab and Joseph's back in her will."

"And you tear up that paternity report."

He shrugged. "I'm beginning to like the kid. Playing papa to him won't be that hard a job."

"And Lori?"

Lance's gaze locked with hers. "Lori Who?" he asked coolly.

Melissa was silent for a long moment. "We have to

talk," she said at last. "Things have been happening too fast."

"Be my guest." He indicated the chaise longue and Melissa stretched out on it.

For a brief moment she remembered that in all the sudden moves of the last few days she had neglected to call Richard Channing. He would be wondering what had happened. Then the thought crossed her mind that telephones worked two ways. She hadn't called him, but then neither had he called her.

"So talk," Lance suggested.

"It's hard to know where to begin." Melissa gestured to indicate the luxury surrounding them again. "Angela always seems to be one jump ahead of us when it comes to wheeling and dealing."

"Neither one of us is an innocent babe. We can handle her."

Melissa smiled sadly. "That's where you're wrong, Lance. We have no plans. She's got them all."

"And she doesn't bother to hide them," he reminded her. "That gives us an edge. As long as you're sitting on the Agretti harvest, you have real leverage with Angela."

For a moment, Melissa wished she could discuss this with Richard. His mind was like Angela's—devious, capable of far-seeing planning. His strategy would be a match for hers any day. But how could Melissa ask him to help her if the planning had to include Lance?

"You see what she's doing," she said after a moment. "After that blowup with Chase— the one we've only gotten hints about— Angela decided she had to have us around as a happily married couple again. She had to have an heir because Chase has his two, and, in her anger with you, she'd cut you and Joseph out. But neither of us is happy being Angela's puppets.

And until we take charge of our own lives, that's all we'll ever be."

He sat down on the bed facing her. "I've got plans," he assured her. "They're just as simple and cold-blooded as Grandmother's. And I think I can get my mother to help us with them."

"Julia's even more her puppet than we are."

"No. Something happened to my mother that day at the cemetery when Grandmother had that fit and disinherited us. I've talked to my mother since then. She's . . ." He paused. "It's as if what Grandmother did hurt her more than it hurt us."

"That's because we're young enough to be flexible."

"Whatever is was, the shock almost blew her away."

Melissa frowned. "She seems all right now."

"Now, yes. Now that we're back at Falcon Crest. Back in Grandmother's will. But my mother's still bitter about what happened. You and I, we bounce back. She doesn't. There's a grudge there. I think we can make it work for us."

"How?"

"Right this minute, she and Chase are trying to work out how many tons of grapes they'll have to buy from the outside. This is the moment of decision. It's the moment for us, too, because the first orders for outside grapes will go to the Agretti vineyard."

"There are other grapes."

"But it's my mother who decides which varietals and how much of each. She's the one who can shape the Falcon Crest order to favor the Agretti grapes. With her on our side we can't lose."

Melissa listened less to the sense of what Lance was saying than to the fact that he kept using words like "our" and "we." Was she hearing the truth or was he as tricky as his grandmother? Were she and Lance really a "we," with a tight communal bond of interest like a real family? Or was he playing with her the way he had so often before?

"I've got a few surprises for Grandmother," her husband was saying. "Once the harvest is over and Falcon Crest's whole next year is totally committed, she's going to find that she *has* to buy grapes from us. That's when we show her who's boss."

Melissa listened, but said nothing. Most of her decisions these days had been made for her, either by Richard or by Angela. Now Lance wanted to play the dominant role. Melissa felt outclassed by the first two people. But she had a hold over Lance that could keep him under her control.

His usefulness to Angela Channing hung by a thread called Joseph. Let Lance really fulfill his promises of what "we" would do with "our" plans, and Melissa would be content to go along with him. Yes, Richard would suffer. But in her heart she had always known she could never control Richard. Lance was a different matter, however.

Let him strut and connive. As long as he played his role as husband and father, Melissa would back him up. But the instant he reverted to his old ways, Lance was dead.

Chapter Sixty-Seven _____

It was a perfect September morning, cool, a bit breezy, with clear blue skies dotted here and there with slow-moving clouds. Angela Channing woke early and stared out at the scene, almost congratulating herself for such weather. This would be a Founder's Day picnic to remember.

Dozens of casks of wine had been set up under trees near the south gardens, where clumps of trees and beds of flowers were placed like jewels in a background of close-cropped lawn. In the cellar at Falcon Crest mansion, white wines chilled to perfection. In the kitchen, platters of canapés and other finger-food were already being prepared under Chao-Li's careful supervision.

At the far end of the south gardens, one of the house men was already stacking bags of charcoal and piles of hickory logs around the great brick barbecue pit. There would be a shoat, sides of beef and ribs, dozens of capons and hundreds of spicy sausages spitted and ready for broiling.

Angela turned away from the window and let her smile of satisfaction spread to an almost ferocious grin. She had finally pulled it all together! Against all odds, against the cunning of Richard Channing and the strength of Chase Gioberti, against Lance's pigheadedness and Melissa's conniving, she had triumphed!

Yes, Angela thought, there had been setbacks. Emma wasn't here to help them celebrate and Maggie had somehow managed to regain Chase's trust. But there were always a few small defeats in every major victory. Julia had been behaving rather strangely of late. The business with the new *Globe* stock issue hadn't yet been resolved by the broker, but it soon would be. And, of course, over all hung the unsolved murder of Carlo Agretti and the question of who would ultimately control his vast and luscious vineyards.

But here, again, a victory nestled within what seemed like a defeat. The murderer of Agretti might never be known, but the heir to the grapes was at this moment sleeping peacefully in his crib in the West Wing, a healthy, whole, growing baby boy.

Angela sat at her dressing table and stared at herself in the mirror. Founder's Day had always been a special celebration for her. It honored the founding fathers of all the major vineyards in the valley, but most of all it honored Angela's own father, Jasper Gioberti, whose genius had made Falcon Crest and whose daughter would defend it to her dying day.

As she began making up her face, Angie realized that she had done nothing but congratulate herself this sunny morning. She wasn't superstitious, but she knew enough about life to understand that all might not be as rosy as she pictured it. For a tense moment she reviewed each of her enemies—and there were many—trying to anticipate his or her next move.

Then her face relaxed. Today was Founder's Day, a day for celebration, not worry. Today would be her crowning glory, the biggest, finest Founder's Day in the history of Tuscany Valley.

Still, Angela gently knocked the wooden top of her dressing table. Just for luck. Just in case . . .

Harvest or no harvest, by noon Chase and Maggie had finally pulled the family together and were about to drive to the picnic.

"Don't expect me to socialize with Aunt Angela," Maggie muttered to her husband.

"Think of it as a business event," Chase joshed her. "Every other vintner will be there. We deserve our share of picnic, too."

"I'm just putting in an appearance," Cole warned them. "I made a date for one o'clock with the man from the County Agricultural Service to test that new land."

"And I'm coming with you," Vickie chimed in. "Picnics bore me."

"As long as you show up to be counted," Maggie agreed. "I'm sure—"

The phone rang. Chase picked it up. "Mother?" He stared at Maggie and raised his eyebrows. "This is a terrific connection. You sound as if you're next door. What's up in Zurich?"

He listened for a long moment. "But not today, Mother. It's Founder's Day. I can't get into San Francisco till tomorrow. It can wait till then, I'm sure."

Chase glanced at his watch as he listened. "Yes, of course, Mother. Yes, they're all just fine. We were about to leave the house. Yes. Right. 'Bye."

He hung up and continued staring at his wife. "Now what . . . ?" He paused. "Have you ever known Jacqueline to get off a transatlantic call that fast?"

Laughing, the four of them left the house and got in the car.

Long wooden picnic tables had been arranged in the south gardens between the barbecue pits and the serving area where already a few dozen neighbors had congregated to taste the wine and explain to the younger children why they had to content themselves with lemonade.

Dressed in a flowing lawn-party dress of pale green crepe de chine with a wide-brimmed floppy hat to match, Angela Channing moved from table to table, checking cutlery, napkins, glasses and plates. Julia stood nearby, dressed in pure white, appearing almost incandescent, as if lighted from within. Only her grave and motionless face offered a contrast to her otherwise shimmering appearance.

At one point mother's path crossed daughter's. "Isn't that your wedding dress?" Angie hissed in an undertone. "Highly suitable."

"Yes, Mother?" Julia wanted to know. "Would the dress I got my divorce in be more suitable?" She passed on, leaving Angela open-mouthed.

Julia made her way to the casks of wine under a grove of spruce and acacia trees. Quickly, with the expertise of a highly trained vintner, she drew a tiny bit of wine from each cask, tasted it and passed along to the next. She turned to Chao-Li and nodded.

"They're fine," she said. "Ready to serve except that Pinot Noir. Can you cool it a bit more?"

"I have an ice tub, Miss Julia."

"That should do it."

Julia glanced at the cars arriving and the guests in twos and fours strolling through the gardens to greet her mother. In the distance she saw a blue station wagon approaching. On top a roof light seemed to revolve, sending out flashes of yellow light paled by the sun's brilliance.

Julia stared at the automobile, wondering whose it could be.

*   *   *

At the eastern end of the Bay, where the town of Tiburon stands, a small spit of land extends out into San Francisco Bay, its coastline protected by sharp, jagged rocks, its approaches guarded by a double cyclone fence.

Near the point stands a small, extremely modern beach house in cast concrete and safety glass. At noon on Founder's Day, it looked deserted. But, then, it always looked deserted.

Now a heavy, gray-painted Jeep raised dust as it approached the barrier fencing from the outside. A man jumped out and spoke into a metal box by the gate. After a moment the gate sprang open, the Jeep entered and, from somewhere hidden by trees, another man clanged the gate tight shut again.

The Jeep pulled into a cellar-level garage, whose doors dropped shut behind it. Inside, hidden from view, two men hustled Richard Channing out of the Jeep and up a flight of stairs to the living room, with its picture-window view of the Bay, the Oakland Bridge and, to one side, the deserted, rat-infested island called Alcatraz.

Richard's blindfold was whipped away and the handcuffs holding his wrists behind him were snapped open. He blinked and rubbed his wrists. "Is one of you going to tell me what this is all about?"

He stared from one captor to the other. Something in his look made one of the men pull out a small .25-mm Beretta automatic gun and point it Richard's way. He looked ill at ease with the gun, but held it steadily enough. In their white shirts, neat ties and pressed business suits, the men looked more like accountants than gunmen.

"Well?"

"You're in luck, Channing," the man with the gun said. "You've been given an audience."

"I've already seen Denault, as well you know."

"Right." The man paused. "Now meet his boss."

Richard's eyes widened. "Number One? Here in San Francisco?"

The man jerked his head toward a door in the wall. "Through there." He lifted the gun so that its muzzle pointed directly at Richard's head. "And no tricks."

As Richard neared the door some sort of proximity sensor clicked and the door opened automatically. He walked into a room the size of the living room, but lined with books and paintings. At the far window, behind a large desk, a swivel chair stood with its back to him. As he took in the situation, Richard heard the door snap shut behind him.

He took a step farther into the room. "I must protest," he began in a strong, level voice. "There was no need for the dramatics. You didn't need to kidnap me. I would have come quite willingly to state my case."

The swivel chair remained motionless. Richard moistened his lips. He had never met Number One. No one had. This fabled person issued commands by telex or coded letter, never in person or by telephone. Yet Cartel executives of the exalted level of Henri Denault took their orders from Number One and no one else.

Richard took another step toward the desk. "Henri had been fed a lot of half-truths, I'm afraid. For reasons which seem to be personal, Diana Hunter has seen fit to try to damage my work here, just when it showed every promise of tremendous success."

Silence.

Richard began to feel the same anger Denault had stirred in him. Who were these high priests of finance anyway? He didn't need any of them, nor was there any reason to kowtow anymore.

"Do you want to talk or just play games?" he burst

out. "All this security, this anonymity. It doesn't impress me. Henri gave me my walking papers this morning. That's fine with me. But you'll never get my signature on any contract of sale. I can't be intimidated."

Silence.

"I can't be scared off or bought off!" Richard said loudly. "I'm only months away from winning and nothing, not even you, can stop me now!" He could feel himself shaking with rage as he shouted, "Who the hell do you think you are? You don't own me!"

With a tremendous noise, Richard slammed his fist on the desk. As he did so the swivel chair began slowly to turn. He stared at it. Then his eyes went wide with shock.

Legs crossed, a slight smile shifting mysteriously in the shadows, Jacqueline Perrault Gioberti sat almost hidden in the depths of a chair made for a much bigger person. Her petite body exuded the chic of style and power that only the very rich achieve.

"Own you?" she asked. "Richard, I'm your mother. Of course I own you. And the Cartel, too."

Lance stood by the barbecue pits carefully painting sauce over a rack of spare ribs. He winked at Melissa, who stood nearby chatting with Maggie Gioberti. "You like 'em spicier than this?" he asked.

"You know me," she responded, then turned back to Maggie. "If you have a chance, Maggie, when things calm down around here, I'd like to take you inside and introduce you to little Joseph."

"That would be lovely," Maggie said. She glanced past Melissa to see a blue station wagon with a white band and a revolving top light pull off the gravel path and onto the carefully tended lawn of the south gardens.

"Angela won't like that," she mused. "Tire tracks in the lawn?"

Sheriff Robbins and his deputy, Sid Rawls, got out of the front seat of the car. They opened a rear door and escorted Tom Fong into the daylight. He had been freshly bathed and clothed for the event. Neither officer tried to hold him, nor was he in handcuffs. He merely looked around him and nodded to Melissa.

"Hi'ya, Miss Lissa."

"Fong! Are you all right?"

"Fine."

"Not now, miss," Sheriff Robbins said, bustling between them. He glanced around him. "Where's Mrs. Channing?"

"Right here," Angie retorted in an angry voice. "What's the meaning of this, Sheriff?"

"Can we speak to you privately?"

"It's Founder's Day. Won't this wait?"

"Sorry." The sheriff sounded anything but. "Murder doesn't wait."

Taking the initiative, he headed toward the mansion and Angela had no choice but to follow him. Melissa took Maggie's arm. "Here's our chance," she whispered. "Joseph's in the West Wing."

The two women went in a side entrance and up a flight of stairs. Miss Cleeve greeted them at the head of the stairway, holding the baby in her arms and gently rubbing his back.

"He took a full bottle, Mrs. Cumson."

"Great," Melissa said. "Maggie, when was the last time you burped a baby?"

Maggie grinned. "How old is Cole?" She took the tiny child and laid his tummy down across her shoulder. "He's chunkier than I imagined."

"Oh, he's been gaining every day," the nurse assured her.

"Miss Cleeve, why not take a rest; I'll manage for a

while," Melissa said. She watched the nurse go to her room and shut the door behind her.

"That's it," Maggie said as Joseph delivered a healthy bubble. She glanced sideways at Melissa. "I'm honored," she said then, "but could you tell me why I'm the only one you've asked to visit the baby?"

"I can tell you."

Melissa's voice had gone very flat with those words, as if she had come to a hurdle and was trying to decide how to get over it. "Maggie," she began again. "I'm glad you and Joseph are getting along."

"Thank you."

"Because, you see, that baby in your arms . . . he's your grandson."

"I can't believe you," Richard told Jacqueline. "Why did you let Denault adopt me?"

"He had no children. He needed an heir." The petite Frenchwoman shrugged almost carelessly, but never took her eyes off Richard. "In those days I had no money to take care of you. I saw the adoption as a way of giving you what I couldn't afford, but still remaining near you through Denault."

"You sold me."

"Call it what you will. I am here now because you and Denault behaved like typical males. Instead of reaching an agreement, you had a test of willpower and you both lost. I will not have it. You must leave California, but you must not leave the Cartel."

"I like it out here," Richard said stubbornly.

"I am willing to turn over control of the Cartel. It has lost its interest to me, anyway. Think of it, Richard. You would be the new Number One."

He eyed her for a moment. So this was his heritage, was it? This clever woman who'd married half a dozen men and parlayed their money into a financial colossus? Who now was willing to give it all up if he

left California? It didn't make sense. Then suddenly
it did.

Richard's smile was hideous, a mixture of loathing
and triumph. "Wait a minute," he told her. "It's
Chase, not me." He pointed a finger at the woman
who had borne him. "It's him you want to protect.
That's why you want me out of California."

"That is nonsense."

"Would it be the first time a mother favored one
son over the other? To the extent that she'd give the
'bad' son anything to keep the 'good' son safe?"

"Chase can take care of himself."

Richard's smile grew even more twisted between
pleasure and rage. "Can he? And can your grandchildren defend themselves, too?"

"You would not dare threaten Cole or Vickie."

"Mrs. Perrault . . ." He paused and bowed ironically.
"Mother, you leave me no choice, do you? To stay
alive, I have to threaten."

"But you cannot threaten your own brother's—"

"Oh, can't I?" The smile faded. "You pride yourself on being a businesswoman? Here's my deal. Come
near me again. Interfere with my work one more
time. And your dear son and grandchildren will
suffer. Understand? It's in your hands . . . Mother."

Rather unsteadily, Maggie made her way down the
West Wing stairs with Melissa. "I understand," she
kept saying. "That is . . . I guess I understand."

"The reason for keeping it a secret?"

Maggie nodded "But, Melissa! Dear God, why did
you have to tell me in the first place?"

"I had to." The younger woman looked helpless
for a moment. "I guess I had to know that if anything ever happened to me, little Joseph had someone on his side . . . someone I could trust."

"But you said Lance was—"

"He's playing nice now," Melissa interrupted. "It may be for real. But I know Lance. I know Angela. The only person I would trust Joseph to . . . is you."

"*I won't!*" Angela thundered.

Both women looked with startled eyes toward the study of the mansion. Angela Channing stood there in her pale green dress, facing down Sheriff Robbins. "And you can't make me, Sheriff. So clear out of here."

"Mrs. Channing," he said almost helplessly, "I'm not asking that much. I want the whole family gathered here. You can have your Founder's picnic. But—" he glanced at his watch—"in one hour, let's say two P.M., all of them have to be in this room. Otherwise I'm going to have to get warrants. My way we keep it quiet and get it over with sort of discreetly. Do you see my point?"

Angie glared at him. "You're ruining a perfect day."

"The other way I have to bring in judges, the police. It'll be one hell of a mess, Mrs. Channing."

"Blackmail," she snapped. "All right. One hour." She turned on her heel and strode out of the house to rejoin her guests.

The sheriff's glance followed her, then caught sight of Maggie and Melissa. "You ladies, too," he said then. "One hour."

By two o'clock most of the barbecue had disappeared. Those guests who had grapes to attend to had left. But twenty or thirty still milled around, sampling wine, telling jokes, laughing and reminiscing. Angela Channing had gone from one to another of her family and told each of them about the appointment in the study.

As they glanced at their watches, it was Chase who caught sight of a sleek sports car approaching along the driveway from the main road. "Look at this," he told Maggie. "Talk about bloody nerve. It's Channing."

"Who invited him?"

"Nobody, I'm sure." Chase scowled unhappily. "He knows we've put an injunction on that memorial winery of his. He can't open for business and he's got thirty days to dismantle it. He's got no business here in the Valley and certainly not at the Founder's Day picnic."

"Still, he is Douglas Channing's son," Maggie pointed out. She watched her husband's face, wondering how she could keep from telling him that he was a grandfather and could never acknowledge it.

"Douglas Channing and party unknown," Chase replied. "I don't hold illegitimacy against anyone. You know that. But in his case . . ."

Maggie bit her lip. She could never tell him about Joseph, never. He might understand, but he'd never forgive Cole.

"My God!" Chase yelped. "Is that . . . ? The woman with Channing. Is that . . . ?"

The sports car drove to a stop. Richard got out and opened the passenger door to escort Jacqueline from the car. "Chase!" she called. "Maggie!"

Chase's fingers dug into his beard. "Some transatlantic call, Mother. Where'd you make it from, San Francisco?"

Formally, with a touch of reserve, he kissed her cheek. She and Maggie embraced. "And Cole?" Jacqueline asked "Vickie?"

"They're in the house." Maggie glanced at her watch "As a matter of fact, Sheriff Robbins wants us—"

"Maggie." Chase's voice was low but urgent. His glance shifted to Richard Channing's strong, handsome face. The two men faced each other. "We seem to have a gentleman of the press here," Chase said.

"Well, maybe that's putting it too strongly. A former gentleman of the press and not much of a gentleman at that."

"Chase," Jacqueline said, "*ne touche pas.*" Her accent had gotten suddenly very strong. "Don't start wiz heem."

"That's right," Richard said. His lips twisted in that frightening smile of his. "Tell him the rest . . . Mother."

Chase reacted as if slapped. "What?"

Jacqueline glanced about her. "Chase, please. It is true. You two . . . you are brothers."

"Right," Sheriff Robbins said. He glanced around the study at the people gathered there, the pause adding to the tension in the room.

"Here's the problem," he said then. "You folks are all family."

"*He* isn't," Angela said in a baleful voice, eying Richard.

"He surely is," the sheriff insisted.

"Then *she* isn't," Angela added, glancing at Jacqueline.

"More than you know," Chase told her in a somber tone. "Angela, let the sheriff get on with it, will you?"

"Anyway," Robbins resumed, "all of us here in Tuscany Valley are like a family. You know what I mean? And Carlo Agretti was one of ours. So I told myself, I said, 'Would I want to wash all this family linen in public?' And the answer was 'No, I would not.' That's why we're here in this room, to try and get it all sorted out private-like."

"You mean," Chase asked, "you have some new evidence?"

"I mean I have a witness."

The room grew very still. Melissa, seated on the

couch beside her mother-in-law, Julia, grasped the older woman's hand, as if for reassurance. Brilliant in white, Julia squeezed her hand comfortingly.

"At this late date?" Richard Channing demanded. "Are you talking about Fong, here?"

Sheriff Robbins teetered forward on his toes. "Here's how it lays out. I won't go into the details of the murder again," he assured Melissa, "but we always had the problem of how the murderer got into the house."

"Always assuming it wasn't me," Cole put in.

"You came in the front door," the sheriff told him. "But the murderer came in through the cellar."

Melissa blinked. "The cellar? You mean . . . ?"

"The old tunnel from the pump house." Robbins looked around the room. "Nobody had the sense to tell us that, not even you, Melissa."

"I didn't even remem—"

"That's all right," Robbins assured her smoothly. "We found it soon enough. Then all we had to do was find Fong."

He turned to the Chinese, standing next to Rawls. "We asked ourselves, who would know about the tunnel? You would, Melissa, we knew that. And since you and Cole used to play around the place as kids, we figured maybe Cole did, too. But, him being left-handed . . ." He shrugged unhappily. "Anyway, once we got Fong to cooperate, it got a little easier."

The sheriff paused and glanced around the room. His eyes fastened on each of them in turn. At last he said, "One of you made it worth Fong's while to unlock the old pump house and guide you through that tunnel into the cellar. One of you hid down there until Agretti was alone, after Diana Hunter talked to him. Once she left, and Fong went to bed, one of you came up the cellar stairs and into Agretti's den by the side door. You must have had a gun because the first thing one of you did was to make Agretti telephone Cole and get him over to Bellavista."

The silence in the big room was total. Sheriff Robbins repeated his previous performance, eying each of them in turn.

"Then one of you killed Carlo Agretti and set up Cole as most likely suspect. I admit we fell for it. But once we knew Cole hadn't done it, we knew it had to be someone in cahoots with Fong. Someone who'd bought his cooperation and his silence. One of you did that, and Fong is here to tell us which of you it was."

"This is ridiculous!" Richard burst out. "You call this a witness?"

"What else?"

"He's an accomplice," Richard snarled.

"That's right," Chase agreed. "To save his skin he'll tell you anything you want to know."

Robbins smiled very slightly. "Maybe you folks were raised on Sherlock Holmes. You think murder cases get solved by snooping around with a magnifying glass looking for clues. That's not how it works." The sheriff balanced on his toes again. "Informers, accomplices—call them what you want, but without them most murders would go unsolved."

"And you haven't solved this one, either," Lance cut in brusquely. "You're just fishing, Sheriff. And Fong's the bait."

"And my study's not a fishing hole," Angela added bitterly. "I resent this, Sheriff. It's unwarranted. It's harassment. It's totally illegal."

"But the other way," Maggie reminded her, "is going to stir up an awful lot of headlines. He's got us over a barrel. Either we cooperate or he spreads this all over the West Coast."

"That will not be good," Jacqueline piped up, "for the Falcon Crest name, eh, Chase?"

Chase sighed unhappily. "Get on with it, Sheriff."
He glanced at Angela. "One way or the other this is
going to hurt our name."

"Then let's get to it," the sheriff concluded. "Fong,
would you come over here beside me?"

The short, powerful Chinese moved to Robbins'
side. "You all know Tom Fong," the sheriff went on.
"Tell us, Tom, did someone get you to unlock the
pump house and lead them through the tunnel to
the cellar?"

"Yes."

"What did they offer you?"

Fong paused an instant. "Fifty thousand now. Fifty
thousand when I'd skipped the country." He laughed
bitterly. "Not one cent do I see so far. Once I had to
lam out of here, it was too late to collect."

"Tell us what happened the night of the murder,"
Robbins urged.

"Just what you said. I let them into the pump
house. I lead them into the cellar. I go upstairs. This
Miss Hunter shows up. She talks to the old m—, to
Mr. Agretti. She leaves. I lock up and go to sleep."

"You see?" Lance burst in. "He's not witness to
anything."

"Just one thing," Sheriff Robbins corrected him.
"Fong, do you see in this room the person you let
into the cellar?"

"Yes."

"Can you point them out to us?"

"Yes."

"Do so."

Tom Fong's glance moved much more slowly than
the sheriff's had from Lance's face, to Angela's, to
Melissa, to Julia, to Chase, to Maggie and Jacqueline,
to Cole and Vickie and finally to Richard.

Slowly his right hand rose, index finger pointing.

Someone gasped. He was pointing directly at the woman in white, Julia Gioberti Cumson.

"You are indicating Mrs. Julia Cumson?" the sheriff demanded.

"Yes."

"She was the one you let into the cell—"

"For God's sake!" Julia burst out. "Let's have an end of this endless, nauseating drivel!"

"Do you deny th—"

"Deny?" Julia's voice rose to a peak. She twisted abruptly on the sofa, let go of Melissa's hand and jumped to her feet. All the light in the room seemed focused on her brilliant white dress, shoes, hat. In one white-gloved hand she held a .9-mm Browning automatic.

"Deny?" she screamed. "Why should I deny it?"

"Look," the sheriff said, "the gun—"

"Is the one I held on Carlo Agretti." Julia nodded once, then seemed unable to stop nodding, three, four, five times. "I toyed with the idea of shooting him. But the noise . . ." She stopped and coughed for a moment. "Besides, I wanted Cole to walk in on it. So it had to be a silent murder."

"Why me?" Cole demanded. "Why set me up?"

"To pay you back for—" Julia stopped herself so abruptly that she began coughing again, the gun waving wildly for a moment from side to side. "Never mind," she said at last. "There's nothing any of you can do about it anymore. Carlo's dead and my grandson will inherit the whole thing, Falcon Crest, the Agretti vineyards . . . all of it. My grandson."

"Mother," Lance began, "stop pointing that gun."

"You were all too soft," Julia sneered. "None of you could stand up to her. Only me." Her glance wavered until she was staring at her mother, Angela Channing. "You let her boss us all. Run our lives.

For what? For her own good, not ours. Only one person could stand up to her. Me."

The Browning automatic was pointed now at Angela, who stood there, a look of horror in her wide-set eyes. "Mrs. Cumson," the sheriff began, "will you give me that gun?"

"Wait till I've finished the job," Julia said in a low, menacing voice. "Not till we're all free of her."

She raised the heavy automatic. "Isn't anybody going to stop her?" Angela cried out. "For God's sake, one of you. Lance! Melissa!"

"Nobody's going to help you now, Mother." Julia spoke with the voice of doom. Her trigger finger began to whiten.

At the same moment, Chase and Richard tackled her from two sides. She started to twist sideways and fall. The three of them went down in a tangle of arms and legs. A shot rang out.

The cemetery sat as it had for generations, a broad sweep of grass and flower beds surrounding the headstones and other monuments. In the distance stood the tan travertine stone that marked the graves of Carlo Agretti and his wife. To the east stood a simple granite monument to Douglas Channing. Farther along was the Gioberti tract headed by Jasper's grave and those of his wife and their son, Jason, Chase's father, Angela's brother.

The newest stone was small. There had even been some controversy over placing it here in Tuscany Valley's cemetery. Some felt that, by rights, it belonged elsewhere. But Chase had insisted and had volunteered part of his own tract.

He stood over the stone now, silently staring down at it. Across the newly sodded grave stood Richard Channing. Neither man spoke. In the distance could be heard the busy hum of work from the vineyards

as hundreds of hands picked the grapes, loaded the
baskets and placed them on trucks. The harvest was
in full swing.

Still not speaking, the two men turned away, walking off on different paths. They left behind the
small stone inscribed:

JACQUELINE GIOBERTI PERRAULT

Both of them continued walking in opposite directions until they were lost from view.

The harvest continued.

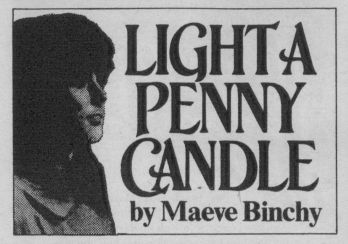